D0179492

**Also available from
Cynthia Eden
and
HQN Books**

Killer Instinct

The Gathering Dusk (prequel to *Abduction*)
After the Dark

For a complete list of books by Cynthia Eden,
please visit www.CynthiaEden.com.

CYNTHIA EDEN

AFTER THE DARK

HQN™

HQN™

ISBN-13: 978-0-373-80192-3

After the Dark

Copyright © 2017 by Cindy Roussos

The publisher acknowledges the copyright holder of the additional work as follows:

The Gathering Dusk
Copyright © 2017 by Cindy Roussos

Recycling programs
for this product may
not exist in your area.

This edition published by arrangement with Harlequin Books S.A.

For questions and comments about the quality of this book, please contact us at CustomerService@Harlequin.com.

www.HQNBooks.com

Printed in U.S.A.

CONTENTS

AFTER THE DARK   7

THE GATHERING DUSK   339

AFTER THE DARK

Over the years, I've met so many wonderful romance readers—at conferences, at signings and, of course, online.
I want to thank all of these readers for their support.
Thank you for reading my books. Thank you for the kind words.
Thank you for telling me that you were able to get lost in my stories—because I think a reader being able to get "lost" in a book is the best compliment that any writer can receive.

CHAPTER ONE

THE SCENE WAS all wrong.

The killer—the balding man in his late thirties—the man who stood there with sweat dripping down his face, a gun held in his trembling hand and a dead girl at his feet…he was *wrong*.

FBI Special Agent Samantha Dark raised her weapon even as she shook her head. She'd profiled this killer, studied every detail of his crime spree. And…

This is wrong.

"Drop the gun!" That bellow came from her partner, Blake Gamble. He was at her side, his weapon drawn, too, and she knew all of his focus was locked on the killer.

They'd come to this house just to ask Allan March some follow-up questions. He'd been one of the custodians at Georgetown University, a university that had recently become the hunting grounds for a killer.

At Blake's shout, Allan jerked. And when he jerked, his finger squeezed the trigger of the gun he held. The shot went wide, missing both Samantha and Blake. She didn't return fire. *Allan doesn't fit the profile. This is all wrong—*

Blake returned fire. The bullet slammed into Allan's right shoulder. Not a killing wound, not even close. Blood bloomed from the spot, soaking the stark white shirt that Allan wore. Allan should have dropped his gun in response to that hit, but he didn't. He screamed. Tears trickled down his cheeks, and he aimed that gun—

Not at Blake, but at me.

"Has to be you…" Allan whispered. "Said…*has to be you…*"

She didn't let any fear show, even as the emotion nearly suffocated her. "Allan, put down the gun." Blake's order had been bellowed, but hers was given softly. Almost sadly. *Put the gun down, Allan. I don't want to shoot you. This isn't the way I want things to end.*

The FBI had been searching for the Georgetown University killer for months. Following the trail left by the bastard—a trail of blood and bodies. But the trail shouldn't have led here.

Allan March was a widower. His wife had passed away two years ago, slowly dying of cancer. He'd been at her bedside every single moment. All of the data that the FBI had collected on Allan indicated that he was a dedicated family man, a caregiver. Not—

A serial killer.

"I'm sorry," Allan whispered.

And Samantha knew what he was going to do. Even as those tears poured down his cheeks, she *knew.*

"No!" Samantha screamed.

But it was too late. Allan pointed the gun right at his own face and pulled the trigger. The thunder of the gunfire echoed around them, and, a moment later, Allan's body hit the floor, falling to land right next to the dead body of Amber Lyle, the twenty-two-year-old college student who'd been missing for three days.

"Fucking hell," Blake muttered.

This is wrong.

Samantha rushed toward the downed man. Her weapon was still in her hand. Her eyes were on Allan. On what was left of his face. *Dear God.*

"THE PRESS IS ripping us apart, Samantha! Ripping us apart!" Her boss glared at her as they stood inside the small FBI office. "You were supposed to be the freaking superstar—a profiler who could do no wrong. But your profile was *shit*. You had us looking for a man who didn't exist. Three women died while we were looking for the killer *you* said was out there!"

Samantha stood, her shoulders back and her spine straight, as Justin Bass berated her. Spittle was flying from her boss's mouth. His blue gaze blazed with rage.

The executive assistant director was far more pissed than she'd ever seen him before. The guy had a temper, everyone knew that truth, but this time… *There's no going back.*

Justin didn't like to look bad. He liked to be the agent in charge, the man with the answers. The suit who handled the press and gloried in the attention he got when his team brought down the bad guy.

"Damn it, Samantha!" Justin snarled, a muscle twitching in his rounded jaw. "Do you have anything to say?"

Did she? Samantha swallowed. Did she dare tell him what she thought? When every single piece of evidence said just how wrong she'd been?

"Take it easy, Bass." Blake spoke on her behalf. He was at her side, sending her a sympathetic glance. "What matters is that the Sorority Slasher has been stopped."

The Sorority Slasher. Samantha hated that name. It

sounded like something from a really bad horror flick. Leave it to the tabloids to glam up a grisly killer.

"We're the fucking FBI," Justin said, stopping to slap his hands down on his desk. "We can't afford to make mistakes."

Her temples were throbbing. She knew exactly who they were.

"Someone has to take the fall for this one. *Three* women died because you were wrong. *You* were wrong, Samantha. The superstar from Princeton. The woman who was supposed to change the face of profiling. FBI brass shoved you down my throat, and you were *wrong*."

She made her jaw unclench.

"You're taking the fall for this one." Justin nodded curtly toward her. "Consider yourself on suspension."

Samantha almost took a step back. Her lips parted— *Don't take the job from me.*

"What?" Blake was the one who'd given that shocked cry. It was Blake who sounded furious as he snapped, "You can't do that! Samantha is the best—"

"Yeah, right, you think I don't know about the hard-on you have for her, Agent Gamble?" Justin fired right back. "You two *never* should have been partners. So take some advice, buddy. Save your own ass. She's a sinking ship, and you don't want to go down with her."

Her boss was a bastard. Lots of men she'd met in the FBI were arrogant assholes. Blake? No, he was a good guy, and that was why she respected him so much.

"Leave your weapon here," Justin ordered her. "And your badge."

She unsnapped her holster, walked slowly toward his desk.

My profile was right. I know it was.

She put her gun on his desk, but when she reached for her FBI badge and ID, Samantha hesitated.

"You know we found pictures of all the victims at his place." Justin's voice was flat. "Souvenirs that he kept."

"Trophies." It was the first thing she'd said since coming into his office. "Not souvenirs, they're trophies." Serial killers often kept them so that they could relive their crimes.

"Shoved in the back of his closet, under the guy's winter boots." Justin shook his head. "Dropped like they didn't matter, and you spent all that time telling us we were looking for a cold, methodical killer. One who wanted to push boundaries and study the pain of his victims. One who wanted to see just how well matched he'd be with authorities. A smart killer, a damn genius. Fuck me, Samantha, Allan March barely graduated high school!"

And that was just one of the many reasons why he was *wrong*.

Her fingers had clenched around her ID. "Did you ever think…" Her voice was too soft, but it was either speak softly or scream. "Did you consider that maybe Allan had been set up?"

Justin's hands flew up into the air in a gesture of obvious frustration. "He shot himself! *Killed* his damn fool self when he blew off half his head! If that doesn't say guilty, then what the hell does?"

Her drumming heartbeat was too loud. "He could have killed himself for a number of reasons." Reasons that were nagging at her. He'd lost his life savings battling his wife's cancer. Extreme financial hardship? Hell, yes, that could lead people to suicide. It could—

Justin yanked the ID from her hand. "Get the hell

out, Samantha. You are done. I won't have you talking this shit in my office—and you sure as hell better not plan on stopping to talk to the reporters outside."

"Director Bass—" Blake began angrily.

"Don't!" Justin threw right back at him. "Not another word, unless you want to be giving up your badge, too."

No, Blake wouldn't do that. The FBI was his life.

She kept her spine ramrod straight as she walked out of the office. When she reached the bull pen, she heard the whispers—from the other FBI agents there, from the cops who'd come to team up with them. Everyone was staring at her with confusion in their eyes.

She was wrong. She screwed up. She let those women die.

This was all going to be on her. Samantha clenched her hands into fists.

She made it to the elevator. One step at a time. Her spine was starting to hurt.

She slipped into the elevator. Pushed the button to go down to the parking garage. The doors were starting to close—

"Samantha." Blake was there. Shoving his hand through the gap between the doors, trying to get to her.

She shook her head. "No." Because she couldn't deal with him right then. He pulled at her emotions, and she already felt too raw.

Blake. Handsome, strong Blake. Blake with his rugged good looks, his jet-black hair, his bright green eyes and that golden skin... Sexy Blake.

Fierce Blake.

Off-limits Blake.

Because her bastard of a boss had been right about one thing. Blake did have a hard-on for her. She'd noticed his attraction. It would have been impossible to miss. An attraction that she more than felt, too. But he was her partner. You didn't screw around with your partner. That was against the rules.

She'd always played by the rules.

And she'd still gotten screwed.

"This isn't on you," Blake gritted out.

Actually, it was. The dead man's blood was still on her clothes because she'd run to him after he'd blown off half his face. His blood was on her—and the deaths of those three women? She knew her boss was going to push those her way, too. Before he was done, she'd be some rogue FBI agent who'd gone off the playbook— and he'd be the shining superstar who'd somehow managed to stop the Sorority Slasher.

Blake stepped into the elevator. Ignoring her request. The doors closed behind him, and his hands curled around her shoulders. "The profile was off. You're not God. You can't predict everything."

"I don't want you touching me." Her words came out stark and hard. Not at all the way she normally spoke to Blake.

He blinked, and, for an instant, she could have sworn that he looked hurt.

"Let me go." She didn't have time to choose her words carefully. She was about to break apart, and his touch was sending her closer and closer to the edge.

His hands fell away from her. He stepped back.

"I'm not dragging you down with me." She licked her lips. "You still have a chance here. You just had the bad luck to get teamed up with me."

"I don't think it's bad."

"Trust me, it is." Her heart was racing far too fast

in her chest. "Just walk away." What had Bass called her? A sinking ship?

The elevator dinged. Finally, she was at the parking garage. Maybe she'd be able to get out of there without the reporters catching her. She stepped toward the elevator's now open doors, but Blake moved into her path.

Her head tipped back as she stared up at him.

"I want to help," Blake said.

There he went being the good guy. "Then let me go."

"Sam…"

"I'll call you tomorrow, okay?" She wouldn't, but, right then, she would have said anything to get away from him. Blake pushed her buttons. She'd always suspected he would have made for an amazing lover—and with her control being as shaky as it was at that particular moment, Samantha was afraid she would cross a line with him if she didn't get out of there.

Once you cross some lines, there is no going back…

A muscle flexed in Blake's square jaw, his green eyes gleamed, but he got out of her way.

She rushed past him. Nearly ran—and she didn't stop, not until she reached her car.

WHEN IT CAME to drinking, Samantha had always had an extremely high tolerance for alcohol. That had come, she suspected, courtesy of her dad. A tough ex-cop, he'd been able to drink anyone under the table.

So she sat in that low-end bar, on the wrong side of DC, and she studied the row of shot glasses in front of her.

"I knew I'd find you here. You always come to this place when you want to vanish."

She looked up at that deep, rumbling voice. A voice

she knew—intimately, unfortunately. *Another line that I crossed a long time ago.* And her gaze met the dark stare of Cameron Latham. *Dr.* Cameron Latham. They'd known each other since their first year at university. Been friends, competitors. They'd gone all through college and graduate school together, earning their PhDs in psychology.

But after graduation, she'd joined the FBI. Samantha had wanted to use her talents to bring down criminals. And Cameron—he'd been bound for the Ivy League and a cushy college teaching job.

And for the college girls whom she knew he seduced. The guy had model good looks, so the women had always flocked to him. Now he had money and power to go with those looks. He'd finally gotten everything he wanted.

He has what he wants, and I just lost what I valued most. Talk about a totally shitty night.

"Guessing the story made the news?" Samantha muttered. This wasn't the kind of bar that had TVs. This was a dark hole made for drinking.

And vanishing.

"It made the news." He pulled out a chair, flipped it around and straddled the seat. "*You* made the news." He whistled. "That asshole of a boss really threw you under the bus."

She lifted another shot glass and drained it in a gulp.

"Drinking yourself into oblivion isn't going to make the situation better…" Cameron cocked his head and studied her.

Her brows shot up at that. "Cam, I'm not even close to oblivion."

He should know better.

"The case is wrong." She slammed down the glass. "Allan March is *wrong*. I don't buy it. The scene was too pat. He was too desperate. That guy isn't the one I was after."

Cameron blinked. "The reporter said plenty of evidence was on hand—"

"Like people don't get framed?" She laughed, and the sound was bitter. "I know all about that. My dad lost his badge because he got pulled into that BS about setting up drug dealers on his beat." Though her dad had always sworn he hadn't been involved in the frame-ups, his protests did little good for his reputation. "People get framed. It's a sad fact of the world." She pushed a glass toward Cameron.

He didn't take it. He never drank much, and when he did drink, it was only the best. Expensive wines and champagnes. Jeez, the guy loved his champagne. When they'd gotten their master's degrees, she remembered the way he'd gone out and bought that fancy bottle of—

"Why would someone want to frame that guy?" His quiet question jerked her from the memory of their past.

She rolled her shoulders. "Because Allan was convenient." *Duh.* Wait, *duh*? Maybe she did need to slow down on the drinks. "An easy target. The custodian who kept to himself. The widower with no close friends. Maybe the perp I'm after wanted the attention off his back, so he tossed Allan into the mix."

Cameron frowned. "Allan…he killed himself."

"That's the part I haven't worked out yet." But she would. "I don't understand that bit. I swear, I actually thought the guy was going to shoot *me*, but then he turned the gun on himself. Weird as hell." She reached for another shot glass. The bartender had done such a lovely job of lining them up for her. "Maybe he had a deal with the killer. I mean, Allan had a daughter, after all. One that needs money for college, money for life. And Allan didn't have any money. He barely had anything at all. Maybe the killer offered Allan money to take the fall. Maybe he was supposed to go out in a blaze of glory." Her eyes narrowed as she considered this new angle. If Allan had gotten a payoff, then perhaps she could find the paper trail. *Follow the money.* "But…Allan was a caretaker." Her voice dropped as Allan's profile spun in her head. "His nature was protective, so in the end, he *couldn't* shoot me. Couldn't shoot at Blake. That wasn't who he was." Her lashes lifted as realization hit her. "He couldn't attack us because *Allan March wasn't a killer.* Instead of shooting us, he turned the gun on himself. The only person he hurt was himself." Excitement had her heart racing.

But Cameron just shook his head. His hair—blond and perfectly styled, as always—gleamed for a moment when he leaned forward beneath the faint light over her table. "Normally, you know I love it when you bounce your ideas off me…"

Her temples were throbbing.

"But the man had a dead woman at his feet. That part made the news, too."

"And no blood on him," she mumbled. Because *that* had been bothering her. *That* was why the scene had been wrong. When they'd first arrived, Allan had been sweating in his white shirt—and there had been no blood on the shirt. *Not until Blake shot him.* "The vic's throat was slit—ear to ear—and Allan didn't have a drop of blood on him. He *should've* had her blood on him." She pushed to her feet. "I have to make Justin listen to me. I'm not wrong. Allan was just a fall guy. The real killer—"

Cameron surged to his feet. His hand wrapped around her arm. "You can't go to your FBI boss with alcohol on your breath and a wild theory spilling from your lips." His voice was grim. "You want more than a suspension? You want to lose the job forever?"

"I want to stop the killer!" Okay, maybe her voice was too loud. Good thing the bar was deserted.

"How many shots did you take?"

She tried to pull away from him.

"No, damn it, let me *help* you." And then they were walking to the door—together. His car was at the curb. That fancy Benz. He had such a plush job. Good for him... He'd gone to Princeton on a scholarship, same as her. Two kids with brains who'd fought their way to the top of the class rank. "I'll take you home. You sleep this off, and tomorrow, tomorrow, I *will* hear your theory, okay? Tomorrow, I will help you."

Nausea rolled in her belly. She didn't think she'd eaten that day, and she really didn't want to vomit all over his plush leather interior. So Samantha sank back into the seat and closed her eyes. She didn't speak while he drove, but all too soon, Cameron was stopping the vehicle. Her eyes cracked open as she peered through the window. "This isn't my house."

"No...because while you were sleeping—"

She hadn't been, had she?

"I drove by your place. Reporters were camped out on your doorstep. So I brought you here."

Her hand lifted and slid over his cheek. She smiled at him. "See, when you want to be, you can be nice."

He laughed, the sound almost harsh. "I know you go

for the good-guy type, but that isn't me." He jumped out of the car. Cameron hurried to her side, but she'd already let herself out, *thank you very much*. A light dusting of snow fell onto her as she stood on the sidewalk. Winters in DC. So very different from her time growing up in the Deep South.

"You can stay in the guest room," Cameron said as they walked toward his front door. He unlocked it and ushered her into the warmth of his house. "Unless, of course…"

She stopped and glanced up at him.

"Unless you want to sleep with me."

Samantha blinked at those words. She hadn't been with Cameron—not intimately—in over a year. *Not since I met Blake.* She and Cameron were safely in the friend zone. A zone she intended to keep occupying. They'd always been better friends than lovers. "I'll take that guest room."

His jaw tightened. He pointed down the hallway. "You know where it is."

Right. Because she knew his place, inside and out, just as she knew hers. "Thanks for being a friend, Cam. I don't have many of those left." She turned from him and began to shuffle her way down the hall.

"Blake Gamble is your friend."

His words stopped her. "I don't know what Blake is," she said honestly. "He was my partner—"

"Come on, Sam. He's just your type. The *good* kind."

She looked over her shoulder. Was that an annoyed tone in his voice? Odd, Cameron *never* sounded angry. Not with her.

"Maybe you don't really want someone good, though," he continued, voice nearly growling. "Did you ever think that? You spend so much time profiling others…you should take a long, hard look at yourself. Why do you *think* you belong with a true-blue sort?"

I know why… "Good night, Cameron."

"We both know you like the dark. Nothing wrong with that. After all…" His lips curved in a mocking smile. "Isn't that your name?"

She hurried down the hallway. Shut the guest room door. And—

The bed was already made, the covers pulled back, and a glass of water even sat on the bedside, as if Cameron had known she'd be there that night.

But he said he only brought me here because reporters were at my house.

Samantha hesitated.

Or maybe…maybe Cameron—in his ever-so-controlling way—had always intended for her to stay at his place after he'd learned about the bloody details of her day. She knew his protective instincts had a tendency to kick into overdrive where she was concerned.

She yanked open the door. Cameron was across the hall—about to enter his bedroom. "You know I hate being manipulated." Her hands were on her hips. Her eyes narrowed on him.

"I do." He nodded. "And I hate for my only friend to suffer alone."

"I'm not your only friend." Cameron had a freaking entourage of women following him around. "Tomorrow, I am so going to kick your ass."

His lips hitched into a half smile. "No, you aren't. But thanks for the warning."

She stepped back and slammed the door shut. Samantha toed off her shoes, ditched her pants, drained that glass of water and fell asleep—wearing just her shirt, her bra and her panties.

IT WAS THE thirst that woke her later. *Always a side effect of whiskey shots.* Samantha's eyes cracked open, and she climbed out of bed, her throat absolutely parched. The empty glass sat by the side of the bed, seeming to mock her. She stumbled to the door, then made her way—as quietly as possible—down the hallway and into the kitchen. After guzzling two glasses of water, she propped back against the counter.

The clock on the microwave told her it was nearing 4:00 a.m. Far too early. Or late, depending on how you wanted to look at it. Unfortunately, now that she was awake, her mind was already spinning, and she knew she wouldn't be able to shut down again and go back to bed.

No blood on Allan. That was why the scene was so wrong. He had a dead woman at his feet, blood splatter all around her, but no blood was on him.

Not until he'd been shot by Blake. And then—once the guy had killed himself, Allan's blood had been *everywhere*. So by the time all of the other agents had swarmed to the scene, the place had looked like a bloodbath.

She put her empty glass in the dishwasher and padded into Cameron's office. She sat down in his leather chair, and it squeaked softly beneath her weight. She didn't bother with a light but just moved his mouse so that his computer would wake up. Illumination immediately flooded out from his screen. His *two* screens. *What an ego.*

A faint smile curved her lips as she typed in the password for his system. Cameron was such a Greek mythology junkie. She knew that Hades was his password of choice—for pretty much everything.

The password got her access, but before she could click the internet icon…

Another file opened on his desk. A file that must have still been in use when Cameron last operated the computer. And that file…

It's the dead girl. A close-up shot of Amber Lyle, the girl who'd been sprawled at Allan's feet. Her eyes were closed, the wound at her neck gaping, and the blood…

Samantha leaned closer to the screen even as every muscle in her body clenched. Cameron shouldn't have that picture. It looked like a crime scene photo. It should be classified. It shouldn't be—

A trophy.

"Samantha?" Cameron's raspy voice came from the doorway. "You okay?"

Her head snapped up. She was behind the computer screens—his desk faced the door. So he couldn't see what she was looking at on the monitors.

But he could see her face. Right there, in the glow of the light, and whatever he saw on her face must have given her away because Cameron sighed. "Found out, did you?"

Her profile for the Sorority Slasher ran through her mind.

Highly intelligent… Cameron was a freaking genius, and he had the paperwork to prove it.

Strong. Fit. Cameron worked out every single day. Not just some light gym work. He was into martial arts, boxing. Hell, he'd even taken up Krav Maga in the last year.

Attractive. His features were absolutely perfect. Sharp cheekbones, deep, dark eyes, sensual lips.

In his late twenties or early thirties... Cameron was twenty-eight.

"I left in a rush before," Cameron mused. "I shut down the computer, but I didn't stop to think that *you'd* possibly get up in the middle of the damn night and come snooping on me." He gave a low hum. "Figured out my password, did you?"

Her lips felt numb as she said, "I've always known your password."

"The Lord of the Underworld."

Her hands inched toward his desk drawer. It was open, just an inch, and she'd caught the gleam of a letter opener in there.

"How will this end, Sam?" Cameron asked her. "Am I really supposed to kill you now?"

It's him. It's him. It's him. Inside, she was screaming.

Cameron took a step toward her. "What do you see on the screen?" Now he sounded curious, not angry. "Is it her? The last one? And she was going to be my last one, by the way. My experiment was over."

"Experiment?" Her left hand had slid into the drawer and curled around the letter opener.

"Um. Yes." He took another step toward her. He hadn't turned on the lights in the room, so he was just a big, dark shadow. "I wanted to see if I could do it, you see. If I could kill. If I could get away with the crimes. And I wanted to see…what are people like…in that last terrible moment? What is it like when they know that hope is gone and they're dying?"

Nausea rolled in her stomach. "Cameron?" She said his name as if he were a stranger, and right then, he was. Not the man she knew. Not her ex-lover. Not her friend. Cameron was a respected professional. He was on the fast track to become the head of his department at Georgetown—after only two years there. He charmed his way past everyone's guard.

He was...a killer.

He took yet another step toward her. She couldn't see his hands. She wished that she could just see his hands.

"There were some surprising results. Would you like to hear them?"

Cameron always enjoyed bouncing ideas off her.

"I felt alive when I killed those women. Interesting, don't you think? That death finally made me feel alive? Until that point, I'd only felt that way, well... when I was fucking you. But that ended when you met Blake Gamble."

She flinched. "Blake and I are just...partners. Nothing more. We haven't been together."

His smile was cold. "Not yet. But I know you, Sam. I know what you want."

This couldn't be happening.

"It was easy to kill." Now his voice was almost musing. "I never hesitated. I mean, I always suspected I was a bit of a psychopath, but as we all know...psychopaths aren't necessarily monsters. They're just...unemotional. Detached. Able to become such great surgeons, CEOs, lawyers...even profilers for the FBI..."

Her phone was in the guest bedroom, and Cameron didn't have a landline. She needed to call Blake. Call Bass. Call the cops.

"Covering up the crimes—well, that was easy, too. All so *easy*. The hardest part? That was staying two steps ahead of you. Because that profile you made up?

The one that your boss called shit?" He was in front of the desk now. "It was dead-on."

She could hear the frantic drumbeat of her heart. Every. Single. Beat. "Show me your hands."

He laughed. "You think I'll hurt you?"

"Show me your hands."

"You were right about Allan." He watched her with a predatory stare. "Allan did need the money and…the guy was sick, too. Dying. I was really just speeding up the process for him. It was all going to work so perfectly." For a moment, he almost sounded sad. Almost. "But even when you were drunk…you were figuring shit out."

"I wasn't drunk."

"Yeah, you were." Another sigh. "I think you might have been better at profiling than you realized. But then, I always said you had that killer instinct."

"Show me your hands." It sounded as if she were begging, and Samantha hated that. "Cameron…"

His left hand came up—

And she surged to her feet because she *knew* he was going to kill her. She swung out with her letter opener, and it caught his hand, sending a wet spray of blood flying.

Cameron bellowed, and then he launched across the desk, coming right at her. They fell back together, slamming into the floor, and that impact was hard enough to knock the breath from her. But she didn't let go of the letter opener. She kept it locked tight with her fingers, and Samantha shoved it right against his throat.

"DROP THE WEAPON! Drop the fucking weapon and put your hands up!"

Samantha blinked at that shout, and she realized that

she was still holding the letter opener in her left hand. She opened her hand and let it fall—the blood-soaked letter opener fell from her bloodstained fingers.

Blood. Blood everywhere. On the floor. On the desk. On me.

"Samantha?"

That wasn't the voice of an angry cop. That was a voice she knew. She squinted, and she saw Blake pushing his way past the first responders as he hurried to her. Her body started to shake.

His gaze raked over her, taking in her bare legs, her shirt—the blood.

"Samantha? What happened?"

Slowly, she shook her head. She *hurt*. Because a lot of that blood…it was hers.

"Samantha!" Blake's hand closed over her shoulder. "What in the hell happened here?"

She licked her lips. "He…he got away…"

CHAPTER TWO

Four Months Later...

ONCE YOU KNEW that monsters lived in plain sight, it was pretty hard to trust anyone.

Samantha Dark's feet pounded along the wooden pier. Her breath heaved in and out of her lungs as she ran. The sun was just rising—starting to slide across the morning sky. This was her routine. This was her sanity. Every day was started with a three-mile run that took her along the Fairhope Pier.

Fairhope, Alabama. Her small-town sanctuary. Her haven.

Her hiding spot.

She reached the end of the pier and stopped, her heartbeat drumming in her chest, as she stared out at the bay. The water appeared so dark today—dark and flat. Across the bay, far in the distance, she could see the skyline of Mobile. That city would be coming alive soon enough.

But she wouldn't be a part of it. She wasn't in for crowds these days. She avoided contact with others like the plague.

Footsteps beat on the wooden pier behind her. Samantha tensed even as she looked over her shoulder. It was just another runner. A woman with a bobbing blond ponytail. She gave Samantha a friendly wave, then turned and headed back down the pier.

Samantha's gaze slid toward the water once more. A yacht was out there, anchored in the bay. Had to be about a forty-footer. It had arrived yesterday. Stayed the night. The owner would probably clear out soon. Head on to a new adventure.

Samantha didn't have adventures any longer. She didn't want them. She wanted the anonymity of small-town life, and that was exactly what Fairhope gave to her. Sure, some tourists flocked to the area in the summer. But in late winter, it was just the locals. Exactly the way she liked it.

She turned on her sneakered heel and began running back down the pier. She passed Mosley, the guy who was always out with his crab trap. He was throwing it into the water. Two fishermen were organizing their bait. They gave her friendly nods. When she reached the parking lot, Samantha turned right and took the path that would lead her toward the little beach that waited. She loved that beach and the trees that twisted near it. Spanish moss hung in the oak and cypress trees, swaying overhead as she ran. Ducks were up ahead, squawking. This scene was as far away from the hustle and bustle of DC as it was possible to get.

Samantha kept running.

It's all I've been doing for the last four months.

Thirty minutes later, she was back at the parking lot. She headed toward her car, but...a man stood there. He'd propped his hip against her driver's-side door. His arms were crossed over his chest, and the light morning breeze tousled his dark hair.

She stopped when she saw him. Her muscles were

shaky from the run, but just the sight of that man with the sunglasses—with his strong shoulders, that dark hair, that hard jaw—had adrenaline pumping through her body. For a moment, she could only shake her head. He shouldn't be there. He didn't belong there.

Samantha realized that she'd frozen, and she forced herself to move forward. Slowly, she closed the distance between them, drawing nearer to the man who'd slipped into more than a few of her dreams…and nightmares. Her breath seemed to burn her lungs. She stopped beside him.

"Blake." She said his name like an accusation. Mostly because it was. "What in the hell are you doing here?" When she'd left DC, she hadn't exactly given anyone a forwarding address. Not even him.

His head tipped back as he straightened. He pulled off his sunglasses, tucking them in his pocket. His eyes—*never been able to forget those green eyes*—met hers…and he smiled.

She shook her head. "No. Whatever it is…*no*. Just get in your car. Drive. Get out of here." She marched toward her car. She'd already pulled out her key and was going to get inside and drive away from him.

But Blake's hand flew out. His fingers curled around her wrist and held tight. "I missed you."

What? Her gaze jerked back to his face. Emotion glinted in his eyes. Emotion she didn't want to read. She couldn't handle his emotions. On good days, she had trouble dealing with the tangle of her *own* emotions. She definitely didn't want to deal with his.

"You can't hide forever," he murmured as his thumb stroked along the inside of her wrist. Her pulse immediately increased beneath his touch.

"I'm not hiding." She could tell lies so easily these days. "I'm living a civilian life. There's a difference." Because her suspension had quickly turned into unemployment. Sure, her profile of the Sorority Slasher had been proved accurate. She *had* perfectly described the perp they were after.

But she'd been found in a serial killer's house. A killer who'd gotten away on *her* watch. And on his way out of town, Cameron had killed again. He'd stabbed a cop who'd made the mistake of pulling him over when Cameron had been racing away from the scene. Bass had blamed her for that death. He'd blamed her for plenty of things.

The fact that she'd been found in Cameron's house, wearing only her shirt and underwear—yes, gossip had spread in the ranks quickly enough about that situation. And that gossip had leaked out to the press. *An agent who screwed a serial killer.* Whispers had dogged her steps.

But even worse than the condemnation from Bass… her own guilt had eaten away at her. Because…*that cop's death is on me.*

She'd let Cameron get away. His escape was on her. She'd kept that secret shame inside for far too long.

"You're a profiler, Samantha. An FBI agent. You hunt killers. You stop them."

She gave him a bitter smile. "Haven't you heard? I fuck them, too." And that was something else that haunted her. She'd thought she knew killers so well. That she understood the criminal mind, but all along… she'd been blind. How the hell was she supposed to trust her instincts any longer? She'd been dead wrong before.

What if she was again?

His hold tightened on her, became almost bruising. Her breath caught because Blake was never rough, not with her. Not with—

"Jesus, Sam." He dropped her hand.

Just seeing him hurt right then. She'd walked away from DC for a reason. She sure hadn't intended to be seeing Blake again anytime soon. Just looking into his eyes made her feel as if someone had ripped open her heart.

The way he'd stared at her…back in DC. When he'd found her, half-naked, covered in blood… Samantha cleared her throat. "Why are you here?" she asked him again.

"Because I need you."

Those words were rough. All rumbly. Her eyes raked over him. She didn't think he meant that he needed her in a personal way. No, he had to mean—

"He's back." A muscle flexed along Blake's square jaw. "He's doing it again."

For an instant, her heart stopped. She couldn't breathe, couldn't move. And then… "No!" A fierce denial. With that cry, her heart began to race in her chest. Her breath came in quick pants. Even though sweat covered her from the run, Samantha was suddenly freezing. "You're wrong."

"I wish that I was. Cameron Latham is hunting again. Playing his sick games. Doing his *experiments*."

Her chill grew worse.

"And I need you to help me stop him."

She shook her head. "You came to the wrong woman. I'm not FBI any longer." Like he'd need that reminder.

"You're the right woman. You're exactly the woman I need."

Her body was so tense her muscles ached.

"No one knows Cameron Latham like you do."

Her cheeks burned. Yes, she knew him intimately.

"You can stop him, Samantha. You can build a new profile on him. You were in his head before, and I know you can get right back there again."

She looked away from Blake and grabbed for the handle of her car door. She yanked it open—

"Unless you don't want to stop him."

Her shoulders stiffened.

"Bass still thinks you let Cameron walk. He doesn't believe that you wanted to put your lover behind bars."

"Ex-lover." How many times had she said that? She glanced up at him, knowing that a glare would be on her face. "As I've said before, Cameron and I hadn't been involved that way in a long time." She climbed into the car. Her hands fisted around the steering wheel.

"Why not?"

His question was so low that she barely heard it.

And since she was already walking on the tightrope of a whole give-him-hell attitude, she offered her former partner a grim smile. *Why not?* "Because of you, of course. I met you and didn't want to be with anyone else."

His shock was plain to see.

Before he could ask any other questions—questions she didn't want to answer—Samantha yanked the car door closed. She started the vehicle and headed out of the lot, leaving Blake behind.

She didn't start shaking until she was nearly home, but then the trembles came, rocking her whole body. *He's doing it again.* She hoped that Blake was wrong. He *had* to be wrong.

Because if Cameron was hunting again, it would only be a matter of time before he came after her.

BLAKE GAMBLE HAD never been the kind of guy to give up easily. Actually, he didn't believe in giving up at all. Especially not when it came to…

Her.

Samantha Dark.

Samantha Fucking Dark. The best profiler whom he'd ever met. Wicked, insanely smart—the woman could dissect a killer from a nearly perfect crime scene. She could see evidence that others missed. She saw motives. She saw monsters. She—

She was the one who stopped the Sorority Slasher. She'd gotten hell from Bass because Cameron Latham had vanished, but Samantha's profile had been dead-on. Every detail she'd given on the killer matched Latham.

His boss thought that Samantha hadn't just been screwing Cameron. Executive Assistant Director Justin Bass had told Blake—on more than one occasion— that he suspected Samantha might have actually even been involved in the crimes with the killer.

Total bullshit. The EAD was dead wrong.

Because I trust her. I have from the moment we were partnered together. She always had my back. The truth of the matter was…he'd taken one look into Samantha's golden eyes and pretty much lost a piece of his soul. No one should have eyes like her. So unusual. So deep. Eyes that saw too much.

She was a pretty woman, beautiful, but she'd always tried to restrain that beauty. She wore suits to work, hiding what he knew was a killer body. Her black hair was always pulled back into a twist. She didn't bother with makeup. Just business, that had been her.

And then everything had been blown to hell for Samantha.

Now here I am, ready to wreck the peace that she's sought for herself.

He sighed as he got out of his car. Samantha's cottage waited right up ahead. He hadn't followed her there. He'd actually gone to the cottage *before* he tracked her down at the pier. When he'd been her partner, he'd learned her habits pretty well. Samantha always enjoyed her morning runs. And the pier? Well, in this small town, he'd figured she'd head for that spot.

Her car waited a few feet away. No sign of her, though. He exited his vehicle, made sure to grab his backpack and tried to figure out just how the hell he was going to convince Samantha to help him.

He took a few steps toward the cottage—a place that was situated high on the bluff that overlooked the bay. Her cottage was surrounded by massive oak trees and plenty of Spanish moss and—

"Why do you think it's Cameron?"

He saw her, sitting on the steps that led up to the cottage. Her hands were on her knees, and her head was bent forward so that he couldn't see her expression.

Her hair was shorter than it had been months before. Her usual twist was gone. The dark locks hung to her jaw, perfectly framing her heart-shaped face. He liked the cut. It made her eyes look bigger and made her look even sexier, though he doubted that had been her intention.

The problem is...I've always found everything about

her sexy. A big problem, when he was supposed to be *only* her partner.

"Blake…" She looked up. "What makes you so certain it's him?"

She hadn't sounded surprised that he'd followed her. He figured Samantha knew it took a lot more to get him off track. He headed toward her, then lowered his body until he was sitting on the steps beside her. His leg brushed against hers.

"The world is full of twisted killers," Samantha continued, her voice both sad and stark. Once more, her head lowered. Her delicate shoulders hunched. "How do you know it's not one of them? Why does it have to be Cameron?"

This was the part that he knew would hurt. "Because he asked for you."

Her head whipped up and toward him. Her eyes widened as she stared at him. "What?"

"He asked for you, at the kill scene."

Her lower lip began to tremble.

Shit. I'm being too cold. Too hard. I'm screwing this up.

Blake cleared his throat and said, "The victim was held for three days, *then* killed. Only before he killed that girl, he made her… He made her record a video."

"That was never part of Cameron's MO. He didn't make any recordings. He just— He took pictures."

Because she'd found his pictures on his computer.

"Maybe his MO has changed."

She stared at him, and he could see the pain in her eyes. He hated that. He *never* wanted to bring Samantha pain. "I have a copy of the video in my bag. I brought my laptop because I wanted you to see that clip." He'd thought it would be the one thing that would convince Samantha to help him. She'd never been able to turn away from victims. Her heart was too soft. Tough exterior, gentle soul. That was his Sam. "Do you want to see it?"

She shook her head... *No.*

Hell, he'd been sure...

"Yes," Samantha said quietly even as she was still shaking her head. "I want to see it."

He reached for his bag, which he'd placed on the ground. He opened it up and pulled out his laptop. It took just a moment to boot.

Samantha slid closer to him. He made sure to keep his breathing deep and easy. He knew the tightrope that he and Samantha had always walked. If she was coming back to him, coming back to *work* with him, he had to be careful to keep his control around her. Samantha pulled at his emotions, a dangerous thing when he was working a case. He needed his focus to be on the killer.

Not on Samantha and the need he felt for her.

"The video doesn't end well," he warned her. His finger was poised over the keyboard. One click, and he'd have the video playing.

"Just get the hell on with it," Samantha muttered. For just an instant, he heard the whisper of the South in her voice. Normally, Samantha had no accent. But when she was angry or really stressed, that Southern drawl would reveal itself.

His finger tapped against the keyboard.

The video began to play.

"I'm Kristy Wales," the blonde woman in the video said. Tears were pouring down her cheeks. Long streaks of black mascara coated her face. "And I'm going to d-die."

Kristy sat in a chair, her hands bound behind her. There was nothing in the background of the video, just a white wall. No sound on the video, just her voice. Shallow cuts covered her arms and her legs. *He'd tortured her.*

"It's…it's because of Agent Dark. She…she didn't finish the ex-experiment." Her gaze cut from the camera to some spot just to the right. There was silence a moment. Then Kristy gave a jerky nod and said, "Dark should have f-finished." Her eyelids fluttered, and then she was looking back at the camera. "She doesn't get to run. It won't stop. He won't stop." Her lips were trembling. *"Make him stop."*

The camera kept going.

But then…Kristy started screaming. *"I did it! I did it! Now let me go, please, please, please—"*

A man walked into the frame. Tall, with wide shoulders, dressed in black from the top of his head down to his feet. A ski mask completely shielded his face and head.

But nothing covered the knife in his hand.

Kristy jerked in the chair. *"I'll do anything! I said what you wanted—I'll do anything! I'll—"*

The man had walked behind Kristy. His hand lifted. He put the knife to her throat.

"I'm sorry! Whatever I did, I'm sorry!" Kristy yelled. *"Please don't—"*

The knife sliced across her throat, moving from the left side in a sweeping slash to the right, ending just beneath her right earlobe. Blood flew out, and Kristy gasped. Her body shuddered and…

She didn't die instantly.

She jerked and twitched a few more moments while the man stood behind her.

Then the video ended.

Beside Blake, Samantha was dead silent. He closed the lid on his laptop. Blake put the computer back in his bag, then he raised his gaze to look at her face.

She'd paled. The faint spray of freckles on her nose stood out—a stark contrast to her too-pale skin. Her eyes were wide.

"We found Kristy in a lake. The video was sent to the FBI. We saw her die before we ever found her body."

She exhaled on a ragged breath.

"Samantha—"

"That wasn't Cameron." She stood up. "You're too good of an FBI agent to think that it was." She turned on her heel and hurried into the cottage.

For an instant, Blake didn't move. But Samantha hadn't slammed the front door shut behind her, she hadn't locked him out, so he took that as a sign that he could follow her. Hopefully. He grabbed his bag and hurried inside.

The place was bright, with plenty of light coming through the big picture window that looked out over the bay. The walls were white. And the furniture—what little of it there was—appeared comfortable, casual. An overstuffed couch, a white chair with a blue blanket thrown over its back.

Samantha stood in front of the window, staring out at the bay below. Through the picture window, he could see the wooden stairs that led down to the small beach that waited at the bottom of the bluff. A moment passed in silence. She remained there, her arms wrapped around her stomach. He was just about to speak when she said, "Why are you really here, Blake?"

Because I want you back. She'd been the best partner he ever had, and his life was pretty much shit without her. But they'd get to that, later. Because right then, hell, yes, they did have business to discuss. "Tell me why it's not him."

Her shoulders stiffened. "Is this some kind of test? You want to see if I've lost my edge over the last few months?"

Actually, he just wanted to see what was going on inside of her head.

"Cameron is left-handed, and that killer in the video was right-handed. Obvious, of course, because when he went behind her, he sliced from the left side across to the right, the typical strike pattern of a right-hander."

"Cameron Latham is a fucking genius." Certified. He'd seen the test scores in the guy's file. "You think he couldn't attack with a different hand if he wanted? I don't buy that. I think he could. I think—"

She looked back at him. "He never called me Agent Dark. We'd known each other too long. Been too... intimate for that."

Blake's hands clenched into fists.

"I was Sam to him. Samantha when he was annoyed. I was never Agent Dark. This guy...the one on that video? It's *not* him. Sure, he had Cameron's build. He had his height. But I mean, if it really were Cameron, why hide the face? Why bother with a mask in that video?" She gave a grim shake of her head. "This isn't him, and I think you know that."

"I know that Cameron Latham disappeared com-

pletely four months ago. Just seemed to vanish from
the face of the earth."

Her expression didn't change.

"*You* said he was alive the last time you saw him."
That had been her story.

"He was." Samantha's voice was flat.

What is she hiding from me? Because he'd known—
from the moment he saw her blood-soaked form in
Cameron's house—that she was hiding something. He
tried pushing her. "So all this time, Cameron has been
alive out there."

"Yes."

"Only, the guy is a killer—he was taking victims
like freaking clockwork before he vanished. Am I really supposed to believe that he just stopped killing?
That he gave that up cold turkey?" It was Blake's turn
to grimly shake his head. "Bullshit. Guys like him don't
stop. They can't stop, not until they're behind bars or
they're dead." Killing was a compulsion. He knew it.

Her gaze held his.

"Tell me I'm wrong," Blake said as he moved even
closer to her. His hands itched to reach out and touch
her. That urge to touch her was always there for him, but
like so many of his urges—especially the more primitive ones that came when he was around Samantha—
he tried to push them back. "Tell me—"

"Cameron isn't like other serial killers. I don't think
there was any compulsion for him. He wasn't driven
to commit the crimes because he *had* to do them. The
murders were a challenge. He wanted to see if he could
get away with the kills." One of her slender shoulders
lifted in a casual shrug. "And he did."

No, he didn't. You found out. You saw the monster.

"The perp on the video…he's different. I think you *knew* he was different, but you still came down here to me." Her lips thinned. "I hate you wasted a trip."

"What's wasting is your talent. You're a good FBI agent—"

"I'm not FBI. No badge. And I'm really not eager to step back into that circus." Her hand lifted, and she was the one to touch him. Her fingers lightly squeezed his shoulder. "I wish you the best of luck on this case. I hope you catch that guy before he hurts anyone else."

He couldn't look away from her golden eyes. "Don't tell me the victim doesn't matter to you." Because he'd *counted* on Kristy mattering. He'd been so sure that once she saw what the other woman had endured—

"What am I supposed to do?" Samantha asked him. "What is it that you want from me?"

Everything. But they'd get to that…soon enough.

YOU CAN'T HIDE from me, Samantha Dark.

He stood in the shadows of a big, arching oak tree. The wind blew against his face as he stared at her cottage. So very far from DC.

Samantha Dark had slipped away from the Bureau. Just vanished. But he'd known that someone knew where she'd been lurking. After all…what were partners for?

He'd just needed the right bait. The right tool. And he'd had to be patient. Had to wait and watch and then…

Then he led me right to you.

FBI Agent Blake Gamble was in the little house with her right then. So predictable. Every move that guy had made—*I saw it coming.*

Samantha Dark was his end goal. She was the one he wanted to face. She was the one who had to pay.

But...

He intended to have a little bit of fun with her before she died. After all, death was the easy part. He'd been taught that lesson by a master. It was the pain, the suffering, the absolute loss of hope—that was the best. That was the rush.

Samantha Dark, before I'm done with you...you will break apart.

Because that was exactly what she deserved.

It was time to let Samantha know that she wasn't hidden any longer. Time to let her know that he'd found her—and that she was about to pay for her crimes.

CHAPTER THREE

"I WANT YOU to come back to DC with me."

Samantha blinked. Her heart raced too fast in her chest, and she couldn't get the image of Kristy Wales out of her mind.

"You say this isn't Latham—"

"It's not." She was dead certain of that fact. A copycat? Yes, she could see that. But this wasn't Cameron.

"Then that's why we need you."

She forced herself to step away from him. A hard thing to do because he always seemed to call to her. "The FBI has plenty of other profilers. Competent profilers who can get the job done. They'll find this killer. You don't need me." Samantha's hand fell back to her side. "I sure hate you came all the way down here for this. You should have called. I could have saved you a trip—"

He grabbed her hand, stepped close to her again, and her drumming heartbeat accelerated even more. "I need you."

"Blake—"

"You're right. The FBI does have other profilers. But they don't have *you*. You looked at that video and then instantly said it wasn't him."

"Because I *know* Cameron!"

His smile was grim and satisfied. "Exactly. You

know the bastard. You know his crimes better than anyone else because you got in his head before."

But he got in mine, too.

"This killer isn't Cameron. The other profilers will be able to handle him." She needed to pull her hand away from him. She needed to put space between them. "You don't want me."

His thick lashes lowered as his gaze swept over her. A tense moment of silence stretched between them. Then Blake gave a hard nod. "I see."

What exactly did he see? Samantha hesitated.

His thumb slid along her inner wrist. "You're afraid."

Her chin notched up.

"That's why you ran down here, isn't it? You ran all the way down here because you're afraid of that bastard."

Smart people would be afraid of a cold-blooded killer, but Blake had her fear all wrong. "My instincts can't be trusted." Her voice came out too husky. "He was close to me, Blake." *I let him in. I trusted him.* "And I didn't see him for what he truly was. Not until it was too late." She pulled her wrist from him because his touch made her uncomfortable. *He* made her uncomfortable. "I can't even judge my own lovers. How the hell can I possibly trust myself when it comes to creating profiles for killers?"

Silence.

She backed away from him. "I can't help you. Go back to DC, find that killer. Use the resources you have up there—"

"I trust you."

Those deep words seemed to reverberate right through her.

"And you want to know why I didn't call? Because

I knew you'd refuse to help me. I knew you'd run away for a reason." A muscle jerked in his jaw. "But the time for hiding is over. We need to go to work, Samantha. We need to find this killer, and we need to give Kristy the justice that she deserves."

THE FIRST STEP was always to survey your territory. To learn your hunting ground. So he spent the morning exploring the city of Fairhope and the land around it. He went on the back roads—and there were plenty of them. He found the abandoned houses, the empty buildings. He surveyed the water because, after all, he'd always loved the water. He knew just how to use it. He bought maps. He made his plans.

Rushing to act wouldn't work for him. He had to be careful. He'd been planning to get Samantha within his grasp for so very long. He couldn't afford to screw up.

He talked to the locals. Some people were always so eager to overshare. He learned more special spots in the area. Secluded spaces. Then, when he was finally ready, he walked along the heart of downtown Fairhope. He strolled down the street, his gaze flickering over the shop windows. An artsy place, one filled with galleries and pottery shops. Restaurants boasted organic food and fine Southern cuisine. Luxury, in a quiet setting. The cobblestone sidewalk beneath his feet appeared to have been recently swept, and, even though it was still February, bright flowers were already planted in the city.

One particular shop drew his eye. A gourmet food and wine establishment. He paused a moment, staring in the window, looking at the cute store clerk who stood just behind the counter. He needed Samantha to know that the hunt was on. He wanted her to understand that he was close. She'd been found.

So perhaps he should send her a little gift...a little note to let her know of his appreciation. He pulled a phone out of his pocket, a burner phone because he knew how to cover his tracks, and he dialed the number displayed so prominently on that shop window.

He watched as the clerk reached for the phone, then he heard her voice, softened by the lightest of Southern drawls, as she answered the line. "Thanks for calling Connoisseur's Delight. This is Tammy. How may I help you?"

Tammy. He smiled and backed away from the shop. After all, he didn't want her to glance up and see him. "Tammy, this is going to be a long shot, but I'm looking for a very special champagne for a friend of mine."

"Well, we sell both fine wine *and* champagne," she said brightly. "And we have a very extensive list." Pride had slipped into her voice.

"Do you now..." He licked his lips. "Well, I'd like to make an order for a friend of mine. If you've got a Dom Pérignon, vintage 1998, then we will be in business." That bottle was special, he remembered that.

So would Samantha.

There was a faint hum, and he heard the click of keys, as if the helpful Tammy were typing in a search on her keyboard.

"If you don't have that one," he said as the moments ticked past, "I can easily order another—"

"No, sir! We have it."

Perfect.

"By any chance...do you deliver?" But he already knew they did. He'd seen that sign on the shop window, too. "Because I would love to surprise my dear friend Samantha with a delivery of her favorite champagne. I'd like to include a card with the package, and I can tell you exactly what her note should say…"

"I WANT TO help her," Samantha said. They were outside now and she'd changed into jeans and a loose blouse. He'd shared more files with her as the morning slipped into late afternoon. Tried to convince her that she was needed in DC.

And, God, she wanted to help that victim. She wanted to stop killers.

But what if I'm wrong again?

The sun was too bright. And the memory of Kristy's face wouldn't leave her mind. "But I'm not FBI, Blake."

"You could be. You know you could fight to get that job back."

He was grim. Determined.

And she was letting fear hold her back. Damn it. She hated being this way. "Blake, I—"

His phone rang, cutting through her words. Immediately, her lips clamped together.

A furrow appeared between his dark brows as he pulled out his phone. "I've got to take this, Samantha. Give me a minute."

"Take all the time you need." She shoved her hands behind her back and stared at the swaying Spanish moss as it blew in the breeze. *A copycat killer.* Why had a copycat started hunting? And why was he deliberately trying to draw her into his crimes? He'd used her name, gotten the victim to say her name for a reason.

He wants me. Goose bumps rose on Samantha's arms as a profile began to slip through her mind. It had been so long since she'd focused on any killer but Cameron, yet...old habits died hard.

This killer wants me. He used the victim because he wanted the message delivered. Kristy Wales was just collateral damage. She didn't matter to him at all.

"What?" Blake's voice was a hard snarl that had her gaze snapping toward him. "When? Shit, hell, yes, I'm near the scene. No, no, don't worry about the local authorities. I'll pull them in. I'm taking lead on this damn thing. If it's Latham, I'll bring him down."

Her mouth seemed to dry up. Blake shoved his phone back into his pocket. His eyes were glittering. "We just got a hit."

She inched closer to him. "A hit?"

"The FBI has been monitoring Latham's credit cards ever since he vanished."

But Cameron wouldn't be dumb enough to use his cards. He would know that the FBI was watching. He'd—

"One of his cards was used ten minutes ago, right here in Fairhope."

Her heart iced. Samantha caught herself even as she was shaking her head.

"I don't believe in coincidences," Blake growled. "You're here...and now his card is being used?" He spun away from her and started marching toward his rental vehicle.

"Wait!" Samantha scrambled after him. "I'm coming, too!" She knew he'd be going to the shop where that card was used, that he'd be talking to the clerks, looking for video feeds—trying to find Cameron.

Something I've been attempting do to for months.

Blake looked back at her. "Thought you were done with the FBI."

She'd tried to be, but a killer was out there—and obviously, he wasn't done with her. "I'm coming with you." This was her town. Her peace.

But she feared that peace was being shattered.

THE BELL JINGLED when Blake pushed open the door to Connoisseur's Delight. A young woman behind the counter glanced up, a wide smile on her face. "Welcome! Please, feel free to browse around and make yourself—"

He flashed his badge. "FBI Agent Blake Gamble, and I need to ask you some questions."

Her blue eyes widened. "The...FBI?"

Samantha was right at Blake's side. They both stepped toward the counter. He could feel the tension rolling off Samantha, and that same energy hummed through his body. After months of inactivity on Latham's cards, suddenly they'd gotten a hit? Hours after Blake had found Samantha at the pier?

No damn way was that pure chance.

He's here. "What's your name, miss?"

Her eyes were still huge in her pale face. "Tammy. Tammy White."

He nodded. "You got an order just a little while ago. The credit card you billed was to Cameron Latham."

Her gaze darted nervously toward Samantha. "Um, was that a stolen card?"

"Tell me about the order."

Tammy's fingers fluttered toward a brightly decorated bag. "The order came in for the Dom Pérignon 1998. He wanted it delivered, and I just finished preparing it."

Blake's gaze raked over the store. "No security cameras here?"

"No...but he didn't come in. The gentleman placed the order over the phone."

Figured. Latham could have made that call from anyplace. But Blake would still get a track going on the shop's phone records and he'd—

"Did you say he ordered a Dom Pérignon 1998?" Samantha's voice was tight. "That's a very expensive champagne."

"It costs four hundred dollars." Tammy licked her lips.

Blake gave a low whistle. "And you didn't think it was odd to get a phone order that big?"

Tammy shook her head, sending her hair sliding over her cheeks. "We get big orders like that all the time. Especially when the high-profile golfers are staying at the hotel down on the Point."

Great.

"That's Cameron's favorite champagne." Samantha's voice was too tight. "Every single time he celebrated, he made sure he had that on hand. I remember the first time he ever got it...it was the night we received our bachelor's degrees."

Blake flattened his hands on the counter. "Who was that order being shipped to?"

Tammy swallowed. "Should I call my manager?"

"Who was getting the order?"

Tammy shoved the bag toward him. "Samantha Dark. He gave me her address. I was going there, but— Go ahead. Just take it. Read the card."

Fury burned in his blood. *The bastard was sending this to Samantha?* He yanked open the bag, shoving white tissue paper out of his way. He pulled out the bottle but barely glanced at it. Instead, his focus was on the small, white card.

"I wrote exactly what he said," Tammy murmured.

Samantha leaned in closer, her arm brushing against Blake's shoulder.

Found you, Agent Dark. See you soon. Then we'll celebrate together.

His back teeth locked together. *Oh, hell the fuck no.*

"Blake," Samantha whispered. "We need to talk, right now."

They needed to find that bastard. Blake would get the local authorities to search with him. They'd tear apart this town.

Samantha caught his hand in hers, and she pulled him back outside. He left the note inside, left a wide-eyed Tammy White for the moment. The bell jingled as the door closed. They stood in front of the shop window, and Samantha stared up at him with an open, desperate gaze.

"Latham," Blake growled. The bastard thought this was some kind of game? Sending her a fancy champagne, telling her they'd celebrate?

"It's not him." Samantha still sounded certain. She looked down the quiet street. A few older couples were walking, window-shopping, not even glancing at them. "Something else is going on. I can see it."

Blake waited, wanting to know exactly what she was thinking.

"I can't be wrong again."

She *hadn't* been wrong before. Samantha might not trust her instincts, but he did.

"Cameron wouldn't use his credit card. He'd know

that you'd find him instantly that way. This guy... Don't you see? He *wanted* us to come to the shop. He wanted us here." She looked around once more. "Is he watching now?" Her voice dropped.

His stare shot around the street.

"He didn't know where I was." Her voice was soft. Almost sad. "That's why he said...*found you*. He didn't realize where I was, not until today."

No, no, shit, he didn't like where this was going, but Blake knew—

"The man in that video wasn't Cameron, but I think it was someone who admired his...work. Someone who admired him."

Fuck. Cameron had been a total mind screwer. Had pulling in another killer been part of his sick "experiment" all along?

"Cameron vanished. I vanished. And the perp in that video was just left with a whole lot of rage. He wanted to take that rage out on someone."

Every muscle in his body ached because his fury was so strong. "You." The perp had mentioned her in the video. He'd ordered that champagne for her... *Agent Dark*.

Her beautiful eyes stared up at him. "I left DC and cut all ties. Maybe that perp couldn't find me. He knew, though, that if anyone was aware of where I'd gone, if anyone could find me..."

No, no, hell, *no*. Blake swallowed. "It would be me."

"You come to town—" her voice was a whisper "—and within hours, Cameron's credit card is used. This guy picks the champagne that he *knows* Cameron favored, and he sends me a message."

Found you.

Her breath sighed out. "I think this guy—whoever he is—I think he followed you here."

"Samantha…"

"I think he killed Kristy Wales—made the video—I think he did it all so that he could catch the FBI's attention."

The son of a bitch sure had caught it.

"Then he waited. He watched and he…hunted." Once more, she peered around the street, as if searching for the killer. "He's still hunting. Because he's found the prey he wants. He's found me."

He was the one to lunge forward and lock his hands around her shoulders. "You're saying that bastard came here to kill you?"

"Kill me…or torture me into telling him what he wants to know."

"Just what the fuck does he want to know?" He glanced back through the shop window. Tammy White hadn't moved.

"Where Cameron is. He wants Cameron. As he said in the video, I screwed everything up. Now *he* wants to set it right."

By hurting her? By killing her? *Hell, no.* That couldn't happen, and suddenly the control he'd always fought to keep with her, it shattered.

She wasn't FBI. They weren't partners. There were no rules stopping him from taking just what he wanted.

The one thing he wanted? The one thing he needed desperately?

Her.

Samantha. She's what I need.

And she was the woman he'd just put in danger.

CHAPTER FOUR

"LET ME GET this straight." Captain Roger Lewis steepled his fingers just beneath his chin. His dark eyes were sharp and hard as they swept over Blake. "You want me to do a full-scale manhunt because you *believe* I've got a potential serial killer on the loose in my town?"

Beside Blake, Samantha stiffened. He saw her tense from the corner of his eye, but he kept his attention focused on the local police captain. After he'd talked to Tammy White, he'd known that he needed to bring the local authorities in right away.

"Cameron Latham?" Lewis's eyebrows rose. "That bastard is *here*?"

Lewis was an older African American man, probably in his early sixties, but still fit and strong. Intelligence glittered in his gaze, and the guy hadn't minced words when he brought Blake and Samantha into his small office.

But the way he talked about Latham...the way the guy's stare had just cut toward Samantha... *Why do I feel as if I'm missing something here?*

Blake cleared his throat. "The Bureau tracked the call that the suspect made—the call came from here in the city. The man who used Cameron's credit card *is* here," Blake stated. He was in Fairhope and he was hunting. "You need to alert all of your patrols to be extra vigilant. This man is extremely dangerous. He's killed before." *Kristy.* "And I think he'll kill again." He exhaled. "Because Cameron Latham's credit card was used in this city, we have to operate under the assumption that he may be present. I'm not saying a copycat isn't at work, I'm saying we need to follow all precautions. Your men should receive an immediate description of Latham, and they need to step up their patrols in the area." Four months ago, everyone had known about Latham, but people—even law enforcement officials—had short memories.

Lewis's gaze cut to Samantha. "Do you think it's a copycat or is the bastard here?'

She inclined her head toward him. "I think we're dealing with an incredibly dangerous man. A man who wants to emulate Cameron Latham. But we can't afford to overlook any possibility. It wouldn't be safe to do that."

"Son of a bitch." Lewis raked his hand over his face. "I'm in a small town for a reason. This shit isn't supposed to happen here." He rose. "I'll alert my men. And if there is *anything* else I can do to help you, say the word."

It was always so much easier when the local authorities cooperated.

Blake rose and offered the other man his hand. "I appreciate that."

Lewis had a strong shake. Very strong. "I trust Samantha's judgment."

What?

The captain inclined his head toward her. "You were

her partner at the Bureau. She told me...you're a good man."

No, he wasn't. Not always.

"It's getting late," Lewis continued. "Why don't you take Sammie back home, and I'll contact my officers?"

Sammie?

But Lewis wasn't hanging around for his response. The captain had already left the office. Blake glanced at Samantha, frowning.

"You're lucky," she murmured, her gaze on Lewis's back. "This small town happens to have the best damn police captain in the state. You can count on him to help you out."

Good to know. "You're close to him?"

A faint smile curved her lips. "He's the only father I've had since I was thirteen. So, yeah, we're close."

Surprise rocked through him. Samantha and her secrets...she always kept him guessing. One day, though, he'd learn all there was to know about her.

"Let's get out of here," she murmured. She rose and headed for the door. "I can't shake the feeling that he's out there, watching."

Blake caught her hand. *I did this. I brought him here.* "Samantha...he's not going to get to you."

She turned toward him, her body brushing against his. "That's the thing. I'd *rather* he come after me. And not pick some other woman like Kristy. I can fight back. I was a trained agent. I don't want anyone else being the victim." Her eyes gleamed up at him. "I don't want anyone suffering because *he's trying to get to me.*"

IT HAD BEEN one crazy day.

Tammy White locked the door to Connoisseur's Delight and stepped into the small alley behind the building. Her car was parked in the garage down the street, about forty yards away. The sun was starting to set, snaking across the sky and turning it a deep red.

The FBI agent had made her nervous. He'd stayed at the store, asking all sorts of questions. And then things had finally clicked for her.

Cameron Latham. Oh, Jesus, she hadn't even recognized the guy's name at first. She heard dozens of names every single day. They didn't stick out for her. So when the caller had placed the order, she hadn't given a second thought to his name.

Until the intense agent and the dark-haired lady had shown up. They'd pushed with their questions, and she'd finally made the connection.

The Sorority Slasher. Cameron Latham. He'd been such a big deal in the news months ago, but the guy had seemingly vanished from the face of the earth. She'd forgotten all about him.

I won't be forgetting now.

Her steps quickened as she headed toward the garage. She couldn't wait to tell her roommate, Jemi, about everything that had happened. Her friend was going to flip. Maybe they should call the news. Or one of those tabloids. Those reporters liked these kinds of stories, right?

"Did she like the champagne?"

The question came from the shadows just inside of the parking garage. Tammy opened her mouth to scream, but a man lunged toward her. He slapped one hand over her mouth even as the other yanked her close to him.

He was handsome. That thought flashed through her

mind as the fluorescent light shone down on them. His face was handsome. His hair was stylish. He had perfect teeth as he smiled at her.

He didn't look evil, but…

He is.

Tammy struggled against him, but his grip was tight. Punishing.

"I hope she liked the gift. I was just so happy to find her that I needed her to understand I was here."

He was yanking her toward a gleaming luxury sedan. A big, fancy car.

"But then I got to thinking…"

She kicked him hard, and his grip slackened on her. Tammy took that opportunity, and she jerked out of his grip. She lunged forward—

But he yanked her back. He spun her around, and his fist slammed into her face.

She heard bones crunch, and she felt wetness— blood—splash over her lips as it poured from her nose. Her whole body slumped, and he seized that moment to lift her up and shove her into his waiting car. Dazed, she didn't even fight him.

This isn't happening. This isn't happening.

"I got to thinking…" He cranked the car. "She's going to need more than a bottle of champagne to realize the hunt is on. She's going to need a victim."

Tammy tried to grab for the door handle.

And that was when his hand flew out, and the knife came toward her.

BLAKE STOOD AT her front door, staring down at her. He'd brought her back from the police station. The ride had been quiet, intense. Too many emotions had seemed to fill the air between them.

Danger was waiting. Samantha could feel it in the air. A killer was coming. There was no more hiding.

Her breath eased out. "Thank you for the ride."

He growled. That was the only word for it—a growl. Rough and animalistic, and the sound made Samantha's heartbeat quicken.

"You think that's the way it ends? I bring you home and I just walk away, knowing some bastard is out there? Someone who seems to be after *you*?"

She didn't want him to walk away. Samantha's hand lifted and pressed to his chest. "Blake—"

"Screw that." His words were ragged. "I'm not playing by the rules any longer. You matter too much."

And then...Blake was kissing her. Samantha's hands flew up and flattened against his chest. She could feel the strength of his muscles beneath her touch. She intended to shove him back. After all, they were partners and they couldn't—

We're not partners, not any longer. I'm not FBI. I'm a civilian. There's no line that we can't cross.

Her hands pressed to him, but she didn't push him back. She'd thought about his mouth for a long time, wondered how he would kiss, how he would taste. Wondered what it would be like to just let herself go with him.

She didn't have to wonder any longer. Samantha's lips parted beneath his, and when his tongue thrust into her mouth, a low moan built in her throat. She found herself rising onto her tiptoes, leaning toward him, wanting more of his kiss.

Still waters run deep. That was the old saying. She'd always suspected he had some very, very deep waters.

Deep water, deep passion. If he just let his control go, if she let hers go…

No.

Samantha stepped back, sliding from his embrace. Her heart was thundering in her chest, and her breasts— her nipples—were tight with arousal. All from one simple kiss. Blake Gamble was dangerous to her. Another truth she'd always known. She felt too much with him. Too much, too fast.

"I'm not going to apologize for that kiss." His voice was a sexy, rough rasp that sent a shiver down her spine.

"Don't remember…asking you to do that." She remembered kissing him back with a wild hunger. "We're adults. We can—"

"I've wanted you from day one."

Her breath whispered out. She'd seen the desire in his eyes, burning hot in that green gaze. But he'd always kept his control around her.

"I played by the rules."

Because he seemed to be the rule-following sort.

His jaw tightened. "And now I've fucking brought a killer to your door." Anger was there, deepening his voice, letting the hint of his Texas drawl slip out.

"Blake, it's not—"

"My fault?" His gaze burned. "You don't need to lie to me. I keep telling you that. When will you believe it? I can handle your truth. I can handle every single secret that you have."

No, he couldn't. He didn't know about her past, and he didn't know everything that had happened the terrible night she realized that Cameron was a killer. If he did know, would he even want to touch her? Would he look at her as if she were the monster?

"I'm not going to stand back, not any longer." The heat from his body seemed to wrap around her. "I want you. I'm not going to let that sick son of a bitch out there—whether it is Latham or someone else—I'm not letting him get you. I may not be your partner anymore, but I'm here. I will always be here for you."

The hero. He had that complex straight to his soul. Too bad she wasn't built the same way. There was a darkness in her, one she'd always felt, like a constant companion who shadowed her every step. Cameron had said she was made for the dark. *We both know you like the dark... Isn't that your name?* His voice floated through her mind, the way it often did. Little things, replaying in her head. *I always said you had that killer instinct.* How many times had she found herself looking over her shoulder in the past few months, certain that Cameron would be there?

"If you don't want me to touch you again, you say the word."

She wanted his touch right then. Wanted to drag him close and kiss him and forget everything else. She'd been playing by the rules during her time at the FBI, and what had that good behavior gotten her? Blame and a swift kick in the ass on her way out of the door.

"But I'm not leaving," he added, when she remained silent. Mostly because she wasn't sure what to say. "And the killer out there? I will hunt him down. I'd just rather do it with you at my side. Because, despite the bullshit that EAD Bass said about you, I know you're the best. We can work together again. We can take this bastard down."

Tempting words. But she already knew what she had to do. "I'll help you find him." Stopping the killer was

as necessary as breathing. She couldn't let a predator like him hunt. The image of Kristy Wales flashed
through her mind. The woman had been terrified, and
her blood…it had sprayed so wide when her throat was
cut. "We'll make our own rules from here on out."

So she'd be back to working with Blake, temporar-
ily. And the desire that was between them? The need
that kiss had just proved was still as hot as ever? What
were they supposed to do about that?

Ignore it, the way they'd done before?

I won't pretend. "I want you," Samantha said. She
could give him that truth. "I just don't know what to
do about that need." Another quiet admission. She did
want him, so very much, and that desire terrified her.

Her last lover had turned out to be a serial killer.
Since then, she hadn't been willing to lower her guard
and trust another man with her body. But if she could
trust anyone…shouldn't it be Blake?

She turned away from him, fumbling with her door.
It took three tries to get the lock open, then she hur-
riedly disengaged her security system. She went inside,
but…Blake wasn't following her.

Samantha glanced back.

His hands were clenched at his sides, and his eyes
glittered with unmistakable desire. Her breath hitched
as she stared at him, and need twisted deep inside of her.

"I think there are a few things we need to discuss."
Again, his voice was rough and dark, sexy.

Samantha licked her lips and tasted him.

If possible, his gaze went even brighter. *Be careful.* The warning whispered through her mind. *You're
about to go too far.*

"I need to talk to you about Latham." His breath

rushed out on a low hiss. "And this time, I don't want you holding back with me."

Oh, hell.

TAMMY WASN'T FIGHTING any longer. A few jabs of his blade and she'd started cooperating quickly. Begging, promising him *anything*.

Before he was done, he'd take everything from her.

After he'd transported her, he'd tied her up, secured her easily, but now her blood was making a pool beneath her body. A gag was shoved in her mouth—just in case she got the urge to scream—and she stared up at him with wide, desperate eyes. The light from his lantern shone on her, illuminating her terror in just the right way…while letting him blend with the shadows around them.

Does she know there's no hope? Or does she still think there is a way out?

He held up her phone in front of her face and snapped a quick picture. "Perfect." He'd taken the phone—and her bag—when he grabbed her in the parking garage.

A low moan came from behind the gag. He lifted up the phone, studying the image. "Not too bad, but I don't know if this angle really is your best. Let's try again." Another shot. Another bloody picture. "Much better." He smiled at her. "You know, I'm really glad I took a few hours to learn my way around your town earlier." Now he nodded. "Always get the lay of the land, that's step one. You have to know where to hide. You have to know how to escape. I mean, otherwise, aren't you just a sitting duck, waiting for the authorities to come?"

Her eyelids had flickered when he said "authorities." Oh, that was cute. She did still have hope. "I'm good on the water," he murmured. "So that helped me. You pay a guy thirty bucks, and you can rent a boat down here for two hours. Gave me time to study your city from land and sea." Then he'd just gone in and set his plan into motion.

Step one. Find Samantha Dark.

Step two. Learn the city.

Step three. Use the right bait. He thought he was staring at the best bait he'd ever seen. He reached into her purse. "Now, if I know those true-blue FBI types, they generally want to give witnesses their card for contacting later...you know, in case you remember any of those pertinent details they love so much." He found the business card in her bag. He lifted it up, smiling when he saw the handwritten number on the back. So incredibly helpful. "They just make it too easy."

He'd be calling that number, soon enough. But first, he had to get the stage set just right. The perfect location. The perfect distraction.

And my bait has to be safe.

He put the card into his pocket and picked up his knife.

She whimpered, a scared, pain-filled sound.

Oh, but he did like that sound. His thumb slid along the blade of his knife. Maybe he did have time to play just a *bit* more.

HE NEEDED TO get his control back, and he needed to get it back *now*.

Blake exhaled slowly as he crossed the threshold and entered Samantha's home. She'd retreated a bit as she stared at him with wide eyes. He shut the door behind him, aware that the tension in his body was just thickening.

He was rock fucking hard for her. He wanted to pull her into his arms again. Kiss her, taste her…strip her.

Have her.

But he knew he was supposed to play things carefully between them. Samantha was important. He'd spent months without her. And if he was finally going to have her back…

Then they needed to clear the air between them. He had to know just what she was facing.

And Samantha needed to know just who he truly was.

"I wanted you from the moment we met."

She stood with her back to the picture window. Her arms were crossed over her chest. At his words, her lips parted.

"You've been in my head for months. A ghost, haunting me." Driving him to the edge. "I can't do it any longer."

Her hair slid over her face as she shook her head. "Do what?"

He closed the distance between them. His hand lifted, and his fingers curled under her chin. "Play the good-guy role." A man could only pretend for so long. Then his true colors would start to show.

"You *are* good, Blake." She gave a little laugh, one that held the faintest edge of desperation. "I'm not wrong about that." Her long lashes lowered, shielding her gaze. "I can't be wrong about you."

Because of Latham. His jaw locked, but he didn't stop touching her. He couldn't. "Did you love him?"

That question had her lashes flying up. She stared at him, that beautiful gaze of hers stark.

"I want to know."

As he waited for her answer, jealousy coiled within him. Dark and twisting. That jealousy had always been there where Latham was concerned. From the moment they'd met, the guy had rubbed Blake the wrong way. *Because we both wanted her.*

"No, I didn't love him...at least, not the way a lover is supposed to. We were far better friends than lovers." Then she gave another bitter laugh. "Though I guess we weren't very good at that, either."

He was about to grind his teeth to dust, but he kept his touch gentle on her. Samantha and Latham. Lovers. That damn image had tormented him too many times. But soon enough, he'd have Samantha. Blake would have her in his bed. And when he did, he'd banish the memory of Latham from her mind.

Before he could speak again, Samantha had pulled away from him. "There are things you don't understand about me. Things that—"

"That *he* did?"

Her head snapped toward him.

Dial back the jealousy. "You think I can't handle your secrets, Samantha? You think *he* could?"

"He didn't mind my darkness." Her gaze skittered to the picture window. "I guess it makes sense now, doesn't it? He liked that part of me. The part that lets me see into a killer's head so easily. The part that thinks about murder and death. He was drawn to all of that because he was the same way."

"You are *not* the same." She needed to see that. "I don't care what crap Latham fed you. You *aren't*."

"He was my first lover."

Every muscle in his body locked down.

"He told me I was perfect, inside and out, and after years of hiding the truth about myself from the world, it was nice to have someone who didn't care about… about the things I'd done." She'd stumbled just a bit over those last words.

And Blake knew that Samantha had more secrets. Secrets that she'd shared with Latham, and those secrets had bound the two together.

"Why won't you trust me?" he gritted out.

She eased out a slow breath, then squared her shoulders. She met his stare, not flinching. "I want you."

Music to his ears. Blake took a step toward her, but Samantha threw up her hand, as if warding him off.

"Wait!"

He had been waiting for her, for months.

"I want you more than I think I've ever wanted anyone."

She was going to break him. He could feel his control splintering. But she'd said wait, and her trembling hand was still in the air.

"But you are *wrong*, Blake. You aren't playing some good-guy role. That's who you are." She bit her lip. "That's who I need you to be. And I can't be wrong about a man I'm with ever again."

"I won't hurt you." He'd never do anything to her. "You can count on me. Don't you know that?"

Her hand fell to her side. "What if I hurt you?"

He frowned.

"You don't know me as well as you think."

Blake closed the distance between them. He curled his hands around her shoulders and pulled her close.

"Only because you keep secrets. You don't have to do that. I can handle anything you've got."

"If you turned away from me..." Her smile was bitter-sweet. "I think it might break something in me."

Samantha could never be broken. Not by him. Not by Latham.

His mouth lowered to hers, but...his phone started to vibrate. He swore when he heard the high-pitched ring. Someone's timing was shit.

He let her go and reached for his phone. With the case, there was no way he could miss any call. There was no "off-duty" time for him when he hunted a killer. Blake didn't recognize the number on his screen, but it had a local area code. His finger swiped over the phone, and he put it to his ear even as Samantha backed away.

Again.

Hell, no. You aren't running. We aren't done. In fact, we're just getting started.

"This is FBI Special Agent Bla—"

Laughter cut through his words. Taunting, cold.

Blake's face tensed.

"I don't care about you, Special Agent. You're just a means to an end. I'm calling to talk with Agent Dark."

He nearly shattered the phone.

"Is she with you?" that taunting voice continued. "I bet she is. I bet you're staying as close to her as you possibly can."

"Who the fuck is this?"

He saw Samantha tense.

"The man you're hunting, of course."

And the bastard had called him?

"I learned Agent Dark didn't get my champagne. I was quite disappointed with that, so I had to let the clerk know just how upset she'd made me. Poor service just can't be tolerated, you know."

What. The. Hell?

Samantha grabbed Blake's arm. *Put him on speaker.* She mouthed the words at him.

Blake lowered the phone and tapped the screen so that she'd be able to hear the call, too. She needed to hear the bastard. The more she learned about him, the better able to profile him she'd be.

"Can she hear me yet?" the voice demanded. "Because I really need her to know what's happening."

"She can fucking hear you," Blake snapped. "But I don't buy your—"

"I'm going to kill her." Flat, cold words. "I've got Tammy White here with me, and I am going to slice her open. I will watch her bleed and beg and die, and it will all be because of you, Agent Dark."

The killer wasn't speaking to Blake any longer. He was talking directly to Samantha. *Because she's the one he's wanted all along.*

The bastard's voice was a rasp. Disguised.

"Do you want that, Agent Dark—Samantha?" He seemed to stumble a bit as he finally used her first name. "Do you want someone else to die because of you?"

"No." Her voice was low, emotionless. "But I don't believe that you have her. If you have her, you'd send—"

The phone vibrated as a text came through. Still keeping the speaker on, Blake swiped to look at the text. He heard Samantha suck in a sharp breath as she saw the brutal picture of a bleeding Tammy White.

"That's my proof," the caller taunted. "Now, be a good agent. Get the coordinates from the pic. They'll tell you where I am. Then *you* come, Samantha. Just you. You come to meet me. You trade yourself for Tammy White, and she'll escape with just a few...cuts."

This was bullshit. "Not happening," Blake swore. Samantha was not going to enter into some kind of deal with that psychopath. Yeah, they'd get the coordinates, all right. Blake was already getting them. Most folks didn't realize that when pictures were taken...if they were using a smartphone to take pics, those phones would actually embed GPS coordinates into each photo. The coordinates were in the metadata that comprised the photo files. To see those coordinates, you just had to view the photo's properties. You could get the coordinates, as long as the person who took that photo hadn't disabled the feature on their phone...

And there they were. The coordinates popped right up, a perfect guide to the killer's location.

"If Samantha doesn't come to me, then Tammy White will die within the next fifteen minutes." Spoken easily. "She's already bleeding quite a bit now. A pool of blood is beneath her. Maybe I cut her too deeply last time."

Samantha's fingers locked around Blake's wrist. "Don't hurt her again. I'll come to you."

Fury swept through Blake.

"You come alone, Samantha. If I see a cop car, if I see a helicopter...I will drive my knife into Tammy's heart right then and there. Her death will be on you."

No, Tammy's death would only be on the sick son of a bitch who got off on torturing her.

"I know the tricks the FBI uses. You'll get the coordinates from the picture I sent...and you'll realize that

I'm on the water. So much wonderful water down here. Makes things easier for me."

Fucking bastard.

"I've left a boat for you all tied up on the old pier near Devil's Hole. You get in that boat—just you. Be in it within ten minutes. Take the boat and come out to meet me. If I hear a chopper, if I hear another boat, if I see any cop cars…my knife is in Tammy. She's dead, and it's because of you, Samantha."

The line went dead.

"No fucking way," Blake gritted. He'd call the local cops, he'd get backup…they'd go in with a full team.

But Samantha shook her head. "You know he wasn't lying. If he sees a team coming, he will kill that woman."

"He's going to kill *you*." Blake believed that with utter certainty. "You think I'm just going to stand there while you walk in blind? You think—"

"I swore the day that I buried my father…" Her shoulders straightened. "No one else would ever die in my place."

Her father?

"Tammy White is a pawn. It's me he wants, and it's me he's going to get."

CHAPTER FIVE

IT WASN'T THE first time that Blake and Samantha had faced down a killer. "Just like old times, huh?" Blake murmured as he shut off the car engine. They were parked at the end of a long, lonely stretch of road. He could see a pier waiting for them. The old, wooden pier was twisted, broken in spots, seeming to sag into the very water itself.

This was supposed to be the site of the trade. The bastard actually thought Samantha was going to walk out to the pier, get on the little boat that was bobbing in the water and head out to meet him...alone.

What a fool. As soon as he'd gotten off the phone with the perp, Blake had been in contact with the FBI and the local authorities. The Bureau had traced the call, triangulating the signal because they *weren't* just going to the drop site based on that text alone. Blake had wanted confirmation—and he'd also wanted backup.

Local FBI agents and Captain Lewis's men were on the way. They'd been given orders to stay back, keeping out of sight, until Blake gave the signal that they were needed. He'd considered bringing in Coast Guard support, but sound traveled too easily over the water, and he hadn't wanted the perp to be alerted to their presence. Blake fully believed if the guy got spooked, he would kill Tammy White.

So the Coast Guard was on standby. Everyone was waiting for the perp's next move.

A move that involved Samantha.

"Not exactly like old times," she murmured as she checked her gun. She'd made sure to arm herself with her personal weapon before she left her house. "This is the first time a killer has wanted to trade for me."

"Latham wants you badly."

She turned her head to look at him. "This isn't Cameron. That wasn't his voice."

"The bastard was disguising his voice." She couldn't be certain they weren't dealing with the SOB. "Maybe he used that credit card because he *wanted* you to know he was in this town. Maybe he ordered the champagne for the same reason. He came here for you."

She tucked the gun into her waistband.

"I don't like this," he said. When they got out of the car, she'd be the one going down those rickety steps to the pier. He'd follow her, keeping to the shadows, watching her every moment. He had night vision goggles so that he could keep his gaze on her every step of the way. Samantha had been trained to deal with hostage situations. They both had.

But...

This is different.

"If I don't go out there, he *will* kill her, Blake. And that girl's death isn't going to be on my conscience. Trust me, I carry enough baggage as it is." She rolled back her shoulders. "He gave us clear orders. I had fifteen minutes to get here. I'm supposed to head out alone. My time is almost up. If I don't go, she dies."

Damn it. *Damn it.*

"If our situations were reversed, you wouldn't even hesitate."

No, he wouldn't. He'd put the victim first because that was what an FBI agent was supposed to do—was trained to do.

"You understand, Blake, so you're going to do your job. You're going to have my back, the way you always have. You're going to trust in me."

That was the thing—he did trust her. He always had and he always would.

"You wanted my help," she said. "Well, you've got it." She reached for the door handle.

He grabbed her, yanked her back.

"Blake—"

He kissed her. Hard. Fast. Desperate. He was angry—with her, with himself. With the bastard who was playing his games out in the bay. For an instant, she kissed him back, but then Samantha was pushing against him.

She had a job to do.

So did he.

Blake pressed his forehead to hers. "If he comes at you, you shoot him. You make sure you're the one who survives."

"I'll make sure Tammy and I both survive." Her breath eased out once more. Then she opened the passenger-side door and slipped away from him.

He immediately reached for his phone and dialed Lewis. "She's going in. Everyone stay in position until you get the signal from me." No choppers were in the air—it was far too quiet that night for the birds to launch. If they went out, the perp would hear them.

"Got it," Lewis growled back. "But you make sure you guard her back."

That was a partner's job, after all.

Blake ended the call and slid from the vehicle. He kept to the shadows as he followed Samantha. The moon was heavy in the sky, and he could see Samantha heading toward the pier. Though the moon was bright, it was hard to see out over the water. Fog was rolling in near the shore. Samantha had told him fog often covered the bay.

Their perp was using that cover to his advantage.

Blake could hear the rush of waves against the shore down below. Samantha was climbing down the wooden stairs that would take her to the pier. Her steps were sure and her hands were empty—he knew she'd tucked the gun into the back of her jeans, the better to hide it from the man waiting for her.

His gaze drifted away from Samantha to the end of the pier. A small boat waited there, so perfectly placed. The killer had obviously planned this moment.

He was watching me. He wanted Samantha. He was willing to kill in order to get her.

And Blake had been the one to lead the bastard straight to her.

SAMANTHA WAS FAR too conscious of the gun's weight at her back as she climbed down the wooden stairs. The pier was located at the base of the bluff, and in that narrow beach area, the wind seemed to make a tunnel, almost moaning around her.

This section wasn't used much. The last big tropical storm had washed away part of the bluff—and the pier. As she eased onto the pier, she saw the missing slats of wood. It swayed beneath her feet, and she was worried she'd tumble into the water at any moment.

She looked straight ahead, trying to see through the

growing fog. The perp had told her to get on the boat. She figured there would be a phone waiting there for her. He would call her, give her more directions. *More orders to follow.* He was a very, very organized killer. Meticulous.

The organized killers were the most dangerous ones.

A piece of wood cracked beneath her foot and gave way, bobbing into the water as she staggered. She was a good swimmer, so she wasn't afraid about taking a tumble into the water. If she had to do it, she could swim out into the bay and find that perp herself.

But…

Something is off. Every instinct had screamed that truth at Samantha as she inched along the old pier. The middle section was completely underwater, the old boards sagging as she sloshed across them.

The perp wanted her. He'd killed one woman to find Samantha's location. He'd abducted a second in order to draw her out. She reached the end of the pier. The boat bobbed beside her, a motorboat that waited for her. She started to ease down into the boat, but then she stilled. *Something isn't right.* That had been the thought she had when she confronted Allan March. A sense that the whole setup was wrong. She'd been correct that terrible day and now…

She retreated back onto the pier. Her head turned, and she gazed through the fog, trying to see if there was another boat out there, one that held the perp as he watched her.

But…

I don't see any lights. It could just be due to the fact that the perp had killed his lights and anchored his boat just beyond her sight. He could be watching her from the water right then, using night vision binoculars. Or...

She looked back toward land. Houses were up there, easily several dozen old cabins that dotted the bluff. A few of those places were condemned—they'd been too damaged in the last storm. Abandoned houses. An abandoned house would be the perfect place to hide with a victim.

Maybe he wasn't in the water at all. At least, not any longer. Maybe he'd been in the water when he brought that motorboat to shore. Maybe he'd taken refuge in one of the houses on the bluff and *then* called her with his little plan.

The better to watch me.

But if that were the case, then why would he want her to get into the boat?

Why...

A phone rang. Its cry was loud, jarring her and making her jump. Her gaze shot back to the boat. She didn't see the phone, but the sound was coming from the small vessel. The perp had left a phone for her to find, just as she'd suspected he would.

Had he placed the phone there, giving her exactly fifteen minutes to reach the boat before he called? Or... *Is he watching me even now? And he realizes that I didn't get into the boat? He's trying to draw me closer.* If she wanted to save Tammy White, she was supposed to get in that boat. She was supposed to climb in and answer the phone. But...

Something is off.

The phone stopped ringing.

Think like the killer. There were some habits that she couldn't break.

And a door seemed to open in her mind. *He's orga-nized. Smart. It's like a game of chess to him. He's con-nected to Cameron. Wants to emulate him...that was what he did with Kristy Wales. He tried to duplicate Cameron's crimes as a way to get to me.*

He wants me.

He...blames me?

Her gaze darted to the boat once more. Oh, hell.

He wants to eliminate me. Everyone else is just col-lateral damage. Everyone else—

The phone rang again.

She spun away from the boat, trying to lunge down the pier as she fled.

SAMANTHA WAS RUNNING away from the boat. As soon as he saw her spin around, Blake took off.

Something spooked Samantha. His gaze shot around him, searching the darkness for any sign of the perp. Maybe Samantha had seen something to make her think the perp wasn't out in the water. Maybe he was up there with Blake, maybe—

That was when he heard the explosion. Deep, rum-bling, quaking like thunder, the explosion seemed to rock everything around him. His gaze flew back to the pier, and he saw the fire, shooting high up—red-and-gold flames. The boat was gone. The end of the pier was gone, and Samantha—she was gone.

HE RUSHED DOWN the stairs. The fire was blazing, crack-ling. *"Samantha!"* He jumped over the last seven steps and hit the small beach at a run. The pier had broken loose in big, thick chunks and those chunks were on fire. He hurried forward—

Another explosion erupted, this one near the middle of the pier, sending chunks of wood flying into the air, making the smoke and fire billow and sending him flying back through the air. He landed hard, but he had the sand to cushion his fall. Blake shoved back up to his feet, his heart racing in his chest.

The son of a bitch set a trap for Samantha. He planted bombs out here, in this secluded spot, and he lured Samantha into his web. He watched, and he waited, and when the time was right, he detonated.

Because he wanted Samantha dead.

Blake didn't head for the remains of the pier. Another bomb could be there, ready to go off at any moment. He rushed toward the water, immediately sinking to his knees in the waves. *"Samantha!"* he bellowed her name as he lunged forward. "Samantha!" The water hit his waist, and he kept going, desperate to find her. He wasn't about to leave that water without her.

Not Samantha. Not—

He saw a hand flash up through the water, about twenty yards in front of him. Then Samantha's head broke the surface.

Time seemed to stop for him. *Alive. She's alive.*

He dived into the water, swimming fast and hard for her as the fire raged on the remnants of the pier. His arms moved in a blur, his feet kicked and soon Samantha reached out to him, curling her arms around his shoulders.

"I'm okay." She was out of breath, treading water. "I had to…stay under until it was clear…"

He yanked her against his body, held her close. A shudder shook him.

"I'm okay," she said again. Her breath still panted out.

"I jumped into the water…right before the explosion… Something was off… Knew it…"

He held her tighter. "He wanted you dead." His hands flew over her, frantic, because he had to be sure she was all right. Whole—safe in his arms.

Her arm curled around his neck. "We can't go directly back to…the beach. He might be waiting."

"Damn straight," Blake said grimly as they began to swim parallel to the shore. That blast and the fire lighting the sky would bring help their way. When Lewis and the others saw those flames, they'd come running. But if he and Samantha went straight back to the beach and the old steps that led up to the bluff, the killer could pick them off when they came ashore…and long before the help ever arrived.

"But what about Tammy?" She glanced back at the flames. "Is she—"

"I don't know." The sooner they got to a safe shore spot and circled back to the SUV, the better. *We can't be the hunted. We have to turn him into prey.* "But we'll get her, Samantha. We'll get her back."

She didn't speak again. They swam in the dark water, and the fire raged behind them.

THE FIRE WAS PRETTY.

He took a moment to admire the way it lit up the sky. Big and bold, rather like the fireworks he'd seen when he spent his summers in Martha's Vineyards.

It had been easy to set the bombs—two of them. One on the motorboat. One just beneath the pier. Almost anyone could make bombs these days, with just a handy internet search, but he'd actually spent time researching bomb-making for quite a while.

One of his "phases" as his father called them. When he liked to explore destruction and death.

Bombs had interested him, once upon a time, but he'd decided they weren't intimate enough. Sure, they could do a lot of damage, very fast, but...

As Dr. Latham had told him, the knife was an intimate weapon.

I only used the bomb because I didn't want to get too close to Samantha. He'd actually seen a story on the news months ago about Samantha Dark and a bomb. She'd barely escaped another case where someone tried to use a bomb to take her out. It had seemed fitting, using a bomb again.

It was dangerous to get close to her. Dr. Latham had gotten close to her...

And now he's gone. She took him away.

He watched the flames crackle. A lot of the fire had already gone out, thanks to that black water. He didn't see Agent Gamble. The man was probably still in the water, still searching for Samantha.

Would she be burned when he found her? Disfigured? The classic beauty Latham had once spoken of gone forever? Oh, he hoped so.

It would be a treat to see Agent Gamble carry her broken body from the bay. To watch as the agent stood there, so lost without her.

But he could hear the scream of sirens, coming in the distance. If he lingered too long, cops would be there, not that the local cops scared him.

He'd completed his mission. Finished what Dr. Latham had started. Now he could evolve. He could go to the next step, he could—

It was the faintest movement that caught his eye.

The fog wasn't as thick near the shoreline, and the moonlight shone down just right…just enough for him to see a man swimming. Strong, hard, a good distance away, not near the burning pier at all.

He could see the man's dark head. He approached the shore, splashing out of the water, and he knew it was Agent Gamble. Agent Gamble turned, stretched out his hand behind him—

No, fucking no.

And his fingers curled around *her* hand. Samantha splashed after him. They ran onto the little beach and hurried toward the cover of the trees.

She hadn't died. She hadn't paid for her crimes. She'd escaped, like a damn cat with nine lives.

Rage twisted in his gut, and he took a lurching step toward them.

But the cry of the sirens came again, louder this time, closer, and he knew that he couldn't finish Samantha right then.

But he'd have his chance with her soon enough. After all, he still had the one thing she wanted. The victim.

"WE CAN'T LET him get away," Samantha said. The wind whipped against her, and she shivered as her teeth began to chatter. When the explosion had first hit, she'd stayed under the water until she thought her lungs would burst. She'd tried hard to swim away from the pier even as the flames lit the sky. "Get the…cops… Search the area. He has Tammy close—"

Blake pulled her against him. She could hear the shriek of sirens. Captain Lewis and his team were rushing to the scene.

"You're freezing." Worry filled Blake's voice.

She was freezing, no doubt, but she was alive, so she'd just suck it up and deal with the cold. "I think he has Tammy in…in one of the abandoned houses on the bluff… W-we have to search for—"

He wrapped his arms around her, held her tight. She could feel the heat of his body, and she wanted to press herself against him. He was warm and strong and she felt safe with him.

"Thought I'd lost you…" His words were so low and…there was something about his tone. Something dark. Dangerous.

Samantha glanced up at him.

"I *can't* lose you."

The sirens were louder. "We have to go," she said, "we have to help find the perp. We need to get Tammy."

He eased back. "We will get her. And that SOB."

In the next instant, his hand had locked tightly around hers. They were running through the trees— twisting pines and old oaks that had limbs heavy with moss—as she and Blake circled back toward his rented SUV. He rushed to the vehicle, and she was right with him. He opened his door and—

Patrol cars screeched to a stop, the sound of their squealing tires and lurching brakes hurting her ears. Bright headlights illuminated the scene, and she heard a rough voice call out, "Freeze! Put your hands up!"

Blake turned in the light, putting his body in front of hers. "FBI," he shouted. "Agent Blake Gamble. The perp is still here. We need to start searching the scene *now.*"

Yes, they did…before the guy vanished into the shadows once again.

THE PERP WAS GOOD, Blake would give him the fuck that. The local cops and FBI agents had fanned out fast, and they'd made short work of searching the abandoned houses on the bluff. One house had shown signs of a squatter, a place littered with old food and debris, but whoever had been there—he was long gone.

They'd found blood in a second house. One with boards on its busted windows and a front door that had been sagging open. Captain Lewis had ordered a crime scene team to the house so they could take care of collecting that bit of evidence.

The problem was…it had been a whole lot of blood. Too much.

If Tammy White is alive, I'm not sure how long she has left.

But the perp—he'd gotten away. Probably just driven away when the cop cars had been screeching up to the scene.

"You didn't get a look at the guy?" Captain Lewis asked him now. He was pacing near Blake's SUV. Samantha stood to the side, a borrowed Fairhope PD jacket wrapped around her shoulders. Lewis had given her that jacket—a jacket that dwarfed her fragile frame.

"Didn't see him," Blake said. "Just the explosion."

Lewis swore. "Hate this shit is happening in *my* town. It's not supposed to happen here. Sammie…" He pointed at Samantha. "You know this is a good town, a quiet place. A *safe* place."

"It's always been my safe place," Samantha said, her words low, just carrying to their little group. "That's why I came back."

Lewis shifted closer to her—and the guy even gave

her an awkward pat on the back. "You needed to come home."

Blake's eyes narrowed. The police captain was built like a former linebacker, and energy seemed to crackle in the air around him. He was over thirty years Samantha's senior, but there was a definite sharpness about him. This guy was no small-town hick. *And this man knows Samantha, very well.* Well enough that concern thickened his voice when he spoke to her. Samantha had said Lewis was the only father she'd had since she was thirteen, and right then, there was no missing the concern in Lewis's eyes. The captain cared for her, deeply.

"We're catching him," Lewis vowed now. "This punk isn't coming here to terrorize my people. He's not going to try to hurt *you*, not on my watch. If your dad knew what was happening…"

Samantha's shoulders stiffened at the mention of her father. Blake wanted to know a whole lot more about Samantha's dad.

"This man is highly intelligent." She spoke without any emotion. "He's a determined killer. Methodical. He's planning out his attacks in careful detail."

"The smart killers are always the most dangerous," Lewis muttered.

She nodded. "I still believe that Tammy White is alive. I think that blood we found was hers. He stashed her in that house so he could come and get an up-close view of my death."

Only, that didn't happen.

"He had a car waiting. He drove off before the cavalry could arrive. There are so many old roads that snake through this town—he was able to slip away clean." Her breath heaved out. "But I believe that the perp is going to make contact with us again."

"Why?" Lewis demanded. "The guy should be running for the hills, covering his tracks. If he's so smart, he knows we're all after him now, closing in, and he—"

"He didn't get what he wanted." Simple words. "He didn't kill me."

And that isn't going to happen. Not on my watch.

Lewis pointed a shaking finger at Blake. "You're FBI! I did some digging on you. You're supposed to be some hotshot…"

He was? Since when?

Lewis took an aggressive step toward him. "Why the hell did you let him get away? If he was close enough for him to nearly kill Sammie, then he was close enough for you to grab!" The captain shook with accusation. "This is on you, *agent*. You should have stopped him! Tammy White would be on her way to a hospital and you—"

"Stop." Samantha's hand curled around Lewis's arm.

Immediately, Lewis seemed to sag in on himself.

"Blake went to help me. When the first bomb went off, I was in the water. He didn't…" Samantha shot him a quick glance. "He didn't know if I was alive or dead. We were partners at the FBI. A partner always watches your back. His job was to come after me. To help me. He jumped into the water for me."

And he wouldn't have gone out without her. But not just because they'd been partners. Because she was so much more to him.

"A partner always watches your back." Lewis's voice had gone soft as he repeated her. "Well, then…" Lewis nodded once, seemingly coming to some sort of decision. "You keep doing that shit, *Agent* Gamble. Because if something happens to Sammie, I'll be coming after you myself." Someone called out for the captain, and he said, "Excuse me. I'll be right back."

Samantha watched him walk away. "Sorry," she said, her voice still lacking emotion. "Sometimes, his protective instincts can come out a bit too strong."

Blake wanted to put his arms around her and pull her against him—the fear was still like acid burning his blood. But there were too many eyes on them. "Sometimes?" he murmured. "Sometimes, *Sammie*?"

Her gaze cut to him. Bright lights illuminated the scene and her suddenly tense expression. "Don't. Only Lewis gets away with calling me that. To everyone else, I'm Samantha or I'm Sam." She paused. "My dad called me Sammie, okay? My dad and Lewis. They worked together, a long time ago. And after my dad died, Lewis was the one who looked out for me." A faint smile curved her lips. "He was the one who ran off my boyfriends. Who made sure that no one ever gave me any trouble." Her smile slipped away. "I could've used him in DC."

You had me. I'd stand between you and trouble.

"He's a good man," she continued, "and a fine cop, but he's been working this small town for over twenty years. Fairhope doesn't get killers like this one. He's going to need our help."

Our. He liked the way she said that.

"I've already put in some calls," Blake said. "We'll get one of our forensic teams to the area." He wanted their team examining any material that was found from the bomb device. But hell, since the bomb had been in the water, the tide could have carried that material all over the bay—making his job so much harder.

Lewis hurried back to them. "My men are going to keep combing the area."

A shiver slid over Samantha.

Lewis frowned at her. "You two need to go home and get changed. We've got this search, for now. And if you really believe this crazy SOB will be contacting you again…"

"He will." Samantha spoke with absolute certainty.

Lewis gave a grim nod. "Then you need to get some rest so that you can be ready for him."

"Lewis—"

"Don't even think of arguing with me, Sammie. My town, my rules. I want you to go home." Lewis was standing firm on this one. But he eased closer to her, and Blake heard his voice soften. "If he's gunning for you, then you need to be at the top of your game. You have to rest."

"But Tammy…"

"You can't do anything for her right now." Lewis's voice was still…well, not gentle, but kind as he spoke to Samantha. "You have to take care of yourself first."

Samantha had always put the victims first, so Blake knew she wasn't happy even as she gritted, "Fine. Your crime scene. For the moment." Her chin lifted. *She's thinking the FBI will be taking over soon, and she's right.*

Blake cleared his throat. "I'm going to contact Executive Assistant Director Bass again about this case. I came down here on a hunch, but now I need more manpower." Not just local cops and fresh-faced FBI agents from the Mobile, Alabama, office. He wanted his team from Violent Crimes there. He wanted agents who were used to dealing with killers of this caliber.

"Executive Assistant Director Blind-ass Bass?" Lewis said. "Yeah, good luck with that."

"Lewis…" Samantha warned.

"The guy fired his best profiler! Hell, no, I don't have confidence in him. But you—" Lewis cocked his head as he studied Blake "—you… I might be able to work with you."

Good, because you have to work with me. "We'll be back at first light," Blake told him. "If you find anything before then, you call me." He rattled off his number, and Lewis put it in his phone.

But then the guy's gaze swept over him. "Just *where* will you be?"

"Excuse me?"

Lewis jerked his thumb toward Samantha. "She's obviously a target. If anyone needs protection…say protection provided by the FBI…" His drawl thickened. "It will be Sammie. That's why I'm asking…*where* will you be? Holed up in some hotel? Or watching her back?"

Blake was starting to like this guy. A straight shooter who didn't waste time with bullshit. "Until we catch this bastard, I'll be staying at Samantha's place."

"Damn straight." Lewis spoke as if it had been his decision. "Like I said, I might be able to work with you." Then he turned on his heel and headed toward the cops who were at the remains of the pier.

Samantha waited until he was gone, then she leaned in close. "You don't…have to stay with me. I assure you, I can take care of myself."

He knew that Samantha was strong. That she could fire a gun better than any other agent. That she could take down men twice her size in a blink. But he also knew…

This is Samantha. And she matters too much. He caught her hand. "You don't get a choice on this. This guy wants you dead." To leave her alone now? Oh, hell, no. "Welcome to protective custody."

CHAPTER SIX

EXHAUSTION PULLED AT Samantha as she stepped out of the shower. When she'd gotten home, she'd smelled like the bay and ash, a revolting combination that still clung to her skin. The adrenaline rush she'd felt earlier was gone, and her body was shaky as she wrapped a towel around herself.

Blake was down the hallway. She'd left him in the guest room. It was a two-bedroom cottage, and she was ever so grateful for that second room right then. She'd told him—numerous times—that she didn't need him to stay with her, but he'd been adamant.

Before, she'd worried about them crossing lines. Partners didn't get to cross lines. But...

They weren't partners any longer. He was in her home.

And she wanted him.

Samantha lifted her hand and rubbed it across the foggy surface of the mirror. Her wet hair hung near her face. Her eyes looked too big. Her skin too pale. She was sporting a few new bruises in various locations— when she'd been in the water, she'd rammed into some chunks of wood. But...

She was lucky. She'd cheated death. Not everyone had the chance to do that.

A knock sounded on the bathroom door. "Samantha?" Blake's voice was a deep rumble. "You okay in there?"

She opened the door. "As okay as could be expected, you know, considering some psycho out there wants me dead."

His gaze dropped to her body—to the towel that covered her. That green stare heated, and his hand came up to grip the door frame. "No one is going to kill you."

That actually wasn't a promise that he could make. No one could save the day every single time. "If I'd been slower to jump off that pier, I'd be dead right now."

She saw his knuckles whiten as he gripped the frame harder.

"It's all about you." His gaze locked with hers. "That's why Kristy Wales died—to get my attention. To get me to get to *you*. Tammy White was taken as bait for you. Every move this guy makes...we both know it's all about you."

Her head tipped back. He'd showered, too, and his dark hair was still wet. He wore a black T-shirt and faded jeans that she knew he'd gotten from the overnight bag he'd brought inside earlier. He looked sexy. Strong.

He looked like the kind of man who could make her forget the hell around her, if only for a little while.

He looked like the best temptation she'd ever seen and that was why she needed to stay very far away from him. "It's not about me." Her hand lifted and pressed to the towel, to the knot she'd made between her breasts. The last thing she wanted was for that towel to slip.

It was the last thing, right?

Samantha cleared her throat. "He's not killing for me. He's doing that for Cameron." Cameron...the ghost who would never leave her alone. Only, he wasn't really a ghost, was he? He was very much alive. He was out there, hunting, hiding. Waiting.

Blake finally backed up a step, and she brushed by him. Her toes curled against the old hardwood floor.

"Has he contacted you?"

Her shoulders stiffened. She was in her bedroom. The brass bed sat in the corner, and her robe was on top of it, tossed over the covers. "If one of the FBI's most wanted called me, don't you think that would be something I'd report?"

"I don't know..."

Those words *hurt*, and she whirled toward him.

He still stood by her bathroom door. "I do know you've been holding on to secrets. Secrets about that night." He took a step toward her. "When I arrived with the police, you'd been sliced, cut several times—"

"I had to get thirty-five stitches," she whispered, her lips feeling numb. Her whole body felt numb, the way it always did when she thought about that terrible night.

He kept closing the distance between them. She backed up until her legs hit the bed.

He kept coming.

Then Blake's hand reached out, and he touched her left arm. His fingers curled around her wrist, and he lifted up that arm. His fingers feathered down her forearm, stopping over the scar left there. "A defensive wound."

That was the type of scar victims normally got when they lifted up their hands to fend off an attacker.

She had a matching scar on her other arm.

"You're a trained FBI agent." His voice was deep and

a little rough. "You know a lot of the others wondered, how did Latham get the drop on you? Why didn't—"

"Why didn't I take him down?" Her stomach clenched. "Trust me, I tried. He carries his own scars now, you can count on that." He'd been so surprised when she'd first slashed at him. His eyes had gone wide. "Cameron is far more dangerous than anyone realizes. He's strong and he's smart and he has no conscience. He killed for sport, just to see what it was like."

"Why didn't he kill you?" He was still feathering his fingers over her arm, and her breath stuttered out. He'd always made her feel too much. Her body was too attuned to him. Too sensitive.

Or maybe I've just gone far too long without a lover.

Her last lover…had been Cameron. They'd come together often over the years. He'd been her first lover, but not her last. None of the others had ever seemed to understand her the way he did. She didn't want romance and candlelight. She needed something basic. Almost primitive. Cameron had given that to her. Pleasure, without the twisted tangle of emotional attachment and fake promises of a happy-ever-after ending.

Then she'd met Blake, and the twisted physical relationship that she'd had with Cameron—almost an addiction on both sides—had come to an end. She'd wanted more than the rough, hot pleasure in the dark, but the elusive more—a connection that was physical and emotional—had been just out of her reach.

Blake wasn't out of her reach now. He was touching her.

"I fought back hard," Samantha said. "I put him off guard, and that's why he didn't kill me." And that was partially the truth. Partially. And…

It doesn't have to end this way, Samantha. Don't you see...we could be perfect together? I've always known...

Tears stung her eyes, and she blinked them away.

Blake was watching her, far too closely, and she saw his gaze sharpen. "Samantha…"

"No." She shook her head. "I don't… I *can't* talk about this right now." She didn't want to talk at all. She could collapse in that bed, but Samantha knew the nightmares would just chase her. They always did.

The thing about profiling killers… Once you learned to think like them, you never learned how to stop. The victims and their pain didn't stop. The terrible knowledge was always in your head.

To stop killers, you became a killer. You looked at the world differently. You even found yourself thinking…

That woman walking alone, she isn't even looking at her surroundings. No one else is on the street. If I ran up behind her, if I moved fast enough, she'd never even have the chance to scream...

Dark, terrible thoughts.

His hand fell away from her. "I should let you get to sleep."

Why? So she could dream about being a killer?

He started to turn away.

"Stay." The line she'd tried never to cross? She was leaping over it right then and there. "Stay with me." They only had a few hours. Not enough time for regret for now.

His face hardened, and she was afraid he was going to try doing the *right* thing. The noble thing. *Don't take advantage—she's too vulnerable.* Samantha could practically see those thoughts on his face.

Screw that.

She would give herself the escape that she craved so very desperately.

She reached for that knot fastened across her breasts, and she let the towel fall to the floor. The cold air hit her, making her nipples pebble. She pushed back her shoulders, lifted her chin, and once more, she said, "Stay."

His hands had clenched, as if he were trying to stop himself from touching her. "If I have you now, I *will* want more."

She'd give him all that she had, but instead of promising that, she said, "Fuck me."

And then he was on her. His arms pulled her against him, strong and hard, and his mouth took hers. There was no pretense of slow seduction. Desperation between them left no room for gentle coaxing. His kiss was wild, frantic, burning with desire.

His tongue thrust into her mouth. A moan spilled from her, and then she was lightly sucking his tongue and pushing her hips against him. She didn't want foreplay. She wanted passion and fire and him driving her into oblivion.

She grabbed the hem of his T-shirt and yanked it up so that she was touching hot, hard skin. He tore his mouth from hers and began to kiss his way down her neck. Her nails raked him and—

His hands locked around her hips. He lifted her up, held her so easily and then put her on the bed. He followed her down onto the bed, kissing a hot path along her neck, over her collarbone, down to her breasts.

When he took one nipple into his mouth, she arched up against him, choking out his name. Her fingers slid into the thickness of his dark hair. Her legs were open, his hips settled between them, and there was no mistaking the long, thick length of his arousal.

She wanted his cock in her.

He was still sucking her breast. Still making arousal heat in her blood and his fingers had worked their way between their bodies. "Oh, baby…" He growled the words. "You're not ready for me."

She was. She needed this. Needed *him*.

His head lifted. His glittering gaze held hers.

Then he bent to press a kiss to her stomach.

He pulled off his T-shirt and dropped it to the floor. She wanted his jeans gone, too, but he wasn't reaching for them. He was putting his hands on the inside of her thighs. Spreading them wider, then lowering his mouth over her sex. She felt the whisper of his breath on her skin, and she tensed.

Then his mouth was on her. Licking, kissing and sucking her and driving Samantha *wild*. While his tongue worked her clit, he pushed two fingers into her, thrusting them in a rhythm that made her lose her breath. Her heels dug into the mattress, and her head tipped back as her whole body tightened. She didn't want to come, not yet, not until he was with her fully, but—

Samantha couldn't hold back her orgasm. It ripped through her, stealing her breath and sending pleasure spiraling through every cell in her body. "Blake!"

Her heartbeat thundered in her ears. Her eyes closed. Aftershocks still trembled through her sex. The bed dipped, the mattress sagged as he slipped away. *Wait… Away?* She forced her eyes open and saw him standing near the bed. He'd ditched his jeans but had taken a foil packet out of his back pocket.

He stared at her, and she'd never seen his face look quite that way. Too stark, too hard, glinting with a fierce desire that should have made her nervous.

Then he was climbing back onto the bed, and her hands reached up to curl around his shoulders.

He positioned his cock at the entrance to her body, and she couldn't help tensing. This one moment... *There is no turning back.* But that was okay. She didn't want to go back. His hands curled around her hips, lifting her up toward him. She was still slick and sensitive, and a gasp slipped from her.

"You ready now?"

More than ready. "No more waiting."

"Hell, no." He sank into her, a long, hard thrust that pushed him balls deep into her. Her legs hugged around his hips, she held tight and she just...let go. Let her control go. Let her worries go. She held on to him, and as he withdrew and thrust into her, she met him eagerly, demandingly. His cock slid over her clit, making her gasp as the pleasure built within her again. Her hands weren't just holding on to his shoulders, she was raking his skin, urging him on with her touch and her gasps and her words. She wanted him to take her hard and long. Wanted that wild oblivion of pleasure once more.

He wasn't treating her with kid gloves like she was some delicate flower. He was taking her—fucking her with a desperation that said he felt the same clawing need that she did, and Samantha loved it.

He kissed her, deep, thrusting his tongue past her lips even as his cock thrust into her body. The angle was just right for her, the need too much to contain any longer, and she erupted, her hips jerking spastically against his, and he was right with her—Blake stiffened above her.

His head lifted, his eyes blazed down at her and she saw the stark pleasure wipe across his face. "Samantha!"

She loved the way he said her name, or rather, the way he'd roared it.

She held him tighter, squeezed him with her sex and rode out that last wave of pleasure. Her heart kept drumming in her ears, racing so very fast. And as that frantic thunder finally slowed, her lashes began to drift closed.

He slid out of the bed and padded toward the bathroom. She couldn't find the energy to look after him, and she wondered if he'd make his way to the guest room.

But he came back to her. He slid into the bed with her. Pulled her against him, cradled her there, making her feel…safe.

Blake wrapped them in covers. He held her easily, and sleep finally pulled her under.

"How will this end, Sam?" Cameron asked her. "Am I really supposed to kill you now?"

She was in Cameron's office, seated at his desk, his two computer monitors in front of her…and pictures of the dead girl tearing her world apart.

Cameron took a step toward her. "What do you see on the screen?" He sounded curious, not angry. "Is it her? The last one? And she was going to be my last one, by the way. My experiment was over."

"Experiment?" Her left hand had slid into the drawer and curled around the letter opener. The letter opener— it wasn't much of a weapon, but it would have to do.

"Um. Yes." He took another step toward her. He hadn't turned on the lights in the room, so he was just a big, dark shadow. "I wanted to see if I could do it, you see. If I could kill. If I could get away with the crimes. And I wanted to see...what are people like...in that last terrible moment? What is it like when they know that hope is gone and they're dying?"

Nausea rolled in her stomach. "Cameron?" She was staring right at a stranger. Not the man she knew. Not her ex-lover. Not her friend.

He took yet another step toward her. She couldn't see his hands. She wished that she could just see his hands. "There were some surprising results. Would you like to hear them?"

Because Cameron—he'd always enjoyed bouncing ideas off her, too.

"I felt alive when I killed those women. Interesting, don't you think? That death finally made me feel alive? Until that point, I'd only felt that way, well... when I was fucking you. But that ended when you met Blake Gamble."

She flinched. For a moment, she almost dropped the letter opener. "Blake and I are just...partners. Nothing more. We haven't been together."

His smile was cold. "Not yet. But I know you, Sam. I know what you want."

No, no, he didn't know.

"It was easy to kill." Now his voice was almost musing. "I never hesitated. I mean, I always suspected I was a bit of a psychopath, but as we all know...psychopaths aren't necessarily monsters. They're just...unemotional. Detached. Able to become such great surgeons, CEOs, lawyers...even profilers for the FBI..."

Her phone was in the guest bedroom and Cameron didn't have a landline. She needed to call Blake. Call Bass. Call the cops.

"Covering up the crimes—well, that was easy, too. All so *easy*. The hardest part? That was staying two steps ahead of you. Because that profile you made up? The one that your boss called shit?" He was in front of the desk now. "It was dead-on."

She could hear the frantic drumbeat of her heart. Every. Single. Beat. "Show me your hands."

He laughed. "You think I'll hurt you?"

She was certain he would. Samantha knew only one of them would make it out of that room alive. Cameron wasn't going to be the type to go down easily. He would hate jail. Prison wouldn't be an option he'd consider. "Show me your hands."

"You were right about Allan." Cameron watched her with a predatory stare. He'd never looked at her that way before. "Allan did need the money and…the guy was sick, too. Dying. I was really just speeding up the process for him. It was all going to work so perfectly." Now he sounded…sad. "But even when you were drunk… you were figuring shit out."

"I wasn't drunk."

"Yeah, you were." Another sigh. "I think you might have been better at profiling than you realized. But then, I always said you had that killer instinct."

"Show me your hands." It sounded as if she were begging, and Samantha hated that. "Cameron…"

His left hand came up—

And she surged to her feet because she *knew* he was going to kill her. She swung out with her letter opener, and it caught his hand, sending a wet spray of blood flying.

Cameron bellowed, and then he launched across the desk, coming right at her. They fell back together, slamming into the floor, and that impact was hard enough to knock the breath from her. But she didn't let go of the letter opener. She kept it locked tight with her fingers, and Samantha shoved it right against his throat. "Stop!" Samantha gasped out the word. "Don't make me do this!" *Don't make me kill you.*

She didn't want to kill...*him.*

He stilled. His gaze—so turbulent—met hers. "This isn't the way we end." His blood was on her. His body pinned hers. She knew Cameron was strong—he'd spent years strengthening his body and his mind. Most people looked at Cameron in his fancy suits and saw just the academic. But she knew the man who had a fourth-degree black belt in Tae Kwon Do, the man who'd studied Krav Maga because he thought a weak body led to a weak mind. He was deceptively strong and incredibly fierce... *But I never knew he was a killer.*

"I don't want to hurt you," she said.

He gave a little laugh. "My blood is on you. Too late. But you know what...let's run a little test."

And her blood seemed to turn to ice. He'd just said he killed those poor women as some sort of experiment. The last thing she wanted was to become another *test* for him.

"I don't think you can do it." His words were soft, almost...seductive. A lover's words. "I don't think you can slit my throat right here and right now."

"Cameron..."

"You're the tough agent. The profiler who actually did know her shit, by the way, but you were mine long before you were those other things." More than a hint of possession thickened his voice. "Just as I was yours."

She kept the letter opener to his throat. She could

slice his skin, but it would hardly do enough damage to carve him open, unless… She'd have to plunge the letter opener into his trachea, slamming it home deep. That would stop him.

"I don't think you can do it. I'm going to give you five seconds to try. Five seconds when I don't fight you back. See if you can disable me in that time. See if you can hurt me, because, Sam, I won't be going to jail. Not even for you."

She stared into his eyes and saw the truth there.

"Five," he whispered.

"You're under arrest," she told him. "Cameron Latham, you have the right to—"

"Four."

"—remain silent. Anything you say will be—"

"Three."

"—used—"

"Two."

Could she drive the letter opener into his throat? Was it even strong enough to do enough damage to stop him?

"One—"

She jerked up her right hand—and the letter opener, yanking it away from his neck—even as she rammed the base of her left hand right at his nose. He wrenched back as the blow came toward him, but she still heard the crunch of cartilage as she broke his nose. He lunged away from her and she rolled quickly, springing to her feet.

He swiped his hand over his nose, smearing the blood on his face. "Nice one." He sounded…admiring.

She shook her head.

"Told you." Cameron gave her a wide smile. "You

couldn't do it. You can't kill me. You're in too deep with me."

"You're going to jail. You're—"

He turned his back on her and walked toward his bookshelves. Big, massive bookcases. Lined with classic books—many expensive first editions. "Killers like certain weapons, but you know that already. I prefer a knife. It's…personal. Intimate. I like the way it feels when it cuts into skin." He reached for a book. Opened it—and she realized the pages had been hollowed out when he lifted a knife from the inside.

"Put it down," Samantha ordered.

He looked at the blade. "You killed before me, did you know that?"

Samantha swallowed and said, "Put down that knife now."

He didn't. Cameron turned to face her, his head tilted. "It was in the line of duty, but you still killed. You took out George Farris before he could hurt you or that precious partner of yours. Blake." His lips twisted when he said the other man's name, disgust flashing on his face. "He was a problem from the beginning. I knew that."

"Blake isn't a problem."

"I'd always wondered what it would be like to take a life. I saw what it did to you. Part of you was…horrified, but I know you, Sam. I know you so well." He took a step toward her. "You didn't just fire once when you shot George Farris. You did it twice—because you liked that rush."

She shook her head.

"You liked the way it felt to have that ultimate control over someone. You liked the way it felt to kill."

"I didn't."

He made a faint humming sound, a murmur of disbelief. "It's just the two of us. Don't forget, I know your very darkest secret. I know all about the man you killed when you were just a child."

"Stop it."

"I held that secret for you, but I have to confess… when you killed again, when you took out George Farris, I was jealous. I wanted to feel what you felt."

She'd felt horror. Disgust. And she felt the same thing now as she stared at Cameron. "I don't want to hurt you," she whispered. But he wasn't giving her a choice.

Cameron smiled at her, his sexy, full smile. The one that had charmed so many women. *He used that charm on his victims. They went willingly with him, blinded by that sexy grin. They never had a chance. I didn't have a chance…*

"Let's see if I want to hurt you." He lifted the knife. "Because maybe you've been holding me back all of these years and I didn't realize it. Maybe you aren't what made me happy after all. Maybe you're what made me weak."

"Cameron—"

He ran toward her, the knife glinting.

CHAPTER SEVEN

"No!" SAMANTHA JERKED upright in bed, her heart heaving, her skin covered in a film of sweat. But Cameron wasn't there. He wasn't coming at her with a knife. And—

I'm not alone.

Blake had sat up beside her, his body warm against hers in that bed. "Samantha?"

Her breath rushed out as she fought to get control. She hated those damn memories. They just wouldn't stop spinning through her head. She didn't dream like normal people did. When she slept, her memories came to her. Memories of the cases she'd worked on. The victims. The killers.

Memories of Cameron.

Because once I get killers in my head, I can't get them out.

"Bad dream?" Blake asked her softly.

Her head turned away from him, and she looked toward the big window that faced the bay. Streaks of sunlight were starting to pour through the window. "Yes." Her voice had gone hollow. "Just a bad dream." She looked at the light for a moment, pulling in strength as she stared at it, then she faced him once more. "I'm going to shower."

I crossed the line. I made that choice.

She slipped from the bed and padded to the bathroom. She shut the door behind her and yanked on the shower faucet, sending the water gushing down. But Samantha didn't get into the shower. She turned to stare at her reflection in the mirror. She'd woken up before the end of that dream—of that memory. Woken up with Cameron lunging at her with the knife, but his attack hadn't just ended at that point. The dream had ended, but in real life...the knife had kept coming.

She glanced down at her arms. Her left arm, then the right. She'd always carry those scars. Defensive wounds that had come when she'd lifted her hands to protect her throat and her face. But...

She'd fought him. Kicking and punching because she knew how to take care of herself. They'd wrecked his perfect study, sending lamps crashing to the floor, breaking his computer, smashing those two precious screens. They'd slammed into the bookshelves and books had rained down on them.

But...

He'd put his knife to her throat. He'd been so strong, maddened with adrenaline, and Cameron had been able to slam her down onto the floor. His knife had pressed to her throat. Their positions had almost been perfectly reversed.

I should have been stronger. I was the trained agent. I should have—

She slammed the door on those thoughts and stared at her reflection once more. Classic victim blaming. She should be stronger, smarter than that. *And I should not blame myself.*

But...she did.

Her golden gaze stared back at her.

"I can't look into those eyes and kill you. Not you." Cameron's voice. Always in her head.

She squeezed her eyes shut. In the end, Cameron hadn't been able to slice her throat open, and she'd used that weakness against him. She'd gotten free of his hold. She'd heaved him off her. She'd grabbed the broken lamp and hurled it at him.

He'd dropped the knife. He'd—

A soft knock rapped against the bathroom door. "You okay?"

Blake…asking nearly the same question he'd asked her hours before.

"Fine." Such a lie. She was far, far from fine, but she wouldn't let herself splinter apart. Her steps were slow as she headed toward the shower. She climbed in, and the hot water pelted down on her. It washed over her body, and she wished she could just wash away her sins. Then she could start fresh without this heavy weight on her soul. A weight that said she was as guilty as Cameron. That he'd been right about her.

The shower curtain was suddenly jerked aside. Gasping, she whirled to see Blake standing there—Blake, who had a pair of jeans hanging low on his hips. Blake, who looked sexy with his tousled hair and a little scary with the hard, determined expression on his face.

"What's wrong?" Samantha said.

"No more lies." His voice was so rough, growling. "You think I can't see it when you lie to me?"

Pain knifed through her, and she grabbed for the shower knob, yanking it hard and shutting off the water until only a *drip, drip, drip* remained. Goose bumps immediately rose on her arms. She reached around him, her hands curling around the white towel that rested on the hook. She pulled it toward her, not bothering to dry off but quickly wrapping the cotton towel around her body. "Don't accuse me of lying without any—"

"You called out his name in your sleep." Red stained his cheekbones. His eyes glittered at her. "I was in bed with you, and you were calling out for him."

Her lips parted. Her heart just seemed to stop. "It wasn't like that." *I should never have let him stay in my bed. I knew the memories would come.* She'd just been so tired. And she'd felt safe with Blake. It had been so long since she'd truly felt safe.

"I know the difference between a woman who is calling out for a man she wants…and a woman who is absolutely terrified."

Cameron did terrify her. Not because of what he'd do to her, but…

What I know he'll do to others. Others like Blake.

"When are you going to trust me?" Blake demanded. "When are you going to get that I'm on your side? I've *always* been on your side."

He had. He'd stood up to Bass for her, tried to get her job back for her. And she'd just held her secrets. *Because I don't want him to turn away.* "I'm not the woman you think I am."

A furrow appeared between his brows. "How do you know what I think about you? You've never gotten close enough to me to find out. You've—"

A phone was ringing. She didn't recognize that sharp ringtone, but Blake must have because his shoulders stiffened. "Fucking hell." He pointed at her. "We aren't finished. This isn't done."

If only it were.

"Son of a bitch." Frustration shook the curse, but he raked his hand over his face. "I called in more FBI resources last night. That's my contact at the Bureau getting back with me." He gave a grim nod. *"But we're not done, understand that."* Then he stalked away, heading into the bedroom. She just stood there a moment, dripping, and she heard the rumble of his voice.

"Josh?…Yeah, man, good to hear from you…No, no, it's not too early. I'll be heading to the crime scene soon…Damn straight I could use you on this one. USERT is exactly what we need at the bay."

She stepped out of the shower. A puddle of water dripped to the mat. USERT…the FBI's Underwater Search and Evidence Response Team. They could definitely use that team in their evidence recovery efforts. Lewis would be glad to have their assistance.

Blake was still talking in the other room, giving the details about last night's explosion. Last night? More like just a few hours ago. She toweled herself off and dressed quickly, drying her hair fast—the shorter cut made that so much easier. In moments, she was wearing clean clothes, feeling a hell of a lot less vulnerable, and she was back in the bedroom with Blake just as he ended the call.

He turned toward her. "That was Josh Duvane. He's coming down with some of his teammates. Should be here by the middle of the day."

That was good. She knew the name—Duvane. He'd been a former SEAL, and a guy who'd often been seen sparring with Blake in the training room. She hadn't been surprised when those two hit it off. They'd exuded that same intense, ex-military vibe. Danger, beneath still waters.

"We should get back to the scene." She nodded toward the window. The sun was definitely rising. "There's going to be a lot of ground to cover."

He tossed the phone onto the bed and crossed his arms over his chest. His muscles flexed. Blake had a killer body, toned and golden, with more than a six-pack. A few scars—faint white lines—sliced over his abs. He hadn't ever told her how he'd gotten those scars.

But then, she'd never asked.

"When do I get the truth?"

His voice still held that thread of anger. Anger directed at her.

Don't ask for what you really don't want to hear, Blake.

He took a step toward her. "What the fuck do I have to do…" Blake rasped, "in order for you to finally trust me?"

"I LIKE TO watch the sun rise." He tapped the knife to his chin. "The sky starts so dark, and then you catch the small trickles of crimson that start to pour through. Soon all you see in the sky is that red, so deep and pure, right before the light comes." He considered the matter for a moment. "I don't really like that light. Too bright for me. But I love it just before the sun rises." Smiling, he glanced back at Tammy. "But what do you think?"

She stared at him, black smudges of mascara tracking down her cheeks. She had a gag in her mouth, blood staining her clothes, and she was tied with her hands behind her. He'd put her in a chair, locked her down good and tight, then set her up so that she'd get that killer view of the sunrise.

"No answer?" He frowned. "Maybe you're more of a sunset kind of girl?"

She gave a low, moaning sound. That sound grated on his nerves. He'd already been through a real pisser of a night as he dodged the authorities and set out to find another hiding spot to use, and Tammy…she just wasn't the woman he wanted. "You're not her."

He had to make a new plan because this—it wasn't working. "They'll be searching now. They know I have you." He'd set their whole world on fire just hours before. "They'll bring in the big guns. More FBI agents will be swarming the area." And they'd be in his way. More people in his path as he fought to get to Samantha Dark. "So annoying." He put down the knife. Picked up his phone. He had lots of phones.

"We're going to make a video," he told her. "It will be short. You'll say exactly what I need you to say." He gave her a big smile. "And then I'll be done with you."

Hope lit her eyes. Such beautiful, wild hope. Just as beautiful as Dr. Latham had said.

"You want out of those ropes, don't you, Tammy?"

She gave a frantic nod.

"You want the pain to stop?"

More desperate nods.

"Then make this video for me. Say what I want, and I'll stop it for you. I'll cut those ropes off you, and you won't have to see me ever again."

The hope just glowed brighter. Almost as bright as the sun. He lifted the phone, aiming the device so he could get her face—and that hope perfectly. "We'll do a practice run first. I'll tell you just what to say. You memorize the words, and then we'll do the video. Understand?"

Her quick nod said, yes, she understood.

Excitement made his fingers tremble. "Start by saying…'You were the one who should have died…'"

FURY AND LUST weren't a good combination. Blake knew that shit, and he was trying to get his control back in place. Samantha stood in front of him, wearing black pants, a black shirt, and looking all too damn sexy as the button-up shirt showed off the curves of her breasts.

She'd been naked when he'd burst into the bathroom. Rage had been riding him hard, and she'd stood there, water dripping down her body, looking like every dream he'd ever had…until he'd gazed into her eyes. There had been pain in her golden stare. Fear.

He didn't want her afraid of him. When would she get that? He would stand between her and any threat. *Always.* Not because they were partners. Because— hell, because it was *her.*

And she was afraid. He could feel the fear in the air around them. Cameron Latham wasn't anywhere close by, but the bastard had left a mark on her, and Blake was tired of it. He wanted the man gone. Behind bars. Dead.

He wanted—

Samantha. Every single bit of her, including the part that Cameron had seemed to lock away.

"He couldn't kill me." Her voice was low, whispering, sliding over his skin like so much silk. "He tried to do it. He had the knife at my throat." Her hand rose and pressed to her throat. An image flashed in Blake's head… Samantha, covered in blood, as she stood in the chaos that had been Cameron's study. Her hand had gone to her throat then, several times as the authorities had swarmed the place, and he'd just thought she was afraid.

He hadn't realized what she'd been silently telling him, all that time.

"I was pinned beneath him on the floor. He could have slit my throat. Killed me. I think...at first, he wanted to do it. Cam—Cameron said I'd been holding him back. For years, holding him back, and he didn't even realize it."

What the fuck? He took another step toward Samantha, but she backed up. That retreat cut him to the quick.

"So he was trying to get me out of his way. He had the knife at my throat. But I saw his eyes change. They'd been cold, calculating, and then he looked up at me. He *saw* me. And he..." Her voice trailed away. She was staring at the floor.

"What the fuck did he do?"

Her gaze lifted. Met his. "He told me he was sorry. That hurting me didn't feel the same. That he wouldn't do it again."

His jaw dropped in shock.

"He was stunned. I could see it. Until that moment, I know he truly believed he was going to kill me in that room. But he couldn't do it. When it came down to it, he just couldn't."

"Because he loves you." Grim words.

"No." Samantha immediately gave a sharp shake of her head. "That wasn't it. I'm not sure he *can* love. I think he can mimic emotions, I think that's what he's done for years, but...love? That isn't what he feels for me. Our relationship is far more complex than that." She hesitated. "I was the one constant in his life. The one person he felt could understand his dark urges. I think he wanted me to keep living because in some way he saw me as…his."

Bullshit, baby. You aren't his. That demented freak isn't ever going to have you.

"Whatever the reason," she continued quietly, "I used that against him."

Damn straight. He was fucking glad she had.

"I heaved him off me. Kicked the knife out of his hand. Attacked him with a fury." Her lips twisted. "Cameron wasn't the stuffy college professor. He's strong. Trained."

He knew that. After the truth about the SOB had been revealed, Blake had made a point of learning everything he could about the man.

"There was a moment when we were fighting, and I could have killed him. I could have taken him out, just as he could have killed me." Her skin had gone pale. "I didn't. He saw that in my eyes—the same way I saw it in his. I *couldn't* cross that line. I couldn't kill him." She gave a bitter laugh. "I guess hurting each other was fine, though. Doing plenty of damage. I had rage and fear on my side, and he had… He had the determination not to go to jail. Cameron doesn't want prison. Prison is hell to him." Her hand rose and pressed to her temple. "He slammed me into the wall. It was a hard hit, and I passed out. He left me there, probably because he didn't know what else to do with me. Maybe because for the first time in his life, Cameron panicked." She seemed to consider her own words for a moment, then added, "When I woke up, I barely had time to stand before you and the others were rushing inside."

Fuck. "I got a text, I thought it was from you—you never said—"

"Never said that Cameron was the one who'd texted you?" She swallowed. "No, I didn't. I told you, he panicked when he left me. That's why I believe he killed the cop who pulled him over when he was speeding away. His instinct was to flee, and he did. But I think before he ran out of that blood-soaked study, he stared at me and he decided he wasn't letting me die."

"Because you were his." Rough words.

"He wanted to make sure I survived. He knew you'd ensure that survival, so he texted you." Her breath expelled on a long rush. "I had the chance to kill him when we were fighting in that study. I could have taken him out, but I hesitated. *I wanted to bring him in alive.*" Her voice was little more than a whisper as she said, "Because of me, a killer escaped. He's been loose for months. He killed that cop. *Because of me.*"

He closed the distance between them. He had to touch her. His hands curled around her shoulders. "Has he contacted you in the last four months?"

"No."

She met his stare directly. Some of the tension eased from his body—

"But I've been trying to find him."

What the fuck?

"If he kills again, that's on me." She pulled from him and marched toward the white door on the right. He'd figured that was a storage closet, but when she opened the door, he saw that it led to a small room, a study. Slowly now, he followed her inside and saw—

"Jesus Christ, Samantha."

Crime scene photos—Sorority Slasher photos—were

pinned to a bulletin board. She'd put a map up of the United States, and pushpins were posted in various cities. Along with short notes about… He leaned in closer and felt his blood chill. "You've been hunting him."

The note near Chicago said: *Spotted at favorite nightclub. Left with a brunette…*

"She looked like me," Samantha said, her voice cold. "I missed him by a day. He always liked that club. I should have tried it sooner. I've hit all his favorite spots, leaving my card with bartenders and bouncers, hotel concierge staff… I just keep missing the bastard at every stop."

She looked like me. He turned toward Samantha. "What happened to the brunette?"

"He fucked her and he walked away."

Blake blinked.

"He's not a typical serial, not in any way." She exhaled. "He can control himself. He kills when he wants to kill. Don't get me wrong, Cameron loves the rush of power, but he isn't killing because of any compulsion. He's doing so because that's his choice. He chooses who lives and dies."

"Sounds like the guy thinks he's fucking God."

He expected her denial. Instead, she nodded. "Cameron thinks he's untouchable. That he's smarter, better than the authorities who are tracking him."

"No one is untouchable." And Latham wasn't God. More like the devil. Blake's gaze jerked away from hers. She had a computer on her desk, and when he went toward it, he saw a stack of files. Blake whistled. "These are confidential FBI files."

"Yeah, well, turns out I still have a few friends there.

They slipped me copies. I'd, uh, appreciate it if you'd not mention this to Bass."

Growling, he looked back up at her. "Why are you doing this? The FBI *is* tracking him—"

"And they're not going to find him. Because he can vanish. He knows how. He doesn't *have* to kill, and his killings are the only thing that raises red flags with the Bureau. Otherwise, he just slips right past the nose of the authorities. They are going by old-school profiles right now...thinking that a serial has to act in a certain fashion. Thinking if he kills again, his MO will be the same. It *won't* be. He isn't the same. Cameron is a chameleon, one who can blend in perfectly anywhere. When he kills, it's about pleasure. His pleasure. Nothing more."

"So that cop he killed after he left you in DC—"

"The cop didn't even register to Cameron. The guy got in his way. So Cameron got him *out* of the way. He isn't afraid of anything or anyone, and that just makes him even more dangerous." Her focus shifted to the map on her wall. "He's out there, probably hiding in plain sight, and planning his next move. I think he knows I've been on his trail. That's what the woman in Chicago was about. A screw-you to me. He knows I'm hunting him, because I *will* stop him. He's just trying to decide what kind of game he wants to play with me."

"That is messed up."

A faint smile curved her lips. "That's Cameron."

And she'd been going after him, all on her own? "Why didn't you tell me—" he waved his hand to indicate the room she'd set up "—about all this? I could have helped you!"

"What did Bass say that day? Oh, right...that I'm

a sinking ship." Sadness flashed on her face. "He was right, and I didn't want you going down with me."

Screw that to hell and back. He marched from around the desk, stopped when he was right in front of her. "I will have your back."

Her mouth parted, as if she'd speak, but then she stopped, pressing her lips together.

"Samantha…"

Her long lashes lifted. "He won't kill me. That's my advantage in this hunt. I can get right up to him and live. But he *will* kill you. In an instant. Cameron always saw you as a rival, even though we hadn't—"

"Slept together?"

She flushed, then nodded. "He was glad that was a line we hadn't crossed."

Now his gaze narrowed on her. "Did you fuck me last night because you wanted me…or because you were trying to send a screw-you message to Cameron Latham?"

Anger burned then, turning her gaze molten. Anger and pain.

"Samantha—"

She shoved against his chest before she calmly answered him. "It was the only thing that felt right under the circumstances." Then she spun on her heel. "Sharing is over. We have a crime scene waiting—and a victim out there, one who needs us."

He'd messed up. Badly. Blake tried again, "Samantha…"

She didn't stop. And he didn't know how to reach her. Blake finished dressing—fast—and soon he was following her to the front door of her cottage. She opened the door.

He grabbed her hand. "Samantha, wait, listen—"

A camera flashed.

"Perfect!" A woman's voice praised. "Now go to video feed."

What the fuck?

A trio waited just beyond Samantha's doorstep. A woman with perfectly styled blond hair, dressed in a stylish suit, and two men—one with a receding hair-line and a video camera on his shoulder and the other a young guy in skinny jeans. The young guy was snap-ping photos, using his flash because they were in the shade on that porch.

"Samantha Dark!" the woman cried out. "Janice Beaufont, from Central News Five. I've learned about the abduction of Tammy White, and I want a comment from you *and* FBI Agent Blake Gamble."

The news crew was there? Lying in wait for them?

And he was still holding Samantha's hand. Shit.

Samantha yanked her hand away from him and whirled to face the other woman. "I *know* who you are, Janice."

Janice smiled at her, but she muttered, "That was *for* the camera."

Samantha's shoulders were tense. "This is private property, and you're trespassing. *Again.* You should know better than that—wait, what am I saying? You *do* know better. I've kicked you off my porch more than a few times in the past."

"Where is Tammy White?" Janice demanded, obvi-ously choosing to ignore Samantha's words. "Is it true that the killer has been communicating with you?" She shoved a microphone at Samantha.

Hell. He would have expected this crap in DC, but in this little town? They really had a hard-edged reporter eager for a story? "Where did you get your information, ma'am?"

"An anonymous source." She turned the force of her smile on to him. "Want to tell my viewers just what happened out there? Doesn't the public deserve to know why the sky was lit up like the Fourth of July?"

"No comment," Samantha asserted before he could reply. "Now get off my property, or I'll get the police captain to remove you."

The woman glowered at her.

"I'm FBI Agent Blake Gamble," he said, wanting to end this scene right now. "And the FBI will be issuing an official statement later, at a press conference. We are not talking about the case at this time, so you need to stop that camera from rolling." He glared. *"Now."*

The reporter huffed out a breath, then she ran her hand across her throat. "Cut!" she barked.

The man with the video camera shrugged his shoulders and moved back. The guy in the skinny jeans wandered away.

Janice braced her feet apart and heaved out what sounded like a long-suffering sigh. "I have been nothing but patient with you, Samantha. I have sat on your story and *sat* on your story so long you would have thought I was a damn hen!"

Blake blinked. Had she just called herself a hen?

"And then this happens." Janice glowered. "A woman is abducted, and you don't even give me a scoop? I thought we were friends!"

"Since when, Janice?" Samantha asked. "You've been hounding me from the moment I came home. And I've been telling you *no comment* that entire time. You keep pulling this crap, showing up at my place unannounced, harassing me—"

"I need this story." She waved away the two eavesdropping men, then leaned in closer to Samantha. "That's why I'm here now. I needed to beat the others to the scoop. This could be my ticket back to the big leagues. Give an exclusive. I'll even let you guide the questions, and I don't normally do that for anyone." Her shoulders heaved as she exhaled. "Word spreads that we have a serial in our quiet town, other reporters will fly in like sharks smelling blood in the water."

Samantha held up her hand. "Who said anything about a serial?"

Janice's eyes went wide. "Seriously? *You're* on the case. Agent Gamble is here… I know you both worked serial crimes when you were at the FBI. I am a professional, after all, and I can certainly do basic research." She sniffed, as if Samantha had personally insulted her.

"For the last time," Samantha said flatly, "I don't have a comment for you. But if that changes, you'll be the first one I call."

"I'd better be," Janice muttered. Then she focused on Blake. She shook her head and held out her hand. "Where are my manners?" She offered him a wide, flirtatious smile. "I'm Janice Beautfont, with Central News Five."

He shook her offered hand, then immediately released her. Blake could practically see the calculation in her blue eyes.

"If *you* should want to comment to me—in an official capacity or even in an unofficial one…" She winked at him. "Here's my card."

He took the card but didn't look at it as he tucked it in his pocket.

Samantha cleared her throat. "Now's the time for you to do that whole vacating the premises thing, Janice. And don't come back, not unless you're called. I mean that. I've played nice with you so far, but that ends. You're crossing the line."

"Understood." But Janice seemed to be focusing only on Blake. "Hopefully, someone will be calling me." Then she turned on her heel and hurried off to meet the two men. A few moments later, they were loaded in their van and driving off.

Samantha stared after them. "We've got a leak in Lewis's department."

Yeah, unfortunately, they did.

"Be on guard with her," Samantha warned him, turning to slant him a hooded glance. "She used to be a reporter up in Chicago—that was her big league. But when she got caught in a compromising position with a certain senator, she found herself bumped from that market. Janice is smart, tough and determined to get back on top. If she thinks this case is her ticket to the headlines, she isn't going to stop."

He absorbed that for a moment. "And she's your... friend?"

Samantha started walking toward his waiting SUV. "Hardly. She's been hounding me from day one for an interview. Between her and the book publishers who keep wanting me to write a tell-all about my 'Life with a Killer'—let's just say I've gotten used to telling folks no."

Once they were in the vehicle, he turned toward her. "A tell-all? About Latham?"

Her smile was bitter. "People love dirt, Blake. It's the nature of the beast. They want to hear all the terrible secrets out there. They want to salivate over someone else's pain."

"And you haven't been tempted to do one of those tell-alls? To set the record straight?"

"Maybe one day." She hooked her seat belt. "After I've caught Cameron and tossed his ass in prison."

CHAPTER EIGHT

THEY WERE BACK at the bomb scene. Samantha was pretty sure that every single patrol car from the city of Fairhope was out there. Police officers walked the area, searching the ground, and Lewis stood in the middle of the scene, barking his orders. She suspected he'd been there all night. Lewis wasn't the kind to give up easily.

A crowd had gathered, a group of onlookers who were being kept just beyond the patrol cars. They were straining their necks to see the action. Instead of looking at the cops, Samantha looked at the crowd. Sometimes, killers really did return to the scene of the crime. They came back because they got a rush out of being close to the investigation. Some killers would even insert themselves into the investigation, acting as if they were volunteers who wanted to help the authorities.

Being that close just made the rush all the sweeter for them.

Samantha caught the arm of a local cop, a woman with short red hair. "Get the names and numbers of every person in the crowd. Check the IDs. Don't miss anyone."

She nodded and hurried off to obey.

She caught sight of a familiar news van, and her lips thinned. Great. Janice and her crew had just arrived at the scene. More vultures to join the crowd. "Keep the reporters back!" Samantha yelled to the retreating cop.

She nodded.

The female officer didn't seem to realize that she had no authority there. And Samantha sure wasn't acting like a civilian, either. That was the problem—she didn't feel like a civilian. She still felt as if she were FBI.

She turned from the crowd and studied the broken pier. For an instant, she could still feel the flames rushing into the air, whipping past her. It had been a near thing. Far too close. Just how many times could you cheat death before you ran out of options?

THE REPORTER WAS his ticket. Janice Beautfont. He'd called her, left a tip, giving her all sorts of juicy tidbits. She'd been so eager to know more. A woman with a desperate edge.

He could use that desperation.

He watched her as she and her crew pushed others out of their way. *Hungry for the story.* So hungry that they left the back of their van ajar. He slipped over to the van. No one was watching him. All of the action was out in the water. He eased the door open just a bit more, and he slipped his little gift inside.

Janice would appreciate it, he was sure. Either she'd put it on the air or, maybe, if she happened to have a conscience, she'd give it to the cops first.

Either way, the message would get delivered.

He stepped away from the van and spotted a uniformed cop slowly making her way through the crowd. *Time to vanish.* He rolled back his shoulders and took off, moving on the old trail that would take him away from the crime scene and away from the cops. He didn't intend to get busted. Not then. Not ever. Latham had told him that prison would be hell, and he had no intention of ever being locked away in a cage.

THE COPS WERE giving her jackshit. Janice glowered at the scene even as sweat trickled down her spine. Sweat in the winter…that was the fucking South for you. She hated this place. She wanted to get her ass back to Chicago. Back to snow. Back to the big leagues. And she would get there, by God.

She would.

"Pack it in!" Janice barked to her team. "I want to get edits going on the videos and get them playing at the station." And there was nothing to see out there, at least, not at that particular moment. She was tired of baking. She'd go to the station, run with some of the footage she'd taken from Samantha's place and then regroup. She could always hit up the police station later. Maybe, *maybe* she'd be able to smooth talk Captain Lewis.

She made her way back to the van, glowering. Her cameraman, John, beat her there, pulling open the back door. He leaned inside to dump his equipment, but then he turned back to her, lifting something up in his hand. "Hey, you left your phone in here."

No, she hadn't. "Not mine." She never went *anywhere* without her phone.

John frowned. "It was right in the back of the van… just sitting there. It's not mine." His finger swiped over the screen.

She saw his face go white. Absolutely white. And he dropped the phone. She heard the screen smash. "John, what in the hell?" Janice scooped up the phone.

A spiderweb-like crack slid across the screen. "What were you—"

She stopped. An image was on that screen. A blood-soaked image of the woman she knew to be Tammy White. After all, she'd been researching the woman ever since she heard about the disappearance, ever since that tip had come through on her line...

Her fingers were trembling.

"That's her," John whispered. "Oh, my God."

Her intern, Billy, strained to get closer.

Yes, yes, it was the missing woman. Janice scrolled through some of the pictures. Saw the video that was waiting, and then her finger hovered over the screen to start play.

"Agent Gamble!" John bellowed from beside her. "Agent Gamble, you need to see this!"

Her gaze flew up to him. She glared.

He glared back. "That woman is a *victim*. Sometimes, you have to turn off the goddamn story."

Agent Gamble was running toward them. Samantha was right at his heels. Janice pasted a smile on her face. "We found something you need to see." She sure wished she'd had time to view the video.

But she still had a scoop. A big one.

Tammy White is dead.

Blake Gamble came to a stop in front of her. She showed him the phone, the images...but her gaze was on Samantha's face. She saw the shock that flashed on the other woman's features. Shock, pain.

Rage.

Samantha Dark wasn't as controlled as she wanted the world to think she was.

"Someone put the phone in our van," she murmured. "I hope it can help the investigation…"

SAMANTHA SAT IN Lewis's office, her gaze on his computer screen. His officers had confiscated the phone, and his tech team—not really a team, just one young cop—had transferred the files on that phone so that they had a copy to view.

The first video file was about to play.

Blake stood behind her. Lewis was sitting stiffly in the chair to her right. The tech guy—Todd Delaney—pressed a few buttons on the keyboard. The file immediately opened.

"You were the one who should have died." Tammy's face filled the screen. She was sitting down, her hands pulled behind her, and she stared straight ahead. "You, Samantha Dark, are the reason I was taken. He was never interested in me. It was you. Always…you."

Nausea rose in Samantha's throat.

Tammy licked her lips—lips that were cracked and raw. "The death of Kristy Wales is on you. How does that feel? Knowing that a woman died because of you?"

Lewis swore.

"Should I stop playback?" Todd asked, jerking a nervous hand through his mop of brown hair. His skin had gone stark white, making his freckles stand out in sharp contrast.

"No," Samantha said flatly.

Blake's hand curled around her shoulder.

"Where is Dr. Latham?" Tammy asked, staring straight ahead. A tear slid down her cheek. "What did you do to him, Agent Dark? Why won't you say?"

I should have killed him.

"How many more people—" Tammy's cracked lips trembled "—will have to die before you pay for your crimes?" She exhaled, a rough, ragged sigh.

The video kept playing.

Tammy gave a faint, hopeful smile. "That's…it, right? I…I said everything this time?"

This time. The man filming Tammy had made her practice her speech.

"I tried really hard," Tammy continued, giving a quick nod and looking so oddly earnest that it made Samantha's heart ache. "I wanted to get it right."

The angle changed—as if someone had just lowered the camera or phone or whatever instrument had been used to film Tammy.

"You got it just right," a low voice rasped.

Tammy's smile stretched. "Then you'll let me go? Y-you said there would be no more pain."

"There won't be." A man walked into the shot. All that could be seen of him was his broad back and the ball cap he'd pulled over his head. "I'll make it fast."

"You'll—"

His hand lifted. Light glinted off the blade he held. Tammy didn't get to say anything else. The blade flew at her, and then her blood—her blood was flying. Spattering—hitting the man who'd hurt her. Hitting the wall near her.

"Dear God," Todd whispered.

The man in the video stood there a moment more, and the knife slowly lowered to his side. Blood dripped from the knife. He didn't glance back at the camera. "I'm coming for you, Samantha Dark. I'll keep killing until I get you."

Then he turned and…being so careful, never once

showing his face, returned for the camera. The angle of the video changed again, focusing once more on Tammy. Tammy slumped in the chair, the wound at her neck gaped open and blood drenched her dirty shirt.

"Fucking bastard," Lewis growled.

Blake's hand tightened on Samantha's shoulder.

The video ended.

I'll keep killing until I get you.

She opened her mouth to speak but just couldn't. The lump in Samantha's throat was too thick. Too hard. She was staring at a dead woman. A woman who'd died *for no reason.* No damn reason at all.

"We're looking for a body," Blake said flatly, no emotion at all in his voice. "We're going to need cadaver dogs. We'll get clothing from Tammy's apartment to help them track her scent. But with so much water in the area, our perp could have just dumped the vic's body. I've got USERT divers from the FBI scheduled to arrive at any time. They'll search and see if they can find—"

Samantha lurched to her feet. Her cheeks were ice-cold, then red-hot. "I need…air." She needed to stop staring at Tammy's horrible final image. *You said there would be no more pain.* "Excuse me." She stumbled for the door.

But Blake moved into her path. "Samantha?" Worry was in his eyes.

"Let me go." She'd never had a reaction like this on other cases, no matter how gory or brutal they were, but this—this was different. This was personal. This was…

How many more people will have to die before you pay for your crimes?

She was going to be sick.

Samantha shoved past Blake. She wasn't an FBI agent. She didn't have to stay strong. She didn't have to act as if seeing a woman die hadn't just ripped out her heart. She yanked open the door to Lewis's office. She could hear voices, phones, everything was so *normal* out there.

But nothing was normal for Tammy White, not anymore. She was dead…her body dumped somewhere. In a shallow grave. In a watery grave.

And the killer…he was probably already hunting again.

She shoved open the door that led outside and immediately ran straight into Janice.

"You watched the video?" Janice asked eagerly. "What was on it? What did it show?"

A woman dying. "Get out of my way. I have *no comment* for you now."

Janice's eyes narrowed. "I helped you! I could have run that video live on the air!"

What a nightmare that would have been. "Leave me alone, Janice. This isn't the time."

"Fine," Janice gritted. "But there'd better be a time later, Samantha. You owe me now, and I expect a payback."

The cameraman was beside her, watching and glaring at Janice. And Samantha remembered that *he'd* been the one to call out to Blake. He'd been the one to report the phone. If that guy hadn't been there, would Janice have run with the evidence on live TV?

Samantha turned away from her. She rushed down the road, trying to take in deep breaths and trying to forget Tammy White's terrible last moments. *But I can't forget them. Just as I can't forget her. She's with me now...*

Always.

"DON'T," CAPTAIN LEWIS said flatly. "Don't even think about going after that woman right now."

Blake whirled toward him. "I think I know how to handle my partner—"

"That's the thing." Lewis ran a hand over his face. "Samantha isn't your partner, not any longer." He nodded toward a too-pale Todd. "Turn off that fucking video. Go get the cadaver dogs. Tell the officers we're..." He swallowed. "We're looking for a body. I'll be right behind you. And make damn sure that the news van is still secure. I want every inch of that thing checked for prints."

"Yes, sir." Todd snapped off the video. He hustled out the door, his body brushing past Blake's.

Blake started to head after him.

"She doesn't want to talk with you right now." Lewis's words were low. "Samantha doesn't like for anyone to see her when she's weak."

Blake glanced back at him.

"Of course," the captain added, "I've never really thought she was weak. She's the strongest person I ever met. This shit with the FBI didn't break her, her father's death didn't break her, and this son of a bitch who thinks he's gonna play mind games with her?" He gave a grim shake of his head. "That guy will find himself way out of his league. Sammie will take him down."

Blake shut the door. It was time to clear the air between them. "The FBI is officially taking over this case." Just so there was no doubt. "My full team will be arriving soon. The executive assistant director will want to take over the investigation."

Lewis grunted. "I'd like to give that asshole a piece of my mind."

Blake's gaze raked the captain. "You're protective of Samantha."

"Like you're not?" Lewis threw right back at him. "Samantha pulls out those kinds of instincts, in the right sort of people." He nodded as if he'd just reached some kind of decision. "Something you need to know about Sammie. She learned early to be careful who to trust in this world. Those close to you can turn on you in an instant. *Especially* someone like you."

The guy had just insulted him. "What the hell is that supposed to mean?"

Lewis rolled back his shoulders. "Her father was a good cop. One of the best I've ever seen. He trained me." A faint smile curled his lips. "He was my friend, and I…I was at his side the day he buried his wife. Cancer took Melanie when Samantha was just five years old." Grief darkened his face. "I'll never forget the sight of her in her little dress, standing at her mother's grave, asking her dad… Asking him when her mommy would wake up."

Shit.

"Harrison Dark loved his daughter. And he loved his job. He loved protecting people, but he… There were some shady cops in the department. He was implicated. Folks said he was on the take. Harry was kicked off the force, and he came back here. His father used to own land here, the place Samantha still has, up on the bluff. Harry came back here, but he swore that he'd prove he was innocent. The guy started a file. He was working to catch the guys who'd set him up. One day, I came to visit him…he had this whole room pretty much wall-papered with evidence that he'd been amassing."

And Blake remembered the small room that Samantha had set up in her home. The way she was tracking Latham. *Like father, like daughter.*

"I made a mistake that day," Lewis spoke slowly. "I went back… I was still on the force in Huntsville. I went up there and I said the wrong thing to the wrong person…" His eyes squeezed shut. "Harry's ex-partner. I *thought* I could trust him. I mean, a partner is supposed to have your back, right?"

Oh, hell. Now he knew why he'd been insulted.

"I was wrong. The partner—Phil Hyde—he was the one who'd set up Harry. The guy got scared that Harry might be getting too close to the truth, because of what I said. He came down here to Fairhope. He was going to take out both Harry and Samantha."

Blake realized his hands were clenched into fists.

"Harry Dark was never a man to go down easily." Lewis swiped his hand over his face. "He took out Phil. Lived long enough for the ambulance to arrive. Samantha—she was thirteen then. Her dad died while she was holding his hand."

The drumming of Blake's heartbeat seemed far too loud. "What happened to her after that?"

Lewis sighed. "Her godfather moved down to Fairhope. He took over the captain's job that had been vacant a few months. He tried to make damn sure he never let her down again." Lewis held his gaze. "So I hope you hear exactly what I am saying to you, boy. I won't trust you, not today and not tomorrow. I won't make that mistake again. I will watch every move that you and your FBI buddies make. If I think you're going to get her hurt, I *will* step in, FBI jurisdiction or not. I don't really give a shit. My goddaughter is what matters to me." He paused. "Are we clear?"

"Crystal clear." And he respected that. "But I think I need to tell *you* a few things now."

"Guess it's your turn…" Lewis murmured. He shrugged.

Yeah, it was. "One… I would *never* turn my back on Samantha. I would never put her at risk. She matters to me. Got it? *She matters.* So I don't give a shit what the FBI brass says, Samantha is my priority on this case. I won't let anyone take her. That prick who thinks getting to her is some kind of game? He'll have to go through me if he wants her. I came too close to losing her on that damn pier. It's not happening again." His voice was grim and rough, and he didn't care. When it came to Samantha, he wanted there to be no mistake about where his loyalties were. *With her.*

"I hear you." Lewis quirked a brow. "But you started with 'one'—and that makes me think you got more to say."

He took a step toward the other man. "Yeah, I do. Two… Thank you for taking care of her." Because he couldn't stand the thought of Samantha on her own, scared, alone, at thirteen—

"When we stood by her father's grave," Lewis spoke slowly, "she didn't ask me when her dad was going to wake up. She wasn't a kid anymore. She stared at his grave, then she looked at me…and she said… She said it should have been her. Seems Phil Hyde was aiming his gun at Samantha. He was going to take her out, make it look like Harry flipped his fucking lid and killed his daughter, then himself. One of them murder-suicides. But Harry…Harry *loved* his girl. He took that bullet for her."

He'd died for Samantha.

"Sometimes," Lewis added, voice gruff, "I worry that a part of Sammie died that day, too."

Samantha wasn't dead, and she wasn't going to be.

"How many bad things can happen to a person…" Lewis asked, musing, "before they start to lose their soul?"

"Samantha isn't losing anything." He stalked back to the door. "Count on it." He grabbed for the knob.

"Agent Gamble!"

He looked back.

"You ever wonder how Samantha understands killers so well?"

Only every fucking day.

"There's a thin line between good and evil. I've seen it myself. After her father died, Samantha had a whole lot of anger building up inside of her. I wanted her to channel that anger. Make sure she used it the *right* way." He nodded. "So I'm the one who started her on the path she's on. I'm the one who taught her to study crime scenes. I'm the one who told her that she could make a difference." Anger glinted in his eyes. "Then you jerks at the FBI turned on her like a pit of vipers."

"I never turned on Samantha."

"Make sure you never do." Lewis's jaw hardened even more. "Because you do something to my baby girl, and badge or no badge, I'll be gunning for you."

Once more, his respect for the other man notched up. "Maybe you should save some of that rage for Cameron Latham."

"Don't think I'm not…" Lewis's smile was sharp. Cutting like a knife. "I'd love to get that man in my sights."

He believed the guy. Blake opened the door and stepped outside. He wanted to find Samantha, but his phone started ringing. Shit. He yanked it out of his pocket, and when he saw the name—Josh Duvane—Blake put the phone to his ear. "Tell me you're in town."

"Just landed."

"Our vic is dead." He kept walking, searching for Samantha but not seeing her anywhere. "I need your team to get in the water." He needed evidence from the bomb scene.

And he needed Tammy. "Our guy is planning to kill again. We have to stop him before he takes another victim."

CHAPTER NINE

THE SUN WAS too bright. Sweat trickled down Samantha's back. *Even in February.* She stood a few yards away from the police station, her hands on the warm bricks as she sucked in air. She'd *never* lost it like that before, not at a crime scene and certainly not in front of other law enforcement personnel. She kept her shit together, kept her control in place. She wasn't—

Weak.

Her shoulders straightened. Her hands fell away from the bricks. *You have to stop him before he hurts someone else.*

If he wanted her, then he should come for her.

Profile him. Focus on him. Stop seeing the victim. That was the problem. Tammy White's pain—the woman's face—they were in her head. She had to stop thinking about the victim and focus on the killer.

You needed a place to work on her...a place to make your stupid video. A quiet spot to kill her.

But once he'd killed the victim...

"You weren't wearing gloves." Her head jerked up. She remembered the video. Remembered seeing him lift the knife. He'd touched Tammy's face, touched *her.* And he'd killed her.

I saw his bare hand when he killed Kristy, too. In that video, the guy had been wearing a ski mask, but nothing had covered his hands. He'd touched her and he'd killed her. Blake had told her that the perp dumped Kristy Wales in a lake. *Maybe he used the water for a reason...* Like to wash away evidence.

Her heartbeat slowed as she thought, as she profiled. The guy liked to get up close and personal with his kills. He liked to *feel* them, so perhaps he was trying to—quite literally—wash the evidence away from the bodies by dumping them in the water. If he followed the same MO with Tammy that he'd used with Kristy, then—

Tammy isn't going to be in the ground. He put her in the water. They'd all been aware of that possibility. With the bay so close, the water was an easy dump site. But she didn't think the case was about easy. The guy *liked* the water. The more Samantha thought about it, the more she realized that was true. *This perp is drawn to water.* He'd even tried to pull Samantha into a watery grave with that bomb of his.

She turned to face the street. Her gaze shot to the left and to the right. The perp had come to Fairhope just for her, so that meant the guy should be close.

"Samantha!" Blake yelled her name.

She jerked and turned to see him hurrying out of the police station. "I'm right here."

He bounded toward her. There seemed to be extra worry in his green gaze as it swept over her, and she wondered just what Lewis had told him. She loved Lewis, but the man had a serious tendency to over-share. He often said that the two of them were opposites. She wouldn't talk enough and he...

Give the man gin, and he'll tell you every secret he has.

Blake caught her arm and pulled her close. "A killer

says he's gunning for you, and you immediately run outside on your own. Great plan."

Her lips thinned. "Maybe offering myself up as bait isn't the worst idea. It could save a life."

"Samantha…" His voice hardened. She could see the warning flash in his eyes. She chose to ignore that warning.

"I'm dead serious. We need him to come right at me, not go for another innocent like Tammy."

His hold tightened on her. "In case you missed it, he *did* come at you. Or are you forgetting the bomb that nearly killed you?"

Hard to forget it. She still had bruises and singe marks. "He's scared of me." She believed that with utter certainty. "And I think I know why." Okay, this was going to be her first profile in a very long time. Bass had tried to tell her she knew jackshit about profiling, but criminals, killers…they were in her blood.

We both know you like the dark. Nothing wrong with that. After all, isn't that your name? Cameron's voice whispered through her mind, and she shivered. Samantha pulled in a long breath, then she spoke, slowly, carefully. "This guy is young, probably only in his early twenties. I think Kristy Wales was his first kill, and he was feeling his way with her, half imitating Cameron and half letting go of the twisted hunger he has inside of himself."

Blake's gaze sharpened on her.

"He doesn't use gloves with his victims. He touches them because what he's doing is intimate. It's personal. That's the same reason he's using a knife…it's a personal weapon." *And it was Cameron's weapon.* "Because he does touch his prey, he dumps their bodies in water, trying to wash away evidence." The guy didn't have a strong grasp of forensic technology. "He's developing an MO with each kill. Abduction, video—the video gives him power, it's a performance. He gets his victims to say exactly what he wants. He probably tells them that if they get their lines *just* right, they'll get to live." She shook her head. "Only, that's never part of his plan. He wants to give them hope and then rip that hope away. He steps in close to kill them so he can better see the hope fade from their eyes." *Because he likes that power.*

Blake was just staring at her.

"What?" Samantha asked, worry gnawing at her.

"Keep going."

Okay. "His MO…abduction, video, killing…then dumping in the water. Our guy is young, and he's probably been around water his whole life. He feels confident near water. A boater, probably. And the way he talks about Cameron, *Dr. Latham*," she corrected, "I…I think he may have been one of Cameron's students at Georgetown."

Surprise flashed on Blake's face.

"He's got a personal relationship with Cameron, like…like a mentor relationship. I took away his mentor, and he's pissed as all hell at me."

Blake seemed to absorb this, and then he asked, "You think Latham realized he had a budding serial killer in his class? Could Latham have been urging the guy on, waiting to see when he'd make his first kill?"

"Like another experiment?" Samantha asked. Her lips pressed together, and she nodded. "Yes, actually, I think he could have been doing just that. Cameron knows people, what makes them tick, what they want most. If this perp was in one of his classes, then Cameron would have figured him out early on." And that was when the fun would have really begun for Cameron. "We'll be looking for a white male, one who came from a boating background, probably a loner, tall, muscled." That part came from the video. "He would have withdrawn from the school after Cameron's disappearance, so it should be easy enough to find someone from Georgetown who fits this MO and…" She licked her lips. "I think he knew Kristy Wales. He wore that mask in her video, and I think he did it because he didn't want her to recognize him. He kept his voice as a rasp, disguising it. He didn't want Kristy to see him for who he really was because he was afraid she'd say something in the video. But Tammy was a stranger to him. She didn't know his name, so he didn't have to hide his identity from her."

Blake gave a slow shake of his head.

Her breath caught in her lungs. "Blake?" He didn't believe her?

"You're pretty fucking incredible, you know that?"

She just stared at him.

"I expect to find you out here, sick or scared or… *something*. But you're profiling him." Pride resonated in his voice.

Goose bumps rose on her arms. "It's easy to think like them. Too easy." And that scared her.

Because…

For just a moment, she remembered a conversation she and Cameron had had one long-ago day. One of their "what if" conversations as they'd called them.

What if you cross a line one day, Sam? He'd given her a probing glance. *What if you stop hunting the kill-*

ers, and you give in to all of those dark emotions that swirl inside of you?

She'd laughed at the question. *I want to put them away. I want to make a difference.*

But he'd shaken his head. *No, you just want to make up for the past.*

"You're not evil, Samantha." Blake's voice pulled her back to the present.

She blinked at him.

"You're not like any of those bastards out there, if that is what scares you." He paused. "You're nothing like Latham."

She sucked in a sharp breath. "You and Lewis did have quite the talk, didn't you?"

Blake gazed into her eyes. "Trust me."

They were so close on that street. His hands were on her shoulders now, their bodies brushing. To passersby, they probably looked like lovers.

Oh, wait, they were. *Another line I crossed.*

"I'm not going to betray you. I'm not going to turn on you. However this case works out, I want you to trust me. No matter what you may see, no matter what twists or turns come...*trust me.* Because the one person I will never betray in this world? It's you."

Her heart was pounding too hard in her chest. "We... we aren't partners—"

"Hell, yeah, we are. But that's not the reason."

"Why?" Her voice had turned into a whisper. "Why me?"

He smiled at her. An actual, real smile that made his green eyes go even brighter. She'd always secretly loved his smiles and the way they made her feel. "You're the profiler. I bet if you tried hard enough, you could get into my head and figure it out."

"You don't like being profiled." He'd told her that before.

But his smile stayed on his lips. "Go ahead," he dared. "Try to figure me out now. Or are you afraid of what you might find?"

Maybe she was. Maybe something about Blake had always seemed too good to be true.

He bent his head and pressed his lips to hers. It was a slow, sensual kiss. Right there, on the street, where anyone could see them. Instinctively, she pushed against his shoulders.

"You're not my dirty little secret, Samantha." His voice was a sensual rumble against her lips. "And I won't be yours, either. I had you in my bed, and that means something to me."

It meant something to her, too.

"It means—" his eyes glinted at her "—you're mine."

BLAKE GAMBLE WAS an asshole. One who was in the way and needed to be eliminated. He watched Blake put his hands on Samantha. Watched the fool agent press his mouth to hers.

Samantha put her hands on his shoulders. She tried to push him back. But did the dumbass take a clue? No, he didn't. He leaned close to her. Whispered some shit to her.

Something that made Samantha…

Scared?

As he watched from the shadows, she pulled away from Blake. Samantha shook her head once, a definite no. But Blake kept talking, and then they headed for his SUV.

The watcher's eyes narrowed as he observed them drive away.

He was tired of Blake Gamble being in his way. Tired of the guy screwing everything to hell and back. He needed to eliminate the SOB. And the best way to do that?

Well, it just might be by using the killer who was hunting in the quiet town of Fairhope, Alabama. It was a quaint place. Neat little streets. At night, the trees in the city lit up—decorated by thousands of miniature bulbs. It was a cute touch, one he was sure Samantha had liked when she was a girl.

After all, darkness had scared her, back then.

Now it would seem that other things scared her.

I scare her. He knew that truth. He'd seen it when he put a knife to her lovely throat. It was her fear that had stopped him. He'd liked seeing the fear in the eyes of the other women. It had given him a sweet rush. But when Samantha had looked at him and her golden eyes had darkened, he'd realized something very important.

He didn't want a world without her. Not Samantha. He didn't care about others. Forming relationships had never been easy for him. Hell, he'd never wanted relationships. But she was different. In some odd way, she seemed to fit him.

She's mine. Possession. It went deep for him. Samantha had given him her secrets over the years; she'd trusted him. She'd learned the truth about killers with him. They shared a special world.

The SUV had driven away. *Blake Gamble, off to*

save the day. Whistling, he crossed the street. A woman glanced over at him and smiled.

He smiled back, flashing teeth that were extra white and capped. He'd made a few changes to himself over the past few months. Nothing too dramatic, no need for that. He'd darkened his hair, not blond any longer but black. He'd let his beard grow out, and he'd colored that, too. The beard had changed the line of his jaw, made it harder, more square in appearance. The beard also made his face appear longer, a nice touch, he thought.

He'd decided to go with blue eyes. Of course, sometimes, he switched those up—he kept lots of colored contacts handy, just in case.

And he'd put on weight—well, muscle. Twenty more pounds. He wore faded T-shirts and loose jeans now, and he kept calloused hands, the kind of hands a man would have if he worked outside a lot.

Not the hands of a college professor. Not some stuffy guy who spent all day lecturing.

He knew how to change…how to alter his speech, how to become nearly anyone at all.

He *had* changed, because he'd wanted to survive. Survive and thrive.

He'd been close to Samantha a few times. He didn't think that she'd noticed. Sure, he'd never talked to her, because that would be too risky. If he talked, if he stood right in front of her, she might see who he really was.

She was the only one who'd ever come close to doing that before.

Well, Samantha and…*one* other person.

The person he was hunting right then. The person he had to find before Samantha did. *I can't let you end his work, Sam. He's not done.*

He reached for the door that led to the police station. *And I'm not done, either.*

His reflection flashed back at him from the glass door. He didn't look the same at all.

Smiling, he headed inside. He walked right up to the counter. "I'd like to speak to Captain Lewis." He'd wanted to meet the man for a long time.

"I'm Captain Lewis." The gruff voice came from the right.

Turning his head, he saw the man marching from his office. Lewis was a few inches shorter than he was, but, despite his age, the guy was fit, with broad shoulders and a quick stride. His dark gaze was assessing.

He almost smiled as he stared at the captain. Almost.

"Who the hell are you?" Lewis demanded.

He strode forward and offered his hand to Lewis. "The guys at the marina told me you were looking for volunteers to help in the search for…" He paused as if it were difficult to say. "For the remains of that woman who went missing. I…I'd like to help."

"I don't know you, son…" Lewis was obviously suspicious.

You taught Sam well.

"That's because I'm new to town. Ex-Navy, working at building the combat ships out of Mobile." He nodded and kept his hand extended. From that angle, the lines of his tattoo were obvious. A trident on his inner wrist. "I've got plenty of dive experience, and I'd like to help out in any way I can."

Lewis slowly lifted his hand. He had a good grip. Strong. "Didn't catch your name."

And you won't, not for a while. Not his real name, anyway. "Brock Chambers." And Brock Chambers *had* served in the Navy. He'd been an excellent diver. And he'd owned one beauty of a boat down in Key West.

It seemed fitting that Brock was currently resting at the bottom of the Gulf, since he'd loved the sea so much.

"All right, Brock. We do need all hands on deck, but I'm running a check on *all* my volunteers." Lewis huffed out a breath. "So give your contact info to the officer behind the desk. The FBI has a team down here now, their USERT guys, but if we need backup in the water and you pass muster, I'll be contacting you."

USERT. He didn't let his expression alter. He'd hoped there would be fewer agents down there. This situation was turning into a clusterfuck.

Someone called for the captain. Lewis turned away.

And he never realized that he'd just met one of the FBI's most wanted criminals.

Cameron Latham smiled as he stood in the middle of the police station.

"Good to see you again, Agent Dark," Josh Duvane said as he stood at the marina. "Didn't realize I'd be running into you here."

Here...that would be the makeshift base that had been set up for the FBI agents. Blake had brought her there to meet the USERT group, but apparently he'd forgotten to tell them a few things.

"You know I'm not with the FBI any longer," she said to Josh, wanting to correct that wrong assumption right away.

His blond brows hiked. "But...when we spoke on the phone, Blake told me you were working the case with him. I thought that meant you were back and—"

"I'm a civilian on this one." She held up her hands.

"Purely freelance work. It's Blake's show." Her smile felt bittersweet. "I'm along for the ride because the killer is trying to get to me."

Josh's face hardened. Josh Duvane…she'd met him a few times, mostly when he'd been training with Blake. Josh was usually quiet, intense. His hazel stare possessed intelligence and confidence. The guy didn't show fear, and she'd heard others say he was the best diver in the Bureau.

"The killer is after you?" Josh's gaze shot to Blake.

"And she wants to be bait," Blake said grimly. "A plan we are *not* following."

It was a plan he should follow. Damn him. Didn't he get that she couldn't have more blood on her hands?

Blake spread out maps on the table in front of them. "Samantha built a profile of the guy. She's certain he's dumped the body in the water, so that's where we start. I've been studying the currents in the bay, and if our guy wanted to make sure the victim stayed down—long enough for any evidence to be washed away—I figure he'd go out through this point." His finger traced over the map, heading away from Devil's Hole and out toward Point Clear. "We need to focus closer to the mouth of the bay. Hell, if the guy didn't want the body found at all, he would have dumped her out there, hoping the tide might drag her out into the Gulf." He looked up at Josh and the two agents with him. "We aren't letting that happen. Recovering the victim as fast as possible is an absolute necessity."

Because the dead could still speak, if they got to Tammy fast enough.

"We've got a boat lined up to take us out," Josh stated with a nod. "The sonar will give us a real-time look beneath the water. Whenever we have a potential hit, a diver will go down. If she's out there, we'll bring her back."

"She's out there," Samantha said with certainty. Her gaze turned toward the water of the bay. So still out there now, almost like glass. She could see boats dotting the water. Fishermen. Yachtsmen. A few guys on sailboats. *She's out there...and he may be, too.*

"Let's get suited up," Josh said to his team, his voice brisk. "Let's bring our vic home."

The other USERT agents turned away. Samantha knew they'd be grabbing their tanks and dive equipment from the shop that waited nearby. But Josh—he was staring at her.

Blake took a protective step toward her. "There a problem here?" And his voice wasn't so friendly any longer.

"Hell, no, we don't have a problem." Josh's gaze held hers. What she saw there made her stiffen. *Sympathy.* She'd always hated looks of sympathy and pity. They tended to piss her off. "Just want Agent Dark to know that she did have a few people in her corner."

"It's not Agent—" Samantha began.

"It should be," Josh retorted.

Her lips thinned.

"Blake wasn't the only one telling Bass he'd screwed up. I was in that line, too."

Wait, there had been a line? Since when?

"You aren't the first person to judge a friend the wrong way." Now there was something else on Josh's face. Something that looked a whole lot like pain. "I made that mistake, too. Trusted a guy with my life, and he wound up turning on me and every man in our unit. Lost two good SEALs that day. And every fucking day since then, I ask myself...why didn't I see the truth about him sooner?"

Josh had just succeeded in surprising her. "I'm sorry."

"And I'm sorry for the shit that went down with you at the Bureau. You got a raw deal." His head jerked toward Blake. "He always said you were a class act, the best at profiling most of us have ever seen. The FBI lost out when they turned on you."

"Tell that to Bass," she said, her lips twisting.

"Blake did. I did. But some dumbasses just don't hear reason very well."

His words warmed her, when she hadn't realized that she was even cold.

"You coming out on the boat with us?" Josh asked her. "On the phone, Blake told me that you grew up in the area. It would be good to have your eyes out there on the water, especially since I've heard there are a lot of boat wrecks out there. Material like that is gonna flash on the sonar, and I'll need help sorting out what we're seeing." He paused. "We could use you."

She glanced back at the water. Once upon a time, she'd known every inch of that bay. The skies were clear now, but things could change in an instant...that was the way down there. Sunny skies one moment. Torrential rain or heavy fog the next. Fairhope was right at the mouth of Mobile Bay. The bay emptied out into the Gulf of Mexico, so that meant their little spot on the map was pretty special. Several rivers led to the bay, giving them a heavy swamp area to the north, while the water deepened and the waves roughened as the bay led farther south.

"Can I count on your help?" he prompted.

"I'll be there." He was right. There were plenty of wrecks out there—small boats, piers—the storms weren't pretty when they ripped into the bay, and far too many materials had found their way into the water.

"Good." He inclined his head toward Blake. "You diving with us?"

Now surprise flashed through her. She hadn't realized that Blake dived—or that he'd ever trained with the USERT team.

Blake nodded. "I'll be suiting up."

Josh turned away and went to join the others. Blake started to follow, but Samantha grabbed his arm. "Can we talk for a moment?" She'd pushed him away back at the station. Things had gotten too intense between them. And when people got too close to her, she tended to have one response—to push away.

She exhaled slowly and waited until the others were gone. "I'm sorry."

"For what?"

Was he really going to make her spell it out? "That I'm not who you want me to be." A woman who'd give herself freely to her lover.

He caught her chin in his hand and tipped her head back so that she was staring straight into his eyes. "You are *exactly* who I want you to be."

Her heart pounded like a drum, echoing in her ears.

"I'm not as good as you seem to think. Trust me, I've got my own dark places, too."

"Yes, but those dark places aren't ever going to send you out to murder innocent women." The words just blurted out of her. "Not like—"

"Latham."

She held his gaze. "I let him get close. I trusted him, for years." When she'd pushed so many others away. "It messed me up. I can't... I can't make any more mistakes."

"You think being with me is a mistake?"

No, she thought being with him was keeping her sane. "What do you want from me?"

And he smiled at her, a long, slow smile. "Are you sure you're ready to find out?"

She wasn't.

Josh called his name.

Blake didn't look back.

"You need to get your tank, Gamble!" Josh yelled.

Blake's hand slid away from her chin. "When we're alone again," Blake said, not looking back at the other man but still focusing totally on her, "I'll show you exactly what I want." He held her gaze a moment longer, then slowly turned away.

She realized she was holding her breath.

Samantha exhaled on a soft sigh. *And maybe I'll show you what I want. What I want...but can't have.*

CHAPTER TEN

BLAKE SAT ON the side of the boat. The farther they'd gone out into the bay, the rougher the waves had become. They'd already hit three dive sites, searching the murky water but turning up nothing. The bottom of the bay was littered with wreckage—old pier pilings that had been ripped away by the last tropical storm, broken boats that had been tossed like debris by the waves. The wreckage kept popping up on the sonar, but so far...

No sign of Tammy White.

His gaze slid to the left. Samantha was with the boat captain, leaning over and pointing at a small screen near the wheel. A faint furrow appeared between her brows. "Here," she said. "This spot...it's good. Drop the anchor here."

The captain nodded and headed toward the front of the boat. Samantha took the wheel, putting the vessel in Neutral as the front anchor was deployed. The captain dropped in the dive flag as Samantha controlled their boat. "Got a reading on sonar," Samantha said, looking back at Blake. "The depth is good here, and we're about twenty minutes from Fairhope. It would have been easy for our perp to get out to this location. To drop the victim and then just slip away. This spot is fairly secluded, so if he wanted a dumping ground, well, this spot would be perfect." She bit her lower lip.

"It's…it's probably the spot I would use, if I wanted to get rid of a body."

"Then that's good enough for me," Josh said as he lowered his body to the side of the boat next to Blake. "You know your killers, ma'am."

The waves lapped against the boat.

Samantha had killed the engine. She stood near the wheel, but her gaze slid over Blake, Josh and the other two USERT divers—Sean Hastings and Fiona Webb. "Be careful down there. As with the other spots, visibility isn't going to be strong. The bay is too murky—"

"That works to the perp's advantage," Fiona muttered.

Yes, it did.

"Don't worry." Josh flashed a half smile at Samantha. The guy was always cocky near the water. "We've got the buddy system in place. And trust me, we've all been in way worse conditions than this." He peered around at the bay. "Way worse." The smile slipped as memories seemed to darken his face. But then he motioned to Sean and Fiona, and they fell back into the water with a light splash.

Blake looked up and saw that Samantha's gaze was on him. "Be careful," she said.

Sounded like she cared. Good. But before he was done with Sam, it would be more than just caring. That was his mission. She just didn't see it yet.

Blake made sure that his mask was in place, all of his gear ready. He pushed his regulator into his mouth and fell into the water, hitting first with his back and then turning to sink beneath the surface. Within seconds, he was no longer aware of the heavy weight of his tank. He cut through the water easily, aware of Josh swimming right at his side. His dive buddy. Right. Josh had been his buddy for years. Sometimes, you needed a friend who could understand the shit that followed you out of battle. Josh had plenty of his own scars. They talked about them some, over cheap alcohol when the memories got too bad. They talked about the things they wished they could change.

And the lives that had been lost.

Blake automatically checked his dive computer. He had plenty of bottom time left, he wasn't worried about that, but checking the dive computer was just second nature to him. Smart diving. No one could take chances in the water, not ever. As they sank lower, following the boat's anchor down, Blake pulled up his flashlight. He kept the flashlight hooked to his BCD on dives. The light cut through the darkness of the water, and as they neared the bottom of the bay, he saw the battered remains of a small, flat-bottom fishing boat. Hell, that must have been what showed up on the sonar.

But the team kept descending because they needed to be thorough. They had to check everything, and Samantha had said this spot was perfect.

Bubbles drifted around them.

Fiona reached the wreckage first. She put her hand on the side of the old boat, pulling herself closer to it, and then—

She jerked back, a fast, hard reflex. Her head whipped toward Josh, and she made a cutting motion with her hand.

Adrenaline flooded through Blake's body as he swam closer to the boat. And…then he saw the ropes. Thick, rough rope that bound something—*someone*— to the wreckage.

It looked as if seaweed were drifting in the water near the boat. But the closer he came, the more he realized… *not seaweed.*

Hair.

Hair was floating in the water. A body was *tied* to the old boat's motor. Tammy White's body was bloated, too white in the glare of his flashlight. Her head bobbed in the water, moving back and forth, and her hair kept drifting around her face.

Blake reached for the dive knife that he'd strapped to his ankle. They'd found Tammy's watery grave.

Now it was time to take her home.

THE WATER BUBBLED near the side of the boat. "They're coming up!" Samantha yelled to the captain. The team hadn't been down long at all. A fast dive, just like the ones before. Frustration heated her blood. She'd been so certain that this spot would be the one. The location, the seclusion…it *fit.*

She saw the edge of a mask appear, and then she was staring at Josh's face. His eyes held hers.

Then Blake broke the surface of the water. She reached out her hand to him, but he shook his head.

Her heart stuttered in her chest.

Josh pushed away his mask. "Like I said, you know your killers."

She locked her gaze on Blake. "You found her?"

He shoved his mask back.

"Yes," Josh said, and his face was grim. "We have her."

Samantha's shoulders sagged.

"Now," Blake said, his voice rough, "we get *him.*"

HE CREPT TOWARD Samantha Dark's house. She was gone, out searching for a body that she wouldn't find, not for a while. He'd made sure that Tammy didn't drift up to the surface—he'd made that mistake with Kristy. He liked to think that he'd learned from his mistakes.

It was time to move again. Time to play again.

He crept toward her house, excitement thick in his blood. Her car was there, but he knew she'd left with Agent Gamble. Her home was secluded, surrounded by all of those thick oak trees and all that swaying Spanish moss. No one would see him there. But then, no one would think to look for him—

At her house.

He went straight to her front door. It was locked, of course, but he was ready. He worked on that lock, sweating a bit until he heard the soft snick that told him he'd gotten inside. He'd worn gloves this time, just in case. But when he actually got ready to kill Samantha…he'd take his gloves off. He liked to feel his victims beneath his hands.

They felt good.

He tiptoed into her house. He'd brought a knife with him; he'd discovered he could never leave the knife behind. It made him feel better, stronger to have it with him. Like a trusted friend. And it fit so well in his hand.

But it wasn't in his hand then. He'd sheathed it and hidden it just inside the jacket he wore. A jacket and a big ball cap. Just in case.

Her house was eerily quiet. It smelled…kind of sweet. Like lavender or one of those other flowery scents women seemed to love. The place was perfectly neat. No dust. Everything arranged just so on her shelves. Samantha liked her order.

He'd be sure and bring chaos to her life.

He trailed his gloved fingers over her couch, then made his way down the narrow hallway to her bedroom. The bedcovers were rumpled. *Not so organized here.* Perhaps she'd left in a hurry.

He saw the indentions on *both* pillows. His eyes narrowed. He hadn't realized just how close Samantha was to her partner. Rage billowed inside of him as he pulled out his knife. Maybe he'd just leave a few surprises for her. He'd cut her home to shreds and let her return to destruction. His knife hovered over her pillow.

Then he heard a creak. Faint, but his head whipped to the right, to the white door that was closed a few feet away. A closet?

His heart was racing. Sweat trickled down his back.

The creak came again.

It's an old house. High on the bluff. Probably just settling. Just the wind...

But he found himself moving toward that door. The sound of his own breathing seemed far too loud as it heaved in and out of his lungs. He reached for the knob. The door squeaked as it opened.

Another room. Smaller, tighter, and...*someone was in there*.

A man stood with his back to him. A man with broad shoulders and dark hair. The guy wore a faded T-shirt and jeans, and he was— He was staring at some kind of map that had been hung on the wall.

The guy hadn't heard him enter. He hadn't moved so much as a muscle.

FBI? It could be Blake Gamble. It was hard to tell for certain from that angle, but the build was right. The hair was right.

He's been sleeping with Samantha Dark. If I take him out, it will tear her apart to find his body. He'd never killed a man, and the guy was big, but...if he snuck up on him, he'd be able to take the fellow out.

Smiling, he lifted his knife and stepped forward.

"She's been looking for me." The man's voice rang out, sounding amused. Almost happy. *Pleased.*

The knife trembled in his hand because... *I know that voice.* He'd heard it often enough. In his favorite classes. In their private talks.

"She's gotten close a few times." The man turned his head, and a faint smile curved his lips. "Almost close enough to touch."

The face was wrong—thicker, fuller. The beard was wrong. The eyes were wrong, but that voice... *That voice is his.*

The man's blue eyes drifted to the knife. "What a good weapon," he murmured. "Tell me, Jason, why did you choose a knife?"

He knows me. It's his voice. Hope bloomed inside of him, but he hardly dared believe. "It...it was your weapon. I wanted...wanted to—"

"To be like me?" He tilted his head and rubbed his chin. It was a move that Jason had seen his mentor make hundreds of times. In the classroom, his office. Whenever he was thinking or puzzling out a situation. "But you aren't me. You're powerful in your own right."

Jason's shoulders straightened. *Yes, I am.*

"So tell me how the knife makes you feel."

Jason swallowed. "Strong. And...close to them. When I see the skin split open for me, it's beautiful." And he stood close enough so that he could feel the warmth of the blood. He needed that warmth.

His mentor nodded.

"You don't look the same," Jason blurted.

Laughter was his response. "When every cop in the country is looking for you, when the Feds put you on their most wanted list, a few things have to change." His fingers slid over his beard. "I've gotten quite used to it now. But, soon enough, I'll take on a new persona. I find that I can change to suit my situation."

It *was* him. Jason could see it now, when he looked hard enough. "I've been searching for you," he whispered. "When you left…" He lifted his hand—it had fisted around the handle of the knife—and pushed it to the side of his head, pressing against his temple. "Everything was messed up. I didn't… I didn't have anyone to talk to. The fucking shrink I was seeing wanted to put me back on the meds."

"Well, that wouldn't have been a good idea." Dr. Latham—*it's Dr. Latham, I found him!*—frowned. "Your mind gets too foggy when you're on the medication. You're not yourself then."

No, no, he wasn't. But no one else understood that. Only Dr. Latham. Dr. Latham had said that if he wanted to be the person he was always meant to be, then he had to stop the drugs. They were making it too hard for him to think. They stopped the urges, but…

Some urges aren't meant to be stopped. Dr. Latham had been the one to tell him that. Dr. Latham had been the one to stop making him feel like a freak. His life had changed the day Dr. Latham picked him from out of a class of one hundred students—he'd been picked for a special psychology experiment—and everything had been different then.

Everything.

"I'm going to kill her," Jason announced. Then he smiled, because that had to be the reason Dr. Latham was there. He'd come to kill Samantha Dark, too. "Samantha Dark will pay for what she did."

Dr. Latham's expression changed, not a fast change—nothing with him was ever fast. It was a change that started with his eyes—*eyes that aren't his*. His gaze hardened. His jaw clenched. His cheeks seemed to go leaner. "Samantha did nothing to me."

Jason backed up a step.

"I'm not in a prison, am I?" Dr. Latham asked him.

Jason shook his head. "No."

"I'm not dead, am I?"

"No." Though he'd feared Dr. Latham was. He'd feared that Samantha Dark had killed him and hidden the body.

"Samantha let me go. Samantha is not my enemy." He paused. His eyes were nearly slits as he said, "She's not your enemy. Do you understand that, Jason?"

No. Yes. Jason nodded.

"You're making mistakes, Jason."

No, he wasn't. He'd killed two women, and the cops hadn't caught him yet. He was too good.

"Samantha had an alarm here at the house. When you came in, it was amateur hour."

He felt his cheeks redden.

"It took you ten minutes just to pick the lock on the front door. Even longer to realize that I was in here, waiting for you. I could have been Agent Gamble. I could have shot you on sight."

Jason shook his head. "No…alarm." It hadn't sounded. There hadn't been so much as a beep when the front door opened.

"I disabled it when I arrived. I arrived through the *back* door, by the way. I got in without leaving so much as a scratch on the lock, something I'm not sure we can say about your work."

So there had been some scratches. The excitement he'd felt upon seeing Dr. Latham began to wane. This meeting was nothing like what he'd expected. *He's not proud of me.* "I almost killed her," he said, his shoulders sagging a little.

Dr. Latham blinked, and all emotion vanished from his eyes. "Yes, I heard about that. I caught a very interesting news segment this morning. Janice something or other on Central News Five had plenty to say." He cocked his head. "Bombs are messy, don't you think? I've never liked fire."

He nodded quickly. "Yes, they are messy. And loud." For some reason, he hadn't expected that part. Loud and messy and not intimate at all. "I was just trying to pay her back. For what she did—for what I *thought* she did," he amended quickly, "to you."

Latham's gaze raked him.

Jason's right foot started to tap nervously.

"No one else cared when I vanished." Latham's voice was quiet. "You did. You've stopped being afraid of your urges, haven't you, Jason?"

Jason's heart raced. This was the mentor he'd missed. "Yes." His foot stopped tapping.

"Good. You should embrace the urges. I don't understand why people fight the dark. We all have it inside of us."

Dr. Latham did. He'd learned that secret one night at Georgetown, when he'd gone into a classroom that should have been empty and he'd seen Dr. Latham dragging out a coed.

He'd had an option then. He could have helped the woman. She'd certainly been alive.

Or…

He'd held the door open for Latham.

"There are some people who need payback. They've quite screwed up my life." Latham gave him another slow smile. "Will you help me, Jason?"

This, *this* was what he'd dreamed about. Latham being proud. Latham wanting him at his side. "I'd do anything for you."

Latham's attention shifted to the knife that Jason still held in his hand. "I think it's time we got you the attention you deserve. The attacks are yours. The glory should be yours, too."

Jason's face ached because his smile was so big. His parents had been so wrong all of those years. His urges weren't to be hidden. They weren't to be fixed. They were going to bring him glory.

"So how about we get started?" Latham asked him. "I know just who your next target should be."

WHEN THEY BROUGHT the body in, the dock was filled with people. News crews—including, of course, Janice—cops, the ME. And…

Hell. Samantha felt her shoulders stiffen. She recognized the man who stood right in the middle of all the reporters. The sunlight glinted off Bass's bald head.

The executive assistant director had made it to town just in time to talk with the press.

"It's all right." Blake's voice was low. "You don't have to worry about him. I'll deal with Bass."

Nice words. But she did have to worry. "He'll block me from the investigation."

"He *knew* I was coming down to get you to consult. He approved it before I left DC."

She glanced at him.

"Grudgingly," Blake admitted. His lips thinned. "But look at what we've accomplished."

Right. *Look.* Their victim was dead and their perp was a ghost. She'd nearly been taken out by his bomb, and wreckage littered the Fairhope shores. She could see where Bass would definitely be lining up to jump on the Samantha Dark bandwagon.

The boat eased closer to the dock. The captain steered the vessel perfectly. She knew dive teams would be going out again. Josh and his crew still had a lot of work to do.

A few moments later, she was stepping onto the dock. The ME and his staff came forward to assist with the removal of…Tammy.

The reporters turned as a swarm, and she wondered if they'd been listening to the marine radio during the search. That would explain why so many folks were on hand, just waiting to pounce.

She tried to slip through the crowd.

"Samantha Dark!"

Her body jerked. That *would* be Janice's voice yelling for her.

"Samantha, can you confirm that the remains discovered today are those of Tammy White?" Janice had pushed her way through the mass on the dock and shoved a microphone toward Samantha's face.

Someone is so ready for the big leagues. "I have no comment."

Janice's face tightened, just a bit. Probably as much as her cosmetic surgery would allow.

She felt Blake brush against her side. Strong, steady Blake. "The FBI will release a formal statement later this afternoon," he said.

He seemed to have missed the fact that one member of the FBI—EAD Bass—already appeared to have been talking plenty with the reporters.

"Agent Gamble!" Bass made his way to them. "I need to speak with you." His gaze dipped to Samantha. *"Only you."*

He was shutting her out already. Not the biggest surprise. A muscle jerked in his jaw. His high forehead was already soaked with beads of sweat. *Welcome to the South.*

She smiled at him. "Bass. Long time no see."

"Samantha." He seemed to grit her name. "I need to have a meeting with my agents right now." His voice was low, not carrying to the reporters, but there sure had been an emphasis on the word *agents*.

He was reminding her of what she was...and what she wasn't.

She held his gaze. "And I have a profile to keep working on. One that will help you and your agents catch this asshole." She gave him a grim nod. Then Samantha stepped around him and left Blake behind. She headed away from the crowd and to the very back of the parking lot. Lewis waited there, one hip propped on the side of his patrol car.

She forced herself to take one slow step at a time until she was in front of Lewis. His gaze raked over her face, then slid back to the group behind her. "Your former boss is a dick."

A quick laugh bubbled out of her.

"Came into my station, throwing his weight around like he owned the freakin' place." His eyes had turned to slits as he stared behind her. "Man needs to be careful. You can't go around making enemies left and right and not expect to get bitten in the ass one day."

Maybe. But Bass had a lot of power and a lot of powerful friends. "I need to go home." It would take hours for the ME to do his exam on Tammy. And Josh and his USERT group—they were heading back into the water. There was very little she could do right then...*other than go and work on the profile.*

"How many times are you going to run?"

Her spine stiffened. "I'm not running. I'm doing my job. Someone has to find the bastard out there." Her words shot out, rapid-fire. "Someone has to—"

He patted her shoulder. "There it is. Good. Just wanted to make sure that fire was still there." And his dark gaze zeroed in on her. "You never let anyone take that away, got it? You're Samantha Dark. No one breaks you. No one undermines you. You make them eat shit, and you make them enjoy every bite."

She could only shake her head. That was just typical Lewis. "What am I going to do with you?"

His face sobered. "You'll tell me that I didn't screw things up too badly with you. That while I wasn't the best stand-in dad, I wasn't the worst. That I made mistakes, but, God willing, I taught you to be strong, too."

Her hand curled against his jaw. The faint stubble there rasped against her palm. Emotion nearly choked her. He'd always been in her corner. Always. When she'd come back to Fairhope, she'd had to physically stop the man from going up to DC to "kick ass and take down too many dumbass names" for her. She swallowed down the lump in her throat. "You didn't make any mistakes." *I did that all on my own.* "And you were the best stand-in dad any girl could ever ask for."

He blinked a few quick times and the moisture in his eyes disappeared. She'd seen him cry only once, at her father's grave. She'd had no tears of her own that day—she'd been far too angry for tears, and she just remembered being grateful that someone had been able to cry for her dad.

Someone had needed to do it.

"Get your ass in the car," Lewis muttered. "You know I hate this emotional shit. I don't even know why you're doing this to me."

Yes, he did. Because she loved him. Just as she knew he loved her. Samantha got her ass into the cruiser. He jumped behind the wheel, and a moment later, they were driving away.

BASS LOCKED HIS fingers around Blake's shoulder in a grip that was too damn hard. Blake glanced down at the executive assistant director's hand. "You're gonna want to move that," he ordered.

Bass had one big, fake smile on his face as he glanced at the reporters who were lingering. "I'll have a news conference this evening at 5:00 p.m." Wisely, he removed his hand from Blake's body. "It will be at the police station, and I will update you all on the White case."

That seemed to satisfy the group, for the moment. They'd all gotten plenty of sound bites, and the remaining reporters nearly ran for the parking lot, eager to get their clips out to the public.

Bass watched them all rush away. For a moment, he

didn't speak. He waited until the reporters were well clear of the scene before his gaze cut to Blake. "Tell me that you know what you're doing."

Easy enough. "I know exactly what I'm doing."

"You convinced me that Samantha Dark could consult on the Wales case, and now we're in this clusterfuck—"

"It's not her fault." It never had been. "She's done nothing but assist with the investigation. Samantha has already created a profile for the man we're after here. One that's dead-on."

Bass's eyes narrowed.

"She thinks he's a former student of Latham's. I've contacted Georgetown, and I've got them pulling his class rosters. Samantha described the guy down to a fucking T. We're looking for a kid who idolized Latham, a guy who—Samantha believes—left school after Latham vanished. The folks at Georgetown told me they'd have that list for me by 3:00 p.m." He glanced at his watch. "So in less than an hour's time, I'm betting Samantha will have exactly nailed the bastard for us." His spine was ramrod straight. "Now if you'll excuse me, I want to get back to the case." He turned on his heel.

"I get that you trust her, Agent Gamble. You made that abundantly clear."

Blake glanced back at the EAD.

"But I don't feel the same way about her."

"Yeah," Blake growled right back. "You made that *abundantly clear.*"

Bass notched up his chin. "She could have stopped Cameron Latham. She was in his house. Right there with him. And Samantha let him walk away. *That's* the reason she's out of the FBI. Because when it came right down to it, her loyalty was with her lover, not with us." His gaze raked Blake. "Maybe you should remember that. If push comes to shove ever again, if it comes down to a choice of saving your ass or of saving his... which side do you think she'd choose then? Do you *really* think you can count on her? Because I don't. And I wasn't going to risk the life of a single FBI agent on that gamble."

"There is no risk." He was certain of that. Blake began to walk away.

"I never said she wasn't a good profiler." Bass's voice rang out.

Blake kept walking. *Uh, yeah, you did.*

"I said that I thought she'd choose him. If hell came calling, if it was us versus him...I said she'd choose him. I stand by those words, and you need to remember them, Agent Gamble. You think she's got your back? Just because you've got hers?"

He did.

"Think again!" Bass yelled.

That guy was such a pain in his ass.

Blake marched straight ahead. He'd go talk to the ME. He'd work the case. He'd get justice for Tammy White. *She* mattered. Bass and his politics? They didn't.

Not even a little bit.

CHAPTER ELEVEN

LEWIS BRAKED HIS car near the entrance to her house. Samantha reached for the door handle.

"Wait!"

Lewis's sharp voice froze her. Samantha glanced over at him.

"Reach into the glove box, Sammie."

Frowning at him, she opened the glove box. She reached inside, and her fingers touched—a holster? Her heart thudded into her chest as she pulled it out.

"That was your dad's," he muttered. "Always kept it in good condition. Cleaned it regularly. Made sure it was in working order."

The weight of the gun was familiar in her hand. A chill skated down her spine.

"You're being hunted, Sammie." He exhaled. "And you need to protect yourself. What better way to do that than with your father's gun?"

She looked up at him. "You're worried about me."

"I'm scared spitless." He blew out another long breath. "And I get that a gun won't be much protection against a bomb, but I had to make sure you had something."

She didn't mention that she had three guns hidden in her house...and a knife currently strapped to her ankle. *You taught me well, Lewis.* "Thank you."

He glanced toward her house. "Want me to come in with you? Search the place?"

"My alarm hasn't gone off." She had it linked to her phone. "And besides, I know how to do my own searches." She waited until he was looking at her. "I can protect myself, you know." She gave a faint smile, hoping to lighten the tension on his face.

Only, it didn't lighten. "You can't protect yourself if you don't see the threat coming. It's the same thing that happened to your father. He didn't see it. *I* didn't see it—"

She caught his hand in hers. "When are you going to stop blaming yourself? You didn't pull the trigger that night. His death wasn't on you."

His gaze lowered. He stared at their linked hands. "And it wasn't on you, either. But that didn't stop your guilt, did it, baby girl?"

Well played. "Lewis…"

He peered up at her. "How about I make you a deal? I'll let my guilt go when you do. Maybe we both need to stop blaming ourselves for the actions others take. Hell, you got that fancy degree in psychology…a couple of them…wasn't that supposed to teach you not to blame yourself?"

"Those degrees were supposed to teach me how to stop killers."

"I think you already knew how to do that long before you left for college." His voice had turned musing. "You always did figure folks out so easy. You could read 'em from fifty feet away."

Not always, she couldn't.

His radio beeped.

"They need you back in town." She pulled her hand

away from his. "Thanks for the ride." She reached for the door, and, holding the holster closer, she climbed from the car. Samantha walked around the vehicle and gave him a little wave. "You'd better call me when you learn something."

"Consider me your inside man." But he didn't smile. "And you call me if you need anything."

She always had.

He drove away, his tires rolling over the shells in her driveway. A lot of people in the area used shells instead of concrete driveways. With the shells, puddles didn't collect from the heavy rains. She stood there a moment, the sunlight trickling through the trees, the sound of the waves hitting the shore a distant sound as it echoed up the bluff.

Then she turned and headed toward her house. She climbed up the porch steps. Pulled out her keys and—

There were scratches on her lock. Faint but discernible. Her finger lifted, and she touched the lock. Little pieces of metal had flecked off the lock because...*the scratches are new*. She glanced over her shoulder. Lewis was gone. She could call him back, have him there in mere moments...

She pulled out her father's gun. Checked it. Loaded, ready to go.

Yes, she could call Lewis. Or she could call Blake. Or she could handle this shit on her own. She'd had the best training in the world.

She slipped around to the back of the house. Her gaze darted to that lock. No scratch marks. She checked her phone and saw that—hell, no wonder she hadn't gotten any sort of alarm. The system was listed as being off-line.

Her jaw locked. She opened the back door, she kept her father's gun at the ready and she went inside.

JUSTIN BASS MARCHED toward his car. A rental, one that wasn't his normal style at all. But he climbed in the four-door sedan and slid behind the wheel. He pulled the door shut, turned on the car and got the air conditioner to blast at him. Who the hell needed an air conditioner in February? *People in freaking Alabama.*

He jerked his car into Reverse. He wanted to floor it and zoom out of there, but Justin was far too conscious of eyes on him. People were always watching. He had plenty of guys gunning for his position at the FBI.

The road twisted and turned as it led back to town. The bay was on his left, gleaming. Water everywhere. The road was damn near deserted, and a sign to the right told him he was taking the "Scenic Route." Like he cared about the scenery.

His GPS was giving him directions, the robotic voice just angering him more and more, and when he missed a turn, he burst out, "Shut the hell up!" He needed to think.

He pulled off the road. Stopped at an old restaurant, one with boarded-up windows, a place that looked as if it had not seen better days in a very, very long time.

The GPS kept ordering him to turn right—like there was any fucking place to go there. He killed his engine and huffed out a breath. Then Justin jumped out of his car and reached in to yank his cigarettes from his pocket. He'd gone four long months without a smoke. His wife had been so proud of him, and now this case—it was breaking him.

He lit up and started to pace. As soon as the nicotine

hit him, he actually felt the calm hit him, too. Okay, he could do this. He could fix things. The media loved him. He always knew how to work them. There had been one reporter, Janice Beautfont, who'd been flirting like crazy with him. He'd use her. Get her to air exactly what he wanted aired.

If Samantha's profile was right, then he'd float the story that *he'd* made the decision to pull her in. That he'd been the one to offer her a second chance. No one needed to know the fact that Blake Gamble had pretty much forced him into that chance. He paced away from the road, moving away from the view of the water. Occasionally, a stray car would buzz past him. Just in case any of the reporters happened to be driving that way, he edged closer to the line of trees on his left. The last thing he wanted was for some reporter to catch sight of him. He'd talk again *only* when he was ready.

He glanced at his watch. Blake had said they'd have the student list by three. He'd wait until that time, and then he'd see where this case went. If they got a name, if they got a face, then he could play the scene triumphantly. Maybe he'd even let Samantha stand behind him at the press conference.

Only…

Damn it, he hadn't been lying to Gamble. He *didn't* trust that woman. She'd been in the home with Latham. She'd let the guy walk. What guarantee did he have that she wouldn't do the exact same thing again?

A twig snapped. He dropped the cigarette. Crushed it beneath his feet, and his hand automatically went to his holster. He stared at the forest before him, a thick line of twisting trees and overgrown bushes. "Who's there?"

SAMANTHA CREPT THROUGH her house. Everything appeared to still be in perfect place. Her books were on the shelves, her furniture untouched. In the kitchen, her glasses were still stacked by the sink. She didn't lower her gun as she paced down the hallway. A quick glance in the guest room showed nothing appeared to have been disturbed. The house was quiet. Still.

Her heartbeat drummed in her chest. She could see her bedroom. The door was partially open. For the life of her, Samantha couldn't remember if she'd left that door open or shut. She'd been heading out with Blake that morning. She'd been stirred up. Desperate. When they'd gone out the front door, Janice had been waiting—

But I'm not worried about the front door. It's the bedroom door that matters. Did I shut it?

Should she call out? Demand that anyone in there surrender? Say that she had a gun?

Or should she just rush in, hoping to use the element of surprise?

I'll try option two. She sucked in a breath and rushed inside, moving soundlessly.

But...

No one was in there. Nothing was out of place. The bed was still tousled, her robe was on the floor. Everything was *exactly* as she'd left it.

She checked the bathroom—nothing. And then her gaze turned to the white door on the right. The door that led to her office. It was shut securely, no light coming from beneath it. It was the only room in the house that she still had left to check. She moved carefully forward, making sure not to step on any of the old floorboards that would creak beneath her weight.

Her fingers curled around the doorknob, and she opened the door. She inched into that little room.

No one was there.

As with the rest of the house's interior, everything appeared untouched. She stalked toward the map she'd made, the one that carefully detailed all of the locations that she'd been tracking Cameron.

Nothing.

Damn it. She was sure someone had been in her house. Someone had broken in and not touched a single thing? How did that make sense?

Then Samantha stilled. Maybe the perp hadn't come to take anything. Maybe he'd come to *leave* something. Like a bomb. He'd set that little boat to blow; maybe he'd left an explosive at her house, too, and she'd walked straight into his trap. *Shit, shit, shit.* She should have thought of the bomb first. She should have realized just what could be happening.

Instead, I was all focused on confronting the perp, on making sure I didn't draw anyone else into the fire.

She started retreating down her hallway, heading for the front door. She was almost there.

The growl of an engine reached her ears. She moved fast, faster. She grabbed for the front door, fumbled with the lock, yanked the door open and rushed down her porch steps. Her gun was still gripped in her hand.

"Samantha!" Blake was there, hurrying toward her as he left his SUV, his face tight and worried.

She grabbed his arm with her left hand. "Someone was inside—"

He immediately tried to lunge for the house.

"No!" She stepped in his path. "Someone *was* inside. But the place is empty now. I'm afraid there may be a bomb in there." Her muscles ached from tension. "We need to call this in and get bomb-sniffing dogs out here, right away."

He pulled her back toward his SUV. Pushed her down behind it. "You thought someone was in your house and you just waltzed in there? What in the actual fuck were you thinking?"

"Oh, I don't know...that I was a former FBI agent who might be able to handle shit." That she was a woman who didn't want the bad guy to get away again.

He yanked out his phone, and a few moments later, he was giving the order to get the K-9 unit there.

She crouched behind the vehicle, her heart still beating far too fast. When he put his phone down, Samantha spoke, slowly, carefully. "I wasn't letting him get away."

Blake's eyes glittered with fury. "I told you that you weren't bait."

Yes, he had said something to that effect. "And I told you that I didn't want anyone else dying for me."

"Samantha..."

"There were scratches on the front lock. Fresh scratches." She remembered the flecks of metal. "If the perp was still in that house, I *was* stopping him. Don't act as if you wouldn't have done the same thing."

His hand curled around her shoulder, and he brought her in closer. "This isn't about me. It's about you. And how many times do I have to tell you...*you* matter to me? Matter too much to lose."

She stared into his eyes. His fury was all around them, but the tension between them wasn't just about rage. If only things were that simple.

"I can't lose you again." Blake gave a shake of his head. "I won't."

"You aren't losing me."

"That had better be a promise," Blake said, and then he was kissing her. A fast, wild, hard kiss. A kiss that sent desire for him scorching through her veins. A kiss that made her remember what it had been like to be with him, all abandon gone, in her bed.

And she wanted to be with him that way again.

She *would* be with him that way again.

Blake eased back. "We aren't staying here tonight." His lips twisted. "We're going someplace secluded. You and me. You aren't going to be bait."

Yes, she was. *How many people have to die in my place?* He didn't understand how much that haunted her.

She could hear the sound of sirens coming toward her. Lewis must have gotten the call about her place— and he was circling back at full speed.

Blake started to pull away from her. Her hand lifted and caught his wrist, holding him close. "What do you want from me?"

"I already told you. I want everything. And tonight, I'm getting it."

The sirens were louder.

And she let him go.

A CAT RAN out of the woods. A stupid, scrawny black cat. Justin swore when he saw it. He'd just had a shit-freak over a cat.

He'd been out of the field too long. Truth be told, he didn't *like* the field. Getting shot at, being targeted— hell, no, he was too old for that hot mess. He was more of a strategist. He could direct his agents—from a safe distance—so that they could get their jobs done. And he could handle the media like a pro.

Justin knew his strengths.

And it's time to get to work on the media now.

Justin marched back to his rental. He opened the door, slid into the front seat. He yanked off his holster and shoved it onto the passenger seat. The thing had been jamming into his side. *Better now.* He exhaled slowly and started to put the key into the ignition and—

Something jabbed into his neck. Hard, sharp. A fucking bee sting? His hand rose to slap at his neck, but…

His fingers curled around a syringe. "What the fu—" His words were slurring. He tried to turn in his seat but got tangled up in the seat belt. The damn thing was tightening around him.

"It's a drug, Bass. A very powerful one," a low voice rumbled from the backseat.

Justin blinked. Some fucker was in his car? Since when? Some fucker who had *drugged* him? From the corner of his eye, he saw a man's tanned hand, the inside of his wrist. Some kind of black tat?

"You're only going to be awake for a few more moments. So you probably shouldn't even try to understand things now. There'll be time to talk later. After all, I never kill my victims right away. There's no fun in that. Nothing to *learn* from that."

Justin slumped in his seat. His body wasn't doing what he wanted it to do. His holster—his gun—they were right in the seat beside him. He just had to reach them. Inches away.

But he was blinking groggily.

"There are so many horses in Fairhope, did you know that? Well, actually, I guess technically most of them are right next door in Point Clear. That's a lovely city, by the way, really picturesque, and it's basically the horse capital around here. They even do big polo games. Quite fancy." That voice was low, amused. "Where there are horses, there is also horse tranquilizer. That's what is running through your veins right now. Don't worry. It won't kill you. Not outright, anyway. I've used it on someone else before. You aren't my first experiment."

Experiment.

Justin tried to talk, desperate, frantic right then because he thought he knew who the bastard was in his backseat. "Ca— Cam…"

His driver's-side door was yanked open. Sunlight poured down on Justin as he fought to keep his eyes open. A second man was there, a man who wore a baseball cap, a guy he couldn't see clearly.

I can't see anything clearly.

He could barely keep his thoughts together.

"We need to move him fast," the other guy said, sounding nervous. "Before any cars happen by. And he's…he's big. I don't know if we should have gone after him…"

"Oh, trust me." The voice from the backseat had turned silken. "If you want your glory, then you go for the big gun. He's exactly the man we want."

Justin's eyes closed. Someone unhooked his seat belt. His body started to fall right out of the car, but—

He never felt the impact with the ground.

CHAPTER TWELVE

"YOUR PLACE IS CLEAR." Blake shut the office door behind him, immediately muting all of the noise from the Fairhope police station. And there was *plenty* of noise out there. Everyone and their mother seemed to be coming forth with tips on Tammy White's killer. Too bad most of those tips were pure BS.

Samantha sat behind Lewis's desk. The police captain was in one of the conference rooms, interviewing the witnesses because he knew most of them personally, and the guy said he could cut through the crap faster if he spoke with the folks himself. The captain had turned over his office to Blake and Samantha.

Giving them privacy. Giving them work space.

Giving Samantha a safe space while the bomb squad and crime techs basically tore apart her house.

"Just got off the phone with the bomb squad," Blake said. "There is no sign of any explosive device at your place."

Samantha tapped her fingers on the old, scarred wood of the desk. "That's good news. I wasn't exactly thrilled about the idea of my home being blown to bits."

Like he was thrilled about the idea of *her* being blown to bits. He marched toward her, moved behind the desk, and then he wheeled her chair around so that she had to face him. He leaned over her, putting them at eye level. Rage still rode him hard, but he was trying to hold it back, for her.

"Want to tell me again why you didn't call me as soon as you realized someone was in your house?" Just so they were extra clear on that point.

"Sure." She stared straight into his eyes, her gaze unflinching. "Because you aren't the only badass with a gun who was trained by the FBI? I'm pretty fierce when it comes to self-defense, and I do know how to pull a trigger."

His jaw locked. "You never go into a dangerous situation without backup. That's FBI 101 and—"

She waved her hand. "Hello? Remember me? *Not FBI and—*"

Something in him snapped. It was all just too much. The bombing at the old pier, the memory of finding Tammy's body—of seeing her hair drifting around her face—of getting to Samantha's home in time to see her running out of her house, fear stamped on her delicate features.

A killer was screwing with them. And she wanted to put herself up as the perfect target. He was so fucking done. He put his hand behind her head and pulled her against him.

His mouth crashed onto hers. He kissed her the way he'd wanted to kiss her back at her house. The way he *always* wanted to kiss her. With all the ferocious need and desire that rode him. When she was near, he wanted. Simple fact. Having her in bed, taking that gorgeous body of hers... Once hadn't satisfied him. The terrifying truth was that he didn't know when he would be satisfied. If he could be. The more he had of Samantha, the more he wanted.

She was in his blood, and he didn't know how to get her out. He wasn't sure he ever would.

His mouth was too rough on hers. He should ease up. He didn't.

He yanked her out of the chair and pushed her up onto the desk so that he could kiss her even deeper, so that he could hold her even closer. Her legs were spread as she perched on the edge of the wood, and he shoved between them. Her hands had come down against his chest, but Samantha wasn't pushing him away. Her fingers curled against him, and he could feel the faint bite of her short nails through his shirt.

He was kissing her like a starving man, and he knew it. Kissing her with a desperate hunger that just wouldn't stop. He'd held back too long with Samantha, and now that he had her, he wasn't letting her go.

He thrust his tongue past her lips. She sucked it, and damn but his dick was as hard as a rock. He had to go out and prepare for the press conference, but all he wanted was to fuck her.

Blake pulled his mouth from hers and kissed her neck, right over her racing pulse. He liked that her pulse was going crazy; it told him that she was just as affected as he was. He wanted her that way. Blake wanted need to blind her the way it blinded him.

"If…if Lewis finds out what we're doing on his desk…" Her voice was husky. Sexy. "Count on him trying to kick your ass."

A kiss from Samantha was worth an ass kicking. The problem was that he wanted far more than a kiss. He wanted her, naked, eager. Desperate. He wanted to sink into her and go fucking wild.

But he could hear voices on the other side of the door.

Cops were out there. Local FBI agents. This wasn't the time.

Even if he wanted her more than he wanted breath.

His eyes closed for a moment as he pulled her sweet scent into his lungs. He tried to get his control back. *Tried.* His hands gripped the desk. *Focus. Breathe.* But every breath just brought her scent to him.

And then he felt her hand, sliding against his cheek. Such a soft, careful touch.

His eyes opened. He knew she'd see the raw desire burning in his stare.

Her gaze widened. She licked her lips.

Hell. He had to kiss her once more. Harder, rougher. She didn't get how very close to the edge he was with her. Knowing that some sick son of a bitch was out there, hunting her? It terrified him, and not many damn things did. He thrust his tongue into her mouth and wanted to thrust his cock deep into her. He wanted—

Blake shoved away from her. "Give me a minute." More like a damn cold shower. That was what he needed. His breath heaved out, and his hands fisted.

He heard her slide off the desk and take a few steps toward him, as if she'd come to touch him.

"Samantha…" His voice held a warning edge.

"You think I don't want you the same way? A need so heavy it seems to claw me apart?"

He looked back at her. Her cheeks were flushed. Her eyes gleamed.

"I do."

That *wasn't* helping him stay in control.

The voices outside were rising. Footsteps passed right beside the door.

"Being with you made me want you even more." Her

confession twisted his guts. If his cock got much harder, the damn thing would be exploding. "When we leave the station, when we are alone, someplace private..." Her gaze swept over him. "There will be nothing to stop us."

Once they were away from everyone else, he'd have her naked within five minutes.

Blake took a step toward her, but a knock shook the door. He froze, his gaze locked with hers.

Samantha cleared her throat. "Come in!"

One of the local FBI agents poked his head inside. "Agent Gamble...we still planning the in-house briefing with the cops before the press conference?"

He nodded grimly. "Yes, I'll be right there. Go ahead and get things organized." He cleared his throat because his voice was too rough and ragged. *That's what happens when my control slips away.* "I just need a few more minutes in here."

The guy slipped away. Blake sucked in a few long, deep breaths.

"You have a job to do," Samantha murmured. "I can wait."

He didn't want her waiting. And it wasn't just *his* job. It was theirs. Or at least, it had been. He'd pulled his control back in place. *Until we're alone. Then that control can go straight to hell.* His head cocked as he studied her for a moment. Before he left the office, he needed to know... "Do you *want* to come back to the FBI?"

"I just... I want to stop killers. I want to help people. My dad believed in justice. Lewis believes in justice. I want to be like them." Her lips pressed together. She was holding back on him again.

His muscles tensed. When would she learn she didn't have to do that?

"May I tell you a secret?"

"You can tell me anything."

But her wistful smile said...*if only.*

"I wanted to help people, my whole life. That's why I studied psychology in school, to understand what could go wrong inside a person. To try to fix..." She shook her head. "I wanted to help, but I always... It felt like my thinking was a bit off. I can profile the killers because I look at a situation and I see how they can attack. I see—too easily—how they can pick the victims. I see what they are." Her breath slid out. "And I fear what I am."

She feared what she was? "You're a talented and strong woman, that's what you are."

"Are you sure about that?"

"Hell, yes, I am."

"I wanted to kill the man who shot my father."

"You were a thirteen-year-old girl, you were terrified, you—"

"So I did."

He tensed. *What?* "I...I thought your father killed him." That was what Lewis had told him.

"I'm the one who killed him. Not my father." She stared straight at him, and he saw the truth in her eyes.

For a minute, he didn't speak. What did she think he'd do? Turn on her? No, no, he saw all too clearly what must have happened. "Self-defense. He'd just tried to kill you. He went after your father, he—"

"No." Samantha licked her lips. Tears gleamed in her eyes. "You're not understanding me. I was afraid of that."

Then who does understand you? Latham?

"Phil Hyde was going to shoot me, yes, but my father jumped in front of me. He took the bullet that should have ended my life." She blinked away tears. Looked beautiful and fragile and strong all at the same time. "My father was dying in my arms, and the man who'd shot him—my dad's ex-partner—stood there, watching. I was screaming for help. But he didn't help me. He just held the gun on us. He waited until he was sure my dad had bled out too much, waited as I shoved my hands against his wound…" She looked down at her hands, frowning as if surprised to see that there was no blood on her. "He waited until my dad was barely breathing. Then he said…'It's done, kid.' He turned to walk away. He was going to leave me alive. I knew right then what he was thinking—"

The way she always seemed to know what killers were thinking.

"Who would believe some traumatized kid? It would be my word against his. And he probably already had an alibi lined up. Folks to swear that he was nowhere near my dad's place. He'd spin the story that I was confused. Broken. That some robber killed my dad and I was just crazy with grief, picking up my dad's old stories about corruption and bad cops, and that I made up the story about him being the shooter. I could see exactly how it was all going down. And I knew he'd walk. He'd get away with killing my father."

His hand was sliding up and down her arm. A soothing caress that he couldn't, wouldn't stop. Her pain was real, living and breathing right between them. Moments ago, he'd been wild with passion, desperate to have her. Now he was desperate to soothe her. She stirred up his protective instincts just as much as she did his lust.

"My dad's gun was at his side. He'd dropped it when he'd been shot." Her breath rushed out. "I got that gun and I yelled for my father's partner to stop. I told him if he didn't drop his weapon and freeze right there, I'd shoot."

Shit. Based on how this story ended, he knew the partner hadn't walked away.

"He laughed at me." Her voice had gone cold. "Told me that I was just a kid and that kids shouldn't play with guns." Her lower lip trembled once more. "I knew if I shot him in the back, I'd have trouble. I mean, it's not self-defense if you shoot someone in the back. And even then, I knew it was…wrong to be thinking that way. But it was as if everything had slowed down for me. Slowed down and become crystal clear. So I waited until he turned toward me. He still had his gun in his hand, but it wasn't aimed at me. I waited, told him to drop the weapon again, and then when he didn't…"

Her words trailed away.

"Samantha?"

She blinked and focused her gaze on him. "I shot him. I was a good shot. The bullet went right into his heart. He didn't get to walk away. And when the cops arrived, he was still holding his weapon. Everyone knew what he'd done." Her eyes squeezed shut. "And my father was the only one to know what I'd done. He lived, just long enough for the EMTs to arrive."

He pulled her close and pressed a kiss to her forehead. "I'm so sorry."

Her laughter was mocking. "Sorry? I just told you that I killed a man—deliberately, not in self-defense, not in—"

"He'd murdered your father. Tried to kill you. And you were a thirteen-year-old child."

Samantha shook her head. "I'm not sure I was ever a child."

She thought she was a killer.

She looked up at him through her lashes. "Months ago, when I shot George Farris, you thought that was my first kill. In the line of duty, it was. But...there was more happening. Shooting George brought back so many memories for me, and I felt like those memories were ripping me apart."

She was ripping him apart. "What do you think I'm going to do? Judge you? Tell you that you were wrong to stop a killer? That you were wrong to protect yourself?"

Her lips parted.

"Don't. Don't even say you weren't protecting yourself. You were. He had a *gun*. You don't know that he would have just walked away from you. *You don't know.* Your dad was bleeding out in your arms, and the man who'd put a bullet into him was right in front of you. I'm glad you shot him."

Her chin jerked up.

"I'm glad because you're here. You're alive with me. And that son of a bitch isn't hurting anyone else. If you had that call to make again—I'd want you to do the same damn thing, understand? You aren't some messed-up killer. You aren't a perp, Samantha. You're a good person. You've done good work at the FBI. You *will* do good work again."

He needed her to believe those words.

He stared into her eyes and realized...

She did it. His heart slammed into his chest. *She trusted me with her secret.* He'd been battering at her for so long, trying to break down the walls that she used to surround herself, and Samantha had just offered up her darkest secret to him.

She was trusting him. "Thank you."

A furrow appeared between her brows. "For what? Dumping my past on you? Making you an accessory after the fact?"

He pressed a light kiss to her lips. "For letting me in."

Her pupils flared. "Blake—"

His phone vibrated. He started to ignore the text, but...

Three o'clock. He could see the time on the big clock that hung on the nearby wall. Damn it, this was a message he couldn't miss. Blake pulled out his phone and read the text there. "You are absolutely brilliant, Samantha." He tapped on the screen, pulling up the information that he'd just received from Georgetown. "Brilliant."

She was staring down at the screen, too. Staring at the picture of a former Georgetown student.

Jason Burke.

Age twenty-two.

Former psychology student. A student who'd been mentored by Cameron Latham.

"I think we've got him," Blake said, excitement thickening his voice. Hell, yes, they had a name, they had a face. He looked up. The same excitement he felt was mirrored in Samantha's eyes. "My contact said Jason withdrew one week after Latham vanished. *One week.*" He needed to get a team to the guy's home in Georgetown. Needed to start connecting all the dots and tear the man's life apart. "This is him." He knew it. Could *feel* it. "You did it."

But Samantha shook her head. "We haven't done anything yet. Not until we have the perp in custody. Not until we have evidence to tie him to the kills."

Time to find that evidence. He backed away from her, started to go toward the door, but stopped. Blake glanced back.

Samantha stared after him with a bit of hesitation plain to see on her face.

"You in this with me?" Blake asked her. He needed her to understand—nothing she'd said changed the way he felt about her. "Because I need you."

Her shoulders straightened. "I'm in this."

"Good. Then let's find this bastard."

"WHERE THE FUCK is he?" Blake demanded. The news conference—a conference that Bass had announced to all of the reporters—was scheduled to have started ten minutes ago, but the EAD had been a no-show.

He paced inside of the police station. He'd called Bass again and again, and he'd just gotten the guy's voice mail.

"Someone has to feed the sharks," Lewis said, nodding grimly. "So why don't one of you Bureau suits get out there and tell them that we know who we're after?"

They did know. Or at least, every bit of evidence they'd amassed in the last few hours certainly pointed to one Jason Burke as being the culprit.

An FBI unit had been sent to the guy's home in Georgetown. The place had been shut up tight, and according to the neighbors, Jason Burke had packed up and headed out of town a few days ago, right at the same time that Blake had traveled down to Fairhope.

They'd gotten a hit on the former Georgetown student's travel. Jason had booked a flight out of DC to Mobile, Alabama. But after that point, the guy had vanished.

Because he'd decided to start killing?

The fellow was even a former boatman, just as Samantha had said. The guy had been raised in New England, the child of two upper-class parents who'd kept a beach home in Martha's Vineyard. According to the family—distant cousins because Burke's parents were both deceased—Jason had grown up spending his summers out in his father's boat. He'd loved the water. Been like a fish.

Blake's phone beeped. He glanced down and realized he'd just gotten a text from Bass. About time. Quickly, he scanned the short message.

Take care of the press. Sick in hotel.

"What?" Bass never missed a chance to take center stage. Blake immediately called the EAD. The phone rang and rang and—

"Don't you understand…" Bass gasped. "Sick. Ate… something…bad."

"We've got a swarm of press here—local and national. And you're vomiting all over your toilet? Get your ass down here."

"You…handle it. You and…Dark." The line went dead.

Blake blinked.

"What's happening?" Samantha asked, her gaze worried.

He shoved his phone back into his pocket. He'd deal with Bass soon enough. For now, reporters were waiting. And they needed the public's help to find a killer. "You and I are going live."

"We're what?" Her jaw seemed to drop.

"Bass said he wanted us doing the press conference. So you're giving the profile, and I'm asking for the public's help." He marched forward and took her elbow so that he could steer her toward the doors that led outside to the waiting ring of reporters. He figured he'd better keep a hand on Samantha, just in case she balked. "We're doing this right now." With his left hand, he shoved open the gleaming glass door. He and Samantha walked out, and the reporters closed in.

JUSTIN BASS VOMITED on the floor. He was as sick as a fucking dog. Everything hurt, and the room kept spinning around him.

"That was really good," an excited voice told him. "You did that just right."

Asshole. He spat on the floor once more. Then Justin looked up, his eyes narrowing on the bastard who stood just a few feet away from him.

Young...too damn young. Had to be in his early twenties. His face was round and unlined. A weak chin. His blond hair was sun-streaked, as if the guy had spent a whole lot of time outdoors. *Some young preppy asshole.* Justin wanted to lift up his fist and drive it right into that guy's face. But his hands were tied behind his back. His feet were bound, too, and the only movement he could manage right then was the retching.

He needed to get his strength back. He had to figure out where he was, and he had to take down the jerk grinning at him.

But he's not the real threat. This guy is following orders. Orders that he knew had come from someone else.

Before he'd blacked out in the car, he'd been sure that he recognized the creep who'd been in his backseat, but things were kind of blurry right now and he couldn't be one hundred percent sure of, well, anything.

"You just… You stay in here," the blond said. He'd taken Justin's phone. Not the smartest move, keeping that thing. As long as it was on, the cops could trace the GPS signal. Sure, he'd played along, and he'd told Gamble exactly what the punk said—mostly because the guy had put a knife to his throat—but when he didn't show up at his hotel in a few hours, his team would come looking for him. They'd trace his phone. They'd find him. And the dumb punk.

He just had to stay alive until then. And hell, he was the fucking executive assistant director…he could manipulate this dumb little shit.

Justin vomited again.

As soon as he got his strength back, he'd go on the attack. He'd get out of this mess, and he'd bring down the man—men?—who'd taken him. If Cameron Latham really was involved…if that memory was right and it hadn't been the drug playing tricks on him…

Bastard, I will make you pay.

Even if it was the last thing that he did.

"We have created a profile for the perpetrator in the death of Tammy White." Samantha stood at the little podium, and her gaze swept around the assembled reporters. Her heart was pounding like mad in her chest, but her voice didn't so much as tremble. "We are looking for a white male, in his early twenties, an individual that we believe is still in the area. He's a highly organized killer, intelligent, fit." She eased out a slow breath. "At this point, this perp is suspected in the death of a second woman as well, Kristy Wales, of DC."

The reporters yelled out questions.

Samantha swallowed.

Blake's shoulder brushed hers. "The FBI has recently identified a person of interest in this case. The individual is Jason Benjamin Burke, age twenty-two, a former student at Georgetown University. I will provide a photograph of him to everyone here. We are asking for the public's help in locating this individual. Mr. Burke is considered armed and dangerous, so *no one*, I repeat, *no one* should approach this man. If you see him, you are directed to call us." Then he rattled off the local number for folks to use.

Samantha wiped her damp palms on her pants.

"Georgetown University?" That was Janice's voice ringing out. "That is Cameron Latham's university."

The man hardly owned the place.

"So are you confirming this killer's linked to Latham?" Janice demanded.

The reporters waited. Samantha's head turned, and she realized that Blake was looking at her, too. He was giving her this moment, letting her take her career back right in front of the press.

Her shoulders straightened. "Yes." Again, no emotion entered her voice. Her drumming heartbeat began to slow. "We believe that the two individuals are linked. Cameron Latham was Burke's mentor at the university. It is possible that he knew of Burke's...darker side."

"Do you think Cameron Latham is in the area?" Janice's voice rose with a hint of anxiety.

Samantha began to deny that possibility, but…

The cameras kept rolling.

Is Cameron here? He shouldn't be. He should have been far, far away. The guy should have fled the US. Gone to a country that didn't have a friendly extradition agreement with the US. But…he hadn't. Instead, he'd been hitting his favorite locales over the last few months. He'd been staying just a step ahead of her.

He'd been…

Hiding, in plain sight.

So she told the truth. "I think that is a possibility that cannot be ignored."

Samantha saw the surprise flash on Janice's face.

"Cameron Latham is a man who values control in every aspect of his life. If he and Burke did have a close relationship, then, yes, it is possible that Latham is either already in the area or he's coming." Her heart rate was a steady beat in her chest. Not too fast, not too slow. "The public should be on the lookout for him, but—" her gaze swept the group "—he will have altered his appearance." Of that, she was certain. When she'd almost gotten him in Chicago, the desk clerk had told her that Latham had been a redhead. "He would have changed his hair color, his eye color, either put on weight or taken it off. He will have adopted a persona that is very different from the one he had in DC. Cameron Latham knows how to manipulate the people around him. He gets them to see only what he wants shown and he—"

"Did he manipulate you?" Janice wanted to know.

Blake moved toward the microphone.

But Samantha touched his shoulder. She didn't need protecting. "Yes." The one word was spoken too close to the mic, and it seemed to echo back to her. "Yes, he did manipulate me. I didn't see his darker side until the end. But I won't make that mistake again, and no one else should, either. He is a very dangerous individual. There's a reason he found his way to the top of the FBI's most wanted list." *And it's not just because he made the FBI look like a bunch of dumbasses.* Well, that wasn't the only reason, anyway.

The reporters kept asking questions. She answered them. Blake answered them. Lewis even came forward for his turn at the microphone.

And then Blake raised his hand, indicating that they were done.

They backed away from the crowd and retreated into the station.

She followed Blake inside, with Lewis at her heels. And Lewis—

"You did good out there, Sammie," Lewis praised. "I didn't so much as see you sweat."

She'd sweated plenty. But she also hadn't backed down. She was more than just the agent who'd slept with the wrong man once upon a time. She was the agent who was going to nail Jason Burke to the wall.

And one day, I'll bring in Cameron.

They strode down the hallway, moving away from the glass doors.

Footsteps padded behind them, and she turned to see Josh Duvane tailing them. When he saw her, he lifted a brow. "So you really think Latham is here?"

Her breath slid out. "Yes, I really do think that."

"Since when?" Blake demanded, voice tight. "How long have you thought the joker was here?"

"He may *not* be here yet, but I believe he's coming."

All of them were focused on her. She shrugged. "It's because of me."

Lewis frowned. "Now hold on..."

"The bombing. The attack that nearly killed me." She rubbed the back of her neck, hating the tension that had gathered there. "Janice reported on the story. I already know the national news picked up that little scene she filmed at my house. I think we've all seen the footage of Blake and me coming out of my place."

Blake winced.

"Cameron would have seen it, too." A mocking smile curled her lips. "He always said it was important to stay updated on current events. He would have seen the news, and when he realized I was almost hurt in that bombing, he would come here."

"To finish the job on you?" Josh asked, nodding. "The story revealed your location, something that has been kept quiet for a long time and—"

"Cameron would have known I was here from the beginning." Her hands were loose at her sides. "And he wouldn't be coming to kill me." Her gaze met Blake's. "He'd be coming...to protect me."

She saw surprise flash on his face. Surprise, then understanding.

"He couldn't kill you," Blake murmured. "Not then, not now."

"He *can't* kill me," Samantha corrected. *He tried.* "And he's not going to let anyone else do it, either."

Josh threw his hands into the air as he started to pace. "Okay, I am beyond confused. You've got some serial out there who—what? Is playing guardian angel for you? 'Cause that's twisted. Even with the weird crap we see on a daily basis, that is some twisted—"

"Cameron thinks he needs me." She was staring at Blake when she said those words. *You're right. I have let you in. I'm not keeping any other secrets.* "I'm the only person in the world he's ever connected with. If he believes I'm in danger, he will act to take out any threat to me. He can't form a connection with another person, and if he loses me, then Cameron fears he will be truly alone."

Lewis whistled. "So this Burke guy that we're all after…he thinks that Latham is his mentor, his good killing buddy, but really…"

She needed them to all understand this point. "Really, Cameron Latham is his greatest threat. If he has the chance, I believe he'll kill Jason Burke. But Jason doesn't realize that. He won't see the threat coming, not until it is far too late."

CHAPTER THIRTEEN

THE BED-AND-BREAKFAST was nice—very nice. Fancy and pricey and currently it was her new home-away-from-home.

Samantha paced near the four-poster bed. The authorities had cleared her house, but Blake had been adamant that she wasn't returning. At least, not that night. He'd even gone so far as to pull rank on her—that FBI protective custody bull again.

She could have argued with him, she knew that, but she also knew that she wanted a safe place to crash. She was exhausted, and when she slept, she wanted to feel safe.

The bed-and-breakfast was close enough to town so that when the ME was finished with his exam, she and Blake would be able to get to his office within ten minutes. Close to the action, but off the beaten path, so that they wouldn't attract attention from reporters.

Local patrol units were out canvasing for Burke and for Cameron. A manhunt was taking place in the surrounding two-hundred miles. While all of that was going down, Samantha was just supposed to wait out the night.

The problem was that Samantha had never been particularly good at waiting.

A knock sounded at the door—the door that connected her room to Blake's. She'd been highly conscious of him in that room, of every whisper of sound and pad of his footsteps. At the knock, she hurried forward and opened the door. It hadn't been locked, a deliberate choice on her part.

He stood in the doorway, wearing a pair of jeans, his dark hair glinting with moisture. She'd heard the roar of his shower, and she'd actually thought about joining him in there.

Things were so...tense between them. She wasn't sure what she was supposed to be doing. How was she supposed to act? She'd given him her most closely guarded secret, expecting the guy to turn on her, but he hadn't.

"Wanted to check on you," Blake said, his deep voice making her breath catch. "Before you went to bed."

Checking on her. Right. How very *gentlemanly* of him. She wasn't in the mood for that. Not after her day. Not even close. "I'm fine." Her words sounded a little angry even to her own ears. Oh, well, why pretend? He'd been the one to say no secrets.

"Something wrong?"

She rolled back her shoulders. "Yes, I think so." She'd showered earlier, too, wanting to wash away the day. But some sins didn't wash away. She was clad in a pair of loose shorts and a T-shirt. She'd thought the shorts did a good job of showing off her legs, and she hadn't put on a bra, deliberately. She'd thought she at least looked semi-sexy. Apparently not, since Blake was there, just seeing if she was *okay* before bed. What had happened to the fierce need they shared at the police station? The whole promise of what would happen once they were away from prying eyes? She wanted his passion. Hot, wild, intense. She didn't want him handling her with kid gloves.

Blake stepped toward her. Samantha held her ground, refusing to retreat. Her head tipped back as she stared up at him.

"You going to share?" Blake pushed. "Or do I get to guess what's spinning through your head right now?"

She'd share plenty. "You don't have to look after me every moment. You don't have to constantly check to see if I'm going to break. I'm not."

His brows rose. "That wasn't what I was doing."

Liar, liar. "I see you. I see you when you're watching me, and you think I don't know."

He laughed. A low, deep chuckle. "You think I watch you because I'm afraid you're about to shatter?"

She licked her lips. His gaze had heated as he followed the quick movement of her tongue. "Is there another reason?"

"Baby, it's always hard as fuck to take my eyes off you. You're gorgeous."

She tucked a strand of loose hair behind her ear.

"I look at you, and I ache. You're under my skin. In my dreams. I can't escape from you."

That didn't sound good. "Do you want to escape?"

"Hell, no."

That was, ah, better.

His gaze swept over her—and it was hot. Very, very hot. Demanding. That stare lingered on her breasts—her nipples were tight and thrusting against the front of her shirt—and her legs. *About time you noticed.* "I told you what you'd be when I got you alone."

Yes, he had.

Mine.

And she wanted to be. She wanted to be his, and she wanted him to be hers. She wanted to let go and forget the killers at the door. Just for a moment. The ME would call, they'd get an update on the case, then it would be back to work.

Stolen moments—that was what they had. What they might always have.

Staring up at him, she reached for the hem of her T-shirt. She yanked it over her head and tossed it to the floor.

His lips parted.

She reached for her shorts. Pushed them down. Then Samantha stood before him, completely naked. Waiting.

"You're…beautiful." His voice was rougher. Darker. *You like the—*

She shut that voice out of her mind. There was no room for Cameron. It was just her and Blake. Only them.

"Your turn," Samantha said, and her voice had gone husky.

She thought he'd strip for her. But he came toward her, scooped her into his arms, held her tight and kissed her. Kissed her with that wild hunger that she loved. The ferocious need that told her he was desperate for her.

She wanted him that way.

She wanted *to be* that way. And she was, with him. With Blake, she felt sexy. She felt…normal. A woman with her lover. A woman who could trust.

He carried her to the four-poster bed. He put her down on it, and she gave a little bounce. A laugh came from her. God, she only seemed to laugh with Blake. Her emotions were like a well that had gone dry except when he was near. He was bringing her back to life, and she didn't even know if he realized that fact.

"Missed that sound." His eyes glittered down at her. "I missed you."

"You don't have to miss me anymore. I'm right here." She rose onto her knees. Her hands wrapped around his shoulders as he stood at the side of the bed, and she kissed him, a long, sensual kiss. She slid her tongue over his lip, then caught that sexy lower lip of his in a light nip.

He growled.

Her hands slid between their bodies. She caught the snap of his jeans and unhooked them. The zipper slid down with a low hiss, and the hot, hard length of his erection thrust into her hands. He'd been the one to seduce her before. Samantha figured this was her chance now. She stroked the length of his erection, moving from base to tip, again and again. He was full, so thick and hot in her hands. His breath blew out as she stroked him. She kissed his chest, moving her body down, moving her mouth down, and then she pressed her lips to his cock.

"Samantha."

She sucked him, licked him and had one hell of a good time exploring his body. Power poured through her—a sensual rush of power that she'd never felt with another lover. She trusted Blake completely in that moment. Anything he wanted—anything she wanted—she knew there was no taboo.

Then his hands were on her, pushing her back, and she hit the bed. He ditched his jeans, grabbed a condom and was back with her in mere moments. He caught her wrists and pinned them above her. He held them there with one of his hands while his other hand positioned his cock at the entrance to her body.

"You push me to the edge."

"I want you over that edge," she told him. She wanted *everything* from him.

"Then here we go." He drove into her, a deep thrust that stole her breath. He filled her completely, and her body closed greedily around him. Withdraw, thrust, in and out, and the old four-poster bed began to squeak.

The passion was red-hot between them. She arched against him, moaning his name. His mouth closed over her shoulder, and she felt the edge of his teeth on her skin. She liked it when he got rough. When he went wild, and he was wild right then. Every hard thrust of his body sent the length of his cock surging over her clit. Again and again, rougher, harder.

And her orgasm slammed into her. It hit her with the force of an avalanche, stealing her breath, and she shuddered beneath him. He held her hands tightly, and he kept thrusting, deep and strong, the power of his thrusts lifting her off the bed, and she loved it.

"Let's do that again," he urged hotly. "You feel fucking fantastic."

So did he.

Blake freed her hands. She started to reach for him, but he withdrew.

Oh, hell, no. "Blake!"

He caught her hips, rolled her over. Samantha came up on her knees even as she automatically grabbed for the headboard to steady herself. He rose up behind her, spread her legs wider apart. "Like this…"

He sank into her again. She was so sensitive from her orgasm. When he sank into her…

"Yes." The word was a hiss of pleasure. *Like this. Exactly like this.* She wanted this to go on forever.

He took her from behind, driving in with fast and hard strokes, and she slammed her hips back to meet him. His hands were around her waist, holding her so tightly that she wondered if she'd have bruises—and she didn't even care. Her orgasm was building again. She wanted to explode, wanted the pleasure to last and last.

His hand slid around her body. His fingers pushed between her thighs. Her hands curled like claws around the headboard. Yes, right there. He was stroking her clit even as he drove his cock into her. Again. Once more, she needed—

Her body stiffened as the climax hit. A climax that rolled through her again and again, and she could barely choke out his name. The pleasure wouldn't stop. It was almost too much for her…

It was perfect.

He pulled her closer, and his cock jerked within her as he came. His mouth pressed to the curve of her shoulder. She could feel the release running through him. She heard the thunder of a heartbeat—hers, his.

Her eyes were closed. She opened them and glanced back at him. His face was cut into hard, predatory lines. He looked rough and dangerous. He was exactly what she wanted. He knew about the shadows in her mind, the shadows that marked her soul, and he didn't seem to care.

He pulled out of her, and she *hated* that loss. "Don't stop," Samantha said. "I want to go again." *And again, and again.*

"Oh, we will." He kissed her. "We will."

"TAMMY WHITE HAD no idea that she was going to work for the last day of her life." Janice Beautfont stared into the lens of her video camera and made sure that her voice was rich with sympathy and just a hint of pain as she stood in front of the Connoisseur's Delight shop. "But she was abducted from this small town, a place that should have been safe for her—and authorities discovered her remains at the bottom of the bay." She gave a sad shake of her head. "Now a manhunt is under way for Jason Burke, a twenty-two-year-old ex–Georgetown University psychology major who is a *person of interest* in Tammy's abduction and brutal murder." She paused just a moment. "Tune in tonight at ten for the latest details on this case as developments continue to unfold." She stared into the camera lens a few more moments and mentally counted down for the transfer back to the station. *Five, four, three, two, one—*

She blew out a hard breath and unsnapped the microphone that she'd been wearing. "Did I sound sympathetic enough? Like I cared?"

John Andrews, her cameraman, frowned at her. It was just her and John working tonight. Billy Wax, her intern, wasn't around for his social media duty. Seriously, if that guy thought he was going to make it in the business, he needed to get his priorities straight. Maybe his jeans were too damn tight or something, because he'd gone on a *date* instead of showing up for the biggest story of the whole freaking year.

And John was still frowning at her. Whoops. Just what had she said to him? "I mean, I care. Of course I *care*." She shot a quick glance over her shoulder. No one was behind her. "I just wanted to make sure that came across in the story."

John opened his mouth to reply.

"It came across," a deep, gravelly voice told her.

Her gaze jumped to the left, to the shadows on the side of the building—and to the man who'd apparently been watching her whole show.

He stepped from the shadows. Tall, broad-shouldered, with dark hair. He was dressed casually, and he walked toward her with a loose-limbed grace. "You handled the segment with tact and class. I was impressed."

She smiled. "Thank you. I always try to present my stories in a way that will do justice to the victims." She studied the man again. Handsome, very handsome. She'd always thought a beard was sexy on a man.

He offered his hand to her, and she saw the tattoo near his wrist. Again...*sexy*. She took that offered hand and lifted a brow. "You a sailor, sir?" She was pretty sure that it was of a trident.

He laughed, a warm rumbly sound. "Former. Right now, I'm overseeing the shipbuilding in the area." His smile faded. "I'm also helping Captain Lewis with the search efforts for the bastard who killed Tammy White."

Oh, he'd just gone all intense. She liked that. Her night was suddenly looking way up.

"Uh, Janice?" John called. "You ready to go?"

The former sailor was still holding her hand. *Ready to go?* Not likely. Especially when her new friend said, "And here I was...hoping you'd get a drink with me. There's a great wine bar right around the corner."

She knew that place very well.

She also knew how she'd be ending her night.

Janice glanced over at her cameraman. He had a wife waiting at home—and a new baby. She knew he was itching to leave. "Go ahead, John! I have an early morning segment. I'll see you then." Her car was in the parking garage a few streets over. "I need to unwind with a drink." She smiled back at the sailor. "And a new friend." She paused a moment. "Just what did you say your name was?"

"Brock Chambers."

"Janice Beautfont." She gave him a slow, considering smile. "And after the day I've had, it is an absolute pleasure to meet you."

His hand slid away from hers, moving in a slow, sensual caress. "Trust me." His smile flashed again. "That pleasure is all mine."

SAMANTHA WAS IN bed next to Blake, his hand curled around her stomach. Her body pressed so perfectly to his. Her breathing was light, easy, and he knew that she was sleeping.

He wanted to slip away into sleep with her, but his job wasn't done.

He pressed a kiss to her cheek, inhaled her sweet scent, then Blake slipped from the bed. He dressed quietly and made his way back to his room. He pulled the door shut behind him, then reached for his phone.

A fast search showed no more calls or texts from Bass. And that was *not* like the executive assistant director. Bass had rented a room at the big hotel up on the Point, a fancy playground that the wealthy had visited for years. He intended to pay Bass a personal visit up there. They needed to clear the fucking air.

Samantha was part of that investigation, and she'd stay part of it. He'd originally thought about booking

Samantha a room at that same hotel, figuring it would be a safe spot, but he hadn't wanted Bass to argue about the situation. So Blake had gotten Samantha the room at the bed-and-breakfast on his own dime. And that place, with its easy Southern charm, it had just seemed like a good fit for her. A place to make her feel...safe.

He wanted safety for her. And while she was sleeping, while she had a few moments of peace, it was time for him to check in with the EAD.

Blake slipped from the bed-and-breakfast, and moments later, he was on the long, winding road that led toward Bass's hotel. Darkness had fallen, but the stars glittered overhead. Thousands of them. It was hard to see that many stars in DC.

Sometimes, it was hard to see anything but the crimes.

He pulled into the hotel's parking lot. Automatically, his gaze swept the lot. He didn't see the rental car Bass had used before. The worry that had been nagging at his gut got worse. He pulled out his phone and called Bass again.

No answer.

Blake marched inside the hotel. He went up to the front desk, flashing his badge and ID. "I need the room number for Justin Bass, right now."

The desk clerk scrambled to comply—not just giving him the room number but even escorting him there. When they stopped in front of room 212, Blake banged his fist on the door. "Bass! Damn it, I don't care if you're puking your guts out over the toilet, we need to talk!"

Silence.

"Bass!"

Nothing. Blake glanced at the desk clerk. "I need in

that room." Every instinct he had was screaming at him. Bass wasn't answering his calls. He'd been a no-show at that press conference. His car wasn't in the lot.

What is happening here?

"I can't give you access—" the clerk began.

Blake lifted his badge and just stared at the guy. "Do you know how the FBI works?"

"Not really."

Good. Blake kept his face blank. "I have reason to believe that the man inside is experiencing health difficulties. He may need an ambulance. Open the door, now."

The guy opened the door. Blake rushed inside.

Bass wasn't in there. His luggage still sat on the foot of the bed, all zipped up. A glance in the bathroom showed no sign of any mess. In fact, it looked as if Bass had barely been in the place at all.

"Maybe...maybe your friend went out to see a doctor?" the clerk asked.

Blake surged past him, yanking his phone out as he headed into the hall. He called Josh, knowing the guy also had a room at the hotel. "Josh," he directed as soon as his friend answered, "meet me in the lobby. We've got a problem."

"Oh, hell." Josh's frustration rumbled over the line. "Did the perp take someone else already?"

"Bass is missing. We need to get a trace on his phone, and we need to figure out exactly when folks saw him last." Because the executive assistant director *never* just disappeared from an investigation. The guy might be a dick sometimes, but he wouldn't abandon a case.

Not unless he wasn't given a choice.

HER VOICE WAS high and keening as she came. Her chest had flushed a dark red, just like her face, and her breasts bounced as she shoved her body against his.

Janice Beautfont hadn't really cared about wine, but she'd been all about a trip to the little room he'd booked at the nearby bed-and-breakfast. A place he'd picked for one reason...

Because I know Samantha is there.

He'd been watching her during the press conference. He'd watched her after. He liked to watch Samantha. Liked to see when she was lying to others.

And to herself.

So he'd seen Gamble bring her to the quaint bed-and-breakfast. And a little cash to the clerk had even gotten the information that they'd booked two rooms. *Still haven't crossed that line yet, have you, Sam?* She hadn't, and she wouldn't.

"You are incredible!" Janice tossed back her hair, panting a bit. "Oh, my God. That was so what I needed today. You have no idea."

A hard, fast fuck with a stranger? Good for her. Sometimes, he needed the same thing.

Her bloodred fingernail trailed over his chest. "Was it as good for you?"

It had been incredibly average for him. He put his hand under her chin, tipped her head up and pressed a kiss to her lips. "You have no idea." When he pulled back, the woman was practically preening.

He slid from her body, marched into the bathroom and cleaned himself off. Her perfume clung to his skin. He didn't like that. The scent was...too strong. He liked more flowery scents. Or...lavender. Lavender was his favorite scent. Samantha always had a lavender scent.

"You coming back?" Janice called.

Of course. I'm not done.

He strolled into the bedroom, still naked, and he climbed back into the bed with her. She snuggled up against him, now totally relaxed, her defenses down. Exactly what he needed. His left hand stretched out and reached toward the nightstand.

"What are you doing?" she murmured.

"Just checking the time." The lie came so easily as his fingers dipped into the nightstand drawer. Her back was to him, so she couldn't see what he was doing.

"It's still early. We have hours to play."

No, they didn't. He had other plans.

"This is a big story that you're covering," he murmured. He pressed a kiss to her shoulder. Frowned at the scent of her body lotion. *Way too strong.* "You think they'll catch the killer?"

"I hope so. Bringing him in would make for killer news." Then she gave a slightly self-conscious laugh. "I don't mean to sound like a heartless bitch." She looked back at him. "I'm not. You just… In this business, you have to put a certain amount of distance between yourself and the story. If you don't, it will tear you apart."

She was more sensitive than he'd believed.

Janice swallowed. "Sometimes, I don't like the things I have to do."

"Then you shouldn't do them."

Her long lashes lowered. "If I didn't, someone else would get the story. Someone would scoop me. That can't happen."

"Because you're driven."

Now her smile was bitter. "Because I was on the top

of the pile, and I got tossed to the bottom. I've been fighting my way back ever since."

Something he could respect.

"So I do things I don't always like."

Now he was curious. "Tell me about those things."

"Samantha Dark." The name seemed to slip from her. She blinked. "That's... I didn't mean to say that." Another nervous laugh came from her. "You sure are... You're easy to talk to."

"I've been told that before." He positioned her in his arms, making sure that her back was against his stomach. "Samantha Dark..." Saying her name made his heart lurch in his chest. It also made his dick hard. *I know you're close, Sam.* "I think I saw you with her on the news. Her and the FBI agent—"

"Her lover?"

His hold tightened on Janice. "Her partner." His words were a correction.

"No, trust me, those two are sleeping together. I got them when they were coming out of her house— together—and look, I know body language. He was touching her the way a lover does, a possessive lover." She gave a little laugh. "And I could see the truth in their eyes. I even started to run with that story on the news, but..."

His whole body had gone tense.

"I didn't see the point in it." Her voice was soft now. "The woman got a raw deal before. Her ex-lover Cameron Latham wrecked her life. I've got an ex who destroyed my career, so I know exactly where she was coming from."

No, you don't. You know nothing.

"So I just ran with the story I had. I'm not into the

gossip rags. What she does in her bedroom is her own business. Just like what I do should have been mine."

He reached for the nightstand drawer once again.

"I think she knew, though," Janice added now, voice musing. "And I would have liked for her to admit that part, at least."

"Knew?" He pulled a knife from the drawer—a knife he'd put inside while Janice had been in the bathroom, freshening up before sex.

"I would have liked for her to admit that she knew Latham was a killer all along. Because I mean, come on, the woman is supposed to be one of the best profilers out there. She *must* have seen signs that the guy was a freak job."

Not necessarily. *Especially since I'm not a freak.* "Sometimes, you don't see any signs."

She made a hum of disagreement. "Wrong. I've come across my share of killers in my time. You see the signs. They're right there in front of your face."

A knife was inches away from her face.

"Janice…" He leaned his body around hers, curving close to her. "You don't see anything." Then he sliced that knife right across her throat.

She never even had the chance to scream. Her blood flew out, soaking the sheets.

CHAPTER FOURTEEN

SAMANTHA OPENED HER EYES, giving a quick gasp. Wakefulness came in a sudden, sharp rush. She could have sworn that she'd heard…something. She rolled over on the mattress, reaching for Blake, but the bed was empty.

He was gone. Maybe in his room? She climbed from the bed, pulling the sheet with her and then wrapping it around her body, toga-style. She tiptoed toward his room, but when she reached for the connecting door, she found it locked. Samantha pressed her ear to the door and heard nothing.

She lifted her hand and rapped on the door. "Blake?"

Again, nothing.

Her eyes narrowed as she turned away from the door. He'd just slipped away without a word? If he'd gotten new evidence on the case, she figured he would have woken her. He *should* have woken her.

Then she stilled. Something *had* woken her. Samantha glanced around her room, but nothing was out of place. Moving quickly now, she donned her clothes, and she took her father's gun out of her small bag.

She put on her holster and she pulled a jacket down to cover the weapon. She opened the door that led to the hallway. Samantha looked to the left and to the right.

No one was out there. But…

Something woke me. She pulled her door shut behind

her and paced down the hallway. She'd taken five steps when she heard…

A gurgle.

And…a thud.

Her steps quickened. She saw that a door on the left was ajar. The gold plate next to that room called it the "Magnolia Room." Each guest room in the bed-and-breakfast had its own name. She'd been staying in the "Azalea Room." Samantha crossed the hall and put her hand on the Magnolia Room door. "Is everything okay in there?"

Another gurgle. No, that did *not* sound as if things were okay.

She pushed open the door with her left hand even as her right instinctively went for her gun. She stepped inside—

Darkness.

The room was pitch-black. The only light came from behind Samantha as it spilled in from the hallway. Fumbling, her hand went to the light switch. The light flashed on and—

Blood. Blood all over the white bedsheets. Blood on the bed's headboard. Blood on the wall near the bed and—

The victim's shoulders jerked. "Get help in here!' Samantha yelled, hoping someone in another room would hear her. "Get help!" She raced across the room. All she could see of the victim was her bare back and the blond tangle of her hair. She scrambled around the bed and—

Janice?

The reporter's throat was sliced open. Blood poured all around her, and Janice's eyes were wide, desperate, terrified. Her lips were opening and closing as she struggled to speak, but the only sound that escaped her was that terrible gurgle. Samantha lunged across the bed, and she put her hands over that deep wound. Janice's blood immediately soaked her fingers. It just kept pumping. Far too much.

I'm losing her. She is dying right now!

It was a brutal attack, one that had gone so deep. *He knew exactly what he was doing.* And the wound was... *Fresh.*

The killer had been there just moments before. He'd sliced Janice's throat, left her to bleed out on the bed because he knew she wouldn't be able to cry out for help, and then he'd just strolled away, even leaving the door to the room slightly ajar.

I was too far away to hear the gurgles she made. So what had woken Samantha?

Dear God...did he knock on my door as he walked down the hallway and left her?

"Who did this?" Samantha demanded.

Janice's body was jerking.

"Janice, look at me. *Look at me.*" There was no time left. She could feel it. "Did Cameron Latham do this to you?"

Janice's wild eyes held hers.

"Was it Jason Burke?" She knew the reporter had gotten a picture of that man at the press conference.

A slow shake of Janice's head.

If it wasn't Jason, it had to be Cameron. Only, he'd changed his appearance like I thought, and she didn't recognize him.

Janice's eyes were closing.

"No!" Samantha yelled. "Don't you do this!"

A shocked gasp came from the doorway. Samantha

looked up and saw an older couple, both well dressed and horrified, standing in the doorway. "Call an ambulance!" Samantha shouted at them. "Get this woman help!"

But…Janice wasn't struggling for breath any longer. Her body had gone still.

He just killed her. He was here minutes ago.

The bastard might not have gotten away, not yet.

Samantha lunged from the bed. She ran toward the door, her gun at the ready. The woman there gave a sharp cry and threw up her hands.

"I'm with the FBI!" Samantha yelled. That was true. She was working with them. Just not *for* them. "Call the authorities! Call Police Captain Lewis!" She shoved the couple out of her way as she ran down the hallway.

When she passed her room, her gaze jerked toward her door and sure enough—*damn it!* She saw the faint swipe of red blood on her door. *He had knocked. The bastard had knocked when he passed because he wanted me to see what he'd done.*

As if she'd needed it, that blood was further proof that Cameron was the killer she sought. She shoved open the back door at the bed-and-breakfast and surged into the lot. Blake's rented SUV was gone; she saw the empty parking spot immediately. A few other cars lined the lot, most with out-of-state tags. But…

No one is out here.

She spun around. "Where are you?" And she knew, she *knew* that Cameron had been there. "Damn it, Cameron, *why*? Why did you kill her? Why the hell did you do it?"

Then she heard the growl of an engine, one coming in fast. She spun around and saw bright headlights aiming right for her. She lifted her gun, her heart racing, and the vehicle slammed on its brakes. She was trapped in that bright field of lights.

An SUV. I know this vehicle—

Blake jumped out and ran toward her. "Samantha!" His frantic gaze flew over her. "Tell me that's not your fucking blood."

She shook her head. "Janice...the reporter...she's dead in there." She pointed to the bed-and-breakfast. "He brought her here...because I was here..." She *knew* he'd picked that place deliberately. "And he killed her while I slept right down the hall."

Blake grabbed her and pulled her close.

Damn you, Cameron, why?

He'd killed before as part of an experiment, or so he said. But now...now he was different. Everything was different.

"BASS'S RENTAL CAR was found parked behind an abandoned restaurant, just three miles from the marina." Blake paced in Lewis's office, his body tight with tension—and so much fury he was about to choke. "We can assume he was taken shortly after the discovery of Tammy's body. And when he made that phone call to me, he was under duress."

"Jason Burke likes to tell people exactly what to say," Samantha murmured. "That's kind of his thing."

"Yeah, but that kid had been taking women. And not killing them right away," Josh fired back. He was positioned near the window, arms folded over his chest, frowning hard at them all. "We're talking about the executive assistant director of the FBI. The guy wouldn't have gone down easily. And his body was transported.

There was no sign that he was dragged away, no marks in the dirt. The only thing we found was a half-smoked cigarette."

"That's because Jason had help," Samantha said simply.

And this was the shit Blake didn't want to hear, but he'd already figured it out for himself.

"Cameron Latham is here," she added. "And he's working with Burke."

"Fuck me," Lewis muttered. He was slumped behind his desk. "This is supposed to be a quiet town. A safe town. It's not supposed to be freakin' serial killer central. We were a number-one tourist spot in the state. Do you know what this will do to us?" His eyes squeezed shut.

Blake wasn't worried about the town losing that number-one spot. He was worried about more victims. "The FBI is monitoring Bass's phone," he said. "The minute it is turned back on, we've got him. They're already triangulating the location of the last call he received." And they'd better be contacting him again about that ASAP. "As soon as we get that—we're on the move."

"On the move…" Josh swiped his hand over his face. "That's great, but what if Bass is already dead? I mean, why the hell would the perp take him anyway? I thought this was all about—" But then he stopped, dropping his hand.

The tension in the room notched up as Blake threw a glare at his friend.

"You thought it was all about me," Samantha finished. She stood near the door, her body held perfectly still.

"You're the one Burke wanted," Josh said, voice softer now. He winced. "I'm sorry, Samantha. I didn't—"

"Cameron doesn't want me dead. That's the last thing he wants." She started to pace.

Blake stepped into her path. She'd washed the blood off her hands. Janice's blood. But she was far too pale, and she wouldn't look him in the eye. "You know him." Fucking intimately. "Tell me, what in the hell is he doing?"

"He's done experimenting."

"What does that mean?" Josh demanded. "And, hell, I thought you said he'd be here to stop Burke, not team up with the guy."

"Appearances can be deceiving." Then she rubbed her eyes. "What I mean is…he *will* turn on Burke. Cameron is just using the guy now. Cameron wanted Bass out of the way, and he got Burke to help him. Cameron won't eliminate Burke until he's done with him."

Blake thrust back his shoulders. "Tell me more."

"Cameron said he was experimenting before. Seeing what it was like to kill. Seeing what his victims experienced. Testing them, testing himself." Her lips pressed together. "He's evolved now. He knows what he likes… and I think Cameron likes killing."

"That's just wonderful." Lewis slapped his desk. "Fantastic."

Samantha shook her head. "No, it's not. Because Cameron is very good at killing." Her gaze finally lifted and met Blake's. "Janice knew Cameron. She'd been researching him, pressuring me to help her co-author a book on him. That was one of the many ideas she pitched to me over the last few months." Sadness flashed on her face. "She was pushy and aggressive, but she was smart, too. I saw that room. I saw…her body. She'd…she'd been with him."

"You're saying she'd fucked Cameron Latham."

Samantha flinched, and Blake realized he'd snarled the words.

Her chin shot up. "Yes, that's what I'm saying. So for her to do that—to get close to him—it means he's substantially changed his appearance."

"You already told us that," Lewis noted grimly. "You warned everyone at the press conference that he'd look different."

"Warning is one thing, but people…they tend to think that they'd recognize a killer. But the bittersweet truth is that they don't. *She* didn't. She let Cameron get close to her, and he killed her."

Now Josh was the one to surge toward her. "How do you know Burke wasn't the one who slit her throat?"

"Because someone had to stay with Bass."

A killing team. This shit is just getting worse by the moment.

"You don't think Bass is dead yet?" Josh asked, hope in his voice.

"I don't. Not yet. But I think he will be, if we don't find him soon." She lowered her gaze to the floor and seemed to puzzle things out for a moment. "Burke is younger…too young for Janice, too fresh-faced in his pictures. She wouldn't have gone with him. Not just walked away." Her gaze lifted and held Blake's. "We need to talk to her cameramen. They're always with her. Maybe one of them saw her hook up with some-one earlier. Maybe they can give us a description, and we can get it out to the public before Cameron changes again." She nodded decisively before she turned toward the door. "We just have to hurry—"

Blake caught her arm. "What would Latham have wanted with Janice? Why did he kill her?"

"He wanted information." She paused. "On me. Maybe even...on us." Her breath came faster as her voice lowered. "I think he killed her, and then I think... he came to my room. He knocked on my door. He left her *blood* on my door because he wanted me to see what he'd done." Her voice went even softer as she said, "Because he knows what I've done."

What she'd done?

Her gaze held his. Pain and shame were in her eyes. *Shame? Oh, hell, no.* "Fuck him. He is going down." Before he could say more, his phone rang.

Samantha flinched.

Snarling, he pulled out the phone, but he saw it was his FBI contact. With Bass missing, he was the lead in the area, and all calls from the Bureau were coming to his cell. He pushed the button to activate the speaker option. "Tell me you tracked his last call."

"We got to within about five hundred yards," Michele Kind said, her voice breaking with excitement. "But that call, according to my maps, it came from the swamp. Way past Five Rivers Delta. You're going to need a chopper or some kind of boat to get there because no roads lead out that far."

"Give us the coordinates," Samantha ordered.

She and Lewis had moved to lean over his computer. Michele rattled off the coordinates for them, and Samantha quickly typed them into the system. Lewis gave a low whistle. "There are tons of old cabins out there. Places that aren't listed on any map. We need someone familiar with the area to show us the best spots. And a chopper ain't going to do the trick, because the damn thing would just be going up and down every five minutes as we searched each cabin. And there aren't a whole hell of a lot of places out there where a bird can land, anyway."

Samantha looked up, her expression tense. "That's not a particularly traveled area. Only certain low-bottom boats can go in that far, so bringing in a big Coast Guard vessel isn't going to happen."

"An airboat," Lewis said, snapping his fingers. "That's what you need." Excitement lit his gaze. "A buddy of mine does an airboat tour up that way, and he goes out five times a day. He knows that area better than anyone damn else." He looked at his watch. "The guy even has a dawn tour that is scheduled to start soon. I'll call him, get him to bump his customers, and we can fill up that boat of his with our team. His boat is supposed to be in the area, so it shouldn't set off any alarms for the perp."

The airboat sounded like their best option. And they'd follow it up with air assistance that would come in when they found their target. "Let's get our asses on that boat." He wasn't sure just how much longer Bass had left.

If he was still breathing.

CAMERON STARED OUT at the water. The sun would be rising soon, chasing away the dark. A pity. After all, he loved the dark.

He put the phone to his ear as he stared at the water. It rang once, twice and—

"Why didn't you come back?"

He nearly rolled his eyes. Jason sounded like a whiny bitch, and he didn't have time for that crap. "You need to kill Bass. Do it now and leave the shack." He refused to call that tiny cabin by any other name. He'd been the one to show Burke the remote spot. He'd found it on a previous scouting trip to the area. *Because I've been watching Sam, for so long.*

"Kill him? But...I haven't played yet."

Played?

"He made the phone call so well. Didn't even fight at all." Jason's words came faster now. "He'll do anything to be let go."

"No, he won't. He's *playing* you. Trying to lull you into a false sense of security. You give him one opening, and the guy will gut you like a pig."

He heard Jason's sharp inhale.

"Don't believe me?" Cameron murmured. "It'll be your funeral." He started to hang up—

"Dr. Latham!"

Desperation had been in Jason's voice. The guy always had such a deep need for recognition. *Someone needs a father figure.* Understandable, since Jason's own father had turned his back on the guy ages ago. His father had known something was off with his only son. He'd sent the kid to shrink after shrink. Like that had done much good.

"I...did a good job so far, didn't I?" Jason pushed. "I found Samantha Dark, I got your attention and I took out those two women."

"You did a great job," Cameron assured him softly. "And you need to keep that up. So listen carefully. Take a knife, go in there with Bass and slit his throat. Leave him tied up, don't give him an instant to escape. Just slit his throat and be done with him."

Silence. Silence meant there was a problem. Cameron pinched the bridge of his nose. Leaving Jason with Bass had been a risk, but he'd needed to get back to town. He'd wanted to see Samantha's press conference up close and personal.

No. I won't lie to myself. I needed to see her...and Blake.

Fucking Blake Gamble. "You have to kill Bass," Cameron said, voice thick. "You kill him, and then you kill Blake Gamble."

"Me? A-alone?"

No, with a damn army. Yes, alone. "Blake Gamble knows where you are." The guy should know. If he didn't, he would soon. The FBI would be realizing that Bass had vanished. They'd start tracing his phone, finding the origin of the last call he'd made. *And that is another reason I need to be far, far away from that little shack. I won't be there when this shit goes down.* "He's going to come for you, so you need to be ready."

More silence.

He forced his jaw to unclench. "I left a gun there for you." Bass's gun. "I put it in the bag that I placed near the front door." It was as if he were guiding a baby. *Time to eliminate the kid.* "When Blake comes for you, don't hesitate to shoot. You take him out, understand? You take him out before he has a chance to hurt you."

"And...then I'll meet up with you?"

"Absolutely." *Hell, no. Authorities are about to swarm you, and when you pull a gun on them, they'll kill you.* "I'm on my way to meet you now. You'll hear my boat coming." Bullshit. He'd hear the cops.

A relieved rush of air filled the line. "Thank you. You…you're the only one who ever understood me."

Oh, I understand you plenty.

"I was so alone when you left. It hurt. It was like someone took a part of me and tossed it away."

Not yet, but I will.

"It was her fault." Anger snarled then, escaping in Jason's tight voice. "Samantha Dark. I know you said she didn't, but—"

"Samantha is not the enemy." He made sure his voice was flat. "She's someone to be protected. She's on *our* side. How many times do I have to tell you that? She isn't coming to hurt you. When you see Samantha, it's because she's there to help. Don't turn the gun on her. Don't even think about that move. Focus on Gamble. He's the threat."

More silence. Damn it.

"But…you'll be here before they are, right?" Jason asked, nearly mumbling.

"I'm trying to get there as fast as I can." The water gleamed. Sunlight trickled across the sky. "It's just that, if they beat me there, I want you prepared. I want you safe." Inspiration hit him. "I want you to repeat these words after me, okay, Jason?"

"Okay…"

"Bass must die."

"Bass must die."

"Gamble must die."

"Gamble must die."

Excitement had quickened in Jason's words, just as Cameron had suspected it would. Getting him to repeat those words…that was incorporating Jason's own MO into the situation.

But the dumbass didn't even realize...

It's the victim who repeats the words.

You're the victim here, Jason. You never should have gone after Sam.

He hung up the phone and stared at the sun. The dark would fade soon.

If Jason followed his orders, more problems would be eliminated. Yet something nagged at Cameron. *What if...at the last moment, the bastard turns and goes after Samantha again?*

What was he going to do if she died?

JUSTIN BASS PULLED at the ropes that bound his wrists. The drug was still in his system, making his muscles tremble. He hated the weakness, but there was nothing he could do about it.

The door creaked open, and he froze, lying on his side on that old, rotten floor. Wooden floor...floor that just happened to have a sharp edge. An edge he'd been sawing his ropes against for the last hour. The ropes hadn't cut—at least, not all the way. He'd felt some of the hemp give, so at least he wasn't bound as tightly as he'd been.

"It stinks in here." That was the punk's voice. High, excited. *Yeah, it stinks because I puked my guts out on this floor.*

The wood groaned beneath the jerk's feet. "I came to set you free."

Because he was supposed to believe that pile of shit? Not likely, but Justin lifted his face up.

The young guy stood in the doorway. His right hand was behind his body.

Are you hiding a weapon, kid?

"Doesn't seem fair, though," the blond muttered. "When I just got you." The guy took a step toward him.

Bass's body went stiff, and he knew the punk was about to kill him. Probably a slice to the throat or a stab to his heart. And it would be all over. Justin rolled his body, moving so that his wrists were hidden behind him, and he jerked with all of his might against the weakened ropes. "Where's the other guy?" He had to talk and keep talking in order to distract the perp and buy time.

"Other…guy?"

"Yeah." Justin tilted back his head. "The one calling the shots."

Red stained the punk's cheeks. "I'm calling the shots. I'm the one with power."

"Lie," he said flatly. "You're just the one he's left to go down for this mess. You're his fall boy. Nothing more, nothing less. The guy set you up so he could escape clean." Another hard yank of his wrists. He could feel that hemp sliding, tearing. "That's why he's nowhere near here, right? He thinks the cavalry is coming to find me, and they are." They'd better be. "But when they get here, *you'll* go down. Not him."

The guy's hand jerked up—and, sure enough, he was gripping a knife. "You don't know what you're fucking saying! Dr. Latham…I mean, Cameron is my *friend*!"

Justin knew exactly what he was saying. And he knew how to keep working the little bastard. Everything he'd needed had been in that one name. *Dr. Latham.* "Cameron Latham? You *think* that bastard is your friend?" His laughter was weak, mostly because he still felt weak. "That psycho is just using you. He's just—"

The knife was at his throat. "That's not what you

say." He felt the prick of the blade on his skin. "That's the *wrong* thing to say!"

He barely breathed. "Then tell me…the right thing… to say."

The guy smiled at him. "I will. Because that's the way it works. I always get you to share a story right before I set you free."

He's fucking insane.

But the knife wasn't at Justin's throat any longer, so he figured that was good. The blond kept the knife in his right hand even as his left fished a phone out of his pocket. He touched the screen and aimed the phone's camera toward Justin. "This is what you say… Listen carefully, and then you're going to repeat after me…"

Asshole.

"Did you hear what I said?" the guy yelled at him. "You're going to repeat after *me*—"

He was trying to hold the knife and the phone. A mistake. And the ropes around Justin's wrists…they'd just given way.

"I heard you." Justin smiled at him. "I just don't give a shit."

The punk's eyes flared wide. He fumbled, the phone dropped—and Justin flew at him.

CHAPTER FIFTEEN

THE AIRBOAT FLEW over the water, moving so fast that Samantha's hair whipped against her face. They were surging through a tunnel of tall grass, skimming right over the surface of the water. No way could one of the Coast Guard's boats have made the trip—the water in the Delta would never have been deep enough for them.

The boat vibrated beneath her, sending her bouncing a bit on the seat. Up ahead, a medium-sized alligator slipped through the water, its tail cutting out behind it. The boat veered a sharp left, heading for the location they'd mapped out with the coordinates provided by the FBI. There were a few old cabins up that way; she'd seen them before. Places that were sometimes used by local fishermen. Places that would be perfect for hiding a victim.

Was Justin Bass still alive? She thought so. She hoped so. But when Jason Burke saw them coming, she knew the guy would panic. Jail wouldn't be an option that he'd considered.

He'd grown up privileged. Living in a cage for the rest of his life—no way would that be the ending he'd pictured for himself.

Tommy killed the airboat's powerful fan. "Got the first cabin coming up to the right."

And there it sat, faded wood, boarded-up windows, perched on stilts in the water.

"Looks quiet," Josh said.

Blake nodded. "Get us closer to check it out." He was already pulling out his weapon. When they got closer, he jumped from the boat and splashed into the water.

THE BASTARD HAD stabbed him. *Shit.* The pain pulsed through Justin even as the blood pumped down his chest. He lunged after the little SOB, but his ankles were still bound, and he slammed into the floor.

"That's not how it works!" the guy yelled at him. "This isn't right!'

Justin grabbed for the ropes around his feet. He jerked at the knots.

And the fucker drove the knife into his back. He roared at the pain. His hand flew back, and he tried to grab the knife, but it sliced right over his palm, cutting deep. Then over his wrist, and the blood sprayed.

But he kept fighting. The perp wasn't used to that. *You don't give the women a chance to fight back, do you?* Justin knocked the knife out of the attacker's hand, and the blond let out a scream as he scrambled back.

Justin *hurt.* Blood was everywhere, and when he tried to yank at the stubborn ropes, his blood-soaked fingers just slid around uselessly.

Footsteps thundered away from him. His hand snapped up. The guy was fleeing. Oh, hell, no. He stretched out and swiped up the dropped knife. It fell out of his fingers once, but he grabbed it again and cut through his ropes. On his second attempt—maybe third?—Justin made it to his feet. He lurched toward the door.

"Cameron warned me…" the bastard cried out.

A gunshot blasted.

It took Justin a moment to feel the burn of the wound, a wound in his stomach. He looked down at his body, even as the knife fell from his fingers.

"Said I had to be careful with you…" Another gunshot. This one hit Justin dead in the chest. "And with Agent Gamble."

BLAKE WAS RUNNING back to the boat when he heard the thunder of gunshots. The little fishing cabin behind him had been empty, but now—thanks to the blasts—they knew where their prey was. *But he's shooting, so we may be too fucking late to save Bass.* He and Josh jumped in the boat with the others. "Follow those shots!" Blake snarled at the airboat captain.

The fan kicked on, and the boat shot forward, barreling fast as it flew over the water. He kept his gun gripped tightly in his hand and his gaze was on the shore. Up ahead, he saw two more cabins. Just as small as the first one they'd searched. With faded wood, slanted roofs, small, twisted piers coming out of them.

And…

A man was there, staggering out of the cabin. Falling. Trying to crawl toward them.

Fuck me, that's Bass.

The boat hadn't even stopped before Blake jumped from it. Samantha and Josh were with him. He saw that they both had their weapons drawn. He heard Lewis's voice barking behind him as the guy gave orders on his phone for their air backup. And, up ahead…

He saw Bass. Crawling on the ground. But behind Bass, coming out of that little cabin—

"Shooter!" Blake roared.

He aimed his weapon, but the bastard had already grabbed Bass. It was a blond male, young, and in the dawn light he could clearly see that he was staring at Jason Burke. The guy looked exactly like his college picture.

Only right then, the preppy college kid was covered in dirt and blood and he had a gun pressed to Bass's head. "Everyone stop!" Jason yelled. "Or I blast his brains out right here!"

Blood soaked the front of Bass's shirt. His eyes were sagging, his face chalk white.

Blake stilled. Samantha and Josh had stopped, Samantha to his left, Josh to his right. Blake glanced back and threw up his hand, making sure that the local authorities who'd come with them also froze. He didn't want some trigger-happy fool screwing this scene to hell and back. Then he glanced toward the perp.

"I'm supposed to kill you," Jason said.

He was staring right at Blake.

"You kill him," Samantha said, her voice ringing out, strong and cold, "and my bullet will be in *your* brain the next second."

Jason flinched.

"You don't want that, do you?" she pushed. "You don't want to die. That isn't what all of this is about."

The gun Jason gripped moved a bit, a tiny fraction, but it was still far too close to Bass's head. And Bass— it was obvious the guy was long past the point of fighting. He was on his knees, his upper body only upright because Jason had one arm locked around his neck.

One arm around his neck, the other hand holding the gun to Bass's head.

Blake didn't have a clear shot at the perp. He needed the guy to move back a little from Bass. Just a little more.

"I know what you want," Samantha said.

"You don't know anything about me!" Jason screamed.

"Sure I do." She kept talking in that calm voice, and Blake knew she was trying to distract the perp.

Josh took one slow step to the right.

"You're smart," Samantha said, and she sounded almost admiring. "You have to be to get away with what you've done. You want the world to know about how clever you are, right? Well, come with us, and they will know. Put down the gun and surrender, and I can get five reporters ready to meet us when we get back to town. They will all hear your story."

Jason's head jerked toward Blake. "But I...I was supposed to kill you."

"Says who?" Blake snarled. *The voices in your freaking head?*

"My friend." And Jason's shoulders stiffened. "He's here. He'll have...my back."

Shit, he'd better not have just told them that Latham was out there. Because as they stood in front of the cabin, there was no cover at all. If Latham was out there, the guy would be able to pick them off. He could fire at any moment.

Jason nodded again. "Yes, he'll have my back... Said so..."

And right then, Blake heard a distant roar.

A wide smile split Jason's face. "He's coming! That's him. That's his boat."

"Drop the gun," Blake ordered.

Jason's smile slipped. "I have to kill you. He said

so. You die." He looked at Bass. "He dies. You both die. Then—"

"Then you take the fall for everything," Samantha called out. "Don't you see that? Cameron is setting you up. He wants you to take their lives so that you're the one who goes down. Only, he isn't planning for you to go to jail. He knows that the instant you fire here… *you're a dead man*."

Jason shook his head. The gun moved another tiny centimeter away from Bass's head. Bass's body sagged more, and Jason seemed to struggle to hold him upright.

"You're expendable to him." Samantha's tone had turned berating. Angry. "Not worth Cameron's time. You imitated his work, and you thought that would flatter him? Wrong. It just pissed him off, and now he wants *you* gone."

"No, *no*! He is my *friend*."

"Cameron is no one's friend. I don't think he has that capacity. He's a user, a manipulator, and he's manipulating you. He wants Bass dead. He wants Agent Gamble dead. You're the means to that end." She took a step forward.

"Samantha…" Blake snarled.

She put down her gun. "We don't have to let Cameron control us. We can be free of him. We can stop playing by his rules."

She'd put down her gun. She'd put down her fucking *gun* and made a target of herself.

"Stand down," Blake barked at her. *"Now, Samantha."*

She took another step forward. "The gun isn't even the weapon you like. I can see the knife wounds on Bass. That's the weapon you like."

Jason nodded. "Dr. Latham told me I'd need the gun… He was right."

"He said to get the gun because he knew that when the FBI agents spotted it, you'd be a dead man. But he was wrong about them, you see. Because these agents don't just go out and start shooting. They're good men. Fair. They will give you a chance if you drop your weapon." She lifted her hand toward him. "Come with me now. Don't play Cameron's game any longer."

Silence. Taut. Dangerous.

And…he saw the change in Jason's face. The tightness. The flare of anger. "He was wrong."

"Yes," Josh called out, speaking for the first time since the standoff began. "Dead wrong." Josh still had his weapon aimed at Jason.

"Wrong about you," Jason whispered as he stared at Samantha. "You aren't on his side. I don't… I don't think you ever were…"

And Blake knew the guy was going to fire even as Jason let go of Bass.

Not firing at the executive assistant director. Jason is going for the target he wanted all along. The woman he blamed for taking Cameron Latham away from him.

Jason jerked his gun up and aimed it at Samantha. Blake was already flying forward. He tackled her, shoving Samantha to the ground, and fired his weapon even as he felt a burn across his arm. He trapped Samantha against the ground, covering her completely. He prepared to shoot again, but—

Bam! Bam!

Josh beat him to the fucking punch.

The bullets flew into Jason Burke's chest, and the

guy jerked back, like a puppet on a string. He rammed into the side of the little cabin and stared with wide, shocked eyes at Blake.

Then he fell, slumping sideways.

Josh rushed toward Bass.

Blake lifted his body up, staring down at Samantha. "What in the hell was that?" Anger cut through him. "You just made yourself a target! You just—"

"I bought Bass time to live." She glared up at him.

"And you almost died." He jumped to his feet and pulled her up beside him. His hands flew over her. No injuries, thank Christ. He yanked her close. "This isn't over." If she thought she'd get to risk herself...*oh, hell, no.*

The distant roar they'd heard before was louder—Jason had mistakenly thought it was a boat's motor, but now the sound was a distinctive *whoop, whoop, whoop*—the helicopter that Lewis had called, coming in to give medical support.

Support that was desperately needed.

Blake and Samantha ran to Bass's side. There was blood everywhere—streaming from slices on the EAD's body and pouring from what looked like two bullet wounds. Samantha bent to help Josh as he tended to the other man, and Blake moved toward Jason Burke. Jason was slumped face-first on the ground, and Josh had already kicked the guy's gun far away.

Blake put his hand on the perp's throat, searching for a pulse.

"Coming...for you..."

Blake stiffened.

Jason's breath wheezed out. "In...his sights...he'll...get...you..."

"Let him come," Blake rasped. "I'm ready."

Jason's breath didn't wheeze any longer. His body had gone still. His final words had been a threat. Blake looked around him. Captain Lewis was running toward the cabin. Samantha and Josh were trying to apply pressure to Bass's wounds.

There was no sign of Latham. No sign that the guy was out there, waiting for his shot.

"Don't worry, Cameron's not here," Samantha said.

Blake's gaze cut toward her.

She kept working on Bass, not even looking up.

"Cameron knew we'd find Bass. He left Jason Burke here so that *we'd* take him out." Frustration was rich in her voice. "And we did." Now her gaze darted up to hold Blake's. "I told you all along… Cameron didn't come here to help Jason. He wasn't looking for some kind of partner in that messed-up kid. He came after Jason for one reason only."

To kill him.

Her lips curled down. "We just did the job for him."

The chopper was closer. He could see it in the sky, could feel the rush of the wind from the blades as the pilot tried to find a place to land out there in the marsh.

"Now…" Samantha's voice rose over the howl of the helicopter. "Now we have to see what he's got planned next."

SAMANTHA STOOD NEAR the tall grass, watching as the helicopter lifted higher and higher into the air. She didn't know whether or not Bass would survive. His wounds had been deep, one far too close to his heart, and there had been so much blood.

Too much.

Josh had gone with him on the chopper. More crime scene techs were rushing in on boats. The little cabin was going to be analyzed from top to bottom, every inch searched for clues.

Jason Burke was dead. She turned and saw his body, still near the cabin. Slumped, legs twisted beneath him. Death by FBI agent.

Blake stood over the fallen man, staring down at the body with tension evident in every tight line of his body. He was just a few feet away from Samantha, but for some reason…it seemed as if the distance was a million miles. *He's furious at me. Hates that I put myself at risk.* But she'd known she could distract the guy, and she'd bought them precious time.

She'd wanted to save both Bass and Burke. In the end, that just hadn't happened.

Her phone rang, vibrating in her pocket. She pulled it out and frowned at the screen: Unknown Caller. What a joke. She knew exactly who was calling her. Samantha put the phone to her ear. "He's dead."

She turned her back on Blake and stared up at the sky. The chopper was high now, she didn't even feel the rush of wind from its spinning blades.

"Isn't that what you wanted to hear?" Samantha asked, when there was only silence on the line. "You called to make sure we put a bullet in Jason Burke?"

"I missed you."

His voice was the same. Deep and sensual. The voice of a lover.

When he was a killer.

Her eyes closed. She heard footsteps crunching behind her. "You wanted Burke to kill Agent Gamble."

"That would have been nice, yes." Cameron's words

were smooth. He'd always been so fucking smooth. "I'm guessing that didn't happen?" A long sigh. "Pity. But that's okay. There are just some jobs you want to take care of yourself."

Her fingers tightened around the phone. "I want you to stay away from him." She opened her eyes. The world was still as chaotic as it had been before.

"If you don't want Agent Gamble brought into the cross fire, then maybe *you* should have stayed away from him." He paused. "Gamble took you away from me, Sam. You think I'll let him have you now? That I'll fade into the sunset and you two can go off living your fucking happy life?"

She took a step closer to the water's edge. "I'm not a thing to be had. Not by you. Not by him. Get that straight."

"You were mine. I knew it. You understood me, all the dark parts. We were alike. We *are* alike."

That was where he was wrong. "You aren't experimenting any longer."

He laughed.

"I'm not so sure you ever were," she whispered. She'd never bought that story from him.

"See…" His voice had turned into a rasp. "You did understand me."

Her heart twisted in her chest. "You just like killing. You like the power."

"My prey is weak. They can't touch me. They can't even come close…no one can. The FBI…they aren't going to find me. They aren't going to catch me. They aren't going to stop me."

Confident bastard.

"But I will stop them." And he laughed. "Bass was the first to fall."

Time to rain on his little sick parade. "Bass is still alive, Cameron."

And she heard it…the fast inhalation of breath that was his sign of surprise. *Didn't see that coming, did you?* "Your little buddy Burke? He didn't go by whatever plan you had for him. He didn't kill Bass." *He came real close, but I won't tell you that.* Because she needed to crack that confidence of his. "And he didn't kill Blake. But he did try to kill *me*."

Silence.

"If you want to come for me, then do it."

"You know I don't want you dead."

"Then what do you want from me?" *Confess to what you've done.* Deliberately, she said, "You left Janice's blood on my door…you wanted me to see what you'd done—"

"You were so close…it was almost like you were there while I was fucking her." He paused. "And killing her."

Her breath eased out slowly. *Got the confession.*

"I'll see you soon, love," Cameron promised her.

The call ended.

She stared at the water.

"We got the trace." Blake's voice was low, controlled, and coming from right behind her. "Let's get in the chopper and get the bastard."

Because a second chopper had been brought in for them. A chopper that waited just a few feet away. Even before they'd left the Fairhope police station, heading out on the airboat, she'd told Blake that Cameron would call her.

He'd have to call. He'd have to make sure that I survive this scene. So they'd taken precautions. They'd had the FBI monitoring her phone.

And now…now they just might have *him*.

CHAPTER SIXTEEN

CAMERON ENDED THE CALL. He smiled. "It was good to hear her voice." He put the phone down on the table. Looked around the house.

Such a nice, homey place. And that view of the water...killer. He could completely understand why Samantha loved the place. Sure, the home was on the small side, but that view...gorgeous.

He paced toward the man who sat—dead silent—in the chair before him. "I realized I needed to take care of you, of course. Couldn't have you running around, telling stories about me. And Samantha...well, I can predict her movements, too. I knew she'd have someone tracing that call. She's so...upright, that way." He let his eyes widen. "Boringly by the book, if you know what I mean."

The man stared back at him. Well, he had to do that—stare. He didn't have a choice.

Cameron had sliced off his eyelids.

A new trick.

And a message.

Samantha, I want you to see what you really are. Stop pretending. Stop hiding. You can't ever hide from me.

"Sorry about the mess," he murmured, glancing at

the man's face. "But I'm a PhD, not an MD. Every new slice is fresh ground for me."

Silence. Only to be expected. "They'll be here soon." Cameron nodded. "So I have to go. Not quite time for my big reunion with Sam. I've got someone else to clear out of my way first. She really needs to see his true colors, and I think this scene…" He waved his hand around the house. "I think this will help. A man can only take so much—" he slapped his gloved hand on the fellow's shoulder "—before he breaks. And believe me, I intend for Blake Gamble to *break*." His grip tightened on the fellow's shoulder. "I had a perfect life before he came into it. He wrecked everything." Rage cracked in his voice. He cleared his throat and continued, "So everything that happens now, it's all on him."

HE WAS IN her home. She'd gotten the address while in midflight. Samantha's stomach was in knots as the chopper flew over the water. Blake was at her side. He had on a headset, and his gaze was directed below. She could feel the fury rolling off him.

Fury, not fear.

I've got enough of that for us both.

Because she knew it wasn't over. There wasn't going to be some easy scene in which Cameron just surrendered to the authorities. He wasn't the surrendering type. He was more the take-everyone-down-with-me sort.

And he was slippery. Always two steps ahead. When they got to her house, would he even be there?

"Local cops were supposed to be at your house." Blake's voice crackled in her headset. Her gaze jerked to his face. "Lewis sent them out last night to keep watch when we went to the bed-and-breakfast."

She'd known a patrol was there.

His lips flattened, and then he said, "They aren't answering their radios."

That knot in her stomach got tighter. "They're dead."

His face hardened. "We don't know that."

She did. "If they were in his way, they're dead." No experiment, but a total change. Cameron wasn't holding himself back any longer. When he'd fled months ago, he'd stopped caring about any rules or restrictions. And she was afraid he liked what he was doing. He'd developed a taste for blood.

And other people's pain.

"More patrols are being sent to your place. Both from Fairhope and neighboring cities. I told them to surround the house but to stand down until we got there." His eyes glittered. The chopper began to lower. "If Cameron is in there, we're taking him down."

But he wants you, Blake. You're the one he's after. Cameron had only missed a target once, and that target had been her. She reached for Blake. Her fingers curled around his hand and held tight. "Be careful."

One dark brow lifted.

"I need you to stay safe." Something happening to him wasn't an option for her.

His hand turned and linked with hers. "And I need you to not make a target of yourself again. You can't trust this guy, Samantha. You can't manipulate him. You can't play mind games with him."

That wasn't—

"If you see him, you fucking shoot him."

That wasn't the way the FBI worked. They took in

the bad guys. They didn't put them down like rabid animals.

"He will kill you," Blake said, certainty in his voice.

She shook her head—

"He *isn't* your former friend. You have to see him the same way you do every other perp."

She saw Cameron for exactly what he was.

"We end this," Blake said grimly. "And he doesn't walk away."

The chopper lowered onto the bluff. She stared at her house, saw the lights flashing from the police cars that were all around it. Ice squeezed her heart. *He isn't going to be waiting inside.* It had taken them too long. There was no way that Cameron would just be sitting there, a grin on his face.

When the chopper neared the ground, she dropped her headset. She jumped out of the chopper and ran with Blake. Uniformed officers hurried to meet them.

"Found the patrol car in the driveway." One of the officers pointed to the left. "No sign of Officer Daniels or McGinnis. Both of them were supposed to be on duty."

That ice around her heart started to spread.

"Keep the perimeter here secure," Blake ordered. "Every side of the house. I'm going in, and you make sure no one else comes out." He glanced at the officers close by. "Cameron Latham is extremely dangerous. We know he's altered his appearance, but just not how significantly yet. Stay on guard. You got it?"

There were quick, nervous nods.

Blake turned toward her.

"We're going in," Samantha said flatly. "You said *I*, but *we*—"

Blake shook his head. "You're staying out here."

The hell she was.

"Two officers are missing. I need to search the house, and I need to do it now." He checked his weapon and wouldn't meet her gaze. "But for all I know, Latham has the house wired to blow."

No. "He wouldn't. Burke was the one who set the bomb, Cameron wouldn't—"

He grabbed her arm and pulled her close. "Why? Because he's your friend?" Anger glittered in his eyes. "You think he wouldn't blow up your house because he *likes* you?"

It wasn't about like. "Cameron hates bombs. He hates fires. That was one of the reasons I knew he'd come after Burke." Samantha fought to keep her voice steady. Blake *couldn't* go in alone. "Cameron's parents died in a fire. That's not something he would ever use. He hates fire."

"Maybe so, but I'm not risking you." He nodded toward the officer behind her. "Keep Samantha Dark here. Put her ass in a patrol car and make sure she stays there until I come back."

He had *not* just said that.

But the cop was nervously putting his hand on Samantha's shoulder. "Ma'am?"

"Don't *ma'am* me!" she snapped back. "Blake, you need me! You need backup, you—"

An SUV rushed to the scene, braking hard. Two men jumped out, men she recognized from the FBI. Special agents who'd worked with her and Blake.

"Tucker Frost and Alex Castell. Bass ordered them down right after he landed in Alabama. And I got the call they arrived just before we took off on the airboat. I told them to stay at the station, to wait and see what developed." Blake's voice was curt. "So I have backup. Don't worry about that."

She was worried about plenty. "Don't shut me out!" The uniformed cop was actually pulling her back then. Damn it, damn it!

"I'm not shutting you out. I'm protecting you."

He was pulling FBI rank on her!

Tucker and Alex had already donned bulletproof vests, vests with *FBI* blazoned across the front. They tossed an extra vest at Blake. He caught it easily, and as he put it on, his gaze found hers once more. Emotion blazed in that stare.

She was right beside the patrol car. This wasn't right. "He's not even inside! Cameron is gone! We need to have men searching the woods—searching the beach!" She looked out at the water. Boats bobbed out there, so many on this cloudless day. "We need to search every vessel! We need to—"

"Put her in the car," Blake said quietly. "And keep a guard on her every moment."

The officer opened the door.

This *sucked*.

Tucker glanced her way, his face worried. And he mouthed the words, *I'll watch his back*.

She and Tucker had trained together, back in the day. The Quantico days. He'd been set for profiling, too, but something had changed, and he'd focused less on behavioral analysis and more on violent crimes fieldwork.

Blake turned away from her, rushing toward her home. Tucker and Alex were right with him as they headed for the house.

And she was trapped in a patrol car, surrounded by cops.

BLAKE WENT IN FIRST, and the scent of blood and death was heavy in the air. Son of a bitch. He glanced to his right and saw Tucker Frost coming in behind him. The guy's face was locked in tight, angry lines.

Walking in and finding a dead cop on the floor was enough to piss anyone off.

And the guy was definitely dead. His throat had been slit nearly from ear to ear, and the blood had already pooled beneath his body. Blake crept toward the body. Where the hell was the dead cop's partner?

It was silent in the house, eerily so.

Not good.

Alex Castell swept to the left, opening the guest room door. No one was inside.

Blake followed the scent of blood forward. And he found missing cop number two.

Only, this guy hadn't been killed with a knife. The gunshot to his chest had taken him out. Blake pressed his fingers to the cop's throat. *No pulse.* And the man's skin was cold to the touch. Lividity had already set in.

While they'd been chasing Burke down in the Delta, Cameron had been killing in Samantha's house.

"Where is he?" Alex barely breathed the words.

Blake motioned toward the hallway. He could see that Samantha's bedroom door was shut. He opened it and went in fast, but—

The room was just as they'd left it. Nothing disturbed.

His gaze narrowed as he stared at the white door that led to Samantha's office. He stalked forward, yanked open that door—

And saw the back of a man's head. Someone was

sitting in Samantha's desk chair, staring at her computer screen.

"Put your hands up," Blake snarled. He could just see the man's dark hair.

The guy didn't move.

"The game is over, Latham." Blake advanced on him. He grabbed the chair, spinning it around. "It's—"

Not Cameron Latham.

"Oh, fuck," Alex muttered. "That is sick."

The man's eyelids had been cut away. His eyes—lifeless—stared straight ahead. His throat gaped open, and blood soaked his shirt.

And the guy…he was familiar. Blake's gaze swept over him, trying to see past the horror, and he realized…

The cameraman. Janice Beautfont's cameraman. He was staring at the guy who'd been on Samantha's doorstep days before. At a guy who'd been tortured to death from the looks of him. Slices were up and down his arms. His hands were tied tightly to the chair arms, and he'd been positioned…

Right in front of the computer monitor.

"Keep searching the house," Blake ordered sharply. "Look in every closet and under every bed. Check the attic, check every single *inch* of this place."

Tucker and Alex moved to obey.

But Blake stayed there. He forced himself to stare at the dead man. The poor bastard. *He cut off your eyelids for a reason.* Blake wasn't good at psychological crap like Samantha, but this one was obvious…

He wants me to see…

Blake looked at the computer. The dead man had been positioned right in front of it. But the screen was black because the system must have gone to sleep. Blake used the back of his hand to lightly brush against the mouse, waking up the system, but trying not to contaminate any evidence and—

Samantha was on the screen. An image of her. Lying in a bed, naked.

And she wasn't alone.

Cameron Latham was with her. Cameron Latham was *fucking* her in that image on her computer. An image that Cameron had wanted Blake to see. That he'd wanted the *world* to see.

Blake's head snapped up. He looked at the bulletin board Samantha had put on her wall, and he realized…

Pictures were on that board. Pictures that hadn't been there before. Every city that Samantha had visited… each city now was marked by a small picture of her. Chicago…she was at a bar, leaning forward intently. New York…she was drinking coffee as she crossed the street. San Diego…she was stepping off a streetcar.

Cameron had been watching her all along.

Blake moved closer to the board. Because there was a picture positioned right over Fairhope, Alabama, too. A picture of Samantha jogging along the pier—the pier that Blake had met her on the very first day he'd come to town.

Words had been written along the bottom of that picture, in thick, black marker.

She was mine first.

He flipped the picture over.

And she will be again.

WHEN SHE SAW Blake stalk out of her house, Samantha's breath left in a low rush. She'd been staring at her home, her body taut, fear thick in her blood, from the moment he vanished. She shoved open the car door and jumped out.

The officer tried to push her back inside. She knocked his hands away. "He's back! It's safe, so just—"

"Three bodies inside," Blake's voice boomed out. "Get crime scene techs in there *now*. Preserve the scene. Get the ME to take care of the dead." His gaze burned as it met Samantha's. "And you come with me." He grabbed her hand before she had a chance to speak, and then he was hauling her toward the SUV that Tucker and Alex had rode up in.

He opened the passenger door and tried to push her inside—but she was done with being pushed. *"Stop!"*

He blinked. She'd…never seen his face quite like that. So tight. His cheeks were hollowed out. His jaw clenched. His eyes too bright with fury.

Samantha licked her lips. "Three men…are dead?"

He nodded curtly. "The two missing cops…and Janice's cameraman. You know, the poor dumbass we were hoping to find because we thought he might be able to ID Latham and tell us about the guy's new appearance." He caged her between the SUV and his body. "Turns out Latham tortured him, for a good long while, judging from the look of things. Oh, and for extra fun, your boyfriend cut off the guy's eyelids."

Her hand slammed into his chest. "He's not my boyfriend."

"No?" He gave a rough laugh. "Guess he doesn't get that clue."

She was missing something. Samantha glanced at her house. "Take me inside."

"No, no, where I'm taking you, it's as far away from here as I can get you. Because he's made a threat against you. He is coming for you. Hell, the guy has apparently been stalking you for months. You thought you were hunting him? No, no, he's been after you, baby. He's *coming for you*." His hands curled around her shoulders. "I'm not going to walk in some house and find your body. I'm not doing that. I won't walk in and find you with slices all over your body because you thought you could *handle* that sick freak."

Her heartbeat was a slow thud in her chest. "Take me inside the house." Because she needed to see the scene.

A muscle flexed along his clenched jaw.

Fine. She would take herself in there. She shoved him back and started marching toward her home. Blake was on the edge of his control. At any moment, she was afraid that control would shatter. Cameron wanted to destroy Blake, she knew it—and she couldn't let it happen.

Blake caught her wrist again and pulled her toward him. His grip was so tight.

She stared into his eyes and knew exactly how to reach him. "Blake, you're hurting me."

Horror came. His gaze flared, and he immediately dropped her wrist, as if she'd burned him. He stepped back.

Samantha didn't move. "Look at me."

Because he was staring at the ground. His face had gone chalk white. He was—

"Did you see that freakin' picture?" a cop muttered as he came out. "On the computer, I swear it was—"

Blake lunged for the guy. He grabbed for the cop's uniform and brought his fist swinging toward the young cop's face.

"Stop!" Samantha yelled.

What in the hell?

Blake froze.

"This isn't you," Samantha said, her voice soft.

His fist dropped.

She looked at the house. Her home. Her sanctuary. And she walked toward it.

"Search the surrounding area," Blake's voice was low, more controlled. About damn time.

She kept walking toward the house. She was almost at her front door when he reached out to touch her. This time, his touch was so careful.

"Don't worry," Samantha told him without glancing back. "I won't be contaminating the crime scene. I just need to see what he left behind." She needed to see the damage he'd done to his victims. She had to see just how far Cameron had fallen.

One cop rushed by her and vomited outside. Right on her flower bed.

She drew in a bracing breath; unfortunately, that breath just brought her the taste of blood and death. "How did it get like this?"

They walked inside together. He was at her side. She saw the first body, the man's slit throat. She noted the ashen color of the skin. "Rigor mortis has set in." He'd been dead for a while, just lying on her floor.

"Killed from behind." All of the emotion was gone from Blake's voice. Only ice remained—the same ice that had numbed her heart. "The guy probably was lured inside, and Latham was waiting to attack."

"It was a fast kill." At least the cop hadn't suffered. "His…gun is missing." His holster was empty.

"Yeah, I know where it is." They went into her den. And she saw the second cop. Dead, near her sofa.

"I'm guessing Latham used the gun he took from the other cop to kill this man."

The scent of blood filled her nose. "Another fast kill." Latham had been into torture before, into seeing just how much pain he could inflict on his victims. "His MO is different now." Because he'd killed Janice quickly, too. Quick and brutal kills.

"Don't be too sure of that." Again, his voice was like ice. As if he were locking down the dangerous emotions burning through him. But you could only hold emotions inside for so long before they exploded. "He took his time with the last guy."

And Blake led Samantha into her bedroom. She didn't breathe when she first stepped inside, but the room looked normal.

"Your study." If possible, his voice was even colder.

The door to her study was open, and when she went inside, she found Tucker standing near her bulletin board. He was staring at it, as if the board held the secrets to the world. She slipped closer and saw...photos.

Of me.

"He knew you were there, every time." Blake was right behind her. "He was hunting you."

"I...I don't think *hunting* is the right word." The pictures had been put into place with her pushpins. Her hand hovered over the map. She saw an indention for another pushpin. Right over Mobile Bay. Fairhope. But there was no picture.

"It's been bagged and tagged," Tucker said quietly. He lifted up his hand, and she saw the evidence bag.

Behind her, Blake gave a low growl.

She was mine first.

She felt her face heat, then go ice-cold.

Tucker turned the bag over so that she could see the back of the picture.

And she will be again.

She took a step back, and her elbow rammed into Blake. His hands came down on her shoulders, steadying her. She looked up at him, knowing there was more. His emotions were too volatile for there *not* to be more.

"The computer," he said flatly.

Afraid of what she'd see, she turned for the computer, but then her gaze got caught on the dead man. "J-Janice's cameraman." Her stutter slipped out, a sign of weakness because she just hadn't expected...this.

Bile rose in her throat, and she thought of the cop who'd rushed outside. She wanted to vomit, right then and there. She wanted all of this to be a terrible nightmare that just *stopped*.

She realized her hands were shaking so she balled them into fists, and then Samantha looked over at the computer.

Blake stepped in her path. "No, you've seen enough. This was a bad fucking idea. There is no reason for you to see more."

What?

"You're done." Once more, he reached for her. Only this time, he tried to push her toward the door.

She wasn't in the mood to be pushed. In the mood to vomit? Hell, yes. In the mood to shatter into a million pieces? Probably so. But not pushed away. Not closed out of this case. "If I'm going to profile him, I have to see everything."

"You don't need to see this."

What was it? She tried to peer around him, but—

Gently, Blake curled his fingers under her chin and

tipped her head back. She could still see the rage burning in his bright gaze, but he was infinitely tender as he touched her. "I can see your pain, Samantha." His voice was low, just for her. "I don't want it to get worse."

How could it get worse? She was in a room with a dead body—a man who Cameron had tortured. If she'd just killed him months ago, this wouldn't have happened. And that guilt was eating her alive.

I tried to bring him in. That was my mistake. I should have—

She slammed the door on that thought. "I need to make a new profile on him so that we can...we can catch him." She'd almost said *kill* him, and that wasn't right. She wasn't a murderer. She wasn't Cameron. "I have to see everything."

"Tucker can do the profile. He's been training more in that area since you left the Bureau."

"Man, I am out of my league with him," Tucker said quickly. "She's the one who knows Latham. She's already in his head. Let Samantha do her job."

But Blake was still blocking her path. Still softly stroking her cheek. "You've come so far," he said. Pain roughened his voice. "I saw how much you hurt in DC. I don't want you hurting again."

"Step aside, Blake." Her voice was flat. She wasn't going to be denied. Wasn't going to be coddled or protected. She was as strong as any man there.

His face tightened, but...he stepped aside.

She had to carefully move around the body—God, that poor man—but then she was at the screen. She realized the cameraman had been positioned right in front of her computer, his eyelids removed—*please, please, let that have been done postmortem*—and arranged as if he'd been forced to watch what was on the screen.

Then she saw the image there. For a moment, she thought she'd faint.

Her. Cameron. Naked. Fucking.

There shouldn't have been an image of them. She'd never known about any pics, certainly never agreed to any videos or cameras being used while they were having sex. And…it had been so long ago since she was with Cameron that way.

The dead man had been positioned to look at that image. And suddenly, the guilt was too much.

Oh, God. I slept with the killer who cut off that man's eyelids. I let him touch me. I trusted him completely. Her legs were shaking, so she locked her knees. The bile was back in her throat, so she swallowed—once, twice, three times. Tears stung her eyes, so she blinked them away. A scream was rising in her soul, but she clamped her lips together.

She wasn't going to show her weakness. Not to Tucker, not to Blake, and most definitely not to Cameron. "He's trying to break me." That was what he was doing. "He's angry at me. Cameron wants me to be weak. He wants to have all the power." She turned from the screen and stared straight into Blake's eyes. "And he's trying to break you. He wants you to see me for exactly what I am."

Blake took her arm. He pulled her from the room. From the room that smelled of death and pain. From the home that had once been her sanctuary. He took her outside, and the sun was too bright. It was too hot. There were too many people.

She wanted to run and hide.

But…she stood still on the bluff. As still as a statue. The waves roared down below. The boats bobbed. And she blinked away the tears that stung her eyes once again.

"What are you?" Blake asked her, his voice seeming to sink into her very skin.

"He thinks…" Her words came out too hoarse, so she tried again, swallowing, making sure there was no emotion seeping out when she said, "He wants you to see that I'm like him. That was what he meant when he said I was his before…that we're alike, deep inside. That I'm as twisted up as he is. That only he can understand me."

"He's fucking delusional."

"No," she said, quite serious. "He never suffered from delusions. He's a narcissistic psychopath, but he's not delusional. He's got a genius-level IQ, and he plans his every movement in advance." Steps ahead, leaps ahead. "He knows you and I are f—that we're intimate." He'd discovered that truth—probably from Janice because the reporter had caught her and Blake as they came out of that very house together. "And he's trying to drive us apart."

"He thinks I'm going to leave you?" Blake gave a bitter laugh. "Hell, no. I'm sticking to you like glue. I *won't* let him hurt you, Samantha."

"He has no intention of hurting me." Blake needed to see that. She glanced at him. "I'm…not afraid of him."

Blake stared at her as if she'd lost her mind. She hadn't. She wasn't delusional, either. "I'm not his target." Couldn't he see that? "*You* are, Blake. You're the one he's coming after next. You're the one he wants." And she couldn't let that happen. "He's not trying to get you to leave me. He left those pictures because he wanted to set you off. He wanted to enrage you."

"Trust me, I'm fucking enraged."

"Enraged, but still controlled." And that was the difference. Even furious, Blake was trying to protect her. "He miscalculated where you're concerned. He can't predict your behavior." And that just might be their saving grace.

"I'm not following you."

She caught his hands and stepped close to him. So close that she saw the gold flecks around the pupils of his eyes. "He thought you'd explode. That you'd turn on me." A jealous lover, burning with rage. "He wanted you to see us like that because he wanted you to see me as a wh—"

"Don't ever say it." He cut her off. "Don't even think it."

Her breath whispered out.

"You trusted the wrong person. It's not your fault he's a 'narcissistic psychopath.'" Blake gave a grim shake of his head. "You're seriously saying that asshole thought I'd flip out on you? That I'd turn on you?" His laugh was bitter. "He has no clue. I'm not some dumbass following the craving of my dick where you're concerned."

"Blake—"

His shoulders thrust back. "He's not winning."

It wasn't a game to her.

"He's not going to break you," Blake continued fiercely. "He's not going to break me. He's not going to break *us*."

She looked into his eyes, and she believed him.

"I won't let him," Blake swore.

And neither will I.

CHAPTER SEVENTEEN

THE SHOWER WATER poured down on her, too hot, pricking her skin, but Samantha didn't care. She'd stayed at the crime scene for hours, until the bodies were moved, until the ME's van had pulled away. Until bag after bag of evidence had been collected.

A crime scene. That was exactly what it had been. Not her home, not anymore. Cameron had taken that away from her.

She didn't want the bastard to take anything else.

Steam rose around her. She put her hand on the shower door. They were in a safe house. At least, it was supposed to be safe. A place the FBI had picked out for her, not in Fairhope, but down the road, nestled out of the city. Nestled out of sight.

The safe house was locked behind a private gate. A security guard was at that gate. Video cameras watched every angle of the house. Not really a house, more of a mini-mansion. There were actually lots of rental houses like that in the area. Sometimes, the rich and powerful liked to play near the bay.

When they played, they wanted protection.

The FBI was utilizing that need for safety.

The shower door opened. Her hand fell to her side.

"How long are you going to stay in there?" Blake asked her, his voice chiding.

Until I wash away the scent of death. No, until she washed the memories out of her head. Unfortunately, they wouldn't vanish easily.

"I just wanted to check on you," he said. He was in his jeans, in a T-shirt. Stubble lined his powerful jaw, and emotions that she was afraid to read glinted in his eyes.

Blake turned away.

He seemed to always be checking on her. Always looking out for her. Always making sure she was okay.

She reached out and caught his hand in hers. "But I don't remember telling you to leave."

He looked back at her. He swallowed. "Samantha..."

Had she ever told him how much she enjoyed the way he said her name? He made it sound sensual. As if her name were a caress.

As if she mattered.

"It was really one hell of a day." She had so many new images to add to her nightmares now.

"Yes, it was." He'd gone stone still.

She didn't want that. She wanted *him*. She tugged on his wrist. "Come into the shower with me."

His gaze slowly swept over her. Heated. "You sure about that?"

"When it comes to you—" he needed to know this "—I am always sure." She would trust him with her secrets, with her life.

With her heart.

He turned toward her and then...then he stepped into the shower, coming right in while still wearing his jeans and his T-shirt.

"Blake!" His name was a surprised cry that broke from her. "Your clothes—"

"They'll dry." He pressed her body against the cold, tiled wall of the shower, caging her there. The hard wall behind her, the hot warmth of his body in front of her. The water thundered down on her. His mouth took hers, and he kissed her, a deep sensual kiss that had her moaning and had her hands digging into the now wet material of his shirt.

Her nipples were tight and hard, stabbing forward against his chest. Her hips arched against him. She wanted him in her, no long foreplay, just the fast, frantic rush of passion. Zero to pleasure because that was the way it was with them. Consuming. Overwhelming.

He kissed a path down her neck, licking her skin, sucking her, nipping her with his teeth. Her head tipped back against the wall. Her nails dug into his shirt. She could hear the wild pant of her breath, and her racing heartbeat seemed to shake her chest.

His hand pushed between her thighs. Two fingers thrust into her. Her eyes squeezed shut, and she shot up onto her toes, gasping. Then she pushed her sex harder against his hand, grinding down.

"I don't like…thinking about you with him…" His words were a rough growl.

Her eyes flew open. For an instant, her heartbeat stopped.

"I don't like knowing he touched you…like this…" His fingers withdrew, then thrust deep, sliding over her clit and sending a surge of pleasure soaring through her. Helplessly, she moaned.

"I don't like knowing he heard that sound…that he heard your pleasure…" His eyes burned. "That he *felt* your pleasure…"

The water still poured down on them. The need was

still bright and hot between them, but a new tension was there, coming from Blake. A dark fury, but...

Not directed at me.

"I want to destroy him. I *will*, Samantha. Know that. I will never let him get near you again."

Neither will I.

"When I saw that picture..." Again, his fingers pulled out of her, thrust back in. He was staring down at her sex, watching her, watching them. "I think I went a little crazy for a moment. I wanted to attack. I wanted to *hurt*."

"Blake?"

He pressed a kiss to her shoulder. "Not you. I would *never* want to hurt you." He looked at her. "You know that, don't you?"

She did. "Make love to me," she said. She needed that distinction. When she was with Blake, it wasn't just fucking. It wasn't just sex for pleasure's sake. More happened with them. More had always been there.

It was time to prove that to them both.

He was in a dark place, she could see it. Could feel the tension all around them. Rage was still there. Jealousy. Possessiveness.

Emotions that could drive a man to kill.

Emotions that could break a man.

But Blake was stronger than that. She knew it. She'd always known that he was.

His fingers withdrew from her, dragging over her clit once more. Samantha bit her lip to keep from crying out because the sensation was so overwhelming. But then his hands were on her hips. He lifted her up, holding her so effortlessly with the strength that she sometimes forgot. She forgot how big and powerful he was.

She forgot that hard ripple of his muscles, the powerful flex of his shoulders.

He held her pinned with one arm while the other yanked open his jeans. His cock sprang toward her, thick and long.

But then he was clenching his teeth. "Condom…"

Her hand pressed to the stubble that lined his jaw. "I'm protected and I'm clean." She'd *never* gone without using a condom with a lover before.

His eyes changed. The desire that had been there before turned ever darker. "I'm clean…"

"Then take me this way," she whispered. "I need to be this way, with you." She wanted nothing between them. No barriers.

And she didn't just mean the condom.

No past. No secrets. Just them. She wanted to open up her soul to him.

Making love. For the first time, that was what she truly wanted to do.

His cock pushed into her, sinking deep, stretching her. She was wet, and he slipped inside so easily, so deeply, until he'd thrust into her, hilt deep. She didn't move at first. Just savored the feel of him inside of her. His gaze was on hers, seeing so completely into her.

Her legs curled around his hips, holding on tight. Her hands shoved up his wet T-shirt so she could touch his hot skin. The heat between them, oh, it was definitely hot enough to burn.

His mouth took hers. Another deep, drugging kiss. He withdrew from her, then thrust deep. Powerful drives of his hips that she matched with a wild force of her own. Deep and sensual, hard and consuming. He took her that way, just as she took him.

And Samantha let herself go.

In and out, he plunged into her. His head lifted, his gaze held hers. Every slow drive of his hips had his cock pushing over her clit. The tension within her built, she couldn't hold back, couldn't stop it, couldn't—

She cried out his name as she came.

His hands clamped tighter around her hips. "That's what I hate most of all...that the bastard had you this way."

He withdrew, thrust—

"He didn't," she whispered. "He never had me this way." She smiled at him, needing Blake to understand the most important thing of all. "Because what I felt with him...it is *nothing* like what I feel with you."

His eyes changed again. The rage, the fury, the possessiveness—all of the darkness that had been trying to swallow him whole—it seemed to vanish.

His control broke. The careful control he'd still maintained gave way with her confession. He pulled her away from the wall, held her in a grip of steel, surged his hips against her, and she felt the hot release from him deep within her body. He kissed her. Wildly, frantically. She kissed him back the same way, her delicate inner muscles greedily clamping down around him.

The water kept surging from the shower, the steam lifted all around them and Samantha knew that she never wanted to let go of Blake.

There were some people in this world who mattered so much that you just never, ever wanted to let them go.

THERE WERE SEVERAL universities in the area. After all, according to the local news, the Gulf Coast of Alabama was a sprawling spot, poised for growth, poised for economic expansion, poised for—

Like I fucking care.

Cameron waited near the psychology building at the University of South Alabama. He'd picked that campus because it was the biggest in Mobile and the most accessible. No guards to check him when he entered. Just an easy walk right to campus. And, because he truly had incredible luck, night classes were in session.

He could have taken his time. Could have studied the students, picked his prey with care. After all, that was the way he *used* to work. He'd pick a student, separate her from the others, make sure that the individual wouldn't be missed, at least, not right away.

And then his experiments would begin. Those experiments had lasted a very long time. He'd learned a great deal about his victims during his experiments. Just as he'd learned some hard truths about himself.

He waited in the parking lot—a dark lot, security should really be improved—until the last class dismissed. Most students came out in little groups. So very smart of them to utilize the buddy system. Walking alone at night was just never a good idea.

All sorts of people could be waiting in the dark.

He stayed in his vehicle, watching as most of the group drove away. Some of the students didn't drive, though. They turned in the direction of the dorms and began walking. Again—in a group. Such a smart move.

And he kept waiting. Because there was always a few...who didn't stay with a group.

Two more students came out. One was a woman who went straight to her car. She didn't glance to the left or the right. *Situational awareness, my dear. You have absolutely none.* It would have been easy to take her. To just run right up behind her. Slam her head into the door of her car. Knock her out and—

She's not the one.

She got in her vehicle and drove away. She'd escaped that night, but he suspected she'd probably be someone else's victim another day.

He was still waiting. Waiting on the one student who would…

Ah, there we go.

The one student who would be walking alone. The others had gone ahead, moving around the curve in the road so they were no longer in sight of the psychology building. But this woman…the woman who was juggling too many books in her hands as she hurried down the large, stone steps in front of the building… she fit the bill.

He slid out of his car, then just waited. After all, he had to be sure no one else was going to interrupt his plans.

The woman hurried under one of the lights near the building, and it shone down on her blond hair. He frowned. He'd never been a particular fan of blondes, but…maybe the blond came out of a bottle. Janice had actually been a natural brunette, a lovely surprise that he'd discovered.

He liked the brunettes best.

His prey didn't head toward the parking lot. Instead, she picked up her pace and hurried toward the trail that led to the dorms. And in her haste, a book slipped from the stack in her hands. She didn't even seem to notice it fall.

He picked it up. He followed her.

It took her a while to hear the tread of his footsteps. He wasn't even being particularly quiet. But she finally looked over her shoulder, and when she saw him, she gave a quick jerk of surprise.

"Miss!" he called, trying to keep his voice gentle, nonthreatening. "You dropped a book when you left the building." He held up the book in his hand. "I tried to get your attention, but I don't think you heard me."

She looked down at the books in her hands, then back at him. And she stopped.

Another mistake.

She turned to face him. Even hurried close. "Thank you!" Her voice was breathless. "My stupid backpack broke right before class, the strap just tore loose, and I have to carry all these books because it was project night." Her breath expelled. "I probably wouldn't have even noticed I'd left that book until I was in the dorm. Then I would have needed to come all the way back here."

My, someone is chatty. Obviously, she'd missed the whole never-talk-to-strangers bit when she'd been a child. "Glad I could help." He glanced at the title of the book, and he had to smile. *"The Psychology of Violence?"* How utterly perfect.

"It's for my graduate thesis. Understanding why certain individuals crave violence." She tucked her other books under one arm and reached for the text he held. "Thanks, again—"

He swung the book at her, hard, fast and brutal. It slammed right into her head. He heard the crunch as her nose broke, and she slipped, falling backward. She hit the cement path hard, slamming her head into the stone.

Cameron crouched over her. "It is your lucky night."

Because he *had* learned something from Burke. The student had taught the teacher. If you want to make the FBI do your bidding, then you have to possess something they want—a victim.

She opened her mouth, probably to scream. *Should have done that sooner.* He clamped his hand over her lips. "You are about to get a once-in-a-lifetime opportunity. A truly firsthand glimpse at the psychology of violence."

Her eyes were wide, terror-stricken.

"You're welcome," he told her.

He had Samantha exactly where he wanted her.

Blake curled his hand around her stomach and pressed a kiss to her shoulder blade. They were in bed, sated, the horrible clawing in his chest finally subsiding. She was with him, and she was safe.

He knew they wouldn't have long together. A few moments of rest, then they'd be back at work again. Back to the police station. Talking to the ME. Analyzing the crime scene reports.

But for that moment, he had her, and that was all that Blake needed. "I should apologize."

"For what?" Her voice was husky, sleepy.

"For nearly losing it at the crime scene. Latham played me."

"No, he didn't." She turned in his arms, rolling to face him. "I told you, Cameron misjudged you. He thought you'd pull away from me, that you'd—" she swallowed "—that you'd give in to rage and jealousy. Dark emotions. Because that's all Cameron knows. The darkness. He doesn't get—"

His laughter sounded bitter to his own ears. "Trust

me, I felt plenty of rage and jealousy." Truth be told, he still did. He didn't want any part of Samantha to be claimed by Latham. He didn't want that freak near her, not even dragging down her thoughts.

"You feel them." She stared into his eyes. "But they don't control you."

For a moment, they almost had. When he'd been there, seeing that image, the dead man next to him… "We can't let him get away."

"I don't think he's running. I think he's going to come right at us." She licked her lips. "He's coming at you."

"Why does he have this hard-on for me?" Blake demanded. "Why is he so bent on taking me out?"

"Because he blames you for taking me away from him." Her voice was low, even. "When I met you, Cameron and I… The intimate side of our relationship ended. I didn't even realize why I'd pulled away from him, but he knew."

Blake waited.

"He knew that something was happening between us. He hated that because I think I was the only person Cameron could connect with. What we had together, it certainly wasn't love. But I think it may have been the closest he could come to that emotion." Her sigh blew lightly against him. "Do you know what psychopaths can do really well?"

He waited.

"Imitate. They see the way others act, they see the way others feel, and, in order to get by in society, they imitate those behaviors. The imitation never goes beyond the surface, but usually the pretense is so good that they can fool everyone around them."

"Cameron was a genius at that."

"Yes." Sadness came and went on her face. "He was."

He pressed a kiss to her lips, needing to touch her, almost needing to...mark her in some way. "So Cameron is going to come at me because he thinks I'm in his way. That I'm stopping him from having you?" *You won't ever have her, bastard. Not ever.*

"No, it's not about having me. It's about him blaming you." She sat up in bed, pulling the covers with her. "He's changed."

A rough laugh escaped Blake. "Yes, I noticed that. Two dead cops, a poor SOB with no eyelids—"

Samantha flinched. "He likes killing. He can do it easily now, with no hesitation, no remorse. I don't think he cares who his victims are. He doesn't have a specific type. He's defying traditional serial behavior."

Wonderful. So the guy was a psychopath with an appetite for blood and pain, and he killed anyone he wanted.

"We can't look at his victims to profile him. He may go back to attacking coeds or he may decide to attack someone else linked to the FBI or to the case. The thing I know for certain now is that he is *clearly* gunning for you."

"Then *I'm* the next victim."

"No."

He rose up next to her. "Look, why the hell not? I can be bait. Shit, you were more than willing to put yourself out there before. I *want* this bastard to come at me. I want him to take a run." He welcomed it. Because when that battle ended, Cameron would be the one in a pool of blood.

"Be careful what you wish for," Samantha murmured.

His eyes narrowed on her.

"He won't come at you directly, at least, not at first. He's profiled you, and while he may have been off about you and your reaction to the crime scene at my house, there are still certain things that he *does* know."

The guy knew jackshit about him.

"He'll use someone else to get to you. That's what I'm afraid of. I'm afraid he's out there, right now, and he's already picking someone else that he can use to manipulate you." She climbed from the bed and dressed quickly. "There is so much ground to cover. He could be anywhere, and I think he's hunting. He's not sleeping. Not waiting. It's dark out, and he likes the dark, so I think he's taking someone else. Or he's about to take someone, and he's going to use that person…" She spun toward Blake. "Against you."

CAMERON TOOK THE phone from his helpful victim. Since she was unconscious, it wasn't as if she needed the thing. He snapped a quick pic, pausing to admire the way the blood trickled from her broken nose, and then he slammed the trunk shut.

His gaze skimmed over the parking lot. Lights were still on in a few of the buildings on campus, but no one was out. No one was watching.

Sometimes, it seemed as if they never were.

He climbed into the vehicle. Not his, of course, but one he'd borrowed. Borrowed, stolen, what-the-fuck-ever. He pulled up the picture, admired it, even started to hit Send, but…

I'm not ready yet.

He had to be sure that he was quite prepared before he invited Agent Gamble to his little party.

CHAPTER EIGHTEEN

BLAKE DRESSED, TOO, acting quickly, with tight, angry movements. Samantha watched him, trying to figure out the right words to say. Blake had argued with her about being bait, and now the guy wanted to use the same tactic? Didn't he get that Cameron had one purpose right then... *And it is to destroy you, Blake.*

"We have to find him before Cameron comes at us." *At you.*

"The guy called you, Samantha. He's been stalking you. All along, you thought you were hunting him, but the bastard has been on your trail."

She'd felt his eyes on her. Unease had slithered through her more times than she could count. When you were being hunted...*you knew it.*

"Cameron likes to control all elements of his environment. He's very meticulous." *Organized to the extreme.* "He'd need a safe base down here, a place where he felt completely secure." But also a place that would allow him the flexibility to leave at a moment's notice. "The picture in Fairhope," she whispered.

"What?"

She paced toward him. "The picture of me jogging in Fairhope. That was a recent picture—I just cut off my hair a few days before you arrived." Because she'd been sick of the heavy weight. She'd wanted a change—

wanted so many things to change. "But the angle was from behind me on the pier."

She was mine first.

"I wouldn't have run right past him." She believed that with utter certainty. "I always look at every person I pass." Occupational hazard. She looked at every person, she wondered about them, gauged them and tried to see past the bright smiles or the tired waves. "I didn't pass him."

"Samantha, you don't know that. You have no way of—"

"I need to see the picture again." They needed to get down to the police station. "I need to study the angle of it. He distracted us." Tricky bastard. "He got our attention focused on the computer screen, on the picture from the past, but the photo we needed to see most was the one of Fairhope." *The present. Because you were saying something with that picture, weren't you?*

From the angle of that photo, she thought he'd been behind her.

"You're the one who said he changed his appearance," Blake reminded her, "so you could walk right past him and never know it was him."

"I don't think so." She'd know him. "He was behind me." She went back to that day, trying to see the moments again. It had been so recent—so very recent. Just a few days, and lives had been wrecked in that short span of time.

Mosley had been out, throwing his crab trap. Another woman had been jogging—a blonde with a bobbing ponytail. And she remembered two fishermen had been on the pier, getting their bait ready for the day.

It had been early. There had been only that small handful of people on the pier with her. But...

"A sports yacht was in the water." She recalled it so clearly. Big, gleaming. *Totally Cameron's style.* "He was behind me. He was on the water. He's been out on the water...sleeping there, traveling there *and hiding* there." Excitement had the words almost tumbling out of her. "When he needs to move, he just moves his boat. He was watching me from a distance. Hell, that's probably how he came to my house. He anchored his boat offshore, then swam to the beach. He climbed up the steps leading to my house, leading to the bluff, and he came in the back of the house." Her words came faster as she figured this out. "The cops on duty..." Those poor, dead men. "They wouldn't have seen him arrive. He got inside, and then...then one of officers probably went in for a quick patrol. Cameron was waiting. He killed the first cop, sliced his throat."

The scene unfolded in her head. Perfectly. Brutally.

"When the first cop didn't come back, the second arrived to check on him. He came inside, looking for his friend. He got to the den, and that was where he found Cameron waiting."

"With the other cop's gun," Blake added grimly.

She nodded.

"How the fuck did the cameraman get here?" Blake wanted to know. "If Latham swam in, no way he dragged the guy with him that way."

No, he hadn't dragged the guy there. "With the two cops out of the way, Cameron had control of the area." *Control. What he values most.*

A furrow was between Blake's dark brows. "He would've needed to leave, to go and get the poor bastard."

No, not necessarily. "Cameron was with Janice. That means he had access to her phone, her contacts. He could have *called* the guy." The guy—he had a name. *John Andrews.* A name, a family. A life. He'd had it all. Samantha eased out a slow breath. "Cameron could have called John and asked him to go there for a meeting."

"John wouldn't have just agreed to meet a killer—"

John hadn't known he was meeting a killer. "I bet Cameron pretended to be one of the cops, offering John an exclusive look at my place. He would have given him a perfect temptation. Cameron always knows what most people want," she said, unable to stop the bitterness from slipping into her voice.

He manipulates everyone.

"Why did he want that guy dead?"

"Because he saw something…" No, *wait.* "Because the cameraman saw *him.*" Her heart raced faster. Yes, yes, that made sense. John had been working with Janice, so maybe when Cameron approached Janice—*John saw you, didn't he, Cam?* "We need to get all of the recordings that John made before his death, particularly that last night with Janice. It's possible that he caught Cameron on one of those tapes." And if he had…

Then we will have you, Cameron.

"I'll get them," Blake swore. "Count on it."

Oh, the wonderful power of the FBI. She missed that power.

They hurried out of her temporary room and rushed to the front of the house—and they found Tucker coming toward them, his face tight.

"Bass is awake. And he's asking for you two." His phone was gripped in his hand. "So I say let's get down there and find out exactly what our boss saw before Jason Burke tried to send him to hell."

"LEWIS, YEAH, YEAH, it's Gamble." Blake paused outside of the safe house. Tucker and Samantha were already loading into the SUV. So much for rest time—there was no rest on a case like this one. "I need you to contact Central News Five. Get all the videos that John Andrews made on the day of his death." He paused. "Samantha thinks the guy may have seen Latham."

Lewis swore. "I don't like this shit. What Latham did to that poor bastard… The ME said it was done *before* Andrews died. Talk about a sick son of a bitch." His disgust and fear carried easily over the line. "You're watching her back, right? You've got my Sammie?"

His eyes were on Samantha right then. "Every single moment."

"Good. He's obsessed with her, you know that? He's not letting go. Sammie thinks the guy won't hurt her. But a twisted freak like him, he has no rules to follow. If Sammie turns on him, he *will* attack her, too. I'm no profiler, but even I can see that human life doesn't mean a thing to him."

No, it didn't. Not usually.

Does Samantha's life matter?

"She thinks he's out on a boat," Blake added. "Get the Coast Guard. Get us boats ready. I want us to start searching every vessel in the area."

Lewis gave a low whistle. "You don't have any idea just how many folks in this area have boats, do you?"

"I don't care. If we have to search every single one, we will."

Samantha motioned toward him.

"He isn't getting away."

He isn't getting her.

EXECUTIVE ASSISTANT DIRECTOR Justin Bass looked like he'd been to hell, and that the trip had been a real bitch.

He was hooked up to half a dozen machines, his body covered in bandages, bruises all over him and his left eye swollen shut. Every breath was a rough rasp, a rasp echoed by the beeping machines.

"Only a few moments," the doctor announced with a warning glint in his eyes. "The patient is not out of the woods, not by a long shot. He needs rest and not—"

"G-give us...t-time alone..." Bass's voice shook. He tried to lift his hand toward the doctor, but his fingers were shaking.

The doctor pinned Blake with a hard glare. "Five minutes. He can't handle more. I spent four hours in surgery repairing his chest—the man needs recovery, not more trauma."

They weren't there to traumatize the guy. They were there for answers.

The doctor backed away. Blake watched him go— they were in the Intensive Care Unit, a series of about half a dozen small rooms that were centered around a nurse's station. The rooms all had big, glass walls so that the nurses could see in to view their patients. The area was quiet, hushed, almost as if the folks there were waiting for death.

"Y-you...sh-shot him?"

Blake stepped closer to the hospital bed. Samantha and Tucker stood a few feet away, not too far; the cramped space wouldn't allow it. Alex Castell had headed to the police station in order to help Lewis get access to the recordings from the news station. They'd wanted to get started on that search right away.

Staring into Bass's eyes, Blake told him flatly, "Jason Burke is dead."

Bass blinked blearily at him.

"Burke was a student of Latham's." He paused just a beat. "Samantha's profile of him was dead-on. The guy lost control when Latham vanished."

"La...tham..." The machines beeped louder. "Knew... h-he was there..."

"Did you *see* Cameron Latham?" Blake asked him.

Bass's eyes closed as the machines kept beeping. "Trident."

He had no clue what that was supposed to mean.

"Guy...in my car...j-jabbed me with something. Wh-when I looked back..." Bass swallowed. "He h-had a tat...on his wrist. Black...trident."

Blake glanced at Samantha.

"H-he was in the back...but that k-kid...the k-kid who stabbed me...sh-shot me..." Bass's eyes flew open. "H-he was at the s-side of my car." He coughed, choking a bit.

"We think Cameron Latham ordered him to kill you at the cabin." Samantha spoke, her voice carrying above the beep and hiss of the machines. "Did Jason Burke say anything to you there? Anything that you believe will help us to track Latham?"

Bass's gaze focused on her. "Wrong..." His voice was a low whisper. His eyes started to sag shut.

"What is wrong?" Blake pushed him. The guy was about to slump into unconsciousness, and if the fellow had anything they could *use*...

"H-he was g-gonna...blow my brains out..." Each

word seemed to be a struggle. Bass lifted his shaking hand and pointed it at Samantha. "You...knew."

Blake stiffened. "Samantha wasn't fucking in on *anything*. I've told you dozens of times that she wasn't working with Latham. She's the one who saved your ass out there. She made herself a target, she—"

"Th-thank you..." Bass said.

Blake's stare jerked to Samantha. Surprise had made her eyes flare wide.

"Say that again?" Samantha asked.

"I'm...f-fucking...on my d-death bed..."

Samantha stepped closer to him. "I doubt that. I think you're too much of an asshole for hell to want you right now."

Bass's lips curled in a faint smile. "Was...wrong," he said again.

"Yes, you were." She stared down at him. "But look at it this way. You're alive, so that means you have plenty of time to make things up to me. I'm thinking... full, official apology. Maybe a new title."

His eyes were nearly shut. "Maybe...something... b-bigger..."

Samantha just stared at him. His breath seemed to even out. After a moment, she glanced at Blake. "He doesn't know anything that can help us. Cameron dumped him with Burke and left the other guy to do his dirty work." She turned away. "Let's go see if Lewis and Alex have those videos—"

The machines beeped louder.

Blake's gaze shot back to the bed.

"H-he thought Latham was his...f-friend...t-told me that..."

"That would be what Latham wanted him to believe."

Tucker spoke up, edging closer to him. "Another mistake that Burke made. You can't trust killers, no matter how personal you think your relationship is to them. They're like snakes. They'll bite the hand that feeds them and never think twice." His gaze shifted to Samantha's face. "And, yes, I'm speaking from personal experience. Doesn't matter if you're the killer's best friend or his fucking blood...anyone can be expendable." He squared his shoulders. "So when you face off with Latham, remember that. Because you still see your friend when you look at him. Every single time you talk about him, you call the guy Cameron. Not Latham. Not Dr. Latham. Not the perp. You personalize him, and that's going to make it harder for you in the end. Believe me, I know."

Samantha cocked her head as she studied him. "I would very much like to hear your story one day, Tucker."

He gave a rough laugh. "It's not very pretty. Most folks wish they'd never heard it."

"I'm not most folks."

"No..." Tucker mused. "You're not." His gaze slanted to Bass. A very much *out* Bass. "You did save his ass, just so we're all clear on that."

"I wasn't the one who took out Burke." She nodded toward Blake. "His bullet hit first, then Josh's followed. I was the one getting slammed to the ground."

Because he'd been frantic.

"I heard you were the one who distracted Burke," Tucker corrected. "You were the one who got him to move the gun from Bass's head. If you'd hadn't, the EAD wouldn't be in this hospital. He'd be in the morgue."

She gave a slow nod.

"So make sure he offers you one fine reward. We need you back to profiling, and I figure the guy's life is worth a reinstatement."

Did she want a reinstatement? Blake would love to have her back at the FBI, but only if that was what Samantha truly wanted.

His phone vibrated, and he looked down, reading the text. "Lewis has the video for us. Let's go." But before he left that little room, he cast one final glance at Bass.

The executive assistant director was battered and bruised. He looked small, pale, hardly the domineering SOB who boasted so much to the media. For the first time in his life, Bass had been made into a victim.

What would that do to him?

You survived, Bass. That makes you one of the lucky ones. He hoped the EAD remembered that in the weeks to come.

"Tammy White had no idea that she was going to work for the last day of her life." Janice Beautfont stared straight ahead. Her voice rang with a perfect combination of sympathy and pain. *"But she was abducted from this small town, a place that should have been safe for her—and authorities discovered her remains at the bottom of the bay."* She shook her head. *"Now a manhunt is under way for Jason Burke, a twenty-two-year-old ex–Georgetown University psychology major who is a person of interest in Tammy's abduction and brutal murder."*

"That woman sure delivered a compelling story," Lewis said, nodding toward the screen that was currently showing the last video that John Andrews had taken, at least, the last video according to the producer at his TV station.

Samantha shoved her hands behind her back as she stared at the screen. Seeing Janice—hearing her—it was surreal. *I swear, I can almost feel her blood on my hands.*

Their core group had assembled to view the video—Samantha, Lewis, Blake, Josh, Alex and Tucker. The USERT members who'd assisted Josh before—Sean Hastings and Fiona Webb—were helping to organize the Coast Guard search that they were hoping to launch soon. They'd be checking all of the vessels in their hunt for Cameron Latham.

But first…

Janice smiled big for the camera. *"Tune in tonight at ten for the latest details on this case as developments continue to unfold."* She stared straight ahead, obviously waiting for the feed to end so that she could cut the scene. A moment later, the camera angle shifted, as if John had lowered the equipment, but…

The video kept going.

Janice blew out a hard breath. *"Did I sound sympathetic enough? Like I cared?"*

Samantha blinked.

"I mean, I care. Of course I care." She shot a quick glance over her shoulder. No one was behind the reporter. *"I just wanted to make sure that came across in the story."*

The angle shifted a bit again, as if John were jostling the camera. *Getting ready to put it up?* It was obvious that Janice thought he'd stopped filming, but he hadn't. Not yet.

"It came across," a deep, gravelly voice announced.

Samantha lunged forward. "Stop!"

Every eye in the room swung toward her. Her heart was racing in her chest. Thundering.

Alex Castell paused the footage. He'd been eager to assist on this end, and she knew it was because the guy was considered one of the tech experts at the Bureau. He was great at retrieving data—and finding images that most others tended to miss. Only this time, she was the one who'd just found their guy. *Because I would know his voice anywhere.*

Josh frowned at her. "Sam?"

Blake came to her side.

"That's Cameron's—that's Latham's voice." And her own voice had gone hoarse. She cleared her throat and tried again. "I know that's him. Begin the footage again, Alex. *We need to focus on that guy.*" And she prayed that John hadn't stopped filming.

As the video rolled again, Janice narrowed her eyes, as if searching for the speaker.

"You handled the segment with tact and class, I was impressed."

Janice threw the speaker a megawatt smile. *"Thank you. I always try to present my stories in a way that will do justice to the victims."*

"John didn't turn to film the guy," Tucker muttered. "Shit!"

The camera jerked once more. "Here we fucking go again." John's voice. A low mutter. And...

He swung the camera down, but not before it panned over and caught Janice—shaking the hand of a tall, dark-haired man.

For an instant, Samantha couldn't even breathe.

"Freeze that frame!" Blake barked.

Alex immediately froze that frame. Then he started tapping on the keyboard he'd connected to the video system.

"Enlarge the image." Blake marched closer to the screen.

"Already on it," Alex said. He kept tapping.

Samantha didn't move. Her gaze locked on the image. Janice, shaking the hand of the man who'd approached her. He was tall, with broad shoulders, his hair was dark and a dark beard covered half of his face.

"Looks like Latham dyed his hair," Tucker mused.

"The beard is a nice touch," Josh added. "Changes up his jaw shape."

"Advance the frame." Samantha wanted to see more. "Slowly."

Very, very slowly, the video continued as Alex advanced the frame. John's camera swung to the ground. The clip ended.

"Rewind it," Samantha ordered. "Play it at regular speed."

The footage rewound.

"You handled the segment with tact and class, I was impressed."

They shook hands. The camera swung toward the ground.

"You a sailor, sir?"

The footage ended.

"A sailor," Samantha whispered. She looked at Blake. "Bass said the guy in his backseat had a trident tattoo on his inner wrist."

Blake's lips parted as he began to speak—

"Son of a bitch!"

Her head swung toward Lewis. He'd jumped out of

his chair. His hands were clenched into fists. "That bastard was *here*!"

"What?" Josh barked. "When?"

Lewis pointed a finger toward him. "Same day you arrived. Guy showed up—big, dark-haired, saying he was ex-Navy and wanted to help with the search for Tammy White." That finger slowly curled back as his hand fisted once more. "He stood right in front of me. Introduced his damn self to me. Hell, I even told him to give his contact info to the desk clerk." His laughter was rough. "Played me for a fool."

Samantha was already running for the door. Her shoes clicked on the tiled floor as she rushed toward the front desk. She slapped her hands on the counter, startling the cop behind the desk.

"Ms. Dark?" Brian Titus frowned at her. Poor guy was always pulling desk duty.

"Give me the contact cards for everyone who came in and volunteered to help on the search."

Brian looked over her shoulder. She knew the others had followed her; she'd heard their thundering steps.

"Give her the cards!" Lewis yelled.

Brian turned away, fumbling with a desk drawer to his right.

"Not like the guy was going to put his actual address down," Josh said. "That would be too easy."

"No." Samantha considered the situation. "That would be arrogant." *Just like Cameron.*

"Name was something with a B…" Lewis tapped his fingers on the counter. "Ben… Brent… Bryce…"

Brian lifted a card. "Brock? I got a Brock Chambers."

She snatched the card right out of his hand. Her gaze

flew over it, reading the address as her insides shook. *609 Persephone Way.* Cameron—still with the mythology obsession. Obviously, the address was pure bull, but there was a telephone number listed on the card, too.

Blake pulled out his phone. She knew he was getting the FBI to run a trace on that number, and, sure enough, that was the order she heard him give. As soon as he ended the call, he put his phone on the counter in front of Samantha. He turned on the speaker option, and he dialed the number that "Brock" had listed on his contact card—the number they were supposed to call if they wanted the guy's help in finding Tammy White.

It rang once, twice.

"He's not going to answer," Josh growled. "I mean, come on, obviously, that number is as bogus as the address—"

On the third ring, the phone was picked up. "Hello?" A deep, familiar voice spoke. There was a slight pause, and then he said, "Agent Gamble, your number just appeared on my caller ID. I know it's you, so don't waste my time with silence."

"And I know it's fucking *you*," Blake snarled right back. "We've got pictures of you—those pictures are going out to the media right the hell now."

Or rather, they would be, as soon as possible. But Cameron didn't need to know that.

Cameron laughed. "I left the number at the station because I wanted you to call me. Though I had just about given up hope of that happening."

"Bullshit," Samantha said, unable to hold back. "You left the number because you were enjoying jerking around the local cops. You actually thought they'd call you in on the investigation, and you liked the idea of being on the hunt for a body. You thought they might lead you to Burke, but—"

"Samantha." Excitement roughened his voice. "I should have known you'd find me first. Gamble was always the clueless one." He sounded so pleased. "Missed me, did you?"

I missed the friend I had. I don't miss the man you are. She drew in a steadying breath and continued, "You wanted the local cops to lead you to Burke. When you realized he was the one hunting here, you wanted them to help you find the guy."

"It was one idea I had briefly." He dismissed that. "But then I located him on my own. If you want the honest truth…"

She laughed. "Can you even give it?" She felt Blake's gaze on her.

"I wanted to meet Lewis. You talked about him so much that I just had to shake the hand of your father figure."

Her stare shot to Lewis. His eyes blazed. Josh was behind him, his face hard and tight. Tucker stood silently at Josh's side. She didn't see Alex. Maybe he was still working on the footage?

"Don't worry, sweetheart," Cameron reassured her. "I wasn't going to hurt him. I know how you feel about Lewis. But getting close to him, well, it was a way for me to get close to you." He made a faint humming sound. She remembered that he'd always made that sound when he was particularly pleased with something. *A grade, a promotion.* "Got to say, the timing of this call is absolutely perfect. I was just about to contact good old Agent Gamble."

"Oh, really?" Blake demanded. "'Cause you're ready to turn your sorry ass in to the FBI?"

Again, Cameron laughed, sounding truly amused. "Good God, no. I was just ready for *you* to come to me. All this running around is quite tiring, so let's just stop that, shall we? You come to me. Unarmed."

"Why would I do that shit?"

His phone gave a little ding as it sat on the counter. A text had just come through.

"Might want to take a look at that," Cameron advised.

Blake picked up the phone. Samantha edged closer to him.

Not another one.

A blonde woman was in that image. Blood trickled from her nose. Duct tape was over her mouth, and her hands were duct-taped to her ankles. She was in a twisted heap, thrown in...a trunk?

"I met a new friend tonight," Cameron announced.

"Damn it, *stop.*" Samantha's voice rang with fury. "Stop hurting her! Stop hurting everyone! Stop doing this!

"Make me..." The low taunt cut right to her soul.

I should have made him stop months ago.

"Agent Gamble..." The whip of wind broke over the line as Cameron spoke once again. "You can save this girl. You see, what I want is for you to come to me. I'll swap you for the coed. A simple exchange. You can save a life today, if you just follow my orders."

Samantha shook her head. *This is just like Burke's deal.* Cameron wasn't going to let the woman go. She could already be dead.

"You're tracking this call, right? Well, this is how it

is going to work. I'll leave the phone on, I'll let the FBI agents home in on my location, but I have conditions."

"He has insanity," Josh muttered.

But Josh was wrong. Cameron was completely sane. Just twisted. And he had very little value for human life.

"I don't know who the fuck that was talking," Cameron said, voice mocking, "but he's obviously an idiot." Again, he paused. "Sam, love, aren't you tired of being with people who just don't understand?" His sigh rustled over the phone. "I am. I miss our talks. I miss the way you could always understand."

Samantha stared straight at Blake.

"I miss you," Cameron said. And he actually sounded as if he meant those words.

Because he does.

But then he cleared his throat. "So here's the deal. I've got this blonde coed, blonde from a bottle by the way. I already checked."

Samantha's eyes squeezed shut.

"And Agent Gamble, if you don't do exactly what I say, I will kill her."

"You don't get to call the shots," Blake snapped at the guy.

"Uh, yes, of course I do. It's not like you'll just stand by and let me torture and kill some innocent woman. That capacity isn't in that true-blue DNA of yours."

"You don't know me." A low growl from Blake.

"Maybe not as well as I'd thought," Cameron allowed. "Because you didn't lose your fucking shit the way I'd hoped at Sam's house."

Her eyes opened. Blake's face was so hard and angry.

"Oh, I *may* have been watching," Cameron murmured.

"From your boat," Samantha said.

A quick moment of silence. Then, Cameron asked, voice only vaguely curious, "Have the agents traced the call already?"

No, I just know how you think, bastard.

He must have taken the silence for assent. "Well, then let's cut to business. Yes, I'm on a boat. And, Agent Gamble, *you* are to come out to the boat. Specifically, I want you to swim out to me. Start at the shore next to the main Fairhope Pier. Go into the water and keep coming. I don't give a shit how tired you get. Keep coming until you reach my boat. Once you get there, I'll let the woman go. I'll toss her into the water, and she'll be free."

The wording he used…*toss her into the water, and she'll be free.* "No," Samantha bit off. "That's not good enough. You have to promise *not* to kill her. If we follow your orders, you can't kill the woman."

He laughed. "It was just semantics, sweetheart."

No, it hadn't been. He'd just promised that once Blake got to the boat, then Cameron would kill the woman and toss her overboard. Semantics, her ass. She knew exactly what he'd meant.

"I'm coming, too." Samantha said.

Blake gave a frantic shake of his head.

But Cameron replied, "Well, of course you are. That's condition number two. For you to swim with him. Just the two of you. No helicopters—I'd hear them, and they'd just make me reach for my knife, and then I might start slicing on the blonde."

There was no *might* about it.

"And no other boats," he added sharply. "Same deal,

I'd see them coming, and they'd just make me kill my coed long before help arrived."

Make me, make me. He was putting the blame for his actions on everyone else. *Take some fucking responsibility, Cam.*

"And once we make the exchange, what happens?" Blake demanded.

"I guess you have to wait and find out." Cameron made a faint humming sound. "So, get moving. If I have to wait too long, I'll start to experiment. It's been a while since I studied pain with my victims."

"Sick son of a—" Josh began.

"And, Sam?" Cameron's voice rose. "It will be good to see you again. Just like old times."

He was about to hang up on them. "Proof of life!" Samantha cried out. "We won't do anything without proof of life. If you really have a victim, let her talk to us right now. You could be making up this whole abduction, you could be—"

A woman screamed. A loud, desperate, pain-filled sound.

"Look what you made me do to her..."

The line went dead. *Made me, made me.* In her mind, Samantha saw Cameron with his knife, torturing, hurting that woman.

Blake's eyes glittered at her.

"Hey, Captain Lewis! Blake!"

Samantha's shoulders jerked as Brian rushed toward them.

"When I heard you say his name, I checked the FBI database." Excitement lit his dark eyes. "Brock Chambers is a real person...got his social security number, his Navy records and his photo..." He pushed some printed papers toward Lewis. "He even looks like the guy we just saw in that video. Tall, dark-haired, and—"

"Latham stole the guy's identity." Blake was still staring at Samantha.

Swallowing, she looked away, trying to focus on Cameron, trying to make a plan. "That may not be all he stole." She bit her lower lip. *Think, Samantha. Think.* "Did Brock own a boat, by any chance?"

Brian nodded, looking damn pleased with himself. *He should. He just scored a home run for us.* "Yeah, yeah, he did—does. A forty-foot yacht called the *Circe*. Supposed to be down in the Keys, though—"

Her heart was slamming into her chest. "It's not. It's right here." The *Circe*. Cameron had probably been unable to resist taking the vessel when he saw the name. It would have been too perfect of an opportunity to pass up.

Blake had picked up his phone and was dialing quickly. A call back to the FBI contact who'd been monitoring the cell. A moment later he said, "Tell me you got the bastard's location."

They had the name of his boat and they had—

He nodded. "Give me the coordinates."

The little group tensed as he took the coordinates.

"Let's mount up," Lewis snapped. "Let's get on the water with the rest of your agents and the Coast Guard. Let's surround that bastard. We will take him down, and there will be no more games. No more of my fucking dead cops left in his wake. He won't hurt anyone else in *my* city."

Going in with a full cavalry was one option, but Samantha shook her head. "You know he'll kill her if we do that." She believed that with utter certainty. She pinned everyone around her with a quick glance. "He wasn't bluffing. If he sees a force coming for him, he *will* kill the victim. There's no reason for him not to do it."

Going in strong would mean just one thing...the blonde woman would be dead. It was just like the setup that Jason Burke had used before with her when he'd tried to lure her onto the pier in hopes of rescuing Tammy White...and Samantha knew it was no coincidence. Cameron was using this tactic deliberately. *Coming full circle.* He'd learned what Burke had done; he'd probably gotten Burke to tell him every single detail of that attack, only now Cameron was perfecting things. Proving that he was better. Always better and smarter than everyone else. Jason Burke had been a pale imitation. Cameron was ready to show he was the real thing. No one could compare with him.

Josh's face reflected his frustration. "The guy is a freaking psychopath! He will get you both on his boat, and then, for all we know, he'll kill everyone out there. Maybe that's what he's planning...to go out with a bang. Only, he wants to take you two out with him."

Samantha's body was so tense her muscles ached. "We're wasting time. He *will* start hurting her if we don't move." Though she feared he'd already begun.

Lewis grabbed her arm. "You can't go out there. If he gets you on that boat, he's not going to let you walk, Sammie. You see that. I know you do." He huffed out a breath. "Shit. Didn't we learn anything from the last damn trade? Perps can't be trusted! It's just a setup to kill!"

"Cameron learned from the last trade." She paused a

moment, then added, voice thoughtful, "I think he even learned from my last big case in Florida."

Blake frowned at her. Then she saw the understanding settle in his eyes. It had been so long since that case… "Hope."

Right. Hope, Florida. A city of sunshine and dark secrets. She and Blake had worked that case together.

A perp had been kidnapping young girls down there—and killing them. And the way he'd gotten away with his crimes for so long? He'd used a boat. No one had focused on the water, and they should have.

Cameron had paid attention to that case, the way he paid attention to all of her cases. "We talked about the perp when I got back. The story had made the news, so it was no secret. He even told me that he thought utilizing the boat had been a genius move for the killer." That was Cameron, all right. He was always learning from the strengths and weaknesses of others. Always trying to push himself. "He probably got the idea to use a boat for his movements from that case."

So many puzzle pieces clicked into place for her. Cameron had gotten the *Circe* from Florida…had he been motivated to go down the Florida coast because of her case in Hope? Had that given him the idea? He'd gone down the coast, heading to the tip of the Keys, then finding the perfect transportation to make himself invisible.

All because she'd told him about the perp in Hope. How that guy had gotten past the radar of the local authorities for so long.

"In that case," Samantha murmured, "FBI Agent Jillian West was lured out to the killer's boat. He wanted her to trade herself for the victim he had." She eased out a slow breath. "When I came home from that case, Cameron couldn't understand why Jillian had taken such a risk." She held Blake's gaze. "I told him… I told him it was because no agent could stand helplessly by while a victim was threatened." A bitter laugh escaped her. "I even told him…I would have done the same thing." And now she was…courtesy of Cameron. "As long as he has his victim, he has power, and Cameron knows that."

A muscle jerked in Lewis's jaw. "When he has you and Gamble, he'll have even more power."

Tucker nodded. "He'll use you both." His sharp gaze flew to Blake. "An FBI agent is a much better bargaining tool than a civilian. He'll think you have more pull, that by threatening the two of you, he'll be able to guarantee his ass safe passage out of this mess."

"No." Blake gave a grim smile as he disagreed with the other agent. "He just wants to attack me. He's tired of playing, and he wants to stare right into my eyes when he kills me."

"Fucking hell," Tucker muttered.

Samantha pulled away from Lewis. She put her hand on Blake's shoulder. "We need to talk, right now. Alone."

His head tilted toward her. "You know I'm right. He took that woman because he knew I'd have to go and try to save her. That's what the FBI does. It's what I do." His lips twisted as he shrugged. "Isn't that what *you* tried to do with Tammy White?"

Yes. But…

"The victims come first for us. They always do."

Her heart thundered in her chest. *But this was different*. This was different because she *knew* Cameron intended to kill Blake at the first chance—

"And if I swim out to him, my gun will be fucking useless. I imagine Cameron will be waiting on his stolen boat, a gun pointed right at my head as I board the vessel. He'll kill me, probably not a straight shot to the heart, because he does like to play a bit with his prey."

Her lips felt numb. "Never realized you were so good at profiling, too."

His gaze drifted over her. "I was taught by the best."

"Blake…"

"He wants you there," Blake continued, his voice holding no emotion, "because he wants you to watch me die, right? For you to see what happens, for you to realize that he was the one in control. That shit fits with his issues, doesn't it? Then I'll be gone, and he'll be left with you…maybe with the poor woman he abducted, too. And at that point, yeah, he'll use you to bargain his way to freedom."

Samantha shook her head. "I'm not letting that happen."

He stepped toward her. His voice lowered. "I'm not, either, because I fucking swear I will not let him hurt you. Not ever."

And I won't let him kill you.

"He thinks he knows me." Blake smiled. Then he glanced at the others, who were watching him in silence. "But he doesn't know *us*." He pointed to Josh. "Get your USERT group. Get Fiona, get Sean. Get your asses in the water, go in at a point he *cannot* see. You take your tanks, and you come up to surround his boat. Samantha and I will keep his attention. You make absolutely sure you get out there, and you get ready to be our backup."

A wide smile split Josh's face. "Hell, *yes*."

"He said no choppers, he said no boats." Blake nodded. "He said nothing he could see...so you make sure your team is invisible. Got it?"

"He'll never see us coming," Josh promised.

"And we'll be ready onshore," Tucker said. He inclined his head toward Lewis. "The captain, Alex and I will be at the ready. We'll have the Coast Guard out a safe distance, and we'll make sure that Latham has no chance to slip away."

Their group would be like a net, closing in on Cameron.

"This is the end for him," Blake vowed. "No more blood. No more games. *The end*."

CHAPTER NINETEEN

BLAKE STOOD ON the beach, the waves coming up to brush over his feet. Bare feet because it would make swimming easier. He'd stripped off his T-shirt but kept on his jeans, and he had two knives holstered on his right ankle. He also had a gun secured to his left ankle, one he hoped would still fire after this trip through the bay. *Taking it, just in case.*

Samantha was at his side, her head tipped back. It was so dark out there, and the only light came from the glistening stars. Like Blake, she'd armed herself. Her shoes were gone and her shoulders hunched forward a bit as she stared out at the dark bay. "I think I can see the light from his boat."

Because Latham was waiting.

"The first day that you found me on the pier, I saw a yacht out in the water. That was the day that photo of me was snapped. He was here even then, watching me." She looked over at Blake. "This isn't going to end well."

"You can stay here. He'll have to deal with me, he'll—"

She stepped toward him. Leaned up on her tiptoes. He bent and took her lips. Needing her taste, needing *her* before hell came.

I won't let him hurt her. I won't let him get away.

"I love you, Blake." She stared up at him, her eyes

gleaming in the dark. "You need to understand that before we go out there. I will do anything to keep you safe. Know that. Trust me."

For a moment, he could only shake his head.

She stiffened and started to back away, but he grabbed her and held tight. "Say that fucking again." Because he needed to hear it—

"I will do anything to keep you safe. I will—"

"No," he snarled. "You said… You said you loved me."

She swallowed. "I've got shit for timing, don't I?"

He wasn't going to complain. "Say it again." He needed those words.

Her body brushed against his. "I love you, Blake Gamble. I love you more than I thought it was possible to love anyone."

His mouth crushed down on hers. *About fucking time.* The kiss was as desperate as he felt. He had the woman of his damn dreams in his arms, a killer waiting, but he also had hope. Because he had her. "Something you need to know, too…" he muttered against her mouth. "You fucking *own* my heart."

He felt the surprise rock through her.

Blake forced his head to lift as he stared down at her. This moment mattered. It mattered because he might not ever have another chance to tell her what he'd held back for so long. "I've loved you when I thought I could never have you. When crossing the lines was an offense that would have cost me my job and I didn't give a damn because I wanted you more than a job, more than breath, more than anything else in this world."

"Blake?" Shock was in her voice. Happiness. Yes,

they could still be happy. They *would* be happy. Latham wasn't going to win.

"When this mess is over, you and I are going away together. We're going to fuck for days, and I'm going to prove to you just how much I love you."

Silence. "You don't have to prove anything to me."

He kissed her once more and knew that their time on the beach had ended. But before he could back away, Samantha's hand fisted in his shirt. "Whatever he says, whatever he does, don't believe him. He's a master at manipulation. Don't fall for his tricks. And if I…" Her breath slipped out as she eased away from him. "If I play his game, know that I am *just* playing. Trust me, completely, just as I'll trust you."

"I'd do anything for you, Samantha. You should know that by now." Trust would be the easy part.

She let him go and began to wade into the water. But then she stilled.

"THERE'S ONE THING you have to promise *not* to do."

His eyes narrowed.

Samantha looked back over her shoulder. "Don't die for me."

He stalked into the tide. "I wasn't planning on dying." She needed to understand this. "But I would kill for you." And that was exactly the way he saw this scene ending.

They went into the water, and he barely felt the cold. He swam forward, strong, determined strokes, and Samantha was right at his side.

The SOB had anchored the boat far from shore, several miles out. He'd wanted them to swim so they'd be tired when they got to the vessel. Tired, weaker.

Latham thought he had every advantage on his side, but he was wrong.

Blake knew Josh wouldn't let him down. Josh and his dive team would take their positions. They'd be ready for him.

And Blake would be ready to handle Latham. His arms cut through the water, and he focused on the boat that waited for him.

SAMANTHA REACHED THE boat first. It was a big vessel, rising out of the darkness. Forty feet, with *Circe* written in flowing script near the bow. The waves were rougher now, and the boat bobbed from its anchor.

Blake was right by her side. His hand settled near her waist.

And then a bright light shone down on them, blinding Samantha.

"Finally, Samantha. I was starting to lose Hope." Cameron's mocking voice drifted to her.

Hope. She knew his word choice was deliberate, a reference to her case in Florida. He'd just confirmed what she'd suspected—the bastard had gotten the idea of using his boat from her investigation down there.

"Though I have to say, you two are both phenomenal swimmers," Cameron praised. "Great form. Made it look so easy." That light didn't waver. "But I bet you're feeling a little winded, hmm? You must be. The waves are getting rougher. A storm is coming."

"Where is the woman, Cameron?" Samantha shouted up at him.

"We'll get to her." The light kept shining on them. Blinding them. Another deliberate tactic to put them at a disadvantage. "I want you to both throw your weapons into the water. And *don't* think of bullshitting me by saying you didn't bring knives and guns with you. I hate it when people insult my intelligence."

She locked her jaw. Didn't move. Blake's hand was still at her back.

"Fine," Cameron called out. "If that's the way you want to play it—"

A woman's pain-filled scream cut through the night.

Samantha grabbed for the ladder, ready to rush up the side of the boat.

"*Stop*, Samantha!" Cameron snarled.

She stilled.

The woman wasn't screaming now, but she was crying. Desperate, heaving sobs.

"I just turned the blade in her side. She's still quite alive. But if you don't follow my instructions, then *I will keep hurting her.*"

Samantha looked back at Blake.

"Lift the weapons up in the light so that I can see them," Cameron ordered, sounding impatient now. "Then throw them into the waves."

Samantha lifted her gun and the knife she'd strapped to her ankle. "Satisfied?" She threw them. They hit the water with a plop and sank beneath the surface.

"It's the hero's turn," Cameron said.

Blake's hand slid away from Samantha's back. He lifted up a gun and a knife—and he tossed them.

"Now strip, Samantha."

Shock rocked through her.

Cameron laughed. "Love, really, stop taking me for a fool. You could have other weapons hidden beneath those wet clothes. So if you're coming on my boat, you're stripping down. Ditch the shirt and the pants and then climb that sweet ass up here. And, Gamble, you stay down there until she's with me. Understand?"

"I understand that you're a fucking dead man," Blake yelled.

"Really? How odd. I feel quite alive."

She yanked at her shirt, fighting to get the wet material over her head. Then her hands went to the snap of her jeans. She shoved the material down, and her pants drifted away in the water. Samantha was clad in only her panties and her bra, and Blake pulled her close.

"I'm okay," she whispered. "It's all right."

"No, it's fucking not." And he...he pushed a blade into her right hand. Based on the weight and the size, she knew he'd given her a folding knife. Probably the one she'd seen him with dozens of times before, a paramilitary folding knife with one wickedly sharp blade. Her fingers curled tightly around the weapon as he promised, "I'll be right behind you."

Samantha nodded. She turned from him, being sure to keep the knife out of sight. She reached for the ladder and slowly began climbing up to the deck. Water poured down her body.

The spotlight stayed on Blake.

She reached the top of the ladder and hauled her body up. The yacht's lights were on up there, and, breath heaving, she slowly straightened.

"Oh, Sam, all of that jogging you've been doing has certainly paid off. You look fucking fantastic."

Her gaze zeroed in on Cameron. Not the Cameron she remembered, but she still would have recognized him...it was in the tilt of his head, the sly curve of his lips, the glint of his eyes, the casual pose of power as he leaned back against the steering wheel...and kept his right hand on the knife that was currently thrust inside of the woman who sat—tears streaming down her cheeks, tied hand and foot—in the captain's chair.

Samantha pulled her gaze off Cameron and focused on the victim. "You're going to be okay."

But…the woman slowly shook her head. *No.*

Samantha kept her hands at her sides. She made sure the knife was out of sight. "We followed your instructions. Now keep your end of the deal. Let her go."

He pulled the knife out of the woman's side. She let out a high, keening cry.

"Samantha, you are being incredibly rude," Cameron chided. "I mean…we've barely spoken in months. I just paid you a compliment. Said you looked fucking fantastic. Yet you have nothing better to say to me?"

"Yes, sorry." She rolled back her shoulders. "I liked you better as a blond."

He laughed. "God, I missed you!" But then his head jerked to the port side of the yacht. "Gamble is climbing up…" He'd left the spotlight positioned on the ladder. "This part is about to get really good."

"Is this another experiment?" Samantha asked as she edged a bit closer to him.

"No, I'm done with experiments." He hoisted the woman up beside him. Because her feet were bound, she staggered a bit. "He's almost at the top of the ladder now…" He winced. "I hope the bastard didn't strip. There is some shit you don't want to see." He put down the bloody knife…and picked up a gun. For a moment, he studied the new weapon in his hand. "Cold, aren't they? Nothing intimate or personal about the blast of a gun, but still, it gets the job done." He was moving toward the side of the boat. Toward Blake. He dragged the woman with him.

"No!" Samantha surged forward, putting herself between him and Blake.

Cameron frowned at her. "What *are* you doing?"

"You aren't shooting him!"

He smiled at her…and then he put the gun to the woman's head. She whimpered.

"I talked to her a bit while I waited for you to arrive. Her name is Veronica Valentine. She's a graduate student at the university. She was working on her master's degree in psychology." His smile widened. "I told her I could teach her so much, especially about the psychology of violence. That's an area of particular interest to her."

Samantha didn't look at the victim, not again. Behind her, she could hear Blake climbing. The water was sloshing off him.

"The first thing I'll teach her," Cameron said, as if sharing a big secret, "is the value of life. You see, I think some lives are worth more than others. But, hey, that's just me." He raised his brows. "Let's see what the true-blue guy thinks. Is *her* life…" He shoved the blonde to the edge of the boat. "Is her life worth more to him than yours?"

And he threw the blonde over the side of the boat.

"No!" Samantha screamed. She lunged toward him, toward the side of the boat as she heard the woman splash into the water. She looked over the edge just in time to see Blake jump off the ladder and dive into the water after the woman.

"She sank like a stone." Cameron made his pleased

humming sound. "Another thing I learned about dear Veronica. The woman can't swim for shit."

Samantha leaped at him again, lifting up the knife Blake had given to her—

But Cameron pointed the gun at her head. "I figured you'd have a backup. It's just so…you."

And he thought he knew her. He thought he knew *everything* about her. While she'd profiled him, he'd profiled her. But which of them was better? Which knew the real truth?

"Drop it," Cameron ordered.

"You won't shoot me." *Look at me. Focus on me. Don't look at the water. Don't worry about Blake. Look only at me.*

His eyes narrowed for a moment, and then… "Oh, hell, you're right. If you're going to die, I swear, it will be personal. It won't be with this damn thing." But in a fast move, using one of his Krav Maga attacks, he struck out at her hand. Her wrist broke, a fast, hard crack, and the knife skittered across the deck.

Then he grabbed her and yanked Samantha against his chest, holding her tightly. His breath blew over her cheek. "I'm sorry. I'll fix that wrist, I promise." He actually sounded remorseful. "I swear, it wasn't payback for you breaking my nose. I just had to get rid of that knife before you decided to be *too* brave."

"I don't need your promises." She risked a desperate glance over the boat, toward the ladder. *Toward—*

"What do you need? Your partner?" He gave a sad shake of his head. "Too bad. Blake went after her. He chose *her*, even though he had to know I was up here, armed, and would be all alone with you." Cameron backed up, moving them away from the side of the vessel, and he hit a button near the wheel. Immediately, she heard the grinding of the anchor being lifted up. "He chose her, and I get to keep you. I warned him that you would be mine again."

He had no clue. "I'm not a thing to be kept." Her wrist throbbed, the pain making her back teeth grind together, but she thought it had been worth it. She'd distracted him...so he hadn't seen when Josh appeared for a moment, his tank gliding near the surface as he went after Blake and the victim.

When you have a team you can count on, everything is different.

"Even if Blake gets her back to the surface, we'll be gone." The automatic anchor was still grinding away as it lifted on its chain. "We'll be—"

She slammed her forehead against his and heard the crunch of bones. *I hope I just broke your nose again. After last time, you should have seen that move coming.* "Guess what?" She jabbed her elbow into his ribs, trying hard to break a few of them. "I'm not sorry, and I *won't* fix you."

He tossed her back, sending her hurtling down a small stack of steps, and then he surged over to grab the wheel. The anchor had stopped grinding. The boat was free to move. He shoved down the throttle and the vessel lurched forward. His laughter rang over the roar of the engine. "Nice one, Sam, but we're going to be alone soon, free and clear and—"

Blake leaped over the side of the boat. She'd known he was there, waiting, because she'd caught a glimpse of him clinging to the ladder. When the boat lurched, he erupted. He ran hard and fast, heading straight for

Cameron. Samantha scrambled to her feet, also charging for Cameron in the same instant.

Cameron glanced back. Surprise flashed on his face. "Tricky bastard!" He lifted the gun, pointing it toward Blake.

But Samantha drove her body against his. The shot fired but went wild. She and Cameron fell onto the deck, limbs tangling. The impact knocked the breath from her. Her head had slammed into one of the stairs, and for a moment the darkness around her deepened.

"Hurting you doesn't make me happy." Cameron yanked her to her feet, his hand around her neck, and the gun muzzle pressed beneath her chin. "So stop making me do this."

Blake had frozen.

The boat kept surging forward. With no one at the wheel, Samantha wondered just where the hell they would all go. *And how Josh and his team can keep up.*

Simple—they couldn't. But at least they'd saved the victim. From this point forward, she and Blake would be on their own.

"Listen up, Gamble. Listen very, very well. If I have to do it, I will put a bullet in Samantha. I will fucking *hate* it," Cameron confessed. "But I'll do it."

Blake's hands fisted. "There's no way out for you."

Cameron laughed. "There's always a way out. You just have to look in the right place to find it." He hummed again. "You let the blonde die, huh? I thought you'd splashed after her. But that must have been her, kicking, trying to survive. The instinct to live is so strong in some people. I've been surprised by how strong. They can withstand almost any pain, as long as they have the hope that they'll live. That they'll escape."

Chill bumps rose on Samantha's body.

"Drowning isn't an easy way to go. I've heard it's quite brutal. And *you* condemned poor Veronica to that fate. I'm truly disappointed in you, Gamble." He pulled Samantha even closer, and the gun muzzle just shoved harder beneath her chin. "Aren't you disappointed in him, Sam? Heroes don't let victims die."

And she knew... She *knew* how Cameron had come to be so twisted. Though the truth had been lurking in her mind for so very long. "It wasn't your fault." She stared at Blake as she spoke, but the words were for Cameron. "It wasn't your fault that they died. Just because you couldn't save them, it didn't mean that you were bad or evil."

His hold tightened on her. *"Samantha, stop."*

"Did your mother cry out for help? Is that what happened? Or maybe it was your father? The fire was raging, and you could hear them...but if you'd gone in, you would have died, too."

The muzzle pressed so hard that she felt the moistness of her blood.

"So you had to stay outside. You had to watch the fire. And that's not what a good boy would have done, is it?" Her gaze held Blake's. His face was locked in tense lines, as if he'd attack at any moment.

But he had to wait for the right moment. And she would try to give it to him.

"Heroes don't let people die, but they died...you had to watch it. Had to hear them and that changed you. I'm so sorry, Cameron." And she was. "I hate what you became. I wish I could have helped you." *Could have seen the truth.*

"They were screaming." He whispered the words.

"I tried to get in… I was outside, just coming home… I tried to get in, but the door was so hot. I didn't want to get burned. It was so fucking hot, and I could smell the fire, and then I could…smell them."

Blake edged closer.

"I didn't cry that day." He was still rasping out the words. "Not when the fire raged, not when the bodies came out. I should have cried, I knew it. Just as I should have tried to save them. It was always like a part of me was missing. The part that would have let me feel." The muzzle jammed harder beneath her chin. "I felt when I was with you, Sam. I felt, and then he took it all away."

"Put down the gun," Blake barked. He wore his jeans, wet and clinging tightly to his body. She didn't see any weapon on him, but that didn't mean he wasn't armed.

Cameron ignored him as he kept talking to her. "I connected with you. When I fucked you, I swear I felt *everything*. Joy, pleasure, love. I love you, Samantha, and when I have you, I can be normal."

"No, you fucking can't," Blake snapped at him. "You can just do a better job of faking it."

Cameron jerked.

"You attached to one person, but what you feel for her isn't love." Blake's voice seemed to thunder in the night. "It's some kind of sick addiction, an obsession. If you loved her, you wouldn't be holding a gun to her. If you *loved* her, you wouldn't have left damn dead bodies in her home. If you *loved* her—"

Cameron started laughing, and the muzzle moved from beneath her chin. "He doesn't understand you at all, does he, Sam?"

She stared into Blake's eyes.

Cameron pressed a tender kiss to her temple. "Does

he know about the man you killed when you were a child? About the way you felt—so good inside—when he died in front of you? How you held your father's gun, cradling it in your hands like it was a special present that night? And when you killed again—the first time you shot in the line of duty—all of those sweet emotions came back. I could see the truth in your eyes. You liked it, just as I like it. We're the same inside. He'll never understand that. He doesn't get to see you like I do. He doesn't know you like I do."

"You're right." Her voice was soft, tender. Sadness swept through her. "He doesn't."

The gun moved again—only this time, Cameron took it away from her completely, and he pointed it at Blake. Because Blake was just steps away, there would be no way for Cameron to miss at such close range.

Besides, he'd always been a good shot. They'd gone to the shooting range together...

"She doesn't really want a hero in her life." Cameron's voice wasn't a rasp now. It was strong, confident. Arrogant. "You were never what she wanted. You were just...a distraction. If you live in the dark long enough, you wonder what the light might be like." He laughed then. "I'll tell you the truth, though. The light is boring as fuck. It's much better to stay in the dark."

He was going to kill Blake. "I'm sorry." She needed Blake to understand. No matter what happened, none of the guilt could be his.

Alarm flared in Blake's eyes. "Samantha—"

But she'd already grabbed the gun, using her left hand, since the jerk had broken her right wrist.

She felt the shock rock through Cameron. She yanked hard, trying to wrench the gun from him.

He snarled at her and fought back, jerking on the gun. She swept her leg beneath him, taking him down, but he was still holding tight to her, and she fell, too.

The gun exploded.

It took Samantha a moment to feel the pain. The blast was so loud. Then…then she heard shouting. Roaring. Her name?

The fire came then, burning in her side. She put her hand on the wound, and blood pulsed through her fingers.

"Look what you made me do!" Cameron screamed.

He still had the gun. He was up on his knees, spinning toward Blake. But he was moving too slowly. Blake launched at him. Their bodies collided with a powerful thud. Blake drove his fist at Cameron, again and again. But Cameron was just taking the blows and laughing. Laughing—then attacking, as if driven by maddened strength.

The gun had flown out of his hand, toppled overboard. The boat was still flying over the water, going straight, heading God knew where. She needed to get control of the boat, needed to help Blake…

And I need to stop bleeding out all over the place.

Samantha grabbed the railing and hauled herself up. Pain burned from her right wrist. Her bare feet slid on the slippery deck, and she almost stepped right on the knife she'd had before. She scooped it up, her bloody fingers curling around the weapon.

Blake and Cameron were locked in a brutal battle. Both men were nearly the same size, the same strength, and their moves—their attacks were even the same. Both had studied the same fighting techniques. Fists pounded, bodies twisted and Samantha crept closer to them. "Stop!"

Cameron didn't stop. He drove the flat of his palm toward Blake's nose. Blake deflected the blow and came in fast with an upper cut.

But, at that moment, the boat hit something, a hard, rough jolt, and Blake went flying toward the port side. Using that moment to his advantage, Cameron rushed toward the wheel, and he came back with a long hook— the kind of hook you typically used when you were bringing your boat in at the dock and you needed to reach for the rope on top of the wooden pilings.

"I will cut you open," Cameron swore as he lifted up the sharp hook. "I'll make your death so painful that you'll beg me to end you."

He rushed right by Samantha, not even glancing her way. He didn't think she was a threat to him. Not injured, not bleeding...he didn't think she'd fight him then.

He was wrong.

Using her left hand, she drove her knife into his back, stabbing deep because he wasn't going to hurt Blake. He wasn't going to win.

He wasn't going to walk away.

He whirled toward her, his face slack with shock. "S-Sam?"

"Fuck you," she whispered. Her side was soaked with her blood.

His face contorted in fury. He drove that hook right at her. She backed away, slipping—and the hook came at her again.

"Samantha!" Blake bellowed.

But the hook hit her. It shoved her right over the side of the boat. She slammed hard into the water, her mouth open, and the waves took her down.

CHAPTER TWENTY

SAMANTHA HAD GONE *over the side of the boat*. Had that bastard gored her with the hook right before she fell?

Shit. Blake immediately killed the engine. The roar died away, the boat rocked and...

Silence.

Blake surged forward. Cameron was just standing there, clutching the hook, staring dumbly at the water below. Blake grabbed him from behind. He locked his arms around the bastard and heaved him back. But Cameron seemed to wake up from his stupor. He swung the hook at Blake—

Blake slammed the guy's head into the railing. Then Blake grabbed the fucking hook, he yanked it right out of Cameron's hands and he shoved the hook up against the bastard's throat.

Cameron stared up at him—and laughed.

"You're done, asshole," Blake gritted out.

"What to do...what to do?" Cameron taunted. "Do you go save the girl? Because I sank my hook so deeply into her..."

Nausea rose in Blake's throat, threatening to choke him.

"Do you play the hero that she's always *thought* she wanted, the one rushing to her aid? Do you dive deep and save her, before she's swallowed by the water?"

He looked over the railing, searching frantically for Samantha, but he didn't see her.

"No screams for help," Cameron said, and there seemed to be…worry…in his voice. "She's under the water." His voice rose. "You have to get her."

He damn well knew it. But he didn't have anything to secure Latham.

"Get her or hold me…you're running out of time. Tick, tick, tick…can't do both. Be the hero or be the agent. Do your job or save the woman that I know you fucking love."

Son of a—

He grabbed Latham's head again. This time, he drove the guy's face into the side of the wheel. Once, twice, three times. Latham's body went slack, and Blake dived for the side of the boat. He jumped in because there was no choice for him. He had to get Samantha. He had to find her. Fear was eating him alive. He dived into the water, then cut right back to the top. "Samantha!" Where the hell was she? *"Samantha!"* He sank beneath the waves again, swimming frantically. He struck out with his hands, searching for her. The waves beat at him, surging hard against him as he swept the area. But she wasn't there. And he wasn't leaving, not until he found her.

I should have jumped in right away. I should have found her. She is my priority. I need—

He touched her. At first, he didn't even realize it was her. It felt like he'd grabbed seaweed, but then he realized it was her hair. *Floating up, just like Tammy White's hair had floated around her.* A dead woman, staring back at him…

No! Samantha wasn't dead. He wouldn't let her die.

The bay wasn't going to be her watery grave. In the murky depths, he couldn't see her, but he touched her. *Samantha.* He pulled her close, and he kicked, surging them up toward the surface. Surging them up—

And he heard the boat's engine, kicking to life once more. The son of a bitch was going to flee.

Be the hero or be the agent.

He'd be the man who'd do anything for the woman he loved. That was who he'd be. Always.

Was Samantha breathing? He pulled her close, squeezed her tightly. "Baby, no, don't do this—"

She coughed out water. Hell, yes, she was alive. His heart started beating again. Relief had him feeling damn near dizzy. He pressed a desperate kiss to her cheek. "You're going to be okay. I'll get you help, baby. I swear—"

The spotlight swept across the water. Latham wasn't leaving. Not yet. He was—

The spotlight stopped on Blake, pinning him there as he kept Samantha's face above the water. And he knew what he had to do. "She needs help, Latham!" Blake yelled.

The light didn't waver. "You broke my fucking cheekbone."

So very glad I did. "Don't leave her like this! She's hurt—badly! *You* did this!"

"She did it to herself." The boat's engine was growling, but Latham wasn't leaving. Maybe he couldn't leave. *Maybe he can't leave Samantha.* Love, addiction, obsession—whatever it was…that connection was chaining him in place.

"Do you really want her to die?" Blake roared.

Silence.

Asking a killer...to save a life. How fucking twisted did things get?

But he was desperate, and for Samantha...he'd do anything.

"Bring her to the ladder."

He swam for the ladder.

"Don't..." Samantha's whisper, barely a breath. "He's...going to kill you."

He was already a sitting duck. The guy would have a perfect shot at them both because Blake was betting the bastard had another gun up there. Latham was always the prepared sort. He wouldn't leave something like that to chance. "Maybe he'll try, but I don't think he'll kill you." And in the end...wasn't that what mattered? That she made it out of this nightmare?

"No," Samantha pleaded, still coughing up water, "don't!"

But he swam closer to the side of the boat.

"Bring her back up." Latham was back to being calm. In control.

Blake climbed the ladder, and Samantha lay limp in his arms. She didn't speak again, and when he put her down on the deck, her eyes were closed.

Latham had a gun pointed at him. *Just like I thought.*

"I learned from Samantha," Latham admitted, lifting up the weapon. "It's best to always have a backup. Isn't that the FBI way?" He looked down at Samantha but kept the weapon trained on Blake. "She's breathing. I can see the rise and fall of her chest." His relief seemed real. Or at least, as real as Latham could get.

"She's breathing, but she's bleeding out." Blake didn't see a slice from the hook. Just the wound from the gunshot. Had the hook missed her when she'd gone overboard?

"I'll take care of her. I always do." Latham bent and brushed his fingers over Samantha's cheek. "Thank you for bringing her back to me." He looked up at Blake and smiled as he rose to his full height. "It's just a pity that her eyes aren't open so that she can see this last moment. I had so hoped she'd be able to witness it."

The bastard was going to kill him. Blake tensed, knowing he'd have only one chance— "Goodbye, Agent Gamble."

Samantha rolled to her side, grabbing Latham's legs. Her arms locked around them, and she yanked, hard. He let out a sharp cry, falling back and slamming down beside her onto the deck.

And in the next breath, Blake was on the bastard. He grabbed the gun and shoved it right between Latham's eyes. "Have fun in hell," Blake whispered.

Latham's eyes widened—and there was no missing the fear there.

"Blake?" Samantha's voice. Weak and worried. "Blake...you can't..."

And the fear eased from Latham's gaze. His lips even started to curl into one of his taunting smiles. "That's right, you *can't* shoot me. Not like this. Not when I'm unarmed. It's not what good *agents* do. And what will Samantha think of you? She'll never look at you the same way. She'll—"

Fuck you, Latham. "I told her I was killing you long before we ever stepped foot on your damn boat." Now it was his turn to smile at the bastard. "But a fast death would be too easy for you. After all you've done, all the lives you've destroyed, you have to pay first."

He heard the shriek of sirens in the distance. Was that Lewis, coming to the rescue? He'd been stationed near shore with a Coast Guard team at the ready. Sound traveled so easily on the water. Had they heard the gunshot? Decided to rush to the rescue? Or had Josh's team radioed them when they'd gotten the blonde out of the water?

"Going to torture me?" Latham taunted. "And here I didn't think that was your style."

It's not, but for you, I'd make an exception. "Hell for you," Blake said quietly, "is going to be a cell. It's going to be solitary confinement. It's going to be you, locked away from everyone else for years. No more games, no more experiments…just a small cell. A cage that you'll be trapped inside as you slowly rot away."

Then he heard the slosh of water. Blake glanced toward the ladder.

Josh tossed his mask onto the deck. His breath panted out. "Hung on to the side…when this bitch took off…" He climbed forward, chest still shaking. "Thought you needed…backup."

He'd had backup. Even shot, nearly drowned, Samantha had been there to watch his back.

"Samantha!" Latham's voice. Sounding…lost. "What's happening?"

"You're going away, Cam," she whispered back. But her voice was filled with so much pain.

Samantha?

Josh rushed forward. He put his hands on her stomach. "She needs help."

"Sam?" Now even Latham was afraid.

The bastard should be.

If Samantha died, Blake would make sure every day of the man's life was agony.

WHEN SAMANTHA OPENED her eyes, she was in a white hospital room. Sunlight poured through the window on the right, trailing over the bed, and on her left…

Blake sat there, holding her hand.

She stared at their linked hands a moment, remembering the night before. The water, the boat, the gunshot blast. She remembered floating in the water, not having the strength to kick up, and then…then she'd been in Blake's arms.

"You're awake." His voice was rough, a little ragged. "Are you in pain?"

A little, but a little pain meant she was alive, so Samantha wasn't about to complain. "Where is he?"

Blake's dark brows rose. "Latham? He's currently enjoying the hospitality of a jail cell, one guarded by three FBI agents and half of Lewis's men. They're making sure that he doesn't get away." He leaned closer to her. His green eyes were turbulent, brimming with emotion. "You weren't supposed to be hurt. You weren't supposed to nearly die for me."

She swallowed. "It…was just a flesh wound." She tried to smile at him. "Don't be so dramatic."

He didn't smile back. "You nearly bled out before help could arrive. They had to airlift you here. You almost died out on that godforsaken boat."

She didn't remember that part. She remembered being on the deck, seeing Josh climb up the ladder. Then he'd been pushing down on her wound, and the pain had been so intense that she'd blacked out. Or so she'd thought.

"I don't want you risking yourself for me, not ever again."

Samantha shook her head, moving it against the pillow. *Can't make that promise.* "I realized…something…" *At the bottom of that bay.* "It wasn't…my fault…that my father died."

"Baby?"

"When you love someone…you want to keep them safe…it's not a sacrifice." *Not even a little bit. No matter the pain.* "It's a…choice… It's love." *He was her choice. Always had been. Always would be.* "I love you."

He pressed a quick kiss to her lips. "Samantha, you own my soul. You have from the moment we met. But, please, I am begging you…don't ever scare me like that again, okay? Next time, let the psychopath shoot *me*. Let him throw *me* overboard, let—"

"We stopped…him?"

Blake nodded.

"Good." *There would be no more deaths on her conscience. No more new additions to her nightmares.* "Now…what?"

"Now you get better." He pressed another kiss to her lips. "Now you get stronger. Now you get back to ass-kicking form." Another kiss. "And when you do… you marry me."

What? That marriage bit hadn't necessarily followed the order she'd expected.

Gruffly, he said, "When you're out of the hospital, I'll do it right…down on one knee, flowers, candy, *anything*. I just want to be with you. I want to love you every single day of your life. I want to give you good memories, I want to make good memories *with you*. I want to show you that the world is more than the night-mares we have…that it can be so much more."

She already knew that. After all, she had him. "I'll say yes—" her fingers squeezed his "—when you get around to asking right."

He smiled at her, a wide smile that lit up his gorgeous eyes. "I'll make sure I remind you of that."

He would.

Not that she'd need reminding. "Chocolate," Samantha said, considering this for a moment. "When you ask…make sure I have chocolate on hand."

His smile slowly slipped away. "I will give you any-thing you want, *always*. Just make me one promise…"

She stared into his eyes.

"Don't ever leave me." She could hear his fear. "Cam-eron was wrong about you, baby. So wrong. There isn't anything dark or tainted about you. You're what's good in the world. You *are* my world. And I need you. I need you to keep going. I need you to help keep me strong. I just…need *you*."

Just as she needed him.

"I love you, Samantha Dark. I'll always have your back. I'll always be at your side."

And she believed him. She trusted him.

Completely.

"Partners for life?" she whispered.

"Partners forever." His lips took hers.

EPILOGUE

SAMANTHA'S HEELS CLICKED on the hard floor as she headed back to see the prisoner. A maximum security facility meant that she'd been searched, ID'd and triple checked until she was close to screaming.

But...

Procedures were procedures.

The guard in front of her typed a code into the keypad and finally—*finally*—she was escorted to the room that waited. The prisoner was already seated, seated and cuffed to the table.

"Hello, Cameron," Samantha said, making sure to keep her voice mild. "You're looking well."

He smiled at her. "Utter bullshit." He glanced down at the orange jumpsuit. "I look horrible in this."

The black was gone from his hair. His tattoo—turned out it had been temporary henna ink—was long gone, too. Clever Cameron. That tattoo had actually hidden the scar she'd given him from their first battle, when she'd sliced at him with the letter opener. Since his arrest, he'd lost his extra weight, trimmed down, and were it not for that garish prison uniform...

He would have looked just like his old self.

"How do you feel?" Cameron asked her. His gaze swept over her, and there was more than a glint of concern in his stare. "All healed?"

"From your attempt to kill me?" She tilted her head and considered that. "Yes, I'm good, thanks."

The guard watched them, standing just a few feet away.

"You look very official," Cameron announced. His fingers drummed against the table. "Back with the FBI?"

"Um, yes…" She sat down in the chair across from him. "Bass was grateful to me. Turns out that people appreciate it when you save their lives."

"Imagine that."

"So he thought it would be…advantageous…to have me back at the FBI. At first, I wasn't so sure about the idea." She shrugged. "But then he told me that I could open my own unit, of sorts. You see, he wants me to help train a new breed of profilers there."

He lifted one brow. "Tell me more."

That's why I'm here. "He thought my connection to you was a weakness. That because of our personal history, I couldn't do my job right."

"But here I am…" He glanced around. "In fucking hell."

"Indeed." She smiled at him and ignored the pang in her chest. "So that got me to thinking…and it got *him* to thinking…perhaps the personal connections that people have to killers, well, those connections aren't a hindrance. They can be an advantage. They can show us more about how to think like a killer, how to capitalize on a killer's weaknesses. How to bring down those killers…"

He leaned back in his chair. "You were faking when Gamble brought you back on the boat. I thought you were *dying*, but you were—"

"Using your emotions—the few you can actually

feel—against you?" She nodded. "I was. Don't get me wrong. I'd been shot and I'd swallowed a gallon of the bay, but I was still strong enough to get to you." She stared straight at him. "And I did."

His jaw tightened. "What about the girl? I've been trying to puzzle that out—"

She was sure that save had pissed him off. He'd planned so carefully. *We planned better.* "We had a team in the water—" *under the water* "—and when you tossed her overboard, they were there to make sure she survived."

He glanced away from her. "So that's it? You're here to tell me about your new job, to gloat because you won—"

"It was never a game." Her voice was soft now.

Cameron looked back at her. "Wasn't it?" He, too, had lowered his voice. As if the place weren't full of cameras and audio equipment—sophisticated equipment that would pick up every word they said.

"We found the real Brock Chambers." Another death. "His body—or rather, what was left of it—washed ashore in Key West."

Cameron smiled. "Guy had a real great boat. Just couldn't help myself."

She didn't smile back. "I think you could have, Cam. That's what hurts me the most. I think, all along, that you could have stopped yourself. You said it was about me. About losing me, but I wasn't what held you in check all of those years."

His lashes lowered. "Yes, you were." And the arrogance was gone from his voice. "I always felt the hunger inside of me. I could feel it growing every single day.

I thought...if I learned more, if I studied more, I could figure it out. I could stop it. I could *beat* it."

She waited.

"Then I met you." He looked up. "You made me... not feel like the freak in the room. You looked at me as if I were normal. I wanted to *be* normal."

"You didn't kill anyone for years. You made it all that time—"

"Everyone has a trigger." He rolled back his shoulders. "You were mine." His gaze swept over her face. "Did you think he was going to kill me?"

Blake.

She didn't answer.

His lips twisted. "Would you have still loved him if he did?"

"Yes." That truth, she would give to him.

His Adam's apple bobbed. "You have him fooled, don't you? You have them all fooled. They think you're so good, but the truth is...you were always just like me."

And that was why she'd come. Why she'd needed this last visit with him. Before she started working on Bass's new profile unit, she'd had to look at the mirror of herself and see if what Cameron said was true.

A personal link to a sadistic killer...could anyone touched by that darkness live with the taint?

Could you go on, have a normal life...be strong? Be happy?

She looked into his eyes. The friend she'd known...it was as if they were meeting for a little catch-up lunch. Friend, lover, killer.

"Goodbye, Cameron." Now she was sad. Samantha stood.

"That's it?" He shot to his feet, too, but the cuffs didn't let him go far.

The guard tensed.

"You gave me a confession for the murder of Brock Chambers. I needed that."

A growl built in his throat.

"And you let me look in the mirror one last time." He'd been her mirror, and she'd seen the truth. "I'm not you. I'm not bent or twisted, and there is no trigger that is going to push me over some edge." She smiled at him. A real smile. "I'm going to stop killers like you. I'm going to stop the ones that want to cause nightmares and pain. And I'm going to use the ones they love to do it. Every killer has a weakness. I'll find them. I'll use them. And then the monsters out there…" Samantha straightened her spine and lifted her chin with determination. "They'll eventually wind up in a place like this, just like you." She nodded toward the guard. "Thank you, I'm done."

She walked away.

"Samantha!"

It felt as if a weight had been lifted from her shoulders.

"Samantha!"

She didn't even have to look back. She'd made her choice.

She didn't need to look into a broken mirror any longer.

HE WAS WAITING for her outside. Waiting in the sunlight. When she saw her, Blake hurried forward. "You okay?"

She smiled at him. For him. "I'm better than okay."

She was free. Free to love, free to be happy, free to live her life in the light.

She rose onto her toes and kissed Blake.

Her partner, her friend…

Her lover.

A man she could trust completely. A man she could love—completely.

Without any fear of ever sliding into the dark.

* * * * *

THE GATHERING DUSK

There are so many people that I need to thank for this book.

For Nick—thank you for walking with me along the beach of Fairhope as I plotted my story and got into the mindset of a killer. Thanks for going with me as I searched for the perfect spot to dump a body...as if that is just a normal activity for us.

For Joan—thank you for the catches on my story. Thank you for always having such a keen eye and for understanding romantic suspense so well.

For Jack—thank you for your patience. You know that your mom often gets lost in her own mind, and you know exactly how and when to pull me back to reality.

For Denise and Kayla—thank you for your editorial insight! It is a pleasure working with you both. I know that you help to make my writing stronger.

And, finally, for my readers— thank you for going on this journey into the dark with me.

CHAPTER ONE

SAMANTHA DARK DIDN'T let her fear show. In her job, there wasn't supposed to be any room for fear. FBI agents were tough and strong and they got the job done—no matter the circumstances. They didn't let nausea twist in their stomachs. They didn't let doubt bloom in their minds.

An FBI agent didn't hold a weapon with too tight a grip with a pounding heart.

But I am.

Samantha tried to steady herself. She forced herself to take a deep breath. Her eyes never left the house nestled so perfectly on the little cul-de-sac. The house with the tall, swaying pine trees in the front yard. The house that had all the blinds pulled down to cover every single window.

It's just a house. Just a house on a street.

"You ready, Samantha?"

At the deep, rumbling voice, Samantha gave a nod. Her new partner, Blake Gamble, was right at her side. He didn't seem scared, didn't seem to be filled with reservation and apprehension—but then, from what she could tell, Blake didn't have room for those kinds of emotions.

She tore her gaze from the house just long enough to send an assessing glance his way. Blake was tall, about six foot two—maybe three inches—and muscled. His wide shoulders told her that he might have played football back in the day, and his hard strength assured Samantha that her new partner worked out far more than the FBI required.

He was handsome, in a rough, rugged way. Square jaw, high cheeks, sensually curved lips...and the greenest eyes that she'd ever seen. Those green eyes were a sharp contrast to his dark, almost perfectly arranged black hair.

Tall, dark and dangerous. Only, Blake wasn't the bad guy...he was the good guy. The real true-blue sort. The kind of a guy that a person could count on... *The kind of partner you need at your side when you're worried the situation is about to go straight to hell.*

She swallowed down her fear and lifted her chin. "I'm ready." They had the all clear to go into that little house, and waiting longer—well, that would just give the man inside a chance to either attack or flee.

He won't get away from me.

George Farris lived in that quiet house on the cul-de-sac. George Farris...a twenty-seven-year-old software designer. A man who hadn't shown up for work in the past two days and who had withdrawn from his friends and his family after exhibiting increasingly paranoid behavior. A man who...

Fits my profile to a T.

"You still think he has the victim in there?" Blake asked her.

"Missy Johnson has been missing for two days." Her voice was barely a whisper. "If he's our guy...he has always kept the victims alive for seventy-two hours."

That was the reason they were moving in on the house. They couldn't afford to waste time. This was it.

"Then let's do this," Blake said, his voice little more than a growl. "I've got your back."

They advanced toward the house. She could see a car sitting in the driveway. Her left hand touched the hood, found it warm. *Used recently, so our perp is probably inside.* It was late afternoon, and there wasn't exactly a way to hide their advance with so little cover. Those twisting pine trees weren't going to cut it—

"Movement," Samantha whispered as her body tightened. "Curtain near the right front window just slid back. He's watching us."

And he'd either panic and try to run…

Or he'd attack.

I made the profile on this guy. He's been deteriorating, losing his humanity more and more. He won't go down easy. He—

The front window shattered and the muzzle of a gun poked through the broken glass. "Go!" Samantha yelled. "Weapon!"

She ducked and ran, even as Blake did the same. A bullet thudded into the ground near her foot, and she felt the heat of another as it seemed to lance across her arm. She ran fast and hard, and she got to the front door even as bullets kept flying. Blake was right behind her.

"FBI!" Samantha shouted. "Put down your weapon!"

If his victim was inside, George Farris could be turning that gun on her.

She nodded toward Blake. One powerful kick, and he had the door flying inward as the lock shattered beneath his foot. She heard the frantic thud of foot-steps running inside and then—

Samantha slammed into Blake, knocking him down just as a bullet sank into the wood near his head.

"Fuck," his deep voice rumbled.

"You're welcome," she said, then jumped back to her feet.

George was rushing down the hallway—she could see the back of his red hair.

"Farris!" Samantha yelled. "Stop! Put down your weapon—"

He swung toward her, his eyes seeming to bulge from his face. Terror and fury strained the lines of his pale skin and—

He's firing.

"Don't," Samantha ordered, but he wasn't listening. *Please, don't.* He was going to shoot. Shoot her, shoot Blake.

Her finger squeezed the trigger, two fast pops that came from a hand gone dead steady. George's mouth dropped open in shock even as a red circle of blood appeared on his chest. His gun fell from his fingers and he staggered back. George slammed into the white wall behind him, and a picture frame fell to the floor, shattering.

Blake rushed forward and kicked the weapon farther away from the downed man. Samantha stood there, her gaze locked on George as he shuddered. Blood bubbled at his lips.

"Where's the victim?" Blake barked at the man. "Where is Missy Johnson?"

Samantha shoved past the shock that had held her in

its tight grasp. She rushed toward George. His bloody lips were curling. He was *smiling*.

"Where is she?" Samantha demanded.

But...

George started wheezing. When she'd fired, there had been no time to think—she'd just reacted. He'd been aiming for her heart and she'd aimed for his.

She hadn't missed.

The wheezing lasted only an instant, and then there was no breath at all. No gasps. No shudders. He was just gone.

Her desperate gaze shot toward Blake. His face was grim, his green eyes flashing as he stared back at her. "Self-defense," he gritted out. "You saved our asses. You—"

Something crashed—a sound that had come from down the hallway. Her head jerked at the noise, but Blake was already moving. He raced down the hallway with his gun drawn. Samantha was right behind him, and she caught sight of the shut door on the left.

There was a thump from behind that door. A pitiful moan and then...

Blake grabbed the knob and thrust the door open. She was two steps behind him and when they got inside that little room, all of the breath left her in a quick rush.

Missy Johnson was huddled in the corner, naked, her hands and feet tied, a gag in her mouth. Cuts covered her body, but she was alive.

Alive.

They'd gotten to her in time. "It's okay," Samantha said, voice soft. She put her gun in its holster and lifted her hands, palms out, toward the terrified woman. "We're FBI agents, and we're here to take you home."

THE LITTLE CUL-DE-SAC was illuminated by a thousand lights.

Samantha sat in the back of an ambulance, her gaze on the house. She'd protested—adamantly and, apparently, uselessly—but the EMT had insisted on checking out her arm.

Turned out that one of George's bullets had grazed her. Not bad enough for stitches, but the EMT had still wanted to patch the wound.

Cop cars and FBI vehicles had swarmed. Yellow police tape was already up, sectioning off the crime scene. Neighbors were out, staring in that kind of numb, shocked horror. The kind that said, *This shouldn't have happened here. We live in a good neighborhood. It's a safe place.*

When would people see? Sometimes, there were no safe places.

News crews were there, too. Reporters who were broadcasting live, almost giddy with the rush of covering a story this big.

A serial killer—taken down by the FBI. A victim rescued. A nightmare ended. Talk about a killer story.

And right in the middle of all that chaos…well, there was FBI Executive Assistant Director Justin Bass. The guy's chest was puffed out, and his authoritative voice rang out clearly as he assured the reporters that his crack team had been confident of their success in locating Missy Johnson, that he'd known all along they would be bringing that victim back alive.

Samantha just shook her head.

"You're all done, Agent Dark," the EMT said, her voice cheerful, her brown eyes gleaming.

"Thanks." Samantha slid out of the ambulance, her

movements slow. Bass was in charge of the circus out there, and she knew he liked to be the only one to handle the press. That was more than fine with her. Samantha didn't exactly enjoy the limelight.

The coroner had arrived earlier, and now she saw the black body bag being wheeled out. The reporters turned as one swarm to get video footage.

Samantha sucked in a sharp breath, one that chilled her lungs.

"You okay, Samantha?"

His voice. A voice that she'd be able to recognize anywhere, anytime. Dark and deep, a voice that sank right beneath a woman's skin.

And made her think about things that—under the circumstances—she shouldn't.

Her head turned and she found herself staring up into Blake's green eyes. Concern was on his face, worry in those eyes.

Samantha made herself smile for him. "Barely a scratch. I didn't even need stitches." The sun was starting to set, and the sky behind Blake was a dark red.

"I'm not talking about your arm."

She lifted a brow.

"That wasn't an easy scene." He stepped closer to her. Instantly, she seemed to feel the heat that swept out from his body. "Taking a life is never easy."

No, it wasn't. Her gaze slid away from him and went back to the house. Except for the broken window out front, the place looked so normal. *But it isn't normal. George Farris probably killed two women in that house.*

I killed him in that house.

Blake's hand rose and touched her shoulder, such a light, careful touch. "Samantha?"

She swallowed. "It's just a house." She turned away from the house and began walking back toward the SUV that waited. They'd driven over together when her profile had paid off and she'd been so sure that George was the man they were after. So sure...

"It's just a house," she murmured without looking back again. "Just a house on a street." *And I killed a man inside.*

She made it to the vehicle. Samantha was reaching for the driver's-side door, but Blake's hand rose, and his fingers—slightly calloused—curled over hers. Startled, she glanced up at him.

"Why don't I drive?" He smiled at her, what she thought of as his million-dollar smile. The smile Samantha was sure had charmed too many women.

She wasn't in the mood to be charmed.

Before she could speak, he leaned in closer to her. "It was...your first, wasn't it?"

Samantha gave a jerky nod. It was her first time to kill in the line of duty. She'd shot a suspect before, but it had been a flesh wound. Nothing like this. "I didn't have a choice."

"No." His voice was even rougher. "You didn't." His smile slipped away. "Why don't you let me drive?" Blake said again.

"You're such a nice guy." That was what everyone said about him. She knew exactly what he was trying to do. *Take care of the agent before she falls apart.* "I promise you, I'm in no danger of breaking."

"Never thought you were." He held her stare. "But leaning on someone else isn't a crime."

No, it wasn't. "Drive," she ordered, and Samantha hurried around the vehicle. She jumped into the passenger side. Pulled on her seat belt, then she just shut her eyes. She didn't want to see the reporters. Bass could keep dealing with them. She'd do her paperwork, close out the case, and she wouldn't focus on the way George Farris's eyes had looked when she shot him. The way the life had just drained out of them at the end. She *wouldn't* think about that.

A few moments later, she heard the engine crank. The vehicle backed up and moved away.

"You're wrong about me."

She didn't open her eyes. Samantha felt so weary. The adrenaline in her system had to be crashing—and the crash was taking her down with it. "Haven't you heard? I'm a profiler. I know people." She knew killers.

But then, she'd known all about killers for a very, very long time.

Since she'd been thirteen and she'd survived a night of blood and hell.

"You don't know me, Sam."

Sam. Just the way he said her name was palpable. Her eyes opened. They were walking a very thin line, she knew it. The attraction was there, just simmering between them. But FBI partners couldn't get personally involved. They couldn't sleep together. They couldn't give in to a hunger that had been there, right from the first touch.

"You're a former soldier," she told him. "Enlisted when you were eighteen. Then went to college, studied criminal justice. You fought the bad guys in the war, then you came home to fight the bad guys on our own soil. You requested to work in Violent Crimes because you're not afraid of a challenge—you want to take down the worst of the worst. A good-guy mentality at its finest." A hero mentality.

He drove in silence.

Her gaze slid to him, and she realized that his hard jaw was tightly clenched. A muscle jerked in his cheek. Uh-oh, someone didn't like being profiled.

Someone looked pissed.

"Sorry," she said. Sometimes, she just did that. Couldn't turn off her brain when she met someone. "People are like puzzles to me. I always... I have this need to figure them out."

He pulled off the road—just pulled right off that quiet highway until they were sitting on the shoulder. He shifted the SUV into Park and then turned to stare at her.

Her brows rose. "Blake?"

"You have me squared away in your head, don't you? The safe guy? The rule follower?"

"Um...there isn't anything wrong with that."

His fingers tapped along the steering wheel. His gaze had turned dark. Turbulent. And that hard stare of his drifted down to the bandage on her arm. "I don't like you getting hurt."

"I don't like being hurt." She tried to lighten the sudden, thick tension between them. She could almost see the line between them—a line they couldn't cross.

"When I saw your blood, I wanted to rip George Farris apart."

Tread carefully.

"The dead don't feel pain," she said. She'd given herself comfort with those words so many times over the years.

"No, that luxury is just for us, isn't it?" Now his gaze

had come back to her face. "You're damn good when it comes to killers. Don't know that I've ever seen anyone work quite the way you do. Bass and the other agents on our team—they weren't looking at Farris."

No, they'd focused their attention on another man, one county over. A man who was recently divorced, a loner now, but… *He didn't fit my profile. He still had too many strong ties. He hadn't been pulling away from society.* Not like George.

"You see things that others don't…" A slight pause. "When it comes to killers."

"You're saying I don't understand you?"

His fingers stilled. "Do you think I'm a killer?"

Oh, yes, she would need to tread *very* carefully here. "Just because you fought and fired in the line of duty, it doesn't mean—"

"You read my fucking confidential files." Anger thickened his voice. It was the first time his anger had been directed at her. She didn't like it.

"No." Samantha fought to keep the emotion from her voice. That was one of her talents. When it came to locking down her feelings and giving the world a perfect mask to view, she was at the top of the class. "I didn't." But his words had just confirmed what she'd suspected when she'd begun to build a profile on him.

I profile my friends. I profile my lovers. I can't turn it off. I wish that I could.

She cleared her throat. "We need to get back to the office." They were just outside of Richmond, and the drive back to DC wouldn't be an easy one, not at this time of the day. "Let's just go, okay?"

He hesitated, and Samantha thought that he was going to push her to determine just how much she really knew about him. She tensed, but he gave a grim nod. He cranked the engine once more. Shifted to Park and—

"Just because you have to fire," Blake said, not looking at her, "in order to save yourself and your partner... That doesn't make you a killer, either."

No, but it did make her someone...who had killed.

CHAPTER TWO

SAMANTHA DARK WAS a mystery.

Blake Gamble watched her as she shut down her computer and carefully arranged all of the items on her desk. She liked to position things just so…the stapler at a ninety-degree angle to her keyboard. The cup of pens just to the right of her mouse. And that little black picture frame…a picture of an older cop in his uniform…

Her fingers skimmed over the top of the photo, as if saying goodbye. She did that every night, right before she left the office.

Then she looked up and her gaze locked with his. There was no flash of surprise in her golden eyes. Absolutely beautiful eyes. Before Samantha, he'd never met a woman with eyes that particular shade. Her straight black hair fell around her face—a beautiful face, but one that she didn't adorn with any makeup. Not that the woman needed any makeup. Her lips were full, naturally a light pink. Her lashes were long, thick. Her cheekbones high.

She wore no-nonsense clothes, usually dress pants and a tailored top. Sometimes a suit. He suspected she was trying to hide her curves, and the first day that he'd come across her—wearing slim-fit athletic pants and a tight top while she worked out at the FBI gym—he'd realized her curves were damn close to perfection.

She'd been sweating, her hair had been pulled back, her bare feet with their bright red toenail polish had seemed to dance over the sparring mat and then—

Then she'd tossed her two-hundred-plus-pound opponent on his ass with barely a blink.

"You're staring."

He still hadn't gotten used to her voice. Soft and husky sometimes, sure with authority other times. But always—*always*—sexy.

He had such a serious problem when it came to Samantha Dark.

"It's rude to stare," she added as she pulled her bag onto her shoulder. "Didn't your mom ever teach you that?"

His shoulders rolled back. "My mom didn't have the chance to teach me much. She died when I was a baby."

She stilled. Sadness flashed on her face, coming and going in an instant. "I'm sorry." Her voice said she truly was.

He pushed to his feet. "Me, too. From all accounts, she was a pretty incredible lady. I wish I'd met her."

"Growing up without a parent... I know how hard it can be."

He'd grown up with a military father who hadn't exactly had a whole lot of room in his life for emotions— or for his young son. But Blake just shrugged. "I made out okay."

"I guess I did, too."

His eyes widened because that was the first personal tidbit she'd ever shared with him. But before he could speak, she was already hurrying toward the door. They shared that little office on the fourth floor of the DC FBI building, an office that looked out onto the busy street. Darkness had fallen, so right then, all he could see were city lights out of the glass, lights glimmering in the night.

Samantha opened the door—and the executive assistant director was standing there, his hand poised to knock.

Because Blake was watching Samantha so closely, he saw the sudden tension that swept through her body.

But Justin Bass just flashed Samantha a broad smile. "Excellent job today, Agent Dark. Got to say, you really impressed me. I was starting to think all the talk about you was just hype, but you proved yourself."

Blake found himself walking closer to Samantha.

Bass's light blue stare drifted to him. "How's this partnership working out?" He gave a low hum. "On paper, you two seemed to be very compatible. Different strengths, different weaknesses—opposites who should be nearly unstoppable when paired together." But his expression was thoughtful as it lingered on Blake.

"The partnership is perfect," Blake said, voice flat. His hand curled around Samantha's shoulder. "My partner saved my ass today. I'll be sure to return that favor for her soon."

Samantha glanced back at him. "Hopefully, you won't have to do that," she murmured.

His lips hitched. "Hopefully."

Bass cleared his throat. "Because there was a shooting... Well, you know how things work in the Bureau. There will be an investigation—just routine, of course—but, Agent Dark, you won't be in the field again until it's all concluded and—"

"I understand," Samantha said quickly. "I didn't want

the case to end this way, sir. I had hoped to bring George Farris in alive."

"Sometimes the perps don't want that." Bass's gaze had suddenly gone distant. "And there isn't a damn thing we can do about it." Then he nodded briskly. "Today was a win—you *saved* Missy Johnson. So go home, get some rest, and I'll call you when it's time for you to get back in here and use that mind of yours to help us catch the next twisted asshole out there."

Samantha brushed by him.

"Agent Dark?" Bass called, stopping her after she'd gone just a few feet. "I'm always curious… Once you get the profile in your head, once you know the killer, inside and out, how do you turn it off? Is there some kind of refresh button that you set in your head?"

She glanced back at Bass. "I wish there was. There's no way to turn it off. Every profile stays with me. Just as every killer does." She gave Bass and Blake a tight smile. "Good night."

She walked away, her spine straight, her shoulders squared.

Bass didn't speak until she'd slipped into the elevator. "You'll have to answer questions about the shooting."

"It was self-defense," Blake said immediately. "He was aiming for her. She was just faster."

Bass nodded. "That's what I wanted to hear." But he seemed to be hesitating.

"Sir? Is there something else?"

Bass's lips thinned. "Be careful with the way you watch her."

Blake blinked. "Excuse me?"

"You're partners. Only partners, understand?"

Then the executive assistant director walked away. Blake stared after him, aware that his hands had clenched into fists.

THE DOORBELL RANG, startling Samantha just as she was climbing out of the shower.

Who in the hell is that?

She toweled off as fast as she could. Then she jerked on a pair of jogging shorts, her bra and an old, faded FBI T-shirt.

The doorbell pealed again.

As she hurried down her narrow hallway, Samantha glanced at the clock. Nearly midnight. Not a normal time for a visit, not by a long shot.

Her heartbeat kicked up. Was it Blake? Coming by to check on her one more time? Being the good stand-up guy that he was? Maybe she was warmed a little by the thought.

Maybe.

Don't go down that path. It is the wrong path to take.

She pressed her eye to the peephole in her door. Blake wasn't out there.

Another man was. A man with stylish blond hair, chiseled features and dark, deep eyes that were staring straight back at her. She fumbled with the locks, then swung the door open. "Cameron? What are you doing here?"

Dr. Cameron Latham. All-around genius, all-around playboy. One of her best friends...

And her former lover.

Definitely a path I won't ever take again.

Cameron let out a long sigh. "I'm here because I had absolutely nothing better to do on a Friday night than to come by and drag you out of a..." His gaze darted to her wet hair. "Shower?"

She stepped back and glanced at his hands. "You have a bottle of wine."

"Yes, it's one of your favorite bottles." He smiled at her and marched right into her apartment. He made himself at home, the way he always did, as he headed into her kitchen. He put the wine down and grabbed two wineglasses from her cabinet. "I figured you could use it tonight."

She shut the door behind him and locked it. Then Samantha leaned back against the wood as she studied him. She and Cameron had met during their first year at Princeton. They'd both been fascinated with the human mind, both determined to unlock all the secrets that rested within a person. She'd gotten her PhD and then immediately joined the FBI, knowing that behavioral analysis—the behavioral analysis of predators—was the work that she had to do.

Cameron had gotten his PhD and gone off to rule in the hallowed halls of academia. He was currently the golden boy at Georgetown University.

She watched as he expertly opened the wine—very, very expensive wine because he had expensive tastes. "That's your favorite, not mine."

His mouth dropped open in mock surprise. "Is it? My bad. I must have grabbed the wrong bottle." He sighed. "Oh, well, guess we have to drink it now. The things I do for my friends."

Her lips twitched, but then she stared at him, feeling a heaviness in her heart. "You know, don't you?"

He poured the wine. It was a dark red. Deep crimson, like blood. "I may have watched the news," Cameron allowed. "I like to do that sometimes, you know. Stay updated on current events. It's a quirk I have." He lifted one brow at her. "A crime scene was featured on the ten o'clock news… Seems a very intrepid FBI agent stopped a serial killer tonight." His gaze slid to her arm. "Got a war wound, do you?"

"It's nothing," she said. She'd taken off the bandage before she got into the shower. Barely a scrape, more of a bruise, kind of like carpet burn. Only…in her case a bullet burn.

He lifted one glass toward her in a salute. "*You* saved the victim. I think that calls for a celebration."

She made herself walk toward him. Samantha pushed her hands down on the kitchen counter, flattening her palms and fingers. "I killed a man tonight."

He put the glass of wine in front of her. She couldn't look away from the bloodred liquid.

"Killed a man," he said, his voice deep, but emotionless. His shrink voice. The professor voice. "But saved a victim. Do you not still consider that a win?"

She didn't touch her wine. "It was my first kill in the line of duty."

He didn't speak. She could hear the ticking of her clock in the hallway. *Tick. Tick. Tick.* Time seemed slow right then, but when she'd shot George Farris, everything had been moving at super speed. The bullets had fired out of her gun so fast…

"How did it make you feel?" Cameron asked her.

Her eyes squeezed shut. "I shot him twice. Why did I shoot twice? Why not just once?"

"Maybe you wanted to make sure he was good and dead." A pause. "Or maybe you liked the way it felt to pull that trigger."

Her gaze flew open. "I did *not* enjoy killing him! He was going to fire at me! He would have shot me, killed me. I did what I had to do, I—"

He lifted his glass—now half-empty to show that he'd certainly been drinking his wine—and tapped it against hers. "And there you go."

She glowered at him. "I hate your mind games."

"No, you love them. Because I'm the only one who can play these games with you. Just as you're the only one who can play them with me." He gave her a smile, one of his rare, real smiles. So much of Cameron was a trick—she'd learned that over the years. His real emotions were often carefully bottled away inside.

Buried deep.

Like hers, Cameron's past wasn't pretty. But they'd moved away from the blood and death from their backgrounds. They'd reinvented their lives.

"You were having yourself a pity party." He took a long sip of the wine. "Unbecoming of someone like you. I was just reminding you of something you already knew, deep down. You didn't kill for some kind of thrill."

"Of *course* not," she gritted out.

"You didn't kill because it was easy."

Her breath caught.

"You did it because you had no choice, so let the guilt go. It'll wreck you if you don't. For the record, I'm not sure if I would enjoy you wrecked."

Her lips curled down. "I know you can be a smooth talker..."

"I don't have to be smooth with you. You can see me for what I am, can't you?"

She held his stare. "Yes." Bright spots and dark.

He nodded. "Now, how about you drink that wine? Then you can tell me all about how you worked up that absolutely killer profile." His smile flashed. "Sure looked as if Bass were having himself one hell of a time on the news. The guy loves a camera. He—"

Her doorbell rang again. The peal seemed to echo through her apartment.

Cameron's smile vanished. "Didn't realize you were…seeing someone, Samantha."

"I'm not." Dating wasn't exactly a priority for her. "You're the only asshole who comes ringing my bell at this hour."

"Obviously, I'm not." He put his glass down, and before she could move away from the counter, he was already marching for the door. "Let's just see what other asshole is paying you a late-night visit."

She spun around. *It's Blake. Blake.* She knew it with utter certainty. She'd mentioned her new partner to Cameron a time or two, but she hadn't gone into specific details with him. Normally, she and Cameron talked about everything. But Blake…

It's private. He's private. The way she felt about Blake wasn't something she'd been up to sharing with Cameron. Mostly because she hadn't wanted him to analyze her.

Ah, there you go, Samantha. Setting yourself up with a man you know you can't have. That's so classic of you. It's a protective instinct, and you know it. You don't want to risk actually giving your heart to anyone, so you focus on someone you can't have. Self-destructive. You've got to stop that… She could practically hear Cameron's voice in her head.

And she could *see* him opening her front door. "Cam, no—"

Too late.

Cameron frowned and said, "Who the hell are you?"

"About to ask the same question," came Blake's curt response.

She hurried toward them. Samantha locked her hand around Cameron's shoulder and pulled him back. "Cameron, this is my partner, Blake Gamble."

Blake's gaze was on her hand. On the hand that she realized was clutching Cameron's shoulder a little too hard. And her partner...he looked pissed.

Samantha swallowed and met his gleaming stare. "Blake, this is my friend Cameron Latham."

"*Dr.* Cameron Latham."

Her gaze jerked toward him.

Cameron flashed a shark's grin as he offered his hand to Blake. "The partner... I was wondering about you."

Oh, shit. She could feel her cheeks burn.

Blake took the offered hand, shook it once. But his attention barely stayed on Cameron for even a moment longer before that gleaming stare was back on her, raking over her body. "Didn't mean to...interrupt." Again, *pissed* was the word that came to mind for her.

"You didn't." She pulled her hand away from Cameron's shoulder. "Cameron saw the news and he came by to check on me."

"That's what friends do," Cameron murmured.

She rolled her eyes at him. Was he baiting Blake? Sure seemed that way. "Come inside, okay?" No sense having this chat in the doorway. She turned, not looking to see if they followed her. "I'd been meaning to introduce you two, anyway."

Samantha heard the click as the door shut. The floor creaked behind her.

"I realized Samantha was working with a new partner," Cameron said, "but she was being a bit...reserved with details about you."

She sat down on the bar stool near her kitchen counter. "Do you want some wine, Blake?" Now she glanced at him.

"Looks like I interrupted," he muttered. "Sorry." His expression was guarded.

Cameron slapped him on the back. "I think you do deserve some wine. After all, you helped to save the girl today, too. What a noble thing to do. True blue." His head cocked as he studied Blake. "Are you the heroic sort? I guess you must be...since you're an FBI agent and all."

"Cameron," Samantha warned. "Trust me, he *doesn't* want to be profiled."

Cameron laughed. "Tried that, did you?"

Blake's attention shifted to Cameron. "You're a profiler, too?"

"Oh, good Lord, no. I'm a professor at Georgetown." He shrugged. "But my PhD is in psychology, so I guess I do know a few things about the twisted paths that minds can take." He smiled. "Samantha and I shared that passion, you see. We always like to know what makes people tick."

"Do you now..." Not really a question from Blake.

But Cameron nodded. "Our minds are interesting. So complex. Take Samantha, for example. I know the way she thinks. Her first kill as an FBI agent. It wouldn't have been easy for her. She would have blamed herself. Would have wanted to punish herself. Why didn't she save George Farris? Why didn't she aim for his shoulder or his leg? In that split second, *why* didn't she make another choice?"

"You *aren't* helping," Blake growled.

Samantha's stomach felt hollow. *Why didn't I?*

Cameron blinked. "Samantha had to protect herself. Self-preservation is one of the strongest human motivators out there."

She could hear the clock ticking again. The tension in the room was uncomfortable. Too high. Too thick.

"Samantha hasn't mentioned your name to me," Blake said suddenly.

Cameron's eyes tightened, just the faintest bit. "Then you must not know her very well yet."

Hell. This mess was the last thing she needed. "I'm tired," Samantha said, rising from the bar stool. *I will kick both of their asses out.* After her day, she wasn't in the mood to deal with testosterone overload. "Thanks for the wine, Cameron, but I'm really done for the night."

He nodded. "Understandable." He walked to her and pressed a quick kiss to her forehead. "If you need me, just call."

Right. "Thanks."

"I can see myself out."

He always did.

Cameron gave a little nod toward Blake. "Agent... interesting to meet you. I'm sure our paths will cross again."

"Count on it," Blake said, the words almost a warning. He stood near the counter, just a few feet away from Samantha. He showed no sign of moving.

But Cameron left. He strode toward the door, even locked it behind him as he left.

Her breath whispered out. "It's been a long day..." Samantha began.

"Yeah, I know." His expression wasn't as hard. No more anger. Just...Blake. "My place is two streets over. I came by because I wanted... I *needed* to see for myself that you were okay."

"I'm a lot tougher than I look," Samantha said. "Promise."

"I have no doubt about that. I was the one who was worried."

"You don't need to be."

He moved closer to her, a gliding, stalking movement. Her shoulders tensed.

"You were involved with him."

"My...you cut right to the chase, don't you?" But then she waved that away. "My personal life really shouldn't—"

"It's in the eyes. The way a man looks at a woman he's known intimately. The way he wants her." Now his smile was mocking. "Trust me, it's something other guys see."

"Cameron and I *aren't* involved that way, not any longer." Not that she had to tell him this. But, well, just so they were clear. "He's my friend. And he's also a very good sounding board for me. When I have crazy theories, Cameron gets them."

"But he doesn't get you."

Her eyes narrowed on him. "There a reason you're asking these questions?"

His hand lifted, as if he wanted to touch her. His fingers were long and strong and she tensed.

Then Blake dropped his hand. "You're my partner. I care about you. I want you happy."

Happy. Now, that was an interesting word. She tried to remember the last time she'd been truly happy.

"Maybe I shouldn't have come here tonight." He rolled back his shoulders. "Didn't mean to cross any lines."

"Didn't you?" she whispered.

His thick lashes lowered. "I don't think I've ever met a woman quite like you."

His response surprised a laugh out of her. After everything that had happened that day, Samantha was surprised she *could* still laugh. "Is that good or bad?"

His lips twisted. "Could be both." Then his lashes lifted and he was staring into her eyes. So much emotion seemed to burn in his gaze.

She found herself holding her breath.

Blake lifted his hand. "Partners?"

Her hand slid against his. His fingers curled around hers and held. "I think we've already established that." Why did her voice have to sound so husky? That wasn't what she'd intended.

"You can trust me, Samantha. I hope you know that. I'll watch your back. I'll hold your secrets."

A quiver slid through her. "What makes you think I have secrets?"

His hand slowly slid away from hers. "Because I can see them in your eyes. Sometimes, you lower your guard, and I get a glimpse of the pain there."

She'd have to be far more careful. Samantha turned from him and walked toward the door. She fumbled with the lock and glanced back at him. "Good night, Blake. Thanks for checking on me."

He nodded. "Thanks for saving my ass." He gave her a little salute as he passed by her.

And Samantha found that she was smiling as she shut the door. It was strange. She wasn't sure if she *had* been happy in the last few months, maybe not even in the last year. Her job had consumed her too much. But she had the oddest suspicion…

Blake could make me happy.

Ridiculous, of course. Other people didn't have that power. If she wanted to be happy, that was her choice. She needed to stop letting the past eat her alive. She needed to stop seeing death and destruction everywhere.

She had to stop seeing monsters.

CHAPTER THREE

BLAKE HEADED OUT of Samantha's building, his steps quick, and his gaze darting around the dark street. An old habit, always checking the scene for threats. Some things that a soldier learned, well, he had a real hard time shutting off.

So maybe that was why he immediately spotted the too-thick shadow near the side of the building. His body tensed and his hand went toward his holster—

"Easy." Cameron Latham, *Dr.* Cameron Latham, stepped from the darkness. He had his hands up as he moved closer to the streetlamp. "I'm not one of your bad guys. I was just lingering because I wanted to talk to you."

He was still tempted to reach for his gun. Something about the guy rubbed him the wrong way.

"I care about Samantha," Cameron said, his voice low but carrying easily. "Like you, I just wanted to make sure she was all right. Taking a life wouldn't be easy for her, not with her past."

Her past. So the guy knew the secrets that Samantha carried. Another point that pissed off Blake. *One day, she'll tell me.*

Cameron stopped when he was about a foot away from Blake. "When you have a past like hers, I guess you do one of two things… You either let the violence enfold you…you let it *lead* you. Or you find a way to fight it."

Blake stared at him. "I don't think Samantha would want us talking about her past, not while we're just standing out here on the street."

Cameron's lips parted. He gave a quick little gasp of surprise. "True blue," he murmured. "What a noble thing to say…don't gossip in the streets. It isn't right."

Blake's jaw locked. This guy knew jackshit about him.

"Or maybe…maybe you just have no clue what I'm talking about." His head tilted as he seemed to assess Blake. "Don't worry, I'm sure she'll tell you," Cameron said, giving a little nod. "In time. Once she knows you better. My mistake. I thought the two of you were closer. It would have explained a few things to me."

Explained things? Blake raked his gaze over the guy. Cameron was close to his height, and he wasn't exactly the stuffy professor sort. The *doctor* looked as if he worked out, and he was dressed casually, in jeans and a black pullover sweater.

"Samantha is a special woman," Cameron added. "I like knowing that she's safe. Tell me, will you keep her safe, Agent Gamble?"

"Samantha does a good job of keeping herself safe."

Cameron looked back at Samantha's building. Blake followed his stare. Her apartment was on the top floor, the corner unit. As Blake watched, the lights in her home went dark.

"She used to hate the night," Cameron murmured. "But I guess that's something that has changed, too. Everything is changing now."

"You know…" Blake drawled, a hint of Texas twang

coming out of his voice, "I can't quite decide what you're trying to tell me tonight. So how about we cut through the games and bullshit—bullshit really isn't my thing—and you just spit out whatever it is that you want to say to me?"

Cameron smiled. "Straight shooter, huh? I bet Samantha respects that about you."

Blake took a step forward.

Cameron laughed and held up his hands again. "Easy, Agent Gamble. All I wanted to say… Samantha is one of the few people I call a friend in this world. It's important to me that she stays safe. I tried to talk her out of joining the FBI, but she wouldn't listen. That's Samantha…she always does just whatever the hell she wants." But he sounded admiring. "I don't like to think of her on the streets alone. I understand the type of criminals she's hunting. They don't play by the rules. They aren't…*straight shooters.*"

"I think you're underestimating me," Blake stated flatly. This guy had no clue who he really was.

"I like that Samantha isn't alone out there. I like that she may have someone she can trust. For her, trust is everything."

She doesn't trust me. Not yet. But I'm working on it.

"Good night, Agent Gamble. It was a pleasure meeting you."

And it was just weird meeting you.

Cameron turned away and began strolling down the sidewalk. He'd just slipped away from the lamppost, gliding back into the dark, when he paused. His head turned as he looked back at Blake. "I certainly hope… I hope there aren't any repercussions from tonight."

"Repercussions?" Blake repeated, voice careful.

"Um…yes, when you take a life, there's a domino effect. What will it do to the killer…to Samantha…? What will it do to the way she reacts to the world around her?"

"She's not exactly a damn killer."

"She's the one who pulled the trigger."

That didn't make her a killer. She was an FBI agent, and she'd just been doing her job.

Cameron gave a sad shake of his head. "What does the act do to the deceased and his loved ones?"

He had an answer for that one. "In this case, nothing. George Farris had no immediate family. His parents were both deceased. The guy started withdrawing from his friends months ago. He barely spoke to anyone at his job, so he sure didn't have any colleagues who were tight with him at the software company. Most people described him as quiet, intense. *Not* the affable sort. Farris isn't exactly going to have a packed funeral." There weren't a whole lot of folks grieving for the guy. It was hard to grieve for a sick, sadistic killer.

"Well, then I guess there isn't anything to worry about. One less monster on the street, and everyone can sleep better tonight." Cameron gave a little wave. "See you around, agent."

Unfortunately, he would.

Blake spared one last look toward Samantha's dark apartment, then he turned, hunching his shoulders, and he headed into the night.

SHE SAW HIS body on the news. Or rather, she saw the bag that held his body. A black body bag, zipped up, filmed and shown on TV by some unfeeling reporter. She'd recorded the footage when it first aired, just hitting the button on her remote because she was sure there was a mistake.

George wasn't dead.

But…

The chirpy reporter repeated the story for her, over and over, as she clicked the remote and replayed the scene. George's little house on that quiet cul-de-sac. And he was a suspected serial killer. A victim had been found—bound and gagged—in his house.

And George had been shot by an unidentified FBI agent.

Shot.

Killed.

She replayed the video once more, then hit the pause button. The image froze on her TV. Her eyes narrowed. Behind the body bag, she saw an ambulance. A woman was in the back of the ambulance, getting her arm tended to by an EMT. The woman wore black pants. A white button-down blouse. *There's blood on that blouse.*

Who was that woman?

Who in the hell was she?

If you're the one who took George, you're going to pay.

She'd make sure of that.

CHAPTER FOUR

SAMANTHA FLASHED HER ID at the guard who'd been stationed at Missy Johnson's hospital door. He gave a quick nod and Samantha straightened her shoulders. She'd woken up at 5:00 a.m., the image of Missy's bloody body in her mind, and she hadn't been able to go back to sleep.

Nightmares sucked. Especially when the nightmare that kept replaying in her head was the moment of the shooting. *Bam. Bam.* The shots fired from her gun and the life left George Farris's gaze again and again.

Clearing her throat, she stepped inside the hospital room. She immediately heard the beeps and buzzes from the machines near the bed. Samantha pushed the curtain aside and pasted a smile on her face. "Missy, I'm—"

A man stood there, tall, with graying hair and deep lines on his face. "My girl ain't seeing anyone right now! That damn guard was supposed to keep the reporters out and—"

"Dad…" A soft voice, coming from the bed behind him. "I don't… I don't think she's a reporter."

His blue eyes narrowed on Samantha.

She lifted her badge.

"She's the one who saved me," Missy said, her voice still soft, weak.

The man's expression immediately changed. In an instant, he went from being fierce and angry to wild with relief. He grabbed Samantha's hand, pumping it. "Agent Dark?"

She nodded.

He yanked Samantha forward and hugged her, hard enough to squeeze the breath from her. "You saved my little girl," he whispered. "Thank you."

He was too tall for her to see over his shoulder. He was big and burly, kind of like a grizzly bear, and when he finally let her ease back so that she could suck in a deep breath, she saw the tattoos that covered his arms.

"My little girl means the world to me," he added. "I owe you."

"No, sir, you—"

"You ever need anything, you call me." He yanked out his wallet and shoved a crisp, white business card into her hand. "My name's Robbie Johnson, and you can believe I'll pay my debt to you." His hard gaze told her he was serious.

She smiled at him and put the card into her pocket. "I appreciate that, Mr. Johnson, but I was just doing my job. As far as I'm concerned, Missy is the real hero. She survived that hell. She's a fighter."

His chest puffed up. "She gets that from me."

Samantha slipped around him. Bandages covered Missy's arms, and she could see the bulk of other bandages poking up beneath her hospital gown. "I wanted to see how you were doing."

Missy lifted the hand that wasn't hooked to an IV. "All stitched up." Dark shadows lined her eyes. "He's... he's really dead, right? I...I didn't dream that? Y-you shot him and—"

"He's dead," Samantha assured her. "He won't hurt you or anyone else ever again."

Missy's breath blew out on a rough exhale. The machines beeped faster. "I was just... I was running, doing my morning jog in the park. He was waiting in the lot, said he had a flat and asked if he could use my phone." Her eyes squeezed closed. "I didn't want to be rude. *Rude.* That's what I was worried about...being rude." Pain and shame flashed on her face. "I gave him my phone and h-he grabbed me." A broken laugh escaped her. "What in the hell was I thinking?"

Her father stiffened. "Missy..."

"I should have just gotten in my car, walked away. Why did I care about being *rude* to some stranger? What—"

Samantha stepped closer to the bed. "You didn't do anything wrong." She'd seen this before—victims blaming themselves. "He was a predator, Missy. You weren't the first woman that he took."

"Just the only one to survive," her father said darkly.

Cold words, but, yes, he was right.

Samantha hesitated as she stared at Missy. She shouldn't be there. Official questioning would come later, but...

I just needed to see her once more. To make sure that she really was okay. "Get some rest," Samantha told her. "You need to focus on healing." She turned for the door.

"Tell me...about them."

Her shoulders stiffened at that soft request.

"The other victims..." Missy murmured. "How did he pick them? Why? *Why did he pick me?*"

Samantha glanced over her shoulder. "You didn't do anything wrong," she said again, her voice calm but strong. "You have to understand that. You didn't cause the attack. You didn't draw his attention. George Farris was the one with the issues. You just—"

"I had the bad luck to get in his path?" Missy licked her lips. "I saw…on the news…" She pointed to the TV that was attached to the right wall of the room. "A guy on the news was saying that serial killers like Farris had…had victim types. Was I…his type?"

Samantha kept her expression blank. "He preferred young blonde women with delicate builds. Probably because he, himself, wasn't an overly big man. Women of that type—he found them easier to control."

Missy's father swore.

"I need to leave," Samantha said. "You *don't* need to hear this now. You have time, Missy. Time for all the bad details later. You survived. You got away—you have time for everything."

"He thought I was weak." Missy's hand fisted over her covers. "That's why he took me."

"No, he thought you were perfect."

Missy's head jerked up.

"He thought you were the perfect woman, Missy." There were things she *wouldn't* say right then, about the way that Farris had arranged the bodies of his victims, how he'd styled their hair. How he'd taken their pictures with such care after he'd mutilated them. "Men like him…they fixate on their ideals of perfection. Blonde, young, delicate like a ballerina—to him, that *was* perfection."

A tear leaked down Missy's cheek as she stared at the bandages on her arms. "I'm hardly perfect now."

Farris had liked to destroy the perfect beauty of his victims. As if he were punishing them.

When she'd created the profile for Farris, an unknown perp at the time, she'd theorized that he chose his victims for two main reasons.

One...their delicate builds made them easier to overpower. That was one of the reasons she'd known that she was looking for a killer with a slight build himself.

Two...he was striking out at someone in particular. Someone who had been personally involved in his life—someone who had been blonde and beautiful and who he had wanted to slice apart.

Samantha found herself heading back to the bed. She waited until Missy's gaze rose to meet hers, and then she said, "You survived a serial killer's attack. You were with him for over twenty-four hours. You have lived through a hell that few people can understand. Will you have some scars? Yes...but scars fade. The fact that *you* are a survivor will never change. Your spirit doesn't change. You are perfect. And soon enough, you'll see that for yourself."

Missy's trembling lips lifted into a smile. "You almost make me believe it."

"We all have scars, Missy." Samantha certainly carried plenty of her own. "They don't matter." She nodded to Missy—and to Missy's father—then Samantha headed for the door. She skimmed past the curtain, curled her fingers around the door handle and pulled it open.

The guard was still outside.

But he wasn't alone.

Blake was there, his brows raised, and his hands shoved into the pockets of his jeans.

Samantha stilled. "Eavesdropping, Agent Gamble?"

"Maybe. A bit."

Shaking her head, she marched past him. Her gaze was on the bank of elevators.

"Does Bass know you're here?" Blake asked her.

She jabbed the button for the elevator. "I was just checking on her. Nothing official about my visit."

"Hmm."

Samantha crossed her arms over her chest as she waited for the elevator to arrive. "What's that supposed to mean?"

"It means I don't think you're very good at staying away from a case, Bass's orders or not."

Fine. So she was a little guilty. "I want to find his trigger."

The elevator dinged.

"What?" Blake asked.

Samantha stepped into the elevator. "The woman who started it all. The woman who stirred all that hate inside of George Farris. The mystery blonde."

Blake didn't follow her. "Samantha…"

"I'm sure there's a clue to her identity in Farris's house. Sooner or later, I'll be cleared on this shooting." She threw up her hand, stopping the elevator doors before they could close. "And then I'm going to find her."

He stepped closer. "How do you know Farris hasn't already killed her? Maybe she was his first victim. Hell, when we start digging in that house, we might very well find her—buried in the basement or in the backyard or—"

"We could," Samantha agreed, cutting through his words. "And then I'll know who she is."

His head cocked as he studied her. "Knowing is important?"

"Knowing gives me his motivation. It helps me to

understand him. He didn't have to be a killer. Something changed him." *I think it was the blonde.* Samantha let her hand drop. "Better move back, Agent Gamble. You don't want to get hurt."

"Trust me, I don't exactly 'hurt' easily." One dark brow shot up. "Why am I suddenly 'Agent Gamble' to you?"

The doors closed before Samantha had to answer. *Because I'm trying to put some distance between us. You're getting too close to me. I'm letting you past my guard.*

I can't do that. It isn't smart. It isn't safe.

Not for either of us.

THE ELEVATOR DOORS dinged when they opened in the parking garage. Samantha hurried out, her gaze automatically sweeping the area. It was early, so the visitors' parking section contained only a handful of cars. The air was crisp and her steps seemed to echo against the concrete as she marched toward her vehicle.

She was almost at her car when she glimpsed the other woman. Standing against a heavy stone column, positioned *under* the security camera, the woman with the red hair and long black coat seemed to just be… waiting.

Samantha stilled. Her head turned as she moved to face the threat. "Are you all right?" she asked the woman. "Is there something I can help you with?" But her words were guarded because alarm bells were going off in her mind, triggering her instincts.

The way she's positioned, as if lying in wait… This isn't some woman who is having car trouble or—

"You're an FBI agent, aren't you?" the woman asked, and what seemed like excitement flashed in her eyes.

Samantha's shoulders straightened. "Who needs to know?"

"You came to visit the victim." A quick smile spread on the woman's face. A pretty woman, classic features, porcelain skin and blue eyes. "Is she doing all right? Will she survive?"

Samantha took a step back and assessed the woman once more. The lady wore designer clothes—high-end, definitely pricey. Her red high heels gave her an extra three inches, but Samantha figured the woman was about five foot three. The way the redhead held herself, the confidence in her stare, the directness of her speech… "Are you a reporter?" Samantha asked. The obvious assumption, but…

"You were at the scene last night," the woman said, nodding. "I recognized you. But you left before answering any questions. Did you leave because of your injury or because you were the one who pulled the trigger and killed George Farris?"

Samantha's gaze swept over the woman, memorizing her. She didn't know all of the reporters in the DC area, but she'd make a point of learning everything she could about this lady. "I have no comment for the press."

The redhead's lips thinned.

"What's your name?" Samantha asked her.

"Hannah Broderick, with Channel Seven." Her smile was broad. "You sure you don't want to tell your side of the story? In cases like this, the last thing you want is for the public to think that they're dealing with some trigger-happy agent."

"We're done with this conversation," Samantha said

flatly. She turned on her heel and headed for her car. She didn't hear the sound of footsteps behind her. As she approached her little coupe, Samantha saw her own reflection in the driver's-side window. Her fingers reached for the door handle and she found herself hesitating. Samantha glanced back—

The woman was gone.

The elevator doors dinged as they closed. Her gaze jerked toward the elevator bank and she saw the light gleam above them as the elevator rose. Her jaw locked and Samantha dug out her phone. She pressed the contact button for Blake, and when he answered, she said, "Watch yourself, partner. A reporter named Hannah Broderick is coming your way."

CHAPTER FIVE

BLAKE CROSSED HIS arms over his chest and stared at the elevator bank. The doors dinged, and when they opened, he found himself gazing at a redhead with vivid blue eyes. She blinked when she saw him, surprise flashing on her face.

"Hannah Broderick?" She fit the description Samantha had given to him.

She nodded.

"Took you a little longer than I expected to arrive." He glanced at his watch. "What happened? Did you have to search a few floors while you were looking for the victim?"

Her breath rushed from between her lips as she slipped out of the elevator. She came right toward him and touched his shoulder. "You spoke to the other agent." Her voice was low and smooth. Probably supposed to be sexy, but he just found it annoying.

Mostly because a reporter was trying to sneak her way into an injured woman's hospital room? *Annoying as hell.*

The elevator doors had closed behind her. He reached around the lady and hit the button to get those doors open once more. "You're heading back down."

Her eyes narrowed on him. "Was your partner the one who pulled the trigger or was it you?"

"Get on the elevator," Blake ordered. "This is not the time or the place for a reporter."

The fury in her stare probably should have burned him. "Don't you think people deserve to know what happened?"

He advanced toward her. She backed up, seemingly an automatic reflex, and he walked her into the elevator. Then he pushed the button for the parking garage. "A killer was stopped, ma'am. That's what happened. When the victim has recovered, *if* she feels like talking…then I'm sure your station will be contacted." He backed out of the elevator. "Now, you have yourself a good day."

The doors slid closed.

"FUCKING ASSHOLE."

The elevator was playing some lame classical music that just grated in her ears. She hadn't found the identity of the shooter, but…

I got close.

Going to the hospital had been pure genius. The news had just served up the name of the hospital for her in their last report, and she'd thought, *If the victim is there, maybe the FBI will be there, too.* She'd been right. The female agent had just walked right up to her.

She'd recognized the other woman. And since the big, dark-haired agent had been lying in wait for her in front of the elevator bank on the third floor…

The lady from the parking garage must have called him and tipped him off. Maybe he's her partner.

A partner who would have been with the other woman when she stormed George's house.

So she had two agents in her sights—one male and one female.

Which one had pulled the trigger?

Which one deserved payback?

She didn't know, so maybe she'd just punish them both.

THE OFFICE DIDN'T feel right without Samantha there. The place just seemed...empty. Blake steepled his fingers as he stared at her empty desk chair. She'd be cleared in the shooting, of that, he had no doubt. He'd already told his side of the story that morning. Samantha should be back in action right the hell away and then—

The office door swung open. "She doesn't exist." Samantha stood there, her chest heaving, her eyes gleaming, faint spots of pink color on her cheeks.

His brows shot up as he rose to his feet. "Bass gave you the all clear to get back to work?" A smile curved his lips. When Samantha was close, there was more excitement in the air. More focus. More—

"Hell, no. I haven't heard a word from him yet." She just waved that matter away.

Blake blinked. "What?"

"The woman. The reporter." She hurried toward him, nodding. "She doesn't exist. There is no Hannah Broderick at Channel Seven. I went down there and talked to the producer myself. She doesn't work for them."

Tension snaked through his body. "Then who the hell was she?" He reached for the phone. He'd call the hospital and warn the guard to be extra vigilant just in case the lady came back.

But Samantha snagged his hand. Heat seemed to lance him at her touch. "I already contacted the hospital. They're moving Missy to another floor and putting a second guard on her." Excitement sharpened her voice. "I think it's *her*."

He stared at her.

"George's trigger? Come on, you know I mentioned this to you only a dozen or so times. His victims were all a certain type."

"Young, blonde, beautiful."

"Petite," she fired right back. "Delicate builds. Fragile in appearance."

"She had red hair, Samantha."

"Like that couldn't be a dye job." Samantha nodded. "Actually, the hair was what made me suspicious in the first place. Do you know how many redheads with blue eyes are roaming around? Natural ones?"

He shook his head, not having a clue on that one.

"Those are recessive traits—the red hair, the blue eyes. I read a story on this once, and only, like, one percent of the population has that combination. It's like finding a freaking four-leaf clover or some crazy shit like that. Needle-in-a-haystack odds."

Samantha had a photographic memory. He'd learned that early on. If she read something once...she had the facts forever.

"I'm wagering she's a natural blonde." Samantha nodded. "More than that, she's the trigger. I know it. She was waiting for me in that garage. She wanted to know who'd killed George. She was there for a reason."

He remembered the woman's eyes. "Because she was pissed."

Samantha nodded. "Anger like that is personal. We need to find her."

She'd already found them.

"She's tied to George Farris. We have to dig in his

files…search his house… We have to find the connection to her because I think she'll be coming after us again. Only, I don't think it will be for a little chat this time."

She was still touching his hand. Blake cleared his throat. "You think she wants vengeance?"

"She wanted to know if I'd killed George."

His shoulders tensed. "She asked me the same thing."

A faint line appeared between her brows. "She's trying to figure out which one of us killed him, because she needs to know which of us *she* will kill."

Sure as hell seemed that way. "Repercussions," he muttered.

Her hand pulled back from him. "What?"

"That's what your friend Latham warned me about."

Surprise flashed on her face. "Cameron warned you about something? When?"

"Outside of your apartment last night. We had a little chat." One that still didn't sit well with him. Cameron Latham wasn't a guy he'd ever see as his friend. Too much tension was between them. *We both want Samantha.* His voice was low as Blake said, "Cameron warned that George's death could have repercussions. That someone close to George would react. Only, I didn't think there *was* anyone left close to the man."

"Someone was left," Samantha said. "His trigger. The woman he's been systematically trying to kill over and over again. The woman who helped to turn him into the killer he is."

The woman who seemed to be gunning for them. "I don't get it. If she's the woman Farris really wanted to kill, then why didn't he go after *her*? Why hurt those other women? Why torture those victims if the mystery lady was the one he actually wanted under his knife?"

Her gaze dropped. Samantha licked her lips, a quick, nervous swipe of her tongue. "Maybe he was afraid of her...or maybe he loved *her*." A bitter laugh slipped from her. "Could be both. Loved her and feared her and he couldn't take that last step, not with her. Because if he killed *her*, if he pushed her out of his life, then there would be no going back. She'd just be gone." Her lashes lifted and she gazed at him once more. "She's dangerous. We have to find her."

The woman had been stalking Samantha in a parking garage. Fuck, yes, they were going to find her.

A YELLOW LINE of police tape sectioned off the entrance to the little house on the cul-de-sac.

The broken window had been covered with cardboard. All of the lights were off. The house appeared... dark.

Beaten.

Dead?

Samantha slammed her car door and walked around the vehicle. They hadn't hidden their ride this time. They'd parked right in front of the house. Secrets were in there—secrets that she intended to find.

Their mystery woman wasn't going to stalk her through the streets. That wasn't a game that Samantha intended to play.

Blake gave a low whistle as he turned and looked at the quiet neighborhood. "Bet the neighbors here will be having nightmares for weeks."

And they'd be trying to sell their property. No one

wanted to be the one who lived next door to a serial killer.

Just not the kind of fame folks wished to have.

She didn't head for the front door. Instead, Samantha went to the back of the house. A patio waited back there. Chairs. A fire pit. A wind chime. It was blowing with the evening breeze, an oddly peaceful sound in the middle of the madness.

The screen door was a few feet away and…

Samantha's eyes narrowed on the screen. "Was that screen cut yesterday?" A small sliver, one near the lock.

Blake had followed her. His arm brushed against her shoulder as he pulled out his gun. "Don't remember, but I'm not taking the chance that it wasn't."

She started to pull her own gun, but…

I don't have it. Hell. Bass still had her gun.

Blake met her stare and nodded. "You stay behind me."

Right. She'd be happy to follow the guy with the gun.

He reached for the screen door. It slid right open. Someone had definitely been inside. Could be some curious neighborhood kid who was a little too interested in death. Could be a nosy reporter.

Could be our mystery lady.

It was dark in the house, but light still spilled in through the windows. The chalk outline of George's body was on the floor. A chair was overturned. But…

Everything else looked normal. Eerily so.

No one was in the living room. The kitchen was empty. Blake began to advance down the narrow hallway.

And Samantha heard the low moan. A weak cry, almost one that sounded pain-filled. Adrenaline flooded through her body. Blake rushed forward.

A weak cry. A woman who'd seemed deceptively fragile.

A woman who knew how to lure her prey to her?

"Don't!" Samantha cried out.

Blake looked back at her. He was a few steps ahead of Samantha in that tight hallway.

The moan came again. And then…"Help…"

Blake nodded toward Samantha. Then he raised his voice and said, "FBI! This is a crime scene. Come out now, with your hands up!"

Silence.

Then…

"Help…" Faint. So weak.

Blake pressed his body against the wall. Samantha did the same. Their eyes met for a moment. She knew he was about to run into the room, gun aimed, ready to face the threat. She'd go behind him, unarmed, yes, but not defenseless.

He gave a fast hand signal to Samantha, and then he was rushing into the room, shoving the door open.

And Samantha heard a faint creak behind her. The softest of sounds.

Her head whipped around and she found herself staring into gleaming blue eyes.

"Shh…" The redhead whispered.

What in the hell?

"Got you," the woman said.

Then she sprang at Samantha with a knife.

CHAPTER SIX

THE DOOR SLAMMED into the wall. "FBI!" Blake roared, but...

No one was in that little back room. No desperate victim. No scheming redhead. Just...

A phone was on the floor and—

"Help..." a voice said, a voice that came from the phone. *A freaking recording.* One that had been left to lure them into that back room. He whirled around. "No one is here, Samantha!"

Shock rolled through him.

Someone *was* there. The redhead was shoving a knife toward Samantha. He hadn't heard the other woman—not so much as a fucking sound—but she was attacking. Going right for Samantha.

"No!" Blake yelled. He started to fire, but the two women lunged at each other. The knife sliced over Samantha's arm, but she didn't stop. She drove her fist into the other woman's face. A hard hit that crunched cartilage.

The redhead howled and lifted the knife again.

Blake surged forward. *"Freeze!"*

She didn't. The knife went straight toward Samantha again. But this time, he had a shot.

He took it.

The bullet blasted into the redhead's shoulder. Blood

splattered onto the wall, onto Samantha. The redhead whirled toward him, her face twisted with fury. "You... *asshole*."

His grip on the gun was dead steady. "The next shot will be to your heart." Amazingly, the woman was still clutching the knife. "Drop that weapon, now."

The redhead moved her body, putting herself between him and Samantha and definitely not *freezing*. Did she think he wasn't serious? Did she think that he wasn't going to drive that bullet straight into her heart?

Then she started laughing. *Laughing*...

"Uh, Blake..." Samantha began.

"There are memories in this house," the redhead said. "So many memories. Can't let anyone else have my memories." The knife—dripping Samantha's blood—was pointed toward the floor.

"Blake." Now Samantha's voice was sharper. "I think we need to all get the hell out of here. Now."

"Drop the knife," Blake ordered. "I won't tell you again."

The redhead smiled at him. "Did you shoot George? The same way you just shot me? You did...didn't you? I thought it was her..." The woman's gaze darted back to Samantha. "But she still hasn't even pulled her weapon. I came at her with a knife, and she didn't even pull her gun. She doesn't have the killer instinct." She focused on Blake once more. "You're the trigger-happy one. You're the one who took him away." She shook her head. "Guns are so cold. You can't feel the pain with them. Can't feel the split of the flesh beneath your hand."

George Farris had enjoyed carving up his victims so carefully. "Is that something George learned from you?" Blake asked her. "You taught him how much *fun* it was to cut up those women?"

Her smile stretched. "I taught him so many things." But her eyelids flickered and the smile faded. "Then *you* took him away."

"No!" Samantha's quiet voice. "It was me! I did it. I'm the one who shot George."

The redhead spun toward her.

"You want to make someone pay?" Samantha nodded. "Fine. Then make *me* pay. I did it. I don't have a gun because my boss took it after the shooting. That's the way things work at the FBI. That's the only reason I haven't shot you already. *I just don't have my gun.*"

The woman took a step toward her. "You're not getting out of here alive," she said, the words barely more than a whisper.

"Of course we are," Blake snapped back. "We're getting out and we're arresting your ass. You'll go with us and you can enjoy some good quality time in a federal cell."

Her head moved in a slow, negative shake. "It won't be any fun without him. I won't be able to watch his work." Her shoulders sagged. "I couldn't let anyone else find his prizes… That was why I came here. You both appearing…" Her breath rushed out. "That was pure bonus."

If she thought going to jail was a bonus, fine. Whatever worked in her demented brain.

The knife suddenly fell from her fingers, clattering to the floor. She tipped back her head. "I'm ready."

"Blake!" Samantha's eyes were wide. "We need to get out of here…*now.*"

The redhead was laughing. Her eyes were still closed.

Her head was tilted back as if she was just waiting for something to happen.

I couldn't let anyone else find his prizes.

Oh, fuck. "Run!" Blake roared to Samantha.

She turned on her heel and took off. He barreled into the redhead, didn't slow, just threw her over his shoulder and kept going. But his touch seemed to ignite her. She fought against him, twisting her body, punching his back.

He ignored her and rushed after Samantha.

The redhead screamed, "No!" She drove her fists into him again. He could see the screen door, still open. *"No, no—"*

Samantha had gone through the door. She looked back at him, fear on her face. She held out her hand, urging him on.

And he felt the explosion behind him. The house seemed to rock around him, and a ball of red-hot fire blasted from behind him. The force of the explosion lifted him up, throwing him through the screen door. The redhead was ripped from his arms as he hurtled forward. Then the ground came up to meet him as he slammed face-first into it.

The impact sent pain shuddering through him, but he shoved that pain right back. Blake started to roll over and—

Samantha was hitting him. Hard, over and over on his shoulders and back.

He grabbed her wrist, holding tight. "What the hell?"

Her eyes were big, so dark and deep. "You were on fire."

He opened her hand, saw the blisters that were already forming there. He surged to his feet, pulling her up with him. Blake stripped off his still-smoldering coat and shirt and stomped at the flames.

The small house was totally engulfed. Broken glass littered the ground where the windows had exploded. The flames reached toward the sky, crackling and hungry.

But over those flames, he could hear laughter. His head turned and he saw the redhead. She was sitting on the ground, her arms curved around her undrawn knees. Her gaze was on the fire. She was smiling.

Slowly, he and Samantha stalked toward her. The woman had just planted a damn bomb—one that had nearly taken them all out, and she was just sitting there, laughing?

Oh, yeah, her lawyer will definitely be using an insanity defense.

When she caught sight of them, her laughter stilled. She looked at Samantha and sadness flashed on her face. "Guess I have to get you next time."

The hell you will.

But Samantha shook her head. "There won't be a next time for you."

The woman rocked back and forth, holding her undrawn knees. "There will be. I'll find you. I never forget. I never let go."

Good to fucking know.

"Lady, you are under arrest," Blake snarled.

Her gaze drifted back to the house. "No one will ever know now. His secrets are mine. My secrets are his. No one will know..."

But Samantha's golden gaze gleamed. "Don't count on it."

LITTLE WAS LEFT of the quiet house on the cul-de-sac. As dawn rose the next morning, Samantha stared at the charred skeleton that remained of the home. Ashes drifted in the breeze.

The fire had been very, very thorough. The arson investigator had already told her he believed several explosive devices had been systematically placed throughout the structure for maximum impact.

Their arsonist—a fingerprint check had revealed her real name to be Nina Miller—had been very, very deliberate. She'd wanted to make certain that no evidence survived the blast.

And she'd nearly made sure that Blake and I didn't survive, either.

But in the end, they'd made it out.

As Samantha stood there, a Mercedes-Benz slowly pulled around the cul-de-sac. She stiffened because she knew that car. It parked behind her smaller vehicle and, a moment later, Cameron unfolded himself from the luxury sedan and headed toward her.

"Went by your apartment." He had a bag of doughnuts in his hand. "When you didn't answer the door, I figured you'd be here." He opened the bag and offered her a doughnut.

She took it. Was it odd to eat doughnuts at such a terrible scene? Maybe. But her starving stomach reminded her she couldn't exactly remember the last time she'd eaten.

Cameron leaned back against her car. His gaze was on the charred structure. "Cut that one pretty close, didn't you, Sam?"

She had to swallow twice before she could force

down the bite of doughnut. "Closer than I would have liked."

He was still looking at the ashes. "I wouldn't have liked it if you died."

His words surprised a quick laugh from her. "Jeez, I don't think I would have liked it much, either."

Slowly, his head turned and his gaze met hers. There was no humor in his eyes. "The world would be darker without you in it."

That just might have been one of the nicest things he'd ever said to her. "Thank you." Cameron could be arrogant. He could be domineering. But…

He was also a friend, one who knew all of her secrets and still didn't stare at her as if she were a freak.

And, even better, he didn't stare at her with pity in his eyes.

"What happened to your hands?" he asked.

She looked at the bandages that covered some of her fingers. "Blake was on fire when he came out."

He caught her left hand. His lips pulled down. "And you hurt yourself helping him."

"He's my partner."

His fingers slid over her wrist, a nearly careless caress. Only, she knew Cameron never made any moves that were actually careless. With Cameron, everything was always carefully planned.

"If someone is going to get hurt," Cameron finally said, "how about next time we let it be him?"

She pulled her hand away from his. "How about there's no next time…and no one gets hurt?"

"Don't think that will happen." He shook his head. "Your line of work seems particularly dangerous."

Yes, it was.

He rubbed the back of his neck.

She made herself take another bite of the doughnut. Then she had to ask him, "Are you…okay, being here?" Because she knew about his past. The fire. The death. Ash drifted in the wind and it had to remind him of the darkness in his life.

The darkness that had changed everything for him.

"You're with me." His head turned toward her. "I've found that I'm often better when you're near."

Her smile came again. "You know, sometimes, you can really be charming." *And a good friend.* She could use a friend.

They sat in silence for a moment, then he asked, "So what's the woman's story? You figured her out yet?"

"She has knife scars all over her body," Samantha said. "They were discovered when she was booked."

"Self-inflicted?" he immediately asked. "Or…?"

"Based on the angles, particularly the wounds on her arms, no, I don't think they *were* self-inflicted. But I do believe she willingly received those cuts."

"You think George gave them to her?"

Samantha nodded. "I think she asked him to, and I think she also asked him to start hurting the other women. She came to the house because she wanted to destroy evidence."

He gave a low whistle. "Evidence that might have implicated her?"

"That's what I believe." She rolled back her shoulders. "But then Blake and I appeared, and her rage took over. It wasn't just about getting rid of the evidence then."

"It was about getting rid of you."

Yes, that was what Samantha believed. "She wanted

THE GATHERING DUSK

us to pay for George's death." And they almost had paid. The explosion wouldn't have just destroyed evidence. It would have killed them.

His stare focused on the burned porch frame. "Pity nothing is left for you."

"She doesn't know nothing is left."

He laughed. "Ah, Sam, you have such a fun mind. I love it when you go all twisted on me." He pushed away from the car. "Going to lie to your prey, are you? Brilliant. Just brilliant."

"I'm going to lock away a killer," Samantha corrected. "Because that's what I do."

The wind blew against her face, tossing her hair over her cheek. His hand lifted and he brushed the lock of hair aside. "Yes, I guess it is."

She moved away from Cameron. His touch didn't feel natural to her any longer. No…it just…

He isn't Blake. That wasn't Cameron's problem. It was hers. She'd deal with it, the way she dealt with all her problems.

"A serial-killing team," he murmured. "Such an interesting element. I would *love* to interview her. I bet she'd make for a fantastic paper topic."

"Maybe you'll get the chance." Her phone vibrated in her pocket, signaling she'd just received a text. "If they want any outside experts brought in, I'm sure you'll be the first on the list."

He always was.

She looked down at her phone. "I need to head down to the Bureau. Bass wants me to start the interrogation on Nina in an hour."

"Because you've been cleared. A justifiable shooting. Never had any doubt."

She glanced up at him. "Justifiable or not…" Her voice lowered. "It still gives me nightmares. It made me remember…too much." The shadows that were in her own mind. The ones she worked to keep so carefully in check.

His stare turned solemn. "You know you can talk to me. I don't judge you, Samantha. No matter what, I will *never* judge you."

She knew that. But… *I can't say the same for Blake. If he learns all my secrets, what will he do?* Things would have been so much easier if she could have just loved Cameron. "I need to go," she said again. "Thanks for the doughnuts."

She reached for the door handle.

But his fingers curled over hers. "It's natural to feel guilt after taking a life."

Yes, she got that. A normal, human reaction. *That doesn't make it any easier.*

His breath whispered over her cheek. "What else do you feel?"

Her gaze cut toward him. There were some things that she couldn't say, not even to Cameron.

But…

In his stare, she swore that…*he knew.*

"There was a rush, wasn't there, Samantha?" he asked. "When you pulled the trigger… When you stopped that very, very bad man… You felt a surge of power, didn't you? He wasn't in control any longer. You were."

Yes, she'd been in control.

"If you want to talk, I hope you know my door is always open to you."

She did know that. She also knew she didn't want to

explore the darkness of her own feelings, not then. She understood killers.

Anyone had the potential to kill, under the right circumstances.

But liking the kill? That wasn't something just *anyone* would experience. "Thank you, Cameron."

He backed away. Samantha slid into her car, and a few moments later, she was driving away from the cul-de-sac.

She glanced in her rearview mirror.

Cameron stood in front of the burned house.

It's just a house on a street. Just a house...

CAMERON WATCHED SAMANTHA drive away. He had no doubt that she'd get a confession. After all, Samantha was very good at her job.

Very, very good.

But he was worried about her. This had been her first kill as an agent and the shooting had stirred up her memories. She couldn't keep her feelings bottled up. She needed to talk and to share.

She needs to tell me all the dark details.

He'd always known that Samantha Dark was like her name. She wasn't meant for a normal life, that fake life of smiles and perfect days. There was more inside of her, a twisting, snaking *dark*, an understanding, even a *need* to explore the tainted side of life.

She hunted killers because her mind understood their motivations far too well. But on this case, she'd crossed a line. Not just thinking like a killer, but finally...

Becoming one.

CHAPTER SEVEN

SAMANTHA SCHOOLED HER features before she opened the interrogation room door. She went inside with her spine straight and her shoulders squared. Her heels clicked on the floor.

Blake was already seated at the little table, his pose relaxed. Across from him, Nina Miller sat, a faint smile curving her lips.

Samantha smiled back at her.

For an instant, she saw Nina's eyelids flicker. But then a mask seemed to fall over the other woman's face. "Why so late to this little party, *agent*?"

"Because I had to stop by George's place and pick up a few things."

Nina smirked. "I don't see anything…"

Samantha laughed as she slid into the chair next to Blake. "Of course you don't. Evidence has to be logged. Analyzed. Studied ever so carefully."

"Why would anyone want to study ashes?" Nina asked. "Seems like a waste of time to me."

Blake leaned forward. "We have you on the arson, Ms. Miller. Arson and the attempted murder of *two* federal agents."

Nina put her cuffed hands on the table. "How did I know you two were going to be there? I certainly didn't mean to hurt anyone." She blinked her eyes, appearing confused. "I mean…I just knew what a terrible, terrible man George Farris was…so I went to his house trying to banish that evil." Her cuffed hands rose and she pressed her fingers to her temple. "I feel so…lost. I…I think something broke in me when I saw that news story." Her hands fell back to the table and she turned her wrists toward her, staring at all the slash marks on her skin. "It reminded me of my past."

The woman was good. Able to turn on and off her act at the blink of an eye. "You haven't asked for a lawyer," Samantha said.

Nina kept staring at her wrists. "I should, right? That's what people do…but…" Her eyes squeezed shut. "My mind is so foggy."

Blake glanced at Samantha, one dark brow raised. She could read his expression perfectly.

Utter bullshit. Neither of them were buying Nina's act.

"Do you seriously think we don't remember the things that you said to us at George's house?" Samantha asked.

Nina looked up at her. "*I* don't remember. Maybe… maybe I should talk to a shrink. Talk to someone who can understand how my mind just…splintered…" A tear leaked down her cheek.

She started this act as soon as I mentioned evidence. Before Samantha had said the one magic word— *evidence*—Nina had been smiling that smug little grin. Samantha leaned toward her. She patted the woman's hand, as if in sympathy. "You are talking to someone who understands. My PhD is in psychology—I totally understand all about the fragile state of the human mind."

The faint lines near Nina's eyes tightened.

"So feel free to tell me everything," Samantha murmured. "Because I sure am ready to listen."

But Nina jerked her hand away from Samantha's. "You won't know my secrets."

Words the woman had said before.

"I found your secrets," Samantha said. "Buried beneath the ash. Did you really think someone like George wouldn't have put those pictures and flash drives in a fireproof safe? I found them beneath the floor of the room that once held Missy Johnson."

Nina paled.

"You knew he was keeping evidence, didn't you? His souvenirs. I mean, even if the kills were *your* idea, he liked to keep the memories close."

Nina shook her head.

Blake settled back in his chair, his gaze drifting between her and Nina.

"You like pain, right, Nina?" Samantha asked.

Nina jumped to her feet. "How *dare* you—"

"Some of your scars are new, some are old. The old scars tell me that you started the pain a very long time ago. Was something bad happening in your life? Did *you* make the first cuts?"

Nina's eyes glittered, but no real emotion showed on her face. *Acting. Just going through the motions, trying to play us.*

And Samantha knew Nina's secret. "You didn't feel alive, did you? Everyone around you felt. You could see it. You could almost taste their emotions. But you didn't feel. Until the first cut. That's when you started to feel. What you felt, it was pain. But to you it was like pleasure, wasn't it? Something to finally cut through the cloud of numbness that was all around you. Something to prove you were *alive*."

Nina shook her head. "You know *nothing* about me—"

"You and George…what happened? Did he find you one day? See what you were doing? Only, instead of being horrified, you found a perfect partner in the boy down the street from you. A boy you could control because he was already in love with you, right?" Samantha nodded. "It would make sense. You're beautiful. You were a little older than him. He was the shy, smart kid, but when we talked to some of the people who went to school with him, they said he was teased because of his size. Teased because he wasn't strong enough for sports or—"

"He was strong enough with me."

Samantha's stomach knotted, but she barely eased out a breath. *It's working. She's talking.* "Because you made him strong. Just like you made him start cutting you. And he liked it, just as much as you did. But then one day, those slices on your skin weren't enough to make you feel, were they? The cloud was back."

"Shut. Up." Nina nearly screamed at her.

"What did you decide the next rush would be? The knife wasn't cutting deep enough…at least, not on you. Originally, I was looking at this all wrong. I thought George was angry, that he wanted to hurt *you*."

"George would never hurt me." She leaped toward Samantha, trying to come right across the table.

Blake shot to his feet, catching her shoulders. "You need to calm down, Ms. Miller."

"Get your hands off me! You can't touch me! I'll have you brought up on charges! I'll—"

"George didn't want to hurt you. You wanted to hurt yourself. But you didn't want to die." Samantha's low words carried right across Nina's screams. "So you found a victim who was similar to you. And you got George to kill her...for you."

Silence.

Samantha didn't dare to breathe. Had she gone too far? Pushed too much? All of her instincts were screaming that she was correct, but...

Maybe I'm not handling Nina the right way.

Blake slowly released the other woman. Nina didn't sit. She stared at Samantha. Nina's eyes were blank, glassy, like a doll's.

"George made videos. Took photos. The killing gave him a rush. He got power from the attack." Samantha kept talking because she knew there was no going back. She needed Nina to break. She needed her to slip up. *Because I don't have any footage linking her to the murders. No evidence at all.* "And then he took another girl...and he killed her, too."

Nina's lips had clamped together. Her body was as stiff as a board.

Blake was still on his feet, but Samantha remained seated. She stayed in the seat to give Nina the feeling of control she knew the other woman wanted. Nina craved control and—

"Did you know he took Missy Johnson?" Samantha asked her, tilting her head. "You were with him for the other attacks—I saw that in the pictures." *I can bluff all day long, Nina.* "But you weren't there when he took Missy." She let her eyes widen. "He took her without you, didn't he? George got a taste for that power rush and he—"

"The bastard should have waited for me!" Nina screamed. "I would have been there! I would have watched out for him—*he would still be with me!* But he took her...said he couldn't wait. She was wrong, though. *Wrong, wrong, wrong.* I'd changed my hair and he didn't even know. I wanted to try someone new. He didn't know—you took him from me and *he didn't know*—"

Once more, she came at Samantha.

And, once more, Blake was in her path. But this time, when Blake touched Nina, she collapsed, sobbing. Deep, wrenching sobs that shook her whole body.

For a moment, Samantha didn't move at all. Shock chilled her skin. *She confessed. I got her to confess.*

Blake looked back at Samantha. A faint smile curved his lips and he stared at her with...pride?

Her chin lifted.

"I want a lawyer," Nina whispered.

Ah, those desperate, guilty words. But they'd come too late. Samantha nodded as she rose to her feet. "We'll make sure you have an attorney present right away." She headed for the door, then, unable to help herself, she glanced back.

Nina was glaring at her.

"Count on it," Samantha said.

Nina's eyes flared and her hands—clawlike—lifted into the air as if she'd attack.

Samantha just kept walking.

Hell, yes. She'd done it.

Told you I'd have those secrets.

"YOU DIDN'T FIND evidence at George's house, did you?" Blake asked her about an hour later, when they were both settled in their office on the fourth floor.

Samantha shook her head.

"Remind me to never play poker with you."

"I'm *fantastic* at poker."

He propped his hip on her desk and stared down at her. "I think you're probably fantastic at a whole lot of things."

You have no idea. She rose from her chair and moved closer to him.

He caught her hand and stared at the bandages that still covered her fingers. "I don't like it when you get hurt because of me."

She just shrugged. "I can handle a few blisters."

His head cocked so that he was staring at her. "I bet you can handle nearly everything that comes your way."

Not everything. She still wasn't sure how to handle him.

His fingers slid over her wrist, then his hand fell away. "When do I get to hear your story, Samantha?"

She should move back. But she didn't. Her skin was still icy and he seemed so warm. "My story?"

"Yeah. When do you tell me about those secrets that I see in your eyes?"

Blake, you don't want to hear about those nightmares. Our job is hard enough.

"When..." he murmured. "When will you start to trust me the way you trust Cameron?"

Cameron was different. Cameron—

A knock sounded on their office door. She jumped back—almost guiltily—as she turned to find the FBI executive assistant director standing there.

Bass nodded toward her. "Heard you got the confession this morning."

"Yes, sir."

"Nice fucking job."

From him, that was high praise, indeed.

"This was a high-profile case. You made the FBI look real good."

She hadn't really cared about how the FBI looked. She'd just wanted to do her job.

"Since you're being cleared on the shooting, it's time to start working on the next case."

Her heart gave a quick jump in her chest. "Another case?"

He strode into the office and tossed a manila file onto her desk. He opened the file and she saw a picture of a pretty young woman staring at her.

"A girl's gone missing from Georgetown University…"

THE KILLER STARED down at his prey. She was a beautiful girl, fit, in the prime of her life.

And she was terrified.

He held the knife in his hand, just watching her. Staring at the terror as it filled her eyes. Her fear seemed to fill the very room around them.

He'd gagged her. After all, it wouldn't do for someone to hear her screams. "This is my first time, you see," he whispered as he let the knife trail over her arm. "I have to be careful. Oh, I'm sure I'll learn plenty as I go… There's always a learning process…"

Behind the gag, she gave a pitiful moan.

"I'm not going to kill you…"

Hope filled her big blue eyes.

"At least not right away," he told her. It had been so easy to get the girl. Georgetown was such a perfect hunting ground. So many women…all young, impressionable… so eager to help him with his new experiment.

Death.

Because he'd decided it was the ultimate experiment.

"I'm going to hurt you first," he told her. It was important that she understood what was happening—every moment. It would enrich the experience for them both. "And you'll tell me what that pain does to you."

She shook her head. Tears streamed down her cheeks.

He let the knife cut into her arm. "You *will* tell me."

Her body spasmed.

And he felt…a rush.

He pulled the knife back and saw the blood dripping from the blade. "Let's try that again," he said.

Her eyes were so wide. So scared.

He slashed her.

And the rush filled his body once more.

Finally, he was becoming what he'd always known he was meant to be.

A killer…

* * * * *

SPECIAL EXCERPT FROM

⬦ HARLEQUIN®
™

I N T R I G U E

*FBI Special Agent Jillian West is reunited with her
childhood best friend, navy SEAL Hayden Black—but
neither could have anticipated the stalker from her past to
resurface…*

Read on for a sneak preview of
ABDUCTION,
from New York Times *bestselling author*
Cynthia Eden's *thrilling series*
KILLER INSTINCT.

"So what's a hotshot FBI agent like you doing in a small town like this?" His index finger slid along her inner wrist, a careless caress.

Or maybe a very careful one. Even he wasn't sure about that.

"Hiding." And this time, her smile broke what was left of his heart. "Because I'm really not so much of a hotshot." She looked down at their hands. "I've got too much blood on me."

Alarm pulsed through him. "Jill?"

"Let me go," she said once more.

Another caress, a gentle touch right over her rapid pulse point, and his hand slid away from her.

"I need to head home," she said, then seemed to catch herself. "Head to the cabin. I rented a place on the beach. The beach is supposed to be good for the soul, right?"

He wouldn't know. The only thing that had ever been good for his soul… Well, that was Jill. She'd changed him, though he didn't think she realized just how much. He didn't think Jill even realized how influential she'd been in his life.

She'd always thought that he'd saved her.

Oh, baby, that could not be further from the truth.

She slipped by him and started walking toward the parking lot.

"Jillian West." Her name pulled from him.

She hesitated.

"We're not kids any longer."

Jill glanced over her shoulder. "I haven't been a child since I was thirteen years old."

No, she hadn't been. He knew that. One terrible act had changed her world.

"I came back to Hope for many reasons," Hayden said. Maybe she deserved that warning. "I didn't expect to see you so soon."

"So soon? Why expect to see me at all?"

Ah, now, that was just cold. "Do you ever think about us?"

She faced him again. "I try not to."

He took that hit straight on his heart. "Really? Because I pretty much think about you every single day." Though the nights were the worst. When he'd been fighting, when he'd been in one hell after another, memories of Jill had always come to him at night.

But a memory wasn't walking away from him right then. No memory, no ghost.

He'd watched her walk away before, but this time things were going to be different. This time he was fighting for Jill.

She just didn't realize it yet.

He wasn't the town troublemaker any longer. Wasn't the boy who'd never been good enough for Jillian West. Now he was back in Hope to prove himself to the person who mattered the most.

To you, Jill. For you. I'm back for you.

Don't miss
ABDUCTION by Cynthia Eden,
available March 2017 wherever
Harlequin® Intrigue books and ebooks are sold.

www.Harlequin.com

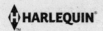

INTRIGUE

EDGE-OF-YOUR-SEAT INTRIGUE, FEARLESS ROMANCE.

Save $1.00

on the purchase of ANY Harlequin® Intrigue book.

Available wherever books are sold, including most bookstores, supermarkets, drugstores and discount stores.

Save $1.00

on the purchase of any Harlequin® Intrigue book.

Coupon valid until May 31, 2017.

Redeemable at participating outlets in the U.S. and Canada only. Not redeemable at Barnes & Noble stores. Limit one coupon per customer.

52614747

Canadian Retailers: Harlequin Enterprises Limited will pay the face value of this coupon plus 10.25¢ if submitted by customer for this product only. Any other use constitutes fraud. Coupon is nonassignable. Void if taxed, prohibited or restricted by law. Consumer must pay any government taxes. Void if copied. Inmar Promotional Services ("IPS") customers submit coupons and proof of sales to Harlequin Enterprises Limited, P.O. Box 3000, Saint John, NB E2L 4L3, Canada. Non-IPS retailer—for reimbursement submit coupons and proof of sales directly to Harlequin Enterprises Limited, Retail Marketing Department, 225 Duncan Mill Rd., Don Mills, ON M3B 3K9, Canada.

5 65373 00076 2   (8100)0 12272

U.S. Retailers: Harlequin Enterprises Limited will pay the face value of this coupon plus 8¢ if submitted by customer for this product only. Any other use constitutes fraud. Coupon is nonassignable. Void if taxed, prohibited or restricted by law. Consumer must pay any government taxes. Void if copied. For reimbursement submit coupons and proof of sales directly to Harlequin Enterprises, Ltd 482, NCH Marketing Services, P.O. Box 880001, El Paso, TX 88588-0001, U.S.A. Cash value 1/100 cents.

® and ™ are trademarks owned and used by the trademark owner and/or its licensee.

© 2017 Harlequin Enterprises Limited

HICECOUP0317

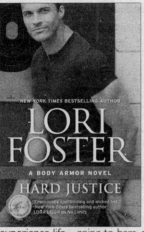

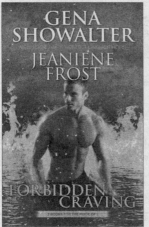